C000082171

TRUST NO ONE

KERI BEEVIS

Boldwood

First published in 2020. This edition first published in Great Britain in 2023 by Boldwood Books Ltd.

Copyright © Keri Beevis, 2020

Cover Design by 12 Orchards Ltd

Cover Photography: Shutterstock

The moral right of Keri Beevis to be identified as the author of this work has been asserted in accordance with the Copyright, Designs and Patents Act 1988.

All rights reserved. No part of this book may be reproduced in any form or by any electronic or mechanical means, including information storage and retrieval systems, without written permission from the author, except for the use of brief quotations in a book review.

This book is a work of fiction and, except in the case of historical fact, any resemblance to actual persons, living or dead, is purely coincidental.

Every effort has been made to obtain the necessary permissions with reference to copyright material, both illustrative and quoted. We apologise for any omissions in this respect and will be pleased to make the appropriate acknowledgements in any future edition.

A CIP catalogue record for this book is available from the British Library.

Paperback ISBN 978-1-83518-003-7

Large Print ISBN 978-1-78513-997-0

Hardback ISBN 978-1-78513-996-3

Ebook ISBN 978-1-78513-994-9

Kindle ISBN 978-1-78513-995-6

Audio CD ISBN 978-1-83518-001-3

MP3 CD ISBN 978-1-78513-999-4

Digital audio download ISBN 978-1-78513-993-2

Boldwood Books Ltd
23 Bowerdean Street
London SW6 3TN
www.boldwoodbooks.com

For Paula Armes and Josephine Bilton – Thank you for believing in me, even during the times I didn't believe in myself.

She has been through hell.

So believe me when I say, fear her when she looks into a fire and smiles.

— E. CORONA

PROLOGUE

My father once argued that it is safer to live in the countryside.

In the big cities, he pointed out, there are dangers around every corner. People are unpredictable and the more of them you have around, the higher the risk of drugs, knife crime, burglaries, rape and murder. Move to the countryside, find a remote location with less people, and the trouble goes away.

I agreed with him on one point. People are unpredictable. But when there are more of them around, it is easier to get help should you find yourself in trouble.

Out in the countryside, all alone, you only need to stumble across one wrong person and no one will be there to raise the alarm. No one will hear you when you scream.

I am reminded of that conversation now as the car travels down the narrow bumpy lanes, headlights cutting a path ahead.

The window is down, the heat of the night warming my skin. There is silence in the car. I need time to think, to compose myself. I have to focus.

Despite the blackness of the night, the low light from the moon, the lack of streetlamps, and the isolation of the property, it is easy to find. I have spent so many nights watching the house, absorbing everything that happened, and trying to pluck up the courage to put things right.

Tonight I will not be a coward and leave.

Tonight it ends.

The car stops just inside the main gate and I gather my things, get out, hiking up the long driveway to the house.

Tonight is for me. It is my responsibility to end this, my chance to put things right, but it is a job I have to do alone.

The property is sprawling and there are no nearby neighbours, but I approach quietly, aware the only sounds cutting the silence are my boots as they hit the dirt track and my shallow breathing. Everything is still and so peaceful; the perfect setting for the spectacle I have planned.

Round and round I go, like a teddy bear, the trickle of liquid soothing as it falls. The heady smell of petrol fills my nostrils, making me giddy with anticipation. As I place the second empty can down and study the building for a final time, I remind myself that I am just putting things right and that tonight I will sleep easier.

The match burns bright, an orange flicker against the darkness that grows quickly in intensity as the flames lick the house.

Did you know that in the UK there are approximately 250 fire-related deaths each year?

And did you know that the response time of the fire brigade will depend on where you live? If you are in a city location, the fire engines will reach you in an average time of seven minutes and eleven seconds; however, out here in the countryside in such a remote location, it can take ten minutes and six seconds.

That is an extra two minutes and fifty-five seconds for the fire to burn. An extra two minutes and fifty-five seconds to make sure that the sinners pay for their crimes.

The flames rise higher and their passionate roar is like music to my ears as the heat burns my skin. Thick smoke billows into the air and I imagine what is happening inside the house. Can only hope the last moments are of terror and remorse.

Glancing at my watch I note the fire has only been burning for four minutes. The fire engines will still be at least six minutes away and by the time they arrive, it will be too late.

I smile to myself.
Living in the countryside isn't all that it's cracked up to be.

1

As the last group left the restaurant, Olivia Blake followed them to the door, setting the sign to closed and turning the lock.

It had been a busy evening, the start of the Christmas party season, with a rowdy table of twelve taking up most of her time. Olivia had humoured them, returning plates to the kitchen when two of the girls, who were outrageously drunk before they had even been served their starters, were insistent they had ordered differently, while avoiding the middle-aged letch who tried to touch her arse as she set down drink and food orders. At the end of the night she had painted on a smile at their generous £4 tip and wished them a happy Christmas, even though it was still almost a month away.

'Feel sorry for me.' Her brother, Jamie, grinned from across the room, where he was wiping down the bar counter. 'I have to put up with this for another three weeks.'

'Oh, pull the other one. You love it!' Olivia finished clearing the table, expertly balancing dishes and glasses, and taking them through to the kitchen, where her mother was loading the dishwasher.

'Thanks for helping out tonight, Livvy. I know you had to cancel plans.'

Olivia set the dirty crockery down. 'It's no bother. It was only a drink out with work and I wasn't really looking forward to it.'

That was the truth. She worked in an estate agents and her colleagues weren't exactly a barrel of laughs. Her boss, Roger, was too tight to shell out for a Christmas meal, so they were supposed to meet for a drink instead. Olivia's only female colleague had phoned in sick, and she had been dreading spending the evening with just Roger and his smarmy protégé, Jeremy.

Her mother calling to say they had a full house in the family restaurant and asking if she could spare a hand had been a welcome excuse to cancel. Roger and Jeremy would have had more fun without her and at least she hadn't had to put up with their snide comments and sexual innuendos all night.

'Is there anything else you want me to help with before I head off?'

Elena Blake shook her head. 'I have it covered. You're welcome to stay the night if you want.' She offered every time, always hoping Olivia would say yes.

'I have Luna waiting at home.' (And a new season of *Mindhunter* she was looking forward to, but she didn't add that bit. Her mother wouldn't appreciate coming second to Netflix.)

'You said Molly's away. I don't like you going back to that big empty house alone.'

'You worry too much, Mum.' Olivia kissed the top of Elena's head before slipping on her coat. 'I'll be fine.'

She called her goodbyes through to her brother, promised her mum she would message once she was home, then stepped out of the back entrance into the cold wind.

She found the envelope pinned under her wiper blade, flapping in the breeze. She didn't take much notice of it until she was huddled inside the car. It was bitter out, with an arctic chill and her windscreen had already started to ice. Turning on the engine and blasting the heater, swearing because she had forgotten her gloves, she glanced at the envelope. It had her name typed on the front.

A Christmas card? Curious, she opened it and pulled out the sheet of notepaper.

A long, long time ago, you did a bad, bad thing.

Everyone's past catches up with them eventually, including yours. Soon.

What the hell?

She would have dismissed it immediately as someone's idea of a joke, but it was addressed to her, so it had been intended for her. Of course that still didn't mean it wasn't a joke. Though she couldn't think who the hell would find it funny.

But if it wasn't a joke, that meant it was a threat. She didn't like that idea and couldn't think of anything bad she had done.

Who had left it on her windscreen? As the car windows began to clear, she glanced around the dark car park warily. No one was around, at least that she could see, and hers was the only vehicle parked there. The envelope could have been left at any point during the evening, but still, unease crept up her spine, and she locked the car doors, figuring better safe than sorry.

Maybe I should take Mum up on her offer of a bed for the night. As soon as Olivia considered the idea, she dismissed it. She wouldn't let herself be spooked by what was obviously a prank. Besides, if she went back inside, her mum would want to know why she had changed her mind, and Olivia wasn't up for explaining.

Elena would only freak out, worrying about her every time she was home alone, and honestly, after a full day at work then a busy evening serving tables, all Olivia wanted was to have a quick shower and slip into her own bed, watch a bit of TV and, Luna's mood permitting, snuggle with her cat.

She pulled out of the car park on to the quiet road. The grassy bank opposite that led up from the river was covered with a sprinkling of frost that, along with the string of overhead fairy lights, made it look decidedly festive.

Turning on the radio for company, she sang along to Starship's 'Nothing's Gonna Stop Us Now', glad she had swerved the work drinks and wondering if Roger and Jeremy were still out in the city bars. She suspected they would be. No doubt getting drunk somewhere on Prince of Wales Road or making their way to a strip club. She shuddered at the thought.

It was while cutting through Thorpe St Andrew that she first noticed the car behind her. She hadn't spotted it initially (probably because she had been too busy with her singalong) and at first she didn't really take any notice. It was almost comforting to not be the only car on the road. But as she headed out into the countryside, towards the Norfolk Broads village of Salhouse, she was aware of the headlights behind her, knew that she had taken half a dozen turns and the car was still on her tail.

Was she being followed?

Jesus, Liv. Get a grip.

It was a ridiculous thought and it was quite plausible that someone else might be taking this route home. The note was making her paranoid. Her attention went back to the implied threat.

A long, long time ago, you did a bad, bad thing.

How long ago was she supposed to have done this thing? When she was in her twenties or possibly even her teens? There was honestly not a single time she could remember wronging anyone.

Everyone's past catches up with them eventually, including yours. Soon.

The last part of the note was definitely a threat. Did whoever wrote it plan to expose this thing that she had supposedly done? In which case, Olivia was intrigued to find out what it was she was being accused of.

Or were they planning on taking revenge? That was the bit she didn't like. Did someone intend to hurt her?

She glanced again at the headlights behind her, aware she was tensing when she pulled off the main road and the car indicated, following her.

She was being stupid.

But what if the person who left the note was the same person who was behind her? What if they had waited for her to finish work before following her home?

Whoever had left the note knew her name. So did that mean they knew that she was home alone, that her lodger was away and her boyfriend was out of town?

She tried to calm her nerves, told herself to stop being ridiculous. This wasn't some stupid movie.

Still, as she turned into the street where she lived, saw the headlights sweep by, she breathed a sigh of relief, annoyed at her overreaction.

The relief was tempered with apprehension when she realised she hadn't left the outside light on. Eager to get inside, she bolted from the car then hotfooted it across the driveway to her front door, fumbling with the key. The quiet location where she lived had its perks, but it wasn't the most welcoming place to return home to in the dark. A couple of years ago, when she had bought the house with her ex-boyfriend, Toby, she had appreciated the high hedgerow and how far apart it was from the other properties on the road; but now things had changed. In the winter, and especially if Molly, her lodger, was away with work, it was a little too secluded for her liking.

Once locked inside, she kicked off her shoes, groaning in relief as she stretched her toes and rubbed at the balls of her feet, quickly messaged her mum, then headed straight upstairs to shower and change into her PJs. Her cat, Luna, commandeered the centre of the bed and Olivia picked her up for a cuddle, before pulling back the duvet.

She was about to turn on the TV when her landline phone rang. The only person who ever used it was her mother, and fearing something had happened in the brief spell since she had left the restaurant, she snatched up the receiver.

'Hello?'

There was silence on the line.

'Mum, is that you?'

A noise – it sounded like scratching – then a low whisper. 'A long, long time ago, you did a bad, bad thing. Everyone's past catches up with them eventually, including yours. Soon.'

2

No one wanted to touch 8 Honington Lane.

The property had been added to the books of Dandridge & Son Estate Agents over eight months ago, and on Olivia's day off, so she hadn't been present when her colleague, Jeremy Fox, had slyly logged it under her name.

Roger hadn't been happy, but Jeremy complained that Olivia had all of the easy properties to sell, accusing their boss of favouritism, something that couldn't be further from the truth. Her other colleague, Esther, point-blank refused to take the house, fixing Roger with a death stare that had him crawling back to his desk with his tail between his legs.

Truth was, Olivia wasn't a great salesperson. Unlike Jeremy, who could sell sandcastles if he had to, she lacked the gift of the gab and had terrible sales patter. It was a wonder Roger had ever employed her and a miracle she still had a job. Even Esther, who was past her prime and put a number of clients off with her glacial comments, doubled Olivia's turnover, and Olivia knew that Roger, be it out of pity or despair, set her up with properties that sold themselves. Just as she knew she had no hope of ever shifting the property on Honington Lane.

The place had belonged to Vera Cadwallader and was being sold by her sons. Given the high price tag that the Cadwallader brothers refused to budge on, and the 1950s time-warp décor that potential buyers refused to look past, viewings had dried up, so it was with great surprise that Dandridge & Son received a new enquiry on Monday morning.

Driving the company car out of the city centre, heading towards the small market town of Swaffham, Olivia flicked through the radio stations after tossing Jeremy's Backstreet Boys CD out of the player. Jeremy, who had only been at the company for just over a year, viewed the car as his own personal vehicle, given that he was the one who drove it most. While she didn't relish the viewing – she was fairly certain that Karen Mortimer would lose interest once she had seen the property – it had been worth it to see the look on Jeremy's face when Roger threw her the car keys.

It had crossed Olivia's mind that Jeremy could be her tormentor, that the note and the phone call were part of some stupid joke he had decided to play on her.

It was no secret that they didn't get along. Olivia thought he was a sleaze (seriously, the man had zero personality and looked like a time machine had sucked him up in the eighties and spat him out again), while Jeremy made it no secret that he disliked her.

Did he hate her enough to torment her with threatening notes and late-night phone calls? He knew her car, would be able to access her home telephone number from the staff file, so it was plausible.

The phone call had spooked her, to the point she had gone downstairs to check all of the doors and windows were locked. If it was Jeremy fooling around, she would bloody kill him.

As she approached the turning for Honington Lane, she refocused her mind on the viewing.

The company website showed just a handful of pictures of the property and they were all outdoor shots of the extensive, albeit overgrown, garden. There were no pictures of the interior, and that was for a reason.

Spotting a car already in the front driveway and assuming it belonged to Karen Mortimer, Olivia parked on the side of the road and headed up to the house. The car was empty and the woman didn't have keys to let herself in, so she had to be having a nose, probably round back checking out the view of open fields from the back garden. If this property ever sold, it would be the garden view that closed the deal.

'Ms Mortimer? It's Olivia Blake from Dandridge & Son.'

When there was no response, Olivia picked her way over broken paving slabs, the cracks filled with weeds, wishing she didn't have heels on. She hated the things, could just about tolerate them when sitting behind her desk. Dressed in her pencil skirt suit and stilettos though, she at least looked the part, even if she was no good at the job.

The client wasn't round the back and Olivia recalled what little information she had on her. The enquiry had come in by email, Karen Mortimer keen to view the house that day. Roger had responded, giving Olivia a patronising pep talk before pushing her out of the door.

She had the client's mobile number and pulled it up now, keen to find out where the woman was. It went straight to voicemail. No personal greeting, just an automated voice urging her to leave a message. So she did, ending the call and glancing around.

Concluding that the car in the driveway didn't belong to Karen Mortimer, but unsure whose it was, given that the property had stood empty for nearly two years, she decided to let herself into the house. The heating wasn't working but it would be better than standing outside in the cold.

She put the key in the front door lock, frowning when it didn't turn. Although she hadn't been here in a while, she had been certain the lock opened to the right. Instead she twisted it left and heard the lock catch. Her frown deepened as she realised it was now locked. The door had been unlocked already. But how?

Neither Cadwallader brother lived locally, though Olivia supposed they could have been back in town. They had no need to visit the house, which was empty of their mother's things, and neither of them struck her as the sentimental type. The house was just extra cash they were waiting on.

Tentatively she twisted the key back, easing the door open. Was that a radio she could hear? Music was coming from somewhere at the back of the house, which suggested someone was inside. But who?

'Hello, Mr Cadwallader, is that you?'

There was no response.

Unease prickled her scalp and the back of her neck. Although there were other houses in the street, they were all set apart with wide gardens that offered privacy. 8 Honington Lane was many things; old-fashioned, dilapidated and unloved, but this was the first time Olivia had ever found it to be creepy.

'Hello? Mr Cadwallader, it's Olivia Blake from Dandridge & Son.'

Perhaps she should go back to the car and wait for her client.

A banging noise and the faint sound of music came from the kitchen, the door at the far end of the hallway. It had to be one of the Cadwallader brothers. They had the radio on and hadn't heard her. Maybe they were finally heeding Roger's instruction to tidy the place up.

Chiding herself for being stupid, she entered the house, choosing to leave the door ajar, glancing at the steep staircase that led up to darkness and the doors along the main hallway, all part open. As she neared the kitchen, the music got louder, the song recognisable.

'It's beginning to look a lot like Christmas'.

It didn't sound like it was coming from a radio. The scratchy sound was more reminiscent of a record player.

She thought back to the note she had received and the phone call repeating the same words.

Everyone's past catches up with them eventually, including yours. Soon.

What if it wasn't an innocent, unfunny prank by Jeremy? The words held a threat. What if Karen Mortimer wasn't who she said she was? What if Karen Mortimer didn't exist? No one wanted this property, yet this woman had insisted that she view it today. And her enquiry had been by email, while the number she had provided had gone to voicemail.

What if it's a trap?

Olivia hesitated, told herself to get a grip. There was nothing sinister here. She was overreacting.

The smell of petrol hit her first, the strong pungent odour clinging to the air. It was also coming from the kitchen and, as she neared, a muffled sound over the top of the Christmas song, followed by the scraping of a chair on the floor, had her ears pricking.

Her brain was screaming *GO*. Something was off, but her feet carried her forward.

She wasn't prepared for the sight that met her.

The kitchen was dated with worn yellow metal units and an ugly pale blue worktop. Ragged checked curtains hung at the windows and door, and clashing blue and pink floor tiles completed the look. A portable record player was on the scuffed fold-down table playing the Christmas song.

One of the blue chairs had been placed in the middle of the room, and that was where her focus was drawn, to the man bound to the chair, lengths of chain wrapped around his body, holding him in place despite his struggles. His hair was wet, plastered to his forehead, his clothes were too, and his face was twisted in anguish as he screamed into the gag tied across his mouth. Both the legs of the chair and the jean-clad legs of the man tied to it, were licked by orange flames that were rising fast.

For a moment Olivia couldn't move. The distressing scream that tore from the man as he managed to spit the gag out, spurred her into action. She rushed forward to help him, but jumped back as the flames leapt out at her.

The heat and the sound conjured memories she had tried to bury. The overwhelming fear, as she tried to register what was happening, paralysed her limbs. As she watched, frozen to the spot, the fire took hold, completely engulfing the man. His pitiful screams rang in her ears and the stench of smoke, petrol, and burning flesh filled her nostrils as the flames incinerated him.

More memories surfaced, awful pain-filled memories that threatened to swallow her and made it difficult to breathe.

Have to get out. Have to get out now.

The instruction from her brain finally connected with her shaking legs and she turned and fled from the kitchen, down the long hallway with the half-opened doors, her frazzled brain not even considering that someone might be in one of the rooms, watching and feeding from her reaction.

She tripped on the large stone step down to the path, landing painfully on her knees, scrambled to her feet again, and leaving the door wide open, stumbled past the car and down the long driveway into the road.

A horn beeping, the rush of an engine and the screeching of brakes all sounded in her ears, but a second too late as hard metal slammed into her.

3

Food shopping day was one of the highlights of Janice Plum's week. It gave her the chance to get out of the house, have a chat with the checkout staff, and sometimes, if she was lucky, she would bump into one of her village friends and they would have lunch in the cafeteria together, where they would spend the afternoon having a gossip and putting the world to rights.

There was nothing to rush home for. Both her sons were in school and, despite her husband Martin's hinting, she didn't feel inclined to get a part-time job. She had her housework, her Zumba and Facebook to keep her busy, and she wasn't prepared to give any of that up.

As she pushed her trolley around Sainsbury's, she had one eye on her list, the other looking out for familiar faces. Although it was only the first week of December, the store was already playing Christmas songs and she drummed her fingers on the handle of the trolley, humming along quietly as she scanned the shelves.

After paying at the checkout, a little disappointed that she hadn't seen any of her friends, she decided to treat herself to a pot of tea and a mince pie anyway. Her shopping bags in the trolley next to her table, she used the store's complimentary Wi-Fi to log on to her Facebook account, and snapped a picture of the drink and mince pie, uploading it to her profile with the caption,

A little treat after my hard workout this morning.

Truth was, she had only managed ten minutes of her Zumba fitness DVD, due to her mother ringing for a chat, but her Facebook friends didn't know that.

She had a quick skim through her newsfeed, liked a couple of memes and forwarded a chain email offering Christmas hugs, then clicked on to Fern St Clair's profile. Her old school friend had so far ignored her attempts to contact her by Messenger and WhatsApp, though Janice knew she had read both messages.

Fern had been active on Facebook too, posting a couple of pouty selfies and a man-hating rant that looked vague enough, but would most likely be directed at the married boss she had been sleeping with for the past three years.

Janice liked the post with a sad face and added a comment:

Here if you want to talk, hun. Xxx

As she finished her second cup of tea, she planned out her afternoon. There was no housework left to do and, eager as she was to put the tree up, she knew the boys would be disappointed if she decorated without them. It was Christmas tradition in the Plum household that they always did the tree together.

Janice glanced at the box of hair dye poking out of the top of one of the shopping bags.

She had bought a shade called Cherry Crush. She would be a vivacious redhead for the festive season. Maybe she would colour her hair this afternoon and give Martin a surprise when he came home.

Deciding that's what she would do, she checked her mince pie photo on Facebook, pleased to see it already had two likes, plus a comment from her friend, Mandy:

Go ahead, Janice. You deserve it, babe. Xxx'

Janice liked the comment, replying with a heart emoji, before slipping her phone back into her bag and wheeling her trolley out to the car park. The Wham! song 'Last Christmas' was stuck in her head and she hummed it as she clicked her keys at her car and loaded the boot. She had just returned the trolley to the loading bay and was about to climb in the driver's seat, when she noticed the piece of paper stuck under her front wiper blade.

Frowning, she plucked it up, assuming it was someone having a go at her for parking over the white line. (Hardly her fault. Supermarkets needed to start making the spaces bigger.) Instead of a note, it was an envelope with her name on it, and her insides went cold as she slipped inside the car and closed the door, locking it. She glanced around, but there was no one paying her undue attention.

She quickly ripped the envelope open, knowing from the last two she had received that this one would contain a veiled threat of some kind. She read the words, her mouth dry.

Does Martin know he is married to a murderer?

He will. Soon.

For a moment she couldn't get her breath, panic clawing at her belly as she reread the note. The mince pie she had eaten was threatening to make its way back up.

The words were more direct than the last two notes she had received. They had all arrived with her name typed on the front, no stamp. They had been hand-delivered and left in places where only she would find them, but this was the first one that named her husband and also the first one that mentioned murder.

Suspiciously, she glanced around again. No one was watching her, the nearby cars all empty. She carefully refolded the note and put it back into the envelope, her hands shaking. She slipped the envelope into her bag, took out her phone and pulled up Fern's number.

It rang several times before cutting into voicemail, Fern's husky voice telling her to leave a message.

'Fern, it's me, Janice. Look, I really need to talk to you. I've received another note. Please call me.' She ended the call, willed her old friend to get in touch.

It had been possible to ignore the first two notes because the threat was vague, possibly even a prank. But this one was different. Whoever had sent it was making a serious accusation.

The worst bit was, it was true.

4

Her mother had come to the hospital as soon as she had received the call.

The whole situation was a little surreal and Olivia felt like she was viewing it down a tunnel. They were in the A&E department, where she had been rushed by the driver of the car that had hit her outside of the Cadwallader house. She had been lucky not to have broken anything, walking away from the accident with sore ribs, a bruised arm, and concussion.

The police were at the house. She knew from the snippets of conversation she had overheard that there was an officer on his way to speak with her. An ambulance had been sent to the house too, along with a fire engine. The latter would be needed, but the ambulance was unnecessary. They were too late to save the man.

Although Olivia had tried her best to explain events to her mother, she wasn't sure that she entirely grasped the seriousness of what had happened. It wasn't until they were sat in a room with Detective Constable Upton that it finally began to dawn on Elena exactly what her daughter had witnessed.

'Why do you think my Olivia had anything to do with this?'

'We are not saying she did,' the DC gently pointed out, his tone calm against Elena's frantic one. 'At this stage, we are just trying to establish if there is a connection between Olivia being called to the house for the viewing and the victim being set on fire.'

He turned to Olivia. 'We've spoken with your boss, Mr Dandridge. According to him they haven't been able to trace Karen Mortimer, the viewer of the property. She isn't answering her mobile phone or replying to any emails. You say there was definitely no trace of her at the house?'

'Nothing. I tried to call her too. When it went to voicemail... well, that was when I decided to go inside.' Olivia faltered, lacing her fingers to stop them trembling. The too recent memory of what had been waiting for her still etched clearly in her mind. 'There was a car parked in the driveway,' she recalled. 'I assumed it belonged to Mrs Mortimer.'

'We think the car was the victim's. We have an ID from the registration paperwork, but it will probably be a couple of days before we can officially identify him.'

'Someone did that to him.' Olivia murmured the words, as much to herself as to the DC. Of course someone else had been responsible. This wasn't a suicide. The man hadn't chained himself to a chair and set himself on fire. She had been so focused on what had happened, it was the first time it really occurred to her that the man had been murdered.

She remembered his screams over the song playing as she entered the kitchen, making the scene she witnessed so surreal. 'There was a record player.'

'I'm sorry?' DC Upton looked at her blankly.

'There was a record player. It was in the kitchen.'

The detective narrowed his eyes. 'We didn't find a record player.'

'It was right there on the kitchen table. There was a record playing on it. A Christmas song.'

'Are you sure, Miss Blake?' DC Upton asked carefully, glancing at Elena. 'The doctor said you took a nasty bump to the head.'

'I know what I saw and heard,' Olivia snapped, anger heating her cheeks. ''It's beginning to look a lot like Christmas'. That was the song. Bing Crosby or Frank Sinatra.'

'Or it might have been Perry Como,' her mother interjected. 'I like his version.'

'Whoever! It was playing right there on a record player on the kitchen table.' Olivia huffed, noting the detective's sceptical look. 'I'm not going crazy. It was there. I saw it!'

'Okay, okay.'

She suspected the detective didn't actually believe her and that he was making a show of writing it down on his pocketbook just to appease her.

The music had definitely been playing, but there was no trace of the record player. She recalled it hadn't been very big, portable in style, opening up like a suitcase.

Had she been lured to the house intentionally? To witness a murder?

And if the record player had been there while she was in the house, but removed before the police arrived, that meant that the killer had been inside the house with her.

'This was intentional.'

DC Upton looked up from his notebook. 'What do you mean?' he asked carefully.

'Someone lured me to that house. They wanted me to find that man, didn't they?'

'You're to come back home while the police investigate.'

'Mum, I don't need to move home.' Olivia drew in a breath to calm her nerves. She had witnessed an horrific crime. It was understandable she was shaken. And perhaps she was overreacting. Though as she tried to convince herself of that, her mind returned to the note she had received, to the phone call on Friday night, repeating the same words.

A long, long time ago, you did a bad, bad thing.

Were the note and phone call connected to what had happened today?

If it was, her mother would start freaking out.

Olivia decided she would sit on the note for now. It was still possible it was Jeremy playing a joke. Much as she disliked him, she wouldn't get him in trouble with the police.

Still, she wasn't convinced that what happened at 8 Honington Lane today had been a coincidence. The email enquiry then the client not showing up. Walking into the house at the exact horrific moment...

She was going to vomit.

Stop. Try not to think about it.

Another deep breath.

Slow and steady, Liv. Slow and steady. As her breathing evened and the sick feeling passed, she gently shook off her mother's hand and addressed the detective. 'Do you think I was meant to find him... that man today?'

'Miss Blake, we haven't found anything to suggest that to be the case. The house has been empty for a while. It's probable you were in the wrong place at the wrong time.'

'But what about Karen Mortimer?'

'I told you we haven't been able to trace Mrs Mortimer yet.'

'And what if you don't find her?'

'Why do you think we won't find Mrs Mortimer?' The detective seemed to be picking his words carefully.

Olivia looked him directly in the eye. 'I mean, what if this was a set-up? What if Karen Mortimer doesn't actually exist?'

She saw the flicker of hesitation, knew the detective had already considered this possibility. 'It's early days. At the moment we can't rule out anything.'

'Is my daughter in danger?'

'I don't think your daughter is in danger, Mrs Blake.' Upton was quick to calm Elena. 'However, I do agree that it might be a good idea if she wasn't alone, at least for tonight.'

'What?'

'That settles it. You're coming home.'

'I'll be fine. I have Molly.'

'You said Molly was away with work.'

Damn, her mother didn't miss a trick. Olivia had forgotten she had told her mother that her lodger was away on a course. 'Only temporarily. She'll be home tonight.' At Elena's narrowed eyes, she cursed her mother's ability to remember everything. 'Or maybe tomorrow,' she added grudgingly.

'So tonight then you come home.'

'I can't leave Luna.'

'We'll stop by to get your things and you can feed Luna. She's a cat. She will cope for one night.'

'I don't need to come home, Mum. I'm thirty-one. I can take care of myself.'

'You witnessed a murder, Olivia.' Elena was on her feet, a formidable presence even though she was only five foot two. 'And then you were involved in a nasty accident. Tell her I'm right, DC Upton.' It wasn't a request.

'You've had quite an ordeal today,' the detective began diplomatically. 'I don't think it would be a bad thing to be with family tonight.'

Olivia scowled at him, knowing he had sealed her fate.

It wasn't that she didn't want to be around her family. Far from it. She had grown up in a close-knit household with her brother, and parents who loved them unconditionally. After her dad's death, she and Jamie had rallied around Elena and they had become an even tighter unit.

Today had thrown her a curveball though and she wanted time alone to process everything that had happened. She also wanted the comfort of her own home and to sleep in her own bed.

It wasn't to be though and, after the interview with DC Upton had concluded, she followed her mother out to the car park, unaware of the eyes that were watching her.

5

There were five in the bed and the little one said, roll over, roll over.
So they all rolled over and one fell out.
There were four in the bed...

Gary Lamb was an easy kill and the most enjoyable one so far. It had been simple enough to lure him to the house and restrain him in the chair. Listening to him beg and plead for his life, seeing the horror on his face when he realised what was going to happen to him, had made the plotting and the waiting all worthwhile.

The filthy pig had shit himself when I doused him in the petrol and teased him with the lit match, and the smell of his fear had been vile.

Of course I blew it out. We weren't quite ready. The moment had to be perfect.

Then she had arrived and it was showtime.

I have lost track of how many times I have watched the video, but I hit play again, enjoying the look on the bitch's face when she enters the room and finds him chained up and burning alive. His muffled screams, her reaction of disbelief and anguish, and the sounds of our favourite Christmas song playing. It was perfect and you would have loved it.

I know you want me to hurt her for what she did to you, for how she betrayed you, and, trust me, I will, but first there are others who need to be punished, who also hurt you.

I promise you though that she will be there every step of the way, witnessing the consequences of her actions. And when it finally gets to her turn, I will make sure she pays.

6

Olivia had spent her childhood in The Riverside Inn, her bedroom overlooking the tranquil River Green in the suburb of Thorpe St Andrew and it was one of her favourite spots in the city. The old pub restaurant had been adapted over the years, but still retained much of its charm, and pulled in a decent crowd, especially over the weekends.

Downstairs was business, while upstairs was personal, with her mum and brother managing the business and living on the top floor of the old building, and over the years, Olivia had helped in the restaurant. These days she only did the odd waitressing shift when needed, to help the family out.

Dropping her overnight bag on the floor of her old bedroom, she looked out of the window at the stunning riverfront view. People paid a premium for this location and she knew her mother had worked hard to keep the business afloat through difficult times, not willing to sacrifice the place she had built up from scratch with their father.

'Get yourself settled. I'll go put the kettle on and make some lunch.'

'Thanks. I'm not hungry though.'

'You have to eat, Livvy. It's nearly three o clock. What have you had today? Any breakfast?'

'I had a banana first thing.'

'I will make some cheese on toast. You like that.'

Although she guessed seeing someone dying would curb anyone's appetite, Olivia's stomach rumbled at the suggestion. Maybe she should eat a little something. 'Okay, thanks, Mum.'

'You want me to bring them upstairs or do you want to come down to the restaurant?'

'I'll come down. I'll be there in a bit.'

Her room hadn't changed since she had moved out almost a decade ago. The oak furniture was the same and the walls were still papered in a delicate pale blue flower pattern on a cream background. The double bed was made up with her old duvet, her childhood teddy bear sat on the pillow, and she suspected the sheets were freshly laundered. She had always loved this room, how its position caught the sunlight late afternoon, making it a bright and cheerful place. Here in the silence, watching a couple of dog walkers meandering along the riverbank, it was hard to believe everything that had happened just a few short hours ago.

Roger had told her to take the rest of the week off, probably because of the dressing down her mother had given him over the phone. Olivia suspected he was also fearful of attracting negative press, raising the whole issue again of lone female estate agents conducting viewings.

She would stay the night to appease her mum and, truth be told, perhaps she was better here and not alone with her thoughts. Molly was returning tomorrow and she could go home, take some time to recover. Noah would be back in a couple of days too. She had messaged him after leaving the hospital, though downplayed what had happened, just telling him about the accident and that she would spend the night at her mum's. How could she possibly explain what had happened in the house on Honington Lane in a message or over the phone? She would wait until she saw him in person.

DC Upton had told her they would want to speak with her again and Olivia knew she needed to mentally prepare herself for that. She guessed they hoped she would remember more details once the shock had worn off. She closed her tired eyes for a moment, immediately seeing the face of the man she had watched burn to death. The bruises she had from the accident would take a while to heal, but would the trauma of what she had witnessed take longer? And gnawing at the edges of that trauma was guilt. She had stood by and watched him burn.

That guilt weighed heavily, despite being told there was nothing she could have done to save the man. He was already on fire, doused in petrol and the flames spreading quickly, and it would have been impossible to free him from the chains, but still she hadn't even tried. She had just frozen in fear, watched the scene unfold, then fled like a coward.

And she knew why. Absently running her hand over the scars, she recalled the pain of flesh burned by fire.

Shaking the painful memories, she went downstairs, found her mother in the kitchen, the waft of melting cheese making her belly rumble again. The room with its sounds and scents was comforting and familiar, and she watched her mother slice vegetables as she sipped tea and nibbled on her sandwich.

The back-hallway door opened, bringing in an arctic blast.

'Mum, where do you want this?'

Olivia turned at her brother's voice, though was unable to see anything other than the bottom of a pair of jeans and boots beneath a giant Christmas tree. She watched as her mother supervised the positioning of the tree against the back wall of the kitchen, lifting a hand in greeting as Jamie, who, realising she was there, narrowed his eyes. 'What the hell happened to you?'

'Long story, but let's just say I came off worse than the car.' Olivia didn't really want to rehash the morning's events. She was exhausted from talking about them.

'You were hit by a car? Jesus, Livvy, are you okay?'

'I'm fine, honestly. You know me. Anything to get out of work.'

'So what the hell happened?' Jamie was fussing over her, looking for signs of damage.

'I wasn't looking where I was going.'

'You idiot. Were you on your phone?'

'No!'

Jamie held up his hands at her sharp tone. 'I was just asking. As long as you're okay though?'

'She'll be fine,' Elena added. 'A few cuts and bruises, and she's had a bit of a shock. She's going to stay here tonight.'

A bit of a shock? Trust her mother to come out with the understatement of the year.

Fortunately, Elena didn't elaborate and for that Olivia was grateful. She needed a break from talking about what had happened. She would leave her mother to tell Jamie.

'Mum conned you into getting the tree, did she?' she joked, changing the subject.

'Jamie offered,' Elena slipped her arm around his waist and gave him a squeeze. 'He's a good boy to his old mum.'

Not exactly old, Olivia thought. Her mum was only sixty-one and looked good for her age. Although her stylish dark hair now came from a bottle, she was fresh-faced and trim. Jamie took after their mother's Italian side more than Olivia, whose light brown hair and grey-blue eyes were inherited from her father.

'Let's get this tree into place.' Elena instructed, raising her hand at Olivia when she started to get up. 'No, not you, Olivia. Your brother and I have got this. Finish your lunch and you can come help us decorate if you feel up to it.'

The afternoon passed more pleasantly than the morning and it was good to spend time with family. Despite having no appetite, Olivia managed to eat the plate of dinner her mother put in front of her then excused herself, going up to her old bedroom. Everything ached from the accident and the stress of the day had taken its toll. She longed for sleep to pull her under, but the moment she closed her eyes the nightmare images resurfaced: the man on the chair, the flames rising higher, his tortured screams.

She tossed and turned for an hour or so, trying to shake the images and think of more pleasant things, and it was gone midnight when she finally gave up on sleep. Crawling from the crumpled bedsheets, she went to the window and spent a few minutes looking down at the peaceful dark river with boats dotted along the bank. The River Green Christmas lights were up, twinkling white lights between the lamp posts, and everything looked calm.

Eventually deciding that the fresh cool air might do her some good, she pulled her coat on over her pyjamas and padded downstairs. The restaurant was closed, the lights all out and the shutters down. In the kitchen she slipped her feet into her mother's wellies and found the key to the back door. She was about to unlock it when she spotted an envelope on the floor, poking through from under the door. She picked it up, her heartbeat quickening when she recognised her name on the front.

She glanced around the quiet kitchen, fearful of being caught opening the envelope, which was stupid, because the place was empty and her mother and Jamie were in bed. Still, she went over and closed the door to the restaurant, wanting privacy, and flicked on the overhead light, before carefully easing open the envelope with shaking fingers.

There was no note inside, instead a photograph. Olivia pulled it out of the envelope, her mouth dry and terror clawing at her throat as she recognised the picture of the man tied to the chair, the contorted look of anguish on his face as the flames ate his skin. Scribbled across the picture in marker pen were the words,

This is your fault.

She dropped the photo, realised she was going to be sick, and rushed to the sink, where she heaved up her mother's lasagne.

The note was connected, which meant she was right about being lured to the house. But why? And who was responsible? Whoever was targeting her wasn't playing a joke. This was serious. A man had been cruelly murdered.

She puked again, the choking sounding too loud in the quiet kitchen. She had to tell the police, but if she did, would they think she was involved in this?

Backhanding spittle from her mouth, she grasped the counter and took a few moments to steady her nerves. Drawing deep breaths, she talked herself through a plan. She would get the photo, go back to bed, sleep (though realistically that wasn't going to happen), then calmly and rationally talk to her mother and Jamie in the morning, explain about the note, and contact DC Upton. She had his card and he had told her to call him if she remembered anything. He was definitely going to want to know about this.

A crash came from outside and she jumped, letting out a yelp. Leaning towards the window she strained her eyes to try and spot the culprit, her heart almost stopping when the security light came on. *Is someone outside? That photo was hand-delivered.*

Heart hammering in her chest, she slowly backed up, crashing into the centre island. With the light on, anyone outside could see right into the kitchen and watch her every move.

Another sound came, this time the crunch of gravel. She held her breath, waiting for another noise, but heard nothing.

Jesus, Liv. Calm the hell down. It was probably just an animal, maybe a cat or a fox, foraging in the bins. It wouldn't be the first time. The photo had scared the shit out of her. No wonder she was jumpy and overreacting.

She gave it a few more seconds, willed her heartbeat to return to normal then, hearing no further sounds, forced her jelly legs to carry her back over to the sink, knowing she needed to clear the mess up so her mum didn't come down to it in the morning. With the water running she didn't hear footsteps growing louder as they neared the house. As she finished disinfecting the sink, she turned off the tap and replaced the bleach in the cupboard below.

A loud rap on the window had her looking up. The figure standing on the other side of the glass made her scream.

7

'Liv? Open the door.' A familiar voice, the mid-Atlantic twang instantly recognisable. Noah.

Seriously? It was fucking Noah?

Her tension eased, though her heart was still hammering as she rushed to the door, quickly unlocked it. As Noah stepped inside she smacked him hard against the shoulder.

He took a step back. 'Ouch! Steady up.'

'Steady up? You just scared the bloody crap out of me. I thought you were in Devon?'

'I came back to see you. That message you sent scared the crap out of me too.'

'What the hell were you doing out there?'

'I heard a crash round the back so I checked it out.'

Olivia's heart was still racing, the shock of everything that had happened, taking its toll. 'I heard that too. Did you find out what it was?'

'One of the bins was knocked over. Foxes, I guess.'

'You really bloody scared me, Noah, banging on the window like that. Couldn't you have called or messaged me to let me know you were coming back?'

'I did try to call you,' he told her, a little testily. 'Perhaps if you check your phone you'll see I've been trying to get hold of you most of the evening.'

'You have?' Shit, her phone. She had put it on silent in the hospital and had forgotten to change it back.

'Nice wellies by the way.'

Olivia glanced down at her pyjama bottoms tucked into the wellington boots, realised just how ridiculous she looked, and managed a laugh. It sounded slightly hysterical and she couldn't help it when it turned into a sob, the events of the day finally catching up with her.

'Oh Jesus, don't cry.' Noah looked momentarily panicked, though recovered quickly. 'Look, I'm sorry I scared you.' He folded his arms around her, pulled her in close. 'It's going to be okay. You're probably still in shock from the accident.'

She nodded against his shoulder, let him hold her for a moment. He had cut his trip short and come back for her. Given the newness of their relationship, she hadn't expected him to do that, and her reaction had been to lose her temper with him.

Nice going, Liv. 'I'm sorry too. I didn't mean to be a bitch.'

'It's okay.' Noah stroked her hair, was silent for a moment. 'Why are you wearing wellies? Were you off out somewhere?'

The initial shock wearing off, Olivia's mind went back to the photograph, and for a moment she thought she was going to be sick again. She pulled free from his arms, took an unsteady step back.

She guessed she looked like she was about to pass out or something, because Noah was suddenly looking at her oddly, eyes narrowed. 'Liv, are you okay?'

'I'm fine.' Before the words were out of her mouth, her stomach roiled and she ran to the sink, certain she was going to throw up again. Her stomach must have been empty because little came out. To his credit, Noah didn't flinch, holding her hair back and waiting patiently with her until she had finished, his eyes full of questions as she steadied herself on shaky legs.

'So are you going to tell me what that was about? I know you had the accident, but you look like you've just seen a ghost.'

Olivia was mortified and just wanted to go back upstairs. 'I'm sorry, I can't do this right now. I appreciate you driving all the way back, I honestly do, but I'll talk to you tomorrow.'

'Liv?' She could hear him following close behind her, didn't have the energy to tell him everything right now. She turned to tell him that.

Noah's attention wasn't on her though. He was staring at the photograph on the floor, the one she had dropped before running to the sink.

No!

'What's this?'

She rushed to pick it up, almost bashed heads with him as he beat her to it. 'Give me that.'

It was too late. He was studying the picture and the words written across it, a look of shock on his face. 'What the actual fuck? Is this yours?'

When she didn't respond, because seriously, how the hell was she supposed to answer that, he shook his head. 'Do your mum and Jamie know about this?'

'No. I only just found it.'

'If someone put it through the door of your mum's restaurant, they need to know.'

'No, don't wake them. It... it was meant for me.'

He paused, studying her closely. 'What do you mean, it was meant for you?' When she wavered, his green eyes narrowed in suspicion. 'Talk to me, Liv.'

'It came in an envelope with my name on. Someone pushed it under the door.' She stepped around him, snatching up the torn envelope and handing it to him. 'See.'

Noah looked at the envelope then the man in the photo again. 'Do you know who this is?'

'Yes.'

'So it's real then?' He sounded disgusted.

'Yes, but it's not how you think!'

He pulled out his phone. 'I need to make a call.'

'Who to? The police?' Olivia was panicked.

'Let me speak to one of my old contacts.'

'No! Please don't.'

'No? Are you serious?' He looked at her incredulously. 'This isn't something you can keep a secret.'

'Please, Noah. I will call them in the morning, I promise, but not tonight. Please.' Olivia held her breath, waited, finally releasing it when he slowly nodded.

'Okay, no police, not tonight. But you'd better start talking, Liv.'

* * *

They went into the restaurant, choosing one of the back tables away from the doorway that led to the upper section of the building, not wanting to wake Elena or Jamie. Noah poured large measures of brandy from the bottle that Olivia took from behind the bar.

He was initially guarded with her, firing questions at her to the point she honestly believed that he thought she had something to do with the photograph. As everything came tumbling out though and he learnt about the note and the phone call she had received, plus what she had discovered in the house on Honington Lane, his stance towards her softened.

'So that's everything?' As he swirled the brandy in his glass he was studying her, she suspected for any trace of a lie.

She was used to fun Noah, teasing Noah, occasionally pain-in-the-arse Noah. She knew he had served in the police for several years before branching out with his own business, but she had never seen this side of him before and the new harder version unsettled her a little. She broke away from his sharp green gaze to study the hardwood floor. The restaurant had her mother's touch all over it, from the simple vases of gerberas on red check tablecloths, to the low copper lighting, to the brick walls, where pans hung from hooks and shelves were filled with large jars of spices.

'What happened in the past?' His voice distracted her, bringing her back.

'Huh?' She glanced up to meet his eyes again. 'Nothing.'

'Nothing?'

When he regarded her suspiciously, Olivia's shoulders sagged, defeated. She had hoped he would understand and be supportive. Although they had only been involved romantically for the past month or so, they had been friends for longer. She needed him on her side, but this was starting to feel like an interrogation. 'Honestly, I'm not hiding anything. I wish I knew what this was about. You know me, how boring my life is. It's always been that way.'

Her last comment had been added lightly, hoping that mention of her dull life might provoke a smart-arse comment, but this time it didn't come. Noah nodded, his expression still serious, considering. 'Well, someone thinks you did something so we need to know what that is in order to find out who is targeting you.'

'The police are going to think I'm involved. They might think I killed him.'

Noah raised a questioning brow and for a moment she thought he was actually going to ask if she had, but then the corner of his mouth twisted up and he seemed amused by the idea.

'What?'

'He was a big bloke.'

'So?'

'And you're a squirt.'

'I am not a squirt. I'm five foot six. That's hardly a squirt.'

He actually had the nerve to roll his eyes at that comment, but Olivia let it slide. He was back to teasing her again, which was both familiar and welcome. She needed familiar right now.

'I just see it as a bit of a stretch, you overpowering someone twice your size and chaining him to a chair.' Noah was silent for a moment, running his finger around the rim of the brandy glass. He downed the rest of his drink, reaching for the bottle and pouring another measure.

Olivia held out her glass when he offered the bottle. She wasn't a big drinker, but tonight was an exception.

'You're sure you don't know who he is?'

It was the third time he had asked that question and Olivia gave him the same answer. 'No.' This time though, after a moment of hesitation, she added, 'At least I don't think so.'

Noah arched a questioning brow. 'You don't think so?'

'I didn't recognise him.. But that's not to say our paths have never crossed. I can't remember every single person I've ever met. Can you?'

He looked like he was about to challenge her on that with some bull-shit brag that yes he could, but a crash from the kitchen had them both jumping up.

'What was that?'

'Wait here.'

When Olivia ignored him, started to edge towards the door, Noah caught hold of her arm, pulling her back as he stepped in front of her. Normally the move would piss her off, but after the day she had experienced, she was already jumpy. Instead she caught hold of the back pocket of his jeans as she followed him out of the restaurant.

The large kitchen was cold from the breeze blowing through the open back door.

'That was shut, right?' she questioned.

'Yes.'

Noah moved quickly, pulling Olivia behind him when she refused to let go of him. Outside he glanced around, looking for any sign of an intruder. If there had been one, he (or she) was long gone.

'I guess the lock didn't catch,' he said eventually, turning to go back inside.

Olivia knew he didn't believe that and was saying it only to reassure her.

'Where's the photo?' she asked as he closed the door, this time locking it. She glanced at the stainless-steel counter, certain that's where they had left it.

'You had it.'

'No, I clearly remember you took it and wouldn't give it back. I thought you had left it here on the counter though.'

Noah thought about that for moment, nodding. 'You're right. I did.'

They both looked at the counter again then back at each other.

The little ball of dread that had been churning in Olivia's gut started spinning faster. 'So where the fuck is it?' she whispered.

'Honestly, I don't know.' Noah sighed. 'Look it's late and I'm tired. Why don't I stay here tonight.' He must have caught the flicker of hesitation on Olivia's face, because he held up both hands. 'This is not about sex. I just don't think you should be alone.'

'I'm not alone. Mum and Jamie are in the house.'

'You know what I mean.'

Yes, she did, could see the concern on his face. She also knew she could trust him. Nearly six weeks and they still hadn't slept together. Lots of making out, yes, and he had been more than patient, stopping every time she asked him to. She couldn't keep putting it off. Knowing that made her feel both anxious and guilty. What if he didn't want her when he understood why she was holding back?

'Let me stay with you, Liv.'

She wanted him to. She really did. 'Not tonight, okay. It's been a hell of a day and I just need to be by myself to process it.' She found a smile for him, knew it probably looked a little contrite.

He studied her and for a moment she thought he was going to push the issue, but then he nodded. 'Okay, but I want you to promise me you'll lock the door after me and no more going outside.'

8

Fern St Clair sat in her car, parked in the street outside her boss's house, watching and waiting.

Peter was supposed to meet her tonight, but he had called off at the last minute, claiming he had a meeting. His message had been casual and vague on details, so she had phoned him. He hadn't liked that, positively squirming as she pressed him on specifics.

He had been lying, she was sure of it. And she intended to catch him out.

She had come straight from her aerobics class, was still wearing her workout clothes under her thick winter coat. She had discussed the situation with her friend, Meg, who had urged her to confront him. Meg had a lot of attitude, one of the reasons Fern had been drawn to her, and had fired her up, hence why she was now sitting outside his house.

Peter always worked late on a Thursday, so she didn't expect him to arrive home before eight. A light flicked on in the front bay window of the large Edwardian house, lighting up the room and, as she caught sight of Caroline Collins, her breath hitched. Peter had said his wife and kids were away. Visiting family, that was what he had told her. Caroline's car was there though and now Fern had seen her with her own eyes. That was the first part of his lie exposed.

She watched briefly as Caroline flitted round the room, plumping cushions and switching lights on the giant Christmas tree. They had only crossed paths a couple of times over the years and Fern couldn't understand what Peter saw in this mouse of a woman.

As Caroline disappeared from view, she hunkered down in her coat. It was freezing in the car and she didn't want to waste petrol by running the engine. As a distraction, she pulled her phone out of her bag, scrolling through Instagram, then Facebook. That idiot Janice was still on her case, liking and commenting on every single one of her posts.

Fern had ignored the messages she had sent, hadn't even bothered to listen to the voicemail. She didn't have time for losers like Janice Plum.

The pair of them had been tight when they were younger, but Fern had moved on, while Janice was stuck in her rut of a life with her drip of a husband and her gormless kids. She had piled on the weight, had questionable fashion sense, and she had become dull, dull, dull, cramping Fern's style.

Like a leech though, she was proving difficult to shake off, not getting the hint from the unanswered calls and messages to fuck off.

It was tempting to just delete her off Facebook and block her number, but a little part of Fern knew it was best to keep her in reserve. Janice Plum could always be counted on to rally round when needed.

The sound of an engine and the flicker of headlights in her rear-view mirror had her slipping down in the driver's seat. Fern's heart was thumping as the car slowed, and she recognised Peter's Range Rover as it turned into the driveway.

The lying bastard.

He climbed from the car, glancing cautiously around, almost as if he suspected she was there watching. Of course, there was no way he could see her. It was pitch-black outside and she had been careful not to switch the interior light on.

He unloaded bags from the back seat. It looked as though he had been shopping. Christmas gifts maybe. As he slammed the door, clicking the locks, the front door opened and one of his little brats appeared, quickly followed by Caroline.

Fern's cheeks were flushed with rage as he kissed his wife on the lips before following her into the house.

She fired a message off to Meg.

The cheating bastard lied to me. He's home with his wife.

A message pinged back.

You need to confront him. This is your chance. Go tell his wife what a cheat he is.

Fired up as she was, Fern considered the implications of that. She could lose her job, would certainly lose Peter. Was that what she really wanted? She debated for a few moments, looked at the house again, decorated with an elegant string of blue twinkling lights. She imagined the family inside; the cheat, the mouse and their brats. Were they laughing and joking as they discussed their day in the warmth of the house?

Frustrated, she thumped the steering wheel, knew she wasn't going to get out of the car.

Instead she drove home via the supermarket, picking up a bottle of vodka.

Once home she slammed the door, kicked off her trainers, and grabbed the mail off the mat. Walking through to the kitchen, barking orders to Alexa to turn on lights as she went, she threw the mail down on to the growing collection on the table – it was mostly spiralling credit card bills that she was avoiding – and reached in the cupboard for a glass. She opened the vodka bottle, poured a large measure and topped it up with Diet Coke from the fridge.

Shower, dinner (though to be honest, she wasn't really hungry) then she would upload on to her social media accounts another one of the selfies she had taken at the weekend, where she was looking glammed up and gorgeous, pouting for the camera with come-to-bed eyes. The picture would attract plenty of attention from her male friends and she knew it would piss off Peter.

She had finished her drink and just fixed another one, when the doorbell rang.

Peter?

Despite the cosy scene she had just left, there was no doubt in her mind that it was her boss. Perhaps she had misjudged the situation. Maybe Caroline's trip had been cancelled; that was why he had found it harder to get away.

She rushed to the door, threw it open... and was dismayed when she found Janice Plum standing on the doorstep. 'What do you want?' Fern didn't bother to hide her disappointment.

'We need to talk, Fern.'

'I'm busy.' She started to shut the door, and was shocked when Janice stuck her foot out, stopping it from closing. 'What the hell do you think you're doing? I said I'm busy.'

'And I said we need to talk. This is important.'

Fern hesitated, understood from the determined look on Janice's face that she wasn't going to get rid of her easily. Giving in, she pulled the door wide open. 'Ten minutes. And it had better be good.'

She turned and walked back to the kitchen. Heard the door close and heavy footsteps as Janice followed. Leaning back against the counter, she sipped her vodka and Coke, scornfully eyeing her old friend. Whatever did the stupid woman look like in her oversized pink jumper, emblazoned with the sequinned words 'Hot Stuff', that clashed with her bright red hair, and her skinny jeans that were two sizes too small?

'So go on, what is it?'

'I need to show you something.' Janice started rummaging through her handbag, also oversized.

'What?'

'I've been trying to contact you.'

'I know.'

'You didn't reply.'

'I've been busy.' Fern made a point of looking at the clock and sighing dramatically. 'What do you need to show me?' she asked impatiently.

'They're in here somewhere.'

'Well, chop-chop, I don't have all night.'

In frustration, Janice tipped her bag upside down, the contents spilling out.

'Be careful,' Fern scolded, furious as screwed-up tissues and tampons landed on her table. She picked up a lipstick that had clattered to the floor. A dark red shade that she suspected made Janice look more Rocky Horror than Marilyn Monroe.

'Here they are.' Janice waved three letters at her.

Fern snatched them, reading the words, the blood draining from her face as she got to the third one. 'What are these? Some kind of sick joke?'

'I don't think they're funny.'

'Where did you get them? Who sent them?'

'The first two were put through the letterbox, the last one was left on my windscreen.'

'Who have you told?'

'No one.'

The woman was lying. 'Who the fuck have you told?'

'I swear, no one, Fern. I promised I would never breathe a word to anyone and I haven't.'

'What about Martin?'

'He doesn't know. I swear he doesn't.'

'So who the fuck sent these? Someone knows. Unless of course you've done something else I don't know about.'

The dig was cruel, Fern knew that. She was just so bloody mad at Janice right now. Her evening had already gone to rat-shit and it was getting steadily worse. This was bad. If someone knew the truth, it could be the end for all of them.

'I haven't done anything and I didn't tell anyone.' Janice's bottom lip was trembling, at first Fern thought in anger, but then drippy great tears spilled on to her reddened cheeks.

Oh for fuck's sake. She handed a sheet of kitchen roll to the blubbering woman. 'Here.'

'Than–thank you.' Janice wiped her eyes, honked her nose. 'I thought... I thought maybe you got a note too.'

'Nope. Nothing.'

'Are you sure?'

'Of course I'm bloody sure. Do you not believe me?'

Janice's eyes shifted hesitantly to the pile of unopened mail on the table. 'I just...'

Fern followed her gaze, shifted guiltily. 'I'm busy. I haven't had time to go through it.'

When Janice remained silent, the guilt kicked up a notch. 'Okay, okay, I'll look. I'm telling you though, it's all just work stuff and utility bills.'

She sifted through the mail, unease creeping in when she spotted the two white envelopes with just her name typed on the front. No postmark, so hand-delivered.

'You have something, don't you?' Janice accused.

'I never saw these.'

Fern ripped the first envelope open, read aloud the note inside. 'A long, long time ago, you did a bad, bad thing. Everyone's past catches up with them eventually, including yours. Soon.' She glanced at Janice. 'It's the same as yours.'

Janice's face had paled and she fidgeted nervously with the screwed-up piece of kitchen tissue. 'What about the other one?'

Fern opened the second note, drew a sharp intake of breath when she saw the one written word.

'What does it say?'

'It's just...' She couldn't finish the sentence. Instead, she held up the note to show Janice. The one typed word clearly standing out on the paper.

Killer.

9

It seemed almost incomprehensible that someone had stolen the photo out of the kitchen while they had both been in the restaurant, but there was no other explanation. The photo had been on the counter and after the door had been opened, it was gone.

That meant that whoever had left it for Olivia, whoever had set the man in the house on Honington Lane on fire, had been close by watching her, and honestly that, above everything else, freaked the crap out of her.

Noah had agreed not to tell Elena or Jamie, accepting that the situation was already difficult to explain and would only upset Elena. As promised though, Olivia did contact DC Upton and told him about the photograph, plus the earlier note and phone call she had received. He had sounded sceptical on the phone, and struggled to hide his suspicion that Olivia was involved in the man's death in some way when he saw her in person to collect the note, pressing her as though he believed she was sitting on information. He also seemed dubious about the photograph, as if she had made that bit up, and that pissed her off.

After giving her some general safety advice and telling her to contact him if anything else happened, he had left with the note and she hadn't heard anything since.

Over the next few days, a sense of normality returned. Whoever had been harassing her had stepped back into the shadows, and for that Olivia was relieved. Come Monday she was back at work at the estate agents, and she just wanted to put the whole mess behind her and move on.

But then the burning man's identity was revealed in the press on Friday.

She knew him.

It was her lodger, Molly, who had spotted the news article while browsing online. 'His name was Gary Lamb.'

'His what?' Olivia was in the kitchen cooking, the radio on, and only heard part of what Molly had said. Leaving the curry she was making to simmer, she stuck her head round the living room door. 'What did you say? I didn't hear you.'

Molly glanced up from the armchair where she sat, her feet tucked under her. Her blue eyes were sombre. 'The man you found. They've released his identity. It says here he was called Gary Lamb.'

She continued to read the article and Olivia heard the words 'foreman' and 'divorced', but she had pretty much zoned out. She had gone to high school with a Gary Lamb, and although she hadn't seen him since leaving school, her mind was back in the kitchen of 8 Honington Lane, remembering the look in those terrified brown eyes. He had aged, put on weight and started to lose his hair, but she knew. It had been him.

'Livvy, are you okay?' Molly's voice brought her back and she found her lodger looking at her with concern.

'I think I went to school with him.'

'You *knew* him?'

'Is there a picture?'

'Yeah, a small one. Hang on, let me see if I can blow it up.' Molly fiddled with her phone then handed it over.

Olivia stared at the picture, the wafting smell of the curry, that just moments ago had her stomach growling, now making her feel sick, the background noise from the radio irritating rather than entertaining. Yes, she knew Gary from the picture, recognising those narrowed hooded eyes and the pinched expression.

Had Gary's killer known they had gone to school together?

It was too coincidental to believe otherwise.

Which suggested this terrible thing Olivia was supposed to have done had happened when she had been in her early teens.

They had gone to school together, but they didn't hang out, their paths barely crossing. Gary had been a popular kid, though he had a mean streak. He certainly hadn't been in Olivia's circle of friends.

'Are you all right?' Molly took back her phone, studying Olivia carefully. 'Maybe you should sit down. Do you want me to get you a glass of water?'

'I'm okay.'

Molly frowned, her expression concerned. 'You don't look okay. Look, sit down. I'll get you some water.'

Olivia nodded, dropping down on to the sofa. 'Thank you.'

Her lodger had been a lifesaver since her break-up with Toby. She had initially been dubious about her friend moving in, worrying that the close proximity might destroy the easy-going relationship they shared, but the mortgage had been too much to afford on her own salary, and Molly had turned out to be the perfect lodger; discreet, pragmatic, considerate and always on time with the rent money. Plus, she had made the big house feel less empty.

'Should you make the police aware that you knew the victim?' she asked now, handing Olivia the glass.

'I will. I'll call DC Upton in the morning.'

Seeing Gary Lamb's face had brought everything flooding back. Olivia had woken a couple of times during the week in the middle of a nightmare where she was back in the kitchen watching him burn, but the constant loop playing in her head had gradually started to fade. Her mother wanted her to see a counsellor, to talk through the trauma, but Olivia was pretty certain that, given time, she could conquer this by herself. People suffered through far worse every day, like her mother's friend, Jill, who had been mugged at knifepoint, or that girl who was dating her friend Tom's brother. Lola or Lila something. She had survived a car accident then nearly been murdered. Those were the people who needed counselling. Yes, Olivia had seen something horrible, but it hadn't actually involved her.

Liar, a little voice in her head whispered, as she tried to ignore the killer's attempt to contact her.

She must have appeared shocked at the news of the victim's identity because Molly was looking at her with sympathy all over her face. 'Tell you what, how about I pour you a glass of wine and you can sit here and get to grips with all of this while I go finish dinner?'

'You don't have to do that.'

'I want to. Let me help you, Livvy.'

'Thank you.' Molly was a bloody good friend and Olivia would make it up to her. She picked up her phone as Molly disappeared back into the kitchen, fired off a quick message to Noah.

They identified the man I found. I know him.

His reply didn't take long.

Coming over.

He showed up just as they finished eating. Olivia hadn't mentioned to Molly that she had messaged Noah, knowing she wasn't a fan. Olivia was clearing the table, her hands full, when the doorbell rang, followed by impatient knocking. Luna, who had been snoozing on the other end of the sofa, woke with a start and fled for the stairs.

'I'll get it,' Molly yelled from the kitchen, her voice travelling over the sound of Phil Collins, and Olivia heard the bells on Molly's slippers jingling as she went to the door, leaving her no time to intervene.

Sod it. Molly and Noah were both important people in her life and they were going to have to find a way to get along.

'Oh, it's you.'

'Hi, Molly. You're looking lovely this evening. That black jumper really brings out the colour in your eyes.'

'Fuck you.'

So that plan worked well.

Olivia stepped into the hallway, ready to referee. Molly scowled as she took the dirty plates from her. 'I'll go sort these. Looks like you have company.' She threw a scathing look at Noah, who didn't help matters by insolently grinning at her as he kicked his boots off.

'Molly! Damn it,' Olivia snapped in exasperation. 'Just wait a second.'

Ignoring her, Molly stomped off down the hallway to the kitchen, the stomping made slightly ridiculous by the large reindeer slippers she wore on her feet.

'I think she secretly likes me.'

'Really? That's what you think?' Olivia closed the door and followed Noah through into the living room where he was already making himself comfortable in the spot vacated by the cat. Other than DC Upton, he was the only one who knew about the killer's attempts to contact her, was certainly the only one who believed her. 'Luna was just sitting there. You're gonna have a hairy arse.'

He looked at her solemnly. 'How do you know I don't already have one?'

Olivia's eyes widened momentarily, before the grin broke on his face and she realised he was joking. She couldn't help smiling back as she went to join him on the sofa. 'Clown. I told you not to wind Molly up.'

'Sorry. She bites too easily.'

Perhaps she did, but Noah played on that. Had done ever since he had started picking up on Molly's frostiness towards him, which had been worse since Olivia had become involved with him. Molly, for whatever reason, was put out and made continual digs at Noah, which led to Noah calling her the grim reaper, because she mostly wore black. She hadn't forgiven him for that, and had made her feelings known to Olivia that she thought her friend had shitty taste in men.

It was an awkward position to be in and Olivia had tried to play peacemaker, but Molly and Noah were both strong-willed and she despaired of the pair of them.

'Anyway, enough about Molly. How are you holding up?' He smoothed a hand over her hair, lips curving as he pulled her close for a lingering kiss that completely scrambled her brain.

She had fancied Noah Keen the moment she had laid eyes on him, when he had shown up in the restaurant one day with Jamie. The pair of them were friends and Noah had done Jamie a deal on some new security cameras for the restaurant. He was six foot one of lean, tanned ruggedness with an infectious grin and sharp green eyes that didn't miss a beat, and when Jamie had introduced them and Noah had smiled at her, he had sucker-punched her right in the gut.

Olivia had sworn off men. She had been with Toby for eleven years before he cheated on her and other than that, only had under her belt one disastrous alcohol-fuelled fail at a one-night stand. Both were enough to put her off. Noah had flipped her ideas of remaining celibate on its head, and she was both tongue-tied and flustered in his presence.

He was so easy-going that her initial awkwardness had quickly thawed, and they had eased into a steady friendship. Yes, she fancied him, thought she had given off enough signals, but he never once reciprocated. There was no wedding ring, no mention of girlfriends or boyfriends, yet he seemed to want to spend time in her company. That had changed about six weeks ago and although neither of them had yet defined what was going on between them, they had been fairly inseparable since.

He eased away from her now, his expression serious. 'We need to talk about your message.'

'Molly doesn't know about the note or the photo.' Olivia kept her tone down. 'I'd rather keep it that way, okay?'

'We can go down the pub if you want. Or upstairs.'

Olivia considered that. She wasn't really up for the pub, but they could go upstairs. It would give Molly the living room back. Her friend had been so good to her these last few days: it would be a token gesture. 'Okay, upstairs.' Seeing the corner of Noah's mouth curve into a grin, she added. 'To talk, Romeo.'

'Of course.'

'Do you want a coffee?'

'I could use a beer.'

'There's some bottles of Heineken in the fridge.'

'Sold.'

'Go upstairs. I'll be up in a minute.'

Molly was in the kitchen loading the dishwasher and Olivia felt a pang of guilt as she topped up her wine glass and grabbed Noah's beer. 'Thank you for sorting dinner. We're gonna go upstairs and get out of your way. Living room is all yours.'

Molly continued to rinse and stack the plates. She didn't turn round. 'No need to do that. It's your house,' she muttered stiffly.

'It is, but you live here too. We'll go upstairs. You can have Netflix if you want.'

'Maybe.'

'Give him a chance, Molly. Please, for me?'

Molly's shoulders tensed as she stopped what she was doing. Still though, she refused to turn. 'Just be careful, Livvy.'

10

Noah had made himself comfortable on Olivia's pretty lemon duvet, legs outstretched as he leant back against the mound of cushions on top of the pillows (what was the thing with women and cushions?) and was making a fuss of the cat, who was sprawled on his lap, when Olivia walked into the room. She used her foot to push the door shut, before passing him his beer, then set her glass of wine down on the bedside table and flopped down on her back beside him, startling the cat, who bolted off his lap and under the bed.

'Sorry, Luna.' She let out a sigh, closing her eyes and rubbing them with the heels of her hands.

'So, Gary Lamb.'

Her eyes immediately opened. 'You know his name?'

'It's all over the news, Liv.' He took a drink of his beer as he studied her, not bothering to point out that he had already been looking into the man. She had been through a lot these last few days and the stress was showing in her pale face. That she hadn't been sleeping properly was clear in the dark smudges beneath her eyes. He decided to tread carefully. 'You said you knew him?'

'We went to school together.'

'Friends?'

'He was a mean little shit, so no, we weren't friends.' Olivia sat up, picked up her wine and took a sip, and he could see her mind working overtime. 'It makes no sense. We went to the same school, shared a couple of classes, but we didn't hang out together or anything. Why me? What am I supposed to have done that got Gary killed?'

'Nothing ever happened at school? Nothing that involved Gary, or you even?'

'No. Like I said, he was a mean bully. Always picking on the weaker kids, showing off and trying to get a laugh at their expense, but it was standard high school stuff.'

'And you never saw him after school? Didn't run into him in any pubs or clubs? Your paths never crossed?'

'I don't think so.' She frowned. 'I guess we probably crossed each other's paths on nights out, but I don't specifically remember.'

'What about mutual friends? Did you have any of those?'

'I don't remember. Maybe. What would that have to do with it? I left school fifteen years ago.'

'Humour me, okay? I'm trying to figure out a link.'

'You're pretty intense when you go into cop mode.'

A brief smile touched Noah's lips. Intense had never been a word his superiors in the force had used to describe him. Reckless, insubordinate, cocky; those words had all been thrown around before he'd made the decision to leave the police, but never intense. Intense was better suited to his dad. The colonel had been a stickler for rules. Moving from country to country and school to school, rules had been a way of life and Noah had rebelled against every single one of them.

'So no mutual friends, at all?' he pressed, ignoring her comment.

'Hold on, I'm thinking.' Olivia was frowning again, creasing the two little lines between her eyebrows, her lips pursed. 'Fern, I guess would be the only link.'

'Fern?'

'Fern St Clair. We went to school together... used to be friends. She had a thing with Gary's best mate, Howard, for a while.'

'When did you last see her?'

'Crikey, I don't think I've seen her since we left school.'

'Anyone else?'

'By process of elimination, Janice Hardesty. She followed Fern everywhere, loved it when Fern and I fell out.'

'Why did you fall out?'

'I really don't see how any of this is relevant.'

'Just answer the question.'

Olivia huffed a little and shifted her position, lying down again so her head was resting in his lap. 'Fern wasn't a particularly nice person. After she was pretty awful to another friend of mine, I cooled the friendship.' She glanced up at him. 'Are we done talking about her? I haven't seen her in years and she's not someone I really want to spend my Friday night thinking about.'

Fern St Clair and Janice Hardesty. Noah committed both names to memory, as he played with the ends of Olivia's hair. 'What was Howard's last name?'

'What? Why...' When he raised his eyebrows, she rolled her eyes in defeat. 'Peck. Are you done now or do you want to know what Gary used to have for school dinners?'

'We're done.'

'Good, because honestly, I just want to put this really crappy week behind me.'

'I'm happy to help you with that.'

Her grey-blue eyes widened at his suggestion and he recognised the struggle behind them as need battled wariness. Something kept holding her back, but as of yet, he hadn't managed to get to the bottom of it. Reminding himself that he could be patient, he shifted her weight in his lap and adjusted his position, dipping his head to softly, chastely, kiss her on the mouth. She tasted of the wine she had been sipping, her lips warm and inviting. When she relaxed into the kiss, he deepened it. Not too fast, not too aggressive, his hand cupping her face then easing back into her hair, wrapping his fingers around it and tugging gently.

Slow and steady, letting her set the pace. Responding with just light strokes and gentle kisses as she hugged him closer, then broke away from his mouth to nibble at his neck, her fingers moving up into his hair. Need intensified, his hand slipping lower and creeping beneath her jumper, finding warm flesh.

Olivia froze against him, her hand clamping around his wrist. 'No.'

He paused, bit down on the frustration, and carefully removed his hand, freed it from her grip, and pulled away from her, sitting back up on the bed and running his fingers back through his hair. 'Okay, so are we going to talk about this?'

Smoothing down her jumper, she refused to make eye contact with him, so he caught her chin between his thumb and forefinger, gently raised her head so she had no choice. 'Come on. Talk to me, Liv. If this isn't working out for you, I deserve to know.'

Something was eating at her. She was a thirty-one-year-old woman, who had been in a long-term relationship, and she had always struck him as easy-going and comfortable in her own skin.

'No!' She appeared horrified at the suggestion she wasn't attracted to him. 'It's not that. It's...' She swallowed hard, eased away from him, reaching for her wine glass and taking a couple of large sips. Putting it down again, she hugged her knees to her chest, eyed him warily. 'There's something I need to tell you. I haven't been honest with you.'

Noah's heart thumped at that. He thought he knew her, but was now questioning just how well. 'Okay, go on.'

Olivia hesitated, seeming unsure how to begin. As she searched for the right words, a loud crash came from below, followed by a piercing scream.

Her eyes widened. 'Molly!'

Noah was already off the bed, heading towards the door, could hear Olivia behind him. They found Molly in the kitchen, wide-eyed and pale-faced, blood pouring from a gash in her arm.

'Jesus, you're bleeding.' Olivia pushed past Noah, grabbed a tea towel, pressing it to the wound.

'What the hell happened?'

Molly stared at Noah, none of the usual animosity in her eyes. He recognised fear.

'There was someone outside.'

'What do you mean outside? Outside where?'

'In the back garden. I went out to the bin, didn't see him till he knocked into me.' She glanced at Olivia. 'I'm sorry, I was scared and he startled me. I broke the wine bottle. There's glass everywhere.'

'Oh God, I don't care about stupid glass.'

Leaving Olivia to tend to Molly's wound, Noah flicked the switch for the outdoor light and let himself out of the back door. It was freezing outside, a frost already settling on the ground. The back garden was enclosed, the gate that led to the front swinging open. He stepped through into the driveway, checked the front of the house, certain whoever it was had long gone. Still, after he closed the gate, he did a quick sweep of the back garden before going back inside.

Olivia had fetched antiseptic cream and dressing, and was tending to Molly's wound, while Molly sat at the kitchen table, sipping at a glass of water. She still looked a little shaken up and he could see that she had been crying.

'Does she need to go to A&E?'

'It looks worse than it is,' Olivia told him. 'A lot of blood, but it's not too deep. Did you see anyone?'

He shook his head, locking the door. 'Whoever it was is long gone. Are you going to report it?'

'Do you think it's connected?'

Molly glanced between them. 'Connected to what?'

'Umm...' Realising she had tripped up, Olivia looked to Noah in panic.

'There's been a spate of burglaries in Salhouse,' he told Molly, the lie rolling smoothly off his tongue. 'I've picked up quite a bit of work off the back of it.'

'Oh. Livvy never mentioned anything.'

'Sorry, Molly. I've been a little preoccupied.'

'Speak with your police contact tomorrow,' Noah suggested to Olivia. 'He can pass any information on to the right people.'

'Do you think this could have anything to do with what happened to Gary Lamb?' Molly's eyes were wide and she looked scared.

'Why would you think that?'

'Well, it's a bit of a coincidence, you finding him the way you did and now this happening tonight.' Molly's voice dropped to a whisper. 'What if the person who killed Gary saw you in the house? What if they decide to come after you because you're a loose end?'

'That's not going to happen.' Molly might have had a scare, but Noah could see that her words were freaking out Olivia. 'I seriously doubt what happened tonight is connected. It was probably just kids messing around.'

'You said burglars.'

'Well, kids, burglars, but nothing more sinister.' He glanced at Olivia, held eye contact for a moment. They both knew Molly's theory, while wrong, was far too close to the truth. 'I can stay here tonight if you want. On the sofa,' he added, when Olivia opened her mouth to protest.

That conversation they had been having upstairs would have to wait.

'You don't have to do that. We'll be fine.'

'Okay, well the offer is there.'

'Honestly, we're good. We'll make sure all the doors and windows are locked, put on a movie, open another bottle of wine.' Olivia finished dressing Molly's arm, found a smile for him. Noah suspected she was putting on a brave front for her lodger. 'Nothing to worry about at all.'

11

She knows I am watching her now.

The note, the phone call and the photograph have her worried, and I am feeding off her reactions.

Tonight was fun. Unplanned, but fun. An attack on the lodger in the garden, it was inspired. The broken glass, the drama, and the look on Olivia's face. Knowing that her lodger is jittery and will probably be nervous about being alone, it's something else for her to worry about.

The silly bitch hasn't figured it out yet, but give her time and eventually she will.

That infuriates me, you know, finding out just how insignificant you were to her. But I will make her remember, I will make her regret, and I will make sure that you are the last person she is thinking about before she dies.

12

Monday morning's alarm brought with it both dread and relief.

Olivia didn't relish going back to work. She was unsure what reaction she would get from her colleagues and did not want to rehash everything that had happened over the past week. But going back to work was a return to normal and she really needed normal right now.

Aside from food shopping, she had spent the weekend at home. Molly still seemed shaken from the encounter in the garden and Olivia didn't want to leave her alone.

Not that she had any plans to go anywhere. Noah had shown up unexpectedly on the Saturday morning, insisting on fitting fancy cameras to the front and back of the house, but he hadn't stayed. They had no weekend plans, and he didn't attempt to make any, leaving things casually open.

Olivia wasn't sure how she felt about that. While she appreciated that he was giving her space, she also worried that he was losing patience with her. She knew she had to talk to him, that she had already let everything become too big a deal, but she was still building up to that, so she hadn't pushed. Instead, she holed up with Molly for a Netflix marathon, and tried her best to forget about Noah, the notes, and the anguished screams of Gary Lamb.

She didn't sleep well Sunday night and was exhausted before she had even arrived at her city centre office. Esther was off sick, which meant Olivia was stuck all day with Roger and Jeremy. While she had been off, someone had put up a Christmas tree and there was a CD of Christmas songs quietly playing on loop. She was certain this was going to drive her mad before the end of the week.

December was a quiet time for property sales, and with few customers, it was the Roger and Jeremy show as the pair of them engaged in unfunny, occasionally sexist banter.

Olivia kept her head down, having no interest in joining in. She flicked from her home screen on to Google and tried to find out what she could about Gary Lamb.

She had already scoured the news reports and there was no new information available. Thirty-one and divorced, he had worked as the foreman for a building company. His death was being treated as murder and both Cadwallader brothers had been questioned, as had Gary's ex-wife, but if the police did have any leads they weren't being reported.

Olivia was grateful that so far, her name had been kept out of the press, though knew it wouldn't take much for the media to find out her identity.

She turned her attention to social media instead, finding Gary had been prolific on Facebook, Instagram and Twitter. Most of his posts were repeated across the three sites and, given that she could see plenty of them, it seemed he had been lax on privacy. They were mostly memes and there were a dozen a day, but interspersed between the memes were personal posts and it was those that gave the best insight into Gary's life.

He had never been much of a looker, but that hadn't dented his confidence. Age had taken its toll on both his waist and his hairline, but Gary Lamb still considered himself to be both a lad and a ladies' man, and from what Olivia could see, he hadn't changed much from school. The memes bordered on offensive and from the comments it seemed he still liked to play the bully.

One name that repeatedly popped up was Rita Works, liking and commenting on all of his posts, and from the flirty way Gary responded, it suggested the pair of them had probably been involved.

Rita's profile was private and her picture, which was heavily filtered, showed a red-haired woman, her face swallowed up by huge sunglasses, pouting at the camera.

Seeing Roger get up from his desk, she quickly flicked her screen back to her work emails, knowing that her boss disapproved of social media use during work time.

'I'm going to take an early lunch, then head straight on to my appointment,' he announced, slipping into his coat. 'Jeremy, can I leave you to lock up tonight?'

'Sure thing, boss.'

'And, Olivia, you'll have the rest of those properties typed up before you leave?'

'Of course.'

She wanted to salute him behind his back, but knew Jeremy was watching and he would snitch. Roger had decided to revamp all of the property portfolios on purpose just to punish her, she was certain of that. They had all been waiting on her desk for her to retype and he hadn't even gone through the charade of dividing them up between the team. No, he was annoyed that, backed into a corner, he had been forced to give her a few days off.

Roger was all about profit and building his bank balance. Those days off had cost him and now Olivia was paying for it.

The afternoon passed painfully slowly and Olivia tried to keep her head down, concentrating on her workload, and ignoring the popping sound Jeremy kept making as he sucked his cheek. She couldn't see his monitor, but she was fairly certain from his laid-back stance and the fact he kept grinning at his screen that he wasn't doing anything work-related. Whatever it was kept him occupied, though, and that was fine by her.

She was halfway through typing up the final portfolio when her phone vibrated on the desk and Noah's name flashed up on the screen. Picking it up, she read the message.

How was your first day back?

She fired a quick reply.

Same old. Stuck in the office with just Jeremy this afternoon. It's dragged.

As she put her phone down, she glanced across at her co-worker, irritated when she realised he was watching her. 'What?'

He didn't answer her, instead smirking, letting his gaze linger for a few seconds longer before turning back to his screen.

Odious man.

Trying to forget he was there, Olivia finished typing up the portfolio, saved it, and logged off her computer, just as the clock hit 5.30 p.m. She glanced at her phone, noted that Noah hadn't replied to her message. He had been quiet most of the weekend, so she guessed he was either giving her some space or was annoyed about Friday night.

Olivia had to talk to him. He deserved to know the truth. She just wished she hadn't put it off for so long.

She went through to use the toilet at the back of the building while Jeremy started locking up the office. As she washed her hands, her thoughts remained on Noah. She would message him again, she decided, see what he was up to and invite herself over, then she would act like an adult, sit down and talk to him. She couldn't let one humiliating experience define her.

Jeremy had already switched the main lights off and Olivia made her way along the hallway in darkness, cursing him and knowing he had probably done it on purpose. She had almost reached the door that led to the front office when he stepped out of the tiny kitchen, scaring the bejesus out of her. 'Damn it, don't do that!'

'You're a bit jumpy, Blake.'

'So would you be if someone sprang out at you like that.'

'Take a chill-pill, woman. You need to lighten up a bit. A good shag would probably sort you out.'

Olivia's temper spiked, but she kept her tone cool, ignoring his crude observation. 'Is that how you get your kicks, lurking in dark hallways, scaring the shit out of women?'

Although it was dark, she saw him curl his lip and was satisfied that her jibe had hit its target.

'Trust me, you have no idea how I get my kicks.'

There was something in his tone she didn't like. Jeremy Fox was slimy, rude and had a nasty streak, but she had never found him intimidating before.

Not wanting him to see that he was creeping her out, she stuck out her chin and gave him her best haughty look. 'No, you're right, I don't. And I have better things to do than hang around here and discuss your pervy inclinations.'

As she made to walk past him, he moved, so he was standing between her and the door, and a cool sliver of fear iced its way down Olivia's back. This was Jeremy. She had worked with him for a year. She knew him, and yes, he was a bit of a dick, but he wouldn't actually hurt her. He was just fooling around and trying to spook her a little. And it was only working because of everything that had happened over the past week. Which made him an even bigger shit for not cutting her any slack.

Still, as she rationalised, a niggling little voice kept chipping away, reminding her that she didn't actually know him that well. Yes, they worked together, but what did she know of his life outside of work? She knew that he had moved to Norfolk at the start of the year, that he lived alone, that he was good at selling houses, and that he was a sleaze. Beyond that though, she knew nothing about him at all.

'What was it like?'

'What?'

'What was it like?' Jeremy repeated, stepping back so his body was now fully blocking the door. He was taller than her, maybe by half a foot. 'When you walked into the house and found him, that man, what was it like?'

Was he being serious?

'What the hell do you think it was like? He died in front of me.'

'Did you watch his skin melt off? Could you smell him burning?'

'You're disgusting.' Anger overriding the fear, Olivia shoved into him, barrelling him out of the way. As her hand closed on the door knob, fingers dug into her arm, pulling her back.

'I think you were lured there on purpose.' Jeremy's voice was almost a whisper against her ear. 'I wonder why.'

'Let go of me!'

Olivia wrenched her arm free, pushed open the door to the front office. Jeremy didn't follow. He stood in the doorway watching her as she grabbed her coat from the rack and slipped into it, an amused look on his face. She kept a wary eye on him as she picked up her bag, crossed to the front door, part afraid he had locked it. On the other side of the glass it was raining. Commuters were rushing by, some with umbrellas, others hunkered down in coats. They were so close.

She tried the handle, relieved when it opened. Out in the street, she let out the breath she hadn't realised she was holding, fastening the buttons of her coat with shaking fingers. The rain was coming down hard and fast now, slicking down her hair and dripping off the end of her nose. As she reached in her bag for her umbrella, Olivia glanced into the dark window of the office. She could just make out Jeremy's silhouette in the doorway, knew he was watching her. Quickly she turned away, blending into the rush-hour crowd, eager to get back to her car.

The encounter had unnerved her. Was Jeremy playing one of his mind-fuck games or had his intentions been more sinister? Regardless, he had stepped over a line and made her feel unsafe in her workplace. She had to tell Roger.

But what would her boss do?

Ultimately it was her word against Jeremy's. There had been no witnesses and, aside from asking a couple of wholly inappropriate questions, the rest was circumstantial. Yes, Jeremy had turned the lights out. Olivia could say it was to scare her, but Jeremy would point out he was simply locking up. And okay, she had felt threatened when he blocked the door, but other than grabbing hold of her arm, he hadn't actually done anything to her or prevented her from leaving.

Jeremy sold houses by the shedload and was an asset to Roger. There was no way he would be cut loose.

Frustrated, she cut down the side street that led to the car park, ignoring the niggling question of why Jeremy had been so interested in Gary's death. Had he simply been asking out of morbid curiosity? Her mind went back to the note she had received, the one she had found on her car.

She had initially toyed with the idea that Jeremy had put it there as a joke.

Was he somehow involved in Gary's murder?

13

Fern St Clair had started the weekend in denial, but by Monday morning she had reached acceptance. Anger, bargaining and depression had been squeezed somewhere in between, with a good healthy dose of panic.

The anger had followed swiftly after denial, both occurring Friday night. Janice, who had still been in the house, had endured the brunt of both, firstly being accused of sending the notes and playing a cruel joke. Then when logic kicked in and Fern realised it was no joke, she had lashed out at her old school friend, blaming her for everything else. Either she had blabbed or one of the others had blabbed, but regardless of who had done the blabbing, it was still Janice's fault. Then when Fern was on her sixth double vodka and the stupid woman had suggested she might want to ease up on her drinking, she had seen red and hurled her glass at Janice.

Janice was a beast of a woman and she had always had slow reactions, but on this occasion she had somehow managed to duck, the glass smashing against the wall behind her. Shortly afterwards, as Fern had sobbed in rage, Janice had beaten a hasty retreat.

Fern had gone to bed annoyed, woken up furious, and had spent much of Saturday nursing a hangover and pacing like a caged animal. By Sunday she had started bargaining. What was done was done. She would track down the leak and then figure out who had sent the letters. This was blackmail and blackmailers could be paid off.

She was no longer in contact with Kelly or Rachel. And she hadn't spoken with Howard recently. The last time had been several months ago when they had hooked up for sex, something they did on occasion when they were both drunk and horny. They were friends on Facebook, though, and so that was where she started, pinging him a casual message asking for a meet-up. Then, while she waited for his reply, she tried to track down Kelly and Rachel.

Rachel Williams proved to be a fruitless task. Fern hadn't seen her in years and she could have been any one of the hundred Rachel Williamses on Facebook. That's if she was even on there. Kelly Dearborn wasn't on any social media sites, but a Google search eventually tracked her down.

Unfortunately, it didn't provide Fern with any comfort.

Kelly Dearborn was dead and as Fern read the news articles regarding the suspicious house fire in which she had perished, a chill went through her.

Kelly had died in a house fire eighteen months ago.

And now Gary had burnt to death. That couldn't be a coincidence.

Feeling sick, she had messaged Janice the news about Kelly before nipping out to the corner off-licence. Once back she had checked all the doors and windows were locked before pouring another vodka. This called for triple measures.

Janice replied almost immediately with three shocked emojis.

Oh my God. What are we gonna do?

Fern threw her phone on the sofa, not bothering to reply. Why was it always her job to sort out the mess? Janice used her like a crutch.

Sipping the vodka, she checked her message to Howard. He had read it, but not replied. She glanced at his profile picture. The hipster beard and man bun made him look a bit of a prat. Howard had always kept up with the trends, but this new look really didn't work for him.

'Fuck you, Howard Peck!' *Always thought he was something special, that one*. She would give him until the morning and God help him if he hadn't got back to her by then.

Sunday evening was spent in a vodka-fuelled depression. She was still reeling from the uncomfortable revelation that both Kelly and Gary had burnt to death. She slept on the sofa that night. Not through choice, but because she was too paralytic to climb the stairs to bed.

Monday brought with it a monster hangover and disgust that she fallen asleep fully clothed.

After calling in sick at work, she downed a couple of paracetamol with a glass of water then dragged herself upstairs for a shower. It was as she was soaping herself down that she finally reached acceptance.

Someone knew the truth about what had happened and was taking matters into their own hands. Fern was still unsure whether the person who had sent the notes was responsible for Kelly and Gary's deaths, though it was looking likely. That meant she had to find out who was targeting them and then try to resolve this. She needed to round up Howard, Janice and, if they could find her, Rachel, and between them they could make a plan of action.

As she sent a message to Janice, fired off a second snotty one to Howard, her mind wandered back to another familiar name.

To someone who had been the catalyst for everything that had happened that day.

Maybe it was time to have a talk with Olivia Blake.

* * *

Hearing his phone ping, Howard reached into his pocket, expecting it to be Daisy. Irritation creasing his brow when he saw Fern St Clair's face on the screen.

He had seen her message yesterday, hadn't replied because, truth was, he wasn't that interested in meeting up for a quick shag, not since meeting Daisy. Fern had an okay face and a fairly hot body, and yes, she wasn't a bad lay, but she was a seven, tops, compared with Daisy's nine-and-a-half. Howard never scored a full ten, because he liked to think there was always room for improvement.

The problem with Fern, though, was she didn't take rejection kindly. The pair of them had been occasional fuck-buddies for close to fifteen years. Sometimes they met up several times a year, but recently it had been less frequent.

It was no strings attached, but still Howard feared her reaction when she learnt he was hoping to settle down with Daisy. So, in true Howard Peck style, he had blanked her message, hoping she would just go away.

Of course, this was Fern St Clair he was talking about. She was not going to just go away. Nope. He read her message now, his balls shrinking as the angry tone of her words warned him he was in trouble. Howard didn't want to meet up with her, but knew he had to come clean about Daisy. He typed:

I wasn't ignoring you. I fell asleep. When do you want to meet?

Coward. He was just buying himself some time, he rationalised with himself. Fern was mad at him right now and it wasn't a good time to tell her about Daisy. Let her calm down and he would tell her in person. That was better, wasn't it?

Of course, deep down he knew that wouldn't happen. Fern could be quite persuasive and Howard had no willpower. They would fuck and he would do his best to make sure that Daisy never found out.

Fern's reply was almost instant.

Come to my place tonight. 8 p.m. Janice is going to be here too.

Janice? Howard racked his brains. The only Janice he could think of was Fern's trucker of a friend from school. He didn't realise they were still in touch. Why the hell would Janice be there? Was Fern expecting a threesome? Because, while they had tried plenty of kinky shit in the past and Howard was definitely up for the idea of a threesome, he wasn't sure he could get his dick hard for Janice.

She's not really my type. Don't you have any other friends you could invite?

While he waited for a response, he checked Janice out on Facebook anyway, just to see if he could. He hadn't seen her in years. Maybe she had improved with age. A quick glance at her profile picture told him she hadn't.

Fern's reply flashed up on the screen.

Oh, for God's sake. This isn't a hook-up, you idiot. We need to talk.

We do? Relief was tinged with fresh fear. Howard knew that when women said they needed to talk, he was normally in some kind of trouble. He hadn't seen Fern in months. Hadn't seen Janice in years. What kind of trouble could he possibly be in?

It crossed his mind briefly that Fern was the one who had sent him that note last week, the one warning him that his past was about to catch up with him. Howard had screwed it up and binned it, knowing it could have been any one of his psycho exes, but given that they still occasionally met up for a shag, he hadn't suspected Fern. Perhaps she knew about Daisy and was jealous. Not that she had any right to be. What they'd had was a casual arrangement and there was no commitment involved. And it certainly didn't justify writing on his windscreen with red lipstick the word 'Guilty'.

That had really peed him off.

Her next message was annoyingly vague and did nothing to allay his concern.

8 p.m. Don't be late.

Was it Fern who was dicking with him? He toyed briefly with just deleting her off Facebook and blocking her so she couldn't contact him again. Problem with that was she knew where he lived and also where he worked. He couldn't risk her showing up and making a scene.

With hindsight he wished he had said he was busy tonight, but it was too late for that. He would go over to Fern's, find out what this thing was she wanted to talk about, and try to get to the bottom of whether she was the person harassing him. Then he resolved to make a fresh start: no more hook-ups, and he would try to commit to making things work with Daisy.

He would be strong. He could do this.

14

The encounter with Jeremy had unnerved Olivia, playing on her mind all of the drive home. Once inside the car, the doors locked, she had fired a message off to Noah.

Fancy some company tonight? I can bring fish and chips.

She had slipped her phone in her bag, smoothed her damp hair back and glanced around the deserted car park. A figure was standing by the back wall of the walkway. Was he watching her?

Quickly she fired up the ignition, headlights on and catching him in her beam. An older man, in his seventies at least, shopping bags on the floor beside him, and she could see he was taking shelter under the overhead brick ledge. As she backed the car out of the space, a woman joined him, taking some of the bags, and they went back towards the main road.

Jesus, Liv. Stop being so paranoid.

It was Jeremy's fault. Intentional or not, he had made her feel vulnerable, had even scared her a little. If it was his idea of a joke, she hadn't found it funny.

Back home and there was a note on the side from Molly saying she had gone to the gym, but had made a tuna bake. It was in the oven if Olivia wanted to help herself.

The absence of her lodger alleviated the guilt that she was going out. Molly had been understandably freaked out by her encounter in the garden, and part of Olivia felt guilty leaving her in the house alone. She really needed to talk to Noah before she lost her nerve again.

Remembering him, she pulled her phone from her bag, surprised that he hadn't replied to her message. Feeling a little uneasy, she fed Luna, who ate just a couple of bites before disappearing out through the cat flap, then changed out of her work clothes before jumping in the shower. Back in the bedroom and she checked her phone again. Still no reply. This wasn't like Noah. Usually he got back to her quickly.

She dried her hair, ran the straighteners through it, her unease growing. The house felt too big tonight, too empty. Needing noise, she shouted downstairs to Alexa to play one of her favourite playlists, turning the volume up and relaxing a little as music filled every room.

Her phone beeped as she was unplugging the straighteners. Noah at last. She relaxed further as she read his reply, telling her to come over.

After moisturising and squirting on her favourite perfume, she rummaged through her underwear drawer, fishing out one of her better sets, just in case.

She was rooting through her wardrobe deciding what top to put on with her jeans, when the music abruptly stopped. Frowning, she shouted down to Alexa to resume the playlist.

The music restarted. Stereophonics blaring through the speaker system. Putting it down to a blip, she turned back to the wardrobe, selecting a thin navy jumper with a low neckline and threw it on the bed next to the underwear. She had just finished doing up her bra, when the music cut out again.

'Damn it, Alexa.'

Quickly she slipped into the jumper, this time went to the top of the stairs to shout at the stupid Echo. Before she could get her instruction out, a song started playing, but it was nothing from her playlist.

For a moment she froze, holding on to her breath. She recognised the chords instantly, ice in her blood as Perry Como started singing 'It's beginning to look a lot like Christmas'. And for a moment she was back in the hideous kitchen of 8 Honington Lane watching Gary Lamb burning to death.

Her heart pounded, the sound thundering in her ears. Someone was in the house.

'Alexa, stop!'

The music instantly cut out.

'Who's there? Molly, is that you?'

Her question was met with silence.

Feeling vulnerable only half dressed, she grabbed her jeans from the back of the chair, put them on, glancing round the room for a weapon.

Call the police.

She couldn't. They would laugh down the phone at her. *What's your emergency? Alexa started playing a random song.* DC Upton hadn't even believed her about the record player, so no one was going to take her seriously about this.

She took an old tennis racquet from under her bed. It was a pretty useless weapon, but better than nothing. Then she picked up her phone and slipped it in her back pocket.

At least call Noah.

It was tempting, but seriously, what could he do? If she was on the phone to him while checking the house she would be distracted, an easy target. He would probably instruct her to barricade herself in her bedroom and wait for him to get there. That would take at least twenty minutes and she didn't have a lock on the bedroom door.

Better to check the house herself, then get the hell out.

As she crept down the stairs, being as quiet as possible, wishing like hell she had put more lights on, a floorboard creaked below.

She froze again, gripping the handle of the tennis racquet with an iron grasp as she recalled the words on the first note she had received: *Everyone's past catches up with them eventually, including yours. Soon.*

Someone had been in the garden on Friday night, startling Molly. Were they now in the house too?

Olivia glanced at her boots and coat in the hallway, was tempted to grab them and leg it to her car, but she couldn't do that to Molly. Her lodger would be home in an hour or so. If Olivia was going out, she needed to know that the house was secure and Molly would be safe. Plus of course there was Luna, who had disappeared outside. She couldn't have her cat coming back indoors to an intruder.

She pulled her phone from her pocket, put Noah on speed dial, just in case she did need to call him, then gripping the tennis racquet with her free hand she descended the stairs and silently crossed to the living room where the Echo was situated, right next to the TV. She flipped the light switch, illuminating the large room, breathed a sigh of relief once she had checked behind the sofa, knowing there was no one in there.

Back into the hallway and she crept towards the kitchen. Again, the room was empty, though a cool breeze and the scent and sound of rain had her heart going into her mouth. The back door was open.

Gingerly, Olivia crossed the room, her legs like jelly as she reached for the door handle, half expecting someone to grab her arm. She pushed it shut, locked it, checked the utility room, found it empty.

That just left the cloakroom and the coat cupboard. Warily she checked both, wanting to cry with relief when she found them empty.

There was no one downstairs. The house was secure.

She was exhausted.

It was tempting to ask Noah to come to her, but truth was she wanted, needed, to get out of the house. As she put her coat on and slipped her feet into her boots, it crossed her mind that she still had to get to her car.

What if the person who had been in the house was waiting outside for her?

She glanced out of the tiny hall window, saw it was still raining steadily. It was maybe twelve to fifteen steps to her car. She could do this. Grabbing her bag and slipping it over her shoulder, she quietly eased the door open, keys ready to click at her car. Stepping outside of the house she gently closed the door behind her. At the moment the latch caught, she clicked her keys. The beep sounded unnecessarily loud above the splatter of raindrops hitting the driveway. Olivia glanced ahead, focusing on her car, sucked in her breath, then ran for the vehicle.

As she got in and locked the doors, she was certain she saw a figure slip across the front lawn. Without stopping to check, she put the car into gear and accelerated off the driveway.

15

She was so shaken by the encounter, she completely forgot the food she had promised to bring, showing up on Noah's doorstep twenty-five minutes later empty-handed. He opened the door to her, glanced at her empty arms.

'I thought you said you were bringing fish and chips?'

'Shit, I'm sorry... I...'

'Liv, what's wrong?'

'There was a man... Alexa... Someone was in the house.'

'What?' He ushered her inside. 'Why the fuck didn't you call me?'

'I didn't want to bother... I took care of it. Whoever it was had left the back door open.'

'You left the back door unlocked?'

'No... No. I came home from work. I guess Molly must've forgotten to lock it before she went to the gym.'

'Seriously? After what happened on Friday, she forgot to lock the bloody door?' His expression darkened.

'She wouldn't have done it on purpose. And no harm was done.'

'But someone was in the house?'

'Yes, I think so.'

'You think so?'

'Well... I didn't actually see them, but the door... and Alexa...' She trailed off, noting the scowl on his face. 'Look, it's okay. I'm okay. I could really use a drink though.'

'Okay, sit.'

'I'm not a dog, Noah.' Thank God she still had her sense of humour. He didn't look impressed by her joke though and she could tell he was mad at her for not calling him, so she did as she was told, while he disappeared through to the kitchen, returning with a bottle of red wine and two glasses.

Olivia ordered herself to breathe, annoyed she was still shaking. 'I'm sorry I forgot to bring dinner.'

'It's okay. I'll call for a pizza.' He poured wine into the glasses, handed her one. 'Here, drink, then I want you to tell me exactly what happened.'

She went through everything with him while they waited for the pizza, finishing her glass of wine, wanting a second one, but knowing she had to drive home. It was a Monday night and she never drank during the week, but guessed after the day she'd had, she had needed something to relax her.

He remained silent throughout, his steady green gaze on her as she spoke.

'Did you check the cameras?' he asked, when she had finished talking.

'No. I just wanted to get out of the house, then I drove straight here.' Olivia didn't point out that in her panic she had completely forgotten about the cameras. If the intruder had entered through the kitchen, the back-door camera would have caught him.

'Give me your phone.'

She fumbled in her bag, finding it, and gladly handing it over. Noah had gone over the app with her after installing the cameras, showing her how she could view the recorded footage, but she was ashamed to admit she hadn't paid a huge amount of attention. Technical stuff didn't interest her and she had struggled in setting up something as basic as her Echo.

'Look, remember how I showed you?'

Olivia scooted up the sofa and snuggled in closer as he slipped his arm around her, and she watched the screen as he guided her through the camera footage.

'See, so although it's recording 24/7, the cameras only alert you when they pick up movement.'

He flicked through the alerts from the front one, which recorded Molly as she went to her car, threw her gym bag on the passenger seat before getting in and driving away. That had been at 18.12, just a short time before Olivia had arrived home, then Olivia saw her own car pulling into the driveway at 18.29, watched as she exited the vehicle and entered the house. It was weird seeing herself on camera, her hair slicked down by the rain, as she unlocked the door and disappeared inside.

She had been pondering her uncomfortable encounter with Jeremy at the time. It now seemed minor given everything that had happened since. There was nothing else on the front camera until she left the house again to go to Noah's. This time she was on camera only for moments as she ran to the car and sped out of the driveway, and she recalled those agonising seconds where she had been terrified someone might grab her.

Noah clicked on to the back camera. There was only one moment where motion was detected, when Molly had taken rubbish out to the bins shortly before she had gone out.

There was no one in the back garden, no one trying to get inside the house.

But the door had been open.

'I didn't imagine it.' Olivia hated the edge of panic as she watched him switch off the camera and exit the app. 'Someone was in the house, I know they were.'

He laid her phone down on the coffee table, pulled her closer, his hand rubbing up and down her arm. 'You've had a tough few days. It's understandable that you're a little paranoid and on edge.'

'You don't believe me.'

'I never said I didn't believe you. I think you were spooked and I believe you honestly thought someone was in the house.'

Olivia pulled away from him, her temper flaring. 'So how do you explain the Echo, or are you saying that was my imagination too?'

'It's a machine. Sometimes they do unpredictable things.'

'Bullshit. It was the same song that was playing while Gary Lamb was murdered. That is not a coincidence. And how do you explain the door being open?'

'Okay, look.' He picked up her phone again, tapped into the settings. 'I'm going to upload the full camera footage to my Mac and I'll go through it frame by frame. I can't explain your Alexa or the door, but you saw how the app worked. If someone entered through the back door, the motion sensor would have picked them up.'

'You think I'm crazy.'

'I don't think you're crazy. I think you were scared.' When she pouted, he reached his free hand under her chin, raised it so she met his gaze. 'Look at me. I promise, I don't think you're crazy and I'm going to check the full footage. Okay?'

Olivia sulked for a moment, hating how rational he was being. She knew someone had been in the house, that there was no way the Perry Como song would have started playing by itself, but equally she couldn't deny the footage she had seen. Was she seriously starting to lose her mind? She forced a smile for him. 'Okay. Thank you.'

It wasn't Noah's fault he had a batshit crazy girlfriend.

He leant in and kissed the tip of her nose. 'It's gonna be okay, Liv.'

She tried to push it to the back of her mind while they ate pizza, determined not to let the incident ruin the night. The lights were dimmed, low music playing in the background and the flame-effect gas fire lit. Outside the heavy rain pounded the window, an unwelcome reminder that later on she would have to head back out into the cold and the wet, and return home.

She had messaged Molly to let her know she had gone out, not wanting her lodger to worry, though hadn't mentioned where she had gone. Molly wasn't stupid. She would put two and two together, but Olivia didn't want to rub her nose in it. She had also warned her about the open back door and how she thought there had been someone in the house. Before she left to drive home she would message again, make sure the porch light was on. Molly was away on another work trip from tomorrow and Olivia wasn't looking forward to spending the rest of the week home alone. She tried not to dwell too much on that, decided to deal with it tomorrow.

It was Christmas in less than three weeks, but there was no trace of it in

Noah's house. Olivia had been trying to persuade him to at least get a small tree, but he was insistent that he didn't want one. She knew he was going back to Devon for the holiday period and guessed he felt it was pointless.

With a bellyful of pizza and a glass of wine making her relaxed and content, she settled back into the cushions of the sofa, legs outstretched and feet on Noah's lap, enjoying the touch of his thumbs as he massaged the balls of her feet. They had kept conversation light while eating, but now she found him looking at her intently, sharp green eyes ready with questions.

'So, are we going to talk about Friday?'

It was why she had initially come here, to talk to him and tell him everything, but then the whole intruder thing had happened and she had been distracted, exhausted even, needing comfort, not another difficult situation to have to deal with. He had been so patient with her, and he deserved to know the truth.

She knew that, so why did it send jitters skating through her belly?

Her mind wandered back to earlier in the year. February. It had been a few days before Valentine's, her first one single in eleven years. She was determined to put Toby behind her, get back into the saddle, so to speak, and had allowed a couple of her old friends to drag her out into the city for drinks.

She wasn't a fan of the city bars and clubs, preferring quieter more traditional pubs. She needed to get over Toby though, her friends had insisted, so spurred on she had slipped into a little black dress that showed off her curves and her legs, and hit the town, her confidence bolstered by a few glasses of wine and the encouragement of her friends that she was too good for Toby anyway.

It was in one of the city bars that she had met Dominic, had been instantly attracted to him. Looking back now, she did wonder how much of that had been alcohol-induced. He had bought her a couple of drinks then suggested they head back to his city flat.

Comfortably tipsy, and determined to forget Toby, Olivia had agreed. Toby had been her boyfriend for eleven years and her only lover. It was time to start living a little.

Toby was a cheating arsehole. He could be tight, inconsiderate and in the last year of their relationship, they had grown apart to the point he had at times felt like a stranger, but to give him his dues, he had always accepted Olivia the way she was. He had never made her feel like a freak.

His acceptance had perhaps become a shield. Because Toby had accepted her, things had never been an issue, and she had foolishly assumed other men would be the same.

Heading back to Dominic's city pad, by now more than a little drunk and definitely horny, she hadn't considered for a second that he would find her inadequate.

Screw that. He hadn't found her inadequate. He had been repulsed.

Her cheeks heated as she remembered the shame, the humiliation, of his reaction.

The fear of being rejected like that again was sickening. And this time it was ten times worse because she had been seeing Noah for several weeks. Things had been getting more and more serious between them and she still hadn't told him.

She pulled her feet off his lap, drew them to her chest as she sat up, hugging them tightly. She had been so relaxed, but now the tension was back, the sick feeling returning. Glancing at the wine bottle on the coffee table, she wished she could have another glass, needing the Dutch courage now more than ever.

He was still watching her, waiting for an answer to his question, so she bit down on the fear, knew she had to come clean. She owed him that much. 'There's something I need to tell you... about me.'

'Okay.'

'I haven't been honest with you. I'm sorry.'

Noah remained silent, waiting for her to continue. His expression was a little guarded.

Oh God, can I seriously do this?

It was too late to turn back.

'A long time ago there was an accident. I... I was... something happened to me.'

Still that awful silence as he waited for her to elaborate.

'I... it's easier if I show you.'

The room was uncomfortably hot, the sickness in her belly twisting into apprehension. Her cheeks were flaming, her palms damp, as she stood up and slowly lifted her jumper, removed it, letting it drop to the floor, before unbuttoning her jeans and stepping out of them, painfully vulnerable as she stood in his living room wearing just her underwear, humiliation burning through her.

Noah's eyes widened slightly, the only betrayal of his reaction. Other than that, he remained neutral, waiting patiently.

Olivia smoothed her hand down the scars that ran from the underside of her left breast to her waist and down her thigh, down the length of her left arm. Slightly raised, less smooth and darker than her natural skin tone. She had become used to them over the years, accepted they were part of her, which was why she hadn't given them a second thought that night she had accompanied Dominic back to his man pad, foolishly assuming that because they hadn't bothered Toby, they wouldn't bother anyone else.

What an idiot.

Dominic had acted like she was a leper, repulsed by how she looked. That night was now ingrained in her memory and she had been too scared to date again, until Noah.

'There was an accident, a fire. I was fourteen. My friend died and I was in hospital for weeks.' She caught her breath, eyes closed, remembering. Too afraid to open them in case she saw revulsion. 'This is it. This is me. I've had skin grafts. It's not going to get any better.'

Silent tears leaked and she wasn't even aware of them until they dampened her cheeks.

'Why did you think this would be a problem?' He was standing in front of her. She hadn't even heard him get up from the sofa, so caught up in the memories of the fire, of being in hospital, and of that awful searing rejection. His thumbs brushed the tears away. 'Do you really think I'm that shallow?'

'Because the last time I tried to do this, it *was* a problem.' Her voice cracked.

'Liv, open your eyes.' He briefly caught her hands and she was aware of him leaning in closer. 'Open your eyes and look at me.' His words were a brief caress against her temple.

Tentatively she did as asked, met his gaze seeing nothing but compassion mixed with a healthy dose of lust.

He tilted her chin, kissed her firmly on the lips as his free hand slipped down to trace where the scar ran down to her waist. 'I think you're beautiful.'

'You do?'

'I do.'

The tension eased out of her shoulders. This had been such a huge deal to her. The encounter with Dominic had seriously dented her confidence.

'And I want to know all about the accident and what happened, I really do.' He continued to rub his palm up and down over the scar. 'But right now, you're standing in my living room in just your underwear and it's driving me a little crazy.'

His lips curved into a crooked grin and despite herself, Olivia found herself smiling. 'I'm sorry about that.'

'No, really, do not be sorry. I've been trying to get you out of your clothes for weeks, so this is a very pleasant and unexpected surprise.' He kissed her again, pulling her against him as his hands roamed down to cup her bum. 'Stay with me tonight.'

It was a Monday, she had work in the morning, plus of course none of her stuff was here. 'Tonight's probably not—'

He silenced her with another kiss. 'No excuses. Stay with me. You can leave early in the morning and go back home before work. I have an early start tomorrow, so I'll make sure you're up.' As he nuzzled her neck, warm hands still caressing her bum, she had to admit it was tempting. Plus it meant she wouldn't have to go back out in the rain.

'Okay,' she agreed. 'I'll stay.'

Later, in the darkness of the bedroom, she awoke from a dream about Margaret. Noah was asleep beside her, rolled on to his belly, head facing away from her, and she could hear his steady breathing and the pattering of the rain that hit the window.

The combination of unburdening her secret, plus good sex – and it had been good, once she had overcome her initial shyness and hesitancy – had seen her falling asleep quickly, but the dream had woken her.

It was the first time she had dreamt about Margaret in years and she guessed it was talking about her scars and what had happened the night of the fire, that had caused the memories to resurface.

Olivia had been pulled from the flames, but not before suffering serious burn injuries and the healing process had been long and traumatic. She had been the lucky one. Margaret hadn't survived the fire.

Olivia had no recollection of what had happened that night in the cottage. She had quickly lost consciousness and knew nothing about it until she woke up in hospital. Her last memories of Margaret had been happy ones.

But when she fell asleep and dreamt of her friend, that was when she heard the screams.

16

As the daughter of two teachers, many assumed school was easy for Margaret Grimes. She attended with her twin brother, Malcolm, had an older sister in the senior year, her mother taught English and her father took the history classes. To any outsiders looking in, they were the dynasty of St Nicholas High School.

To quiet, sensitive, and eager-to-please Margaret though, nothing could be further from the truth. She felt like the square peg in a round hole. She was academically gifted, but disinterested in the latest fashions, not up to date on the cool bands, TV shows and trends. She had little in common with her classmates. Her brother, Malcolm, was a loner and a trouble-maker, who struggled in classes, and she was expected to be responsible for him, while her father ruled both his household and the classroom by using fear. No one was foolish enough to disrupt one of Mr Grimes' lessons because he would punish students for the slightest thing. And that rule extended to his children too. If anything, he liked to use Margaret, Malcolm and their older sister, Alice, as an example for the other students, almost looking for ways to find fault with them.

At home, things were no better, and behind closed doors the punish-ments were more physical. Forgetting to pray at the dinner table, not removing shoes at the front door, and failure to do chores properly resulted in regular beatings with the belt that Gerald Grimes kept in his study desk drawer. And there was no running to their mother. Marie Grimes stood behind her husband and, although she never dished out the punishments herself, she wasn't interested in giving any sympathy.

As the eldest, Alice suffered the most, rebelling against her father every step of the way, Malcolm was disinterested, seldom even reacting to punishment, while Margaret tried her best to stay on her father's good side. Still, she walked on eggshells around him, terrified of doing something that might upset him.

Alice had always been the constant in Margaret's life, the one person she could turn to, but the more Alice resisted, the further Gerald sought to punish her, and as a result the sisters became further estranged. Alice started staying out late and Margaret knew she was seeing boys – something their father strictly forbade. The results of the late-night make out sessions were evident in the love bites around Alice's neck.

School life was no picnic either, with some of the more popular students learning that Margaret was an easy target. As kids often are, they were discreet with their bullying, careful to do it when there were no witnesses. And when they found they had no resistance, their confidence grew, often setting Margaret up to take the fall with her father. A shove of a text book off her desk, making her look like she had dropped it or kicking the back of her chair, causing her to cry out. Gerald Grimes was always quick to blame his daughter for disrupting the lesson.

Margaret tried her best to keep her head down, avoiding eye contact with the other students, eating her lunch quietly in the corner of the canteen, and praying like hell that Malcolm behaved himself and didn't do anything to draw attention to them. Things seldom happened that way.

All Margaret wanted was to make it through school unscathed then she could take her A levels, go to university and start afresh.

Things moved along miserably, but uneventfully, until October when the opportunity arose for a school trip to Norfolk. It was billed as a Pre-Christmas Extravaganza, with Black Dog Farm opening its doors to welcome students to celebrate ahead of the Christmas period.

Margaret had no interest in going, hadn't expected her father would even want her to, so she was surprised when he announced at dinner one evening that places had been booked for her and her brother.

She tried to reason with him, but of course he took her dislike of the idea as resistance, punishing her accordingly. Malcolm was nonplussed as usual, not really reacting to the idea one way or another, but Margaret was dreading a whole week stuck in Norfolk with her classmates.

As the date grew closer, Margaret's misery increased. School was already a miserable enough affair. A whole week with her fellow classmates would be unbearable.

A few days before the trip, she was given a mild reprieve. Suzannah Chegwin, one of her main tormentors, had come down with flu and would be unable to go. On the day of the trip, Gerald drove Margaret and Malcolm to the school, playing the genial father as he watched their luggage being packed, then waved them goodbye as the coach pulled away.

Margaret had glanced around at the other students. Two of Suzannah's friends, Kelly Dearborn and Rachel Williams were on board the coach, but neither girl was too bad if Suzannah wasn't around. Maybe the weekend would be more bearable than expected. The absence of Suzannah lulled her into a false sense of security. Little did she know that she was just a couple of hours away from meeting the girl who would destroy her life.

17

Monday night had not gone at all how Howard had expected. He had shown up at Fern's, not really sure what exactly he was walking into, just relieved she wasn't expecting him to shag Janice. That relief wobbled when he walked into the kitchen, found Janice sitting on a bar stool at the counter.

Her face lit up as she saw him. 'Hey, Howard. How are you, mate?'

She leapt down from the stool, squeezed him in a hug that nearly broke him, the faint odour of sweat and poorly laundered clothes offending his nostrils. He eased himself free, wanting to excuse himself for a shower. Instead, he gave her a cool smile and settled himself on a bar stool down the other end of the counter, smoothing down his shirt and the lapels of his jacket.

This kitchen was Fern all over, glossy and showy, with little substance. He had to give the woman credit, though. At thirty-one, her arse still looked ripe in her tight jeans and he admired it as she reached down into the cooler fridge to get him a beer.

Just a shame the face has weathered slightly, he thought unkindly, as she handed him the bottle. *With the lights low she could probably still pass for a six-point-five.*

'So why are we here?' he asked, still dubious to the reasons, and watching Janice suspiciously, convinced if he took his eye off her, she might start dry humping him.

'It's about the notes,' Janice announced.

'The notes?' Howard repeated, confused.

Fern looked furious at Janice for stealing her thunder. She had always been about the build-up. 'I know you've received them,' she said coolly. 'We all have.'

Howard wracked his brains. 'You mean the sex notes?'

'Sex notes?' That was Fern and Janice in unison.

'The ones that said I had done something bad.' He broke off, frowned at Fern. 'I thought maybe you had sent them.'

'Me?' She looked affronted at that. 'Why the hell would I send you sex notes?' She was pacing now, that tight arse in those tight jeans difficult to distract his eyes from. 'And they are not bloody sex notes. We've all received them.'

'All?' He looked at her blankly.

'You, me and Janice.'

'You had a note like this.' Janice rooted in her giant handbag, pulled out a crumpled piece of paper and passed it to him. 'Right?'

He read the words, recognising them. 'Okay.' Now he was a little unsure at the course the conversation was taking. 'So who sent them, and why?'

'Do you think we would be standing here having this conversation if I knew who had sent them?' Fern growled.

'But why have we all got them?'

'You honestly can't figure out why?'

'Nope.'

'How about a little refresher? You, me, Janice, Gary, Rachel Williams and Kelly Dearborn. We were fourteen.'

Howard cast his mind back, remembering. 'Oh, that. It was years ago.' Still, the smile he had been wearing disappeared from his face. 'And anyway, Gary's dead, Fern.'

'I bloody know that. And do you know who else is dead?'

'Who?'

'Kelly. She died in a fire, just like Gary did.'

'Really? That's a bit of a coincidence. What are the chances of that?'

'It's not a coincidence, Howard.'

'We're being punished,' Janice piped up, sliding ungraciously off her bar stool and edging closer. 'Because of what we did.'

'What?' Were they being serious? They were being targeted for a stupid prank they had played when they were fourteen years old?

'Are you still in touch with Rachel Williams?'

'Of course not. Why would I be?'

'Because I am trying to track her down. We need to get to the bottom of who is sending us these notes.'

'So back up a minute. Let's be clear. You are saying that Kelly and Gary were both murdered?'

'Yes!'

'So why aren't the police investigating?'

'They are.'

'Yes, but why aren't they investigating the connection?'

'Because they don't fucking know about it.' Fern's face was suddenly in front of his and she looked really peed off. 'You're not getting this? Whoever is targeting us hurt Kelly and Gary. We're being punished. The police don't know their deaths are connected because they don't know what we fucking did!'

'Okay, and say you're right—'

'I am right. Why the hell else would we all be getting these notes?'

'So did Gary and Kelly get notes too?'

'I don't know. How would I know that?'

Howard was quiet for a moment, as he pondered the situation. There was no escaping the fact that someone was targeting them all with the notes, but were they really connected to Gary and Kelly's deaths? He had to admit, it was odd that they had both died in a fire. 'Maybe we should go to the police, tell them what really happened,' he suggested.

Fern's eyes nearly popped. 'Are you having a laugh?'

'We can't do that!' Janice looked equally distressed at the idea. 'What if we go to jail?'

'Why would we go to jail? We were fourteen years old. It was just a stupid prank that went wrong.'

'But we were responsible. It was because of us it happened.'

'We were kids!'

'We killed her!' screeched Janice.

'It was a prank, damn it. A stupid bloody prank!'

'You are not telling. I am not gonna risk going to jail.'

They were face to face now, yelling at each other; Janice, red and sweaty, her features contorted, while Howard could feel the veins in his neck bulging.

Neither one was aware of Fern approaching. The hard slap on the backs of both their heads momentarily shocked them into silence.

'No one is going to tell the police anything. We made a pact never to tell anyone and we are sticking to it.'

'So what the fuck is your plan, Fern?' Howard wasn't liking this one bit. If they went to the police, confessed, he was certain that after all this time they would get away with just a slap on the wrists. By continuing to keep this twisted little secret, he was being further embroiled with Fern St Clair and Janice Plum.

'We sort this problem ourselves,' she told him smoothly.

'And how exactly do you intend to do that?'

'For starters, we need to find Rachel, find out if she is being targeted too.'

'I can help with that,' Janice offered.

'I already looked for her on Facebook.'

'Well let me try and find her. I'm pretty good at tracking people down.'

Yes, you look like the stalker type, Howard decided.

'Okay, you do that,' Fern agreed, before turning to Howard.

His heart sank. *God, she was going to ask him to get involved in her Miss Marple adventures*. He cut her off before she could speak, smiling sweetly. 'I don't really have time to help out, so perhaps you can just drop me an email and keep me updated.'

'You were still in touch with Gary, right?'

'Barely,' he lied. 'We hadn't seen each other in months.' Another lie. He had seen Gary in the pub a couple of weeks back.

Fern's lips thinned. 'He posted on Facebook the week before he died that he'd been out with you.'

Rumbled! Howard scowled. 'So?'

'So find out what you can. Did he have a girlfriend?'

'He was seeing some woman. Rita, I think her name is.'

'Talk to her. What was Gary like in the lead-up to his death? Did he receive any notes?'

'I've never met the woman, Fern. How do you expect me to do that?'

She smiled, almost seductively, at him. 'You'll find a way. You're a smooth operator.'

His ego stroked, he grudgingly relented. 'I can't make any promises.'

'Just try.'

'So what are you going to do then? You can't just use Janice and me to do your dirty work.'

Fern gave him a sharp look. 'I'm going to track down Olivia Blake.'

Janice let out a tiny gasp. 'Olivia? Do you think she has something to do with this?'

Howard thought back to Olivia Blake. Fern's old best friend. Slim, wide-eyed, pretty. At least she had been before the fire. He hadn't seen her since high school.

'I don't know,' Fern admitted. 'But I think it's time I found out.'

18

Noah's alarm cut through the silence of the dark bedroom, abruptly waking Olivia. As she took a moment to adjust to the unfamiliar setting, to remember that she wasn't in her own bed, she heard him grunt, the mattress shifting as he rolled over to silence his phone.

She had been awake for quite a while during the night, her mind working overtime, finally drifting off maybe an hour or two before dawn, and her eyes stung with tiredness when she tried to ease them open.

Wishing she didn't have to go to work, knowing it would be a struggle to get through the day, she closed them again, wanting just a little longer. Noah must have felt the same, because he lay quietly beside her for a few minutes, listening to the pattering rain outside, before giving what sounded like a reluctant groan. The mattress dipped slightly between them as he turned towards her, the warmth of his hard body against her as he eased his arm around her, pulling her close.

Pushing her hair back he trailed kisses down the side of her neck and Olivia let out a murmur of satisfaction. 'Let's just stay here.'

'Mmm, that would be nice.' He playfully nipped her earlobe, before yanking back the duvet. 'Unfortunately we can't, because I promised you I would have you up and out of the house so you're not late for work.'

Olivia groaned. 'Forget what I said last night.'

'Come on. Up.' He gave her a nudge. 'Go have a shower and I'll make you a coffee.'

She found him in the kitchen when she wandered in ten minutes later, his back to her and phone pressed to his ear. She took a moment as she leant against the door jamb to study him: tawny brown hair sleep tousled, wearing just a pair of sweatpants that hung low on narrowed hips.

'I already told you no, the job's over.' He seemed a little agitated, muscles working in those bare broad shoulders as he raised his free hand to shove it in his hair. 'By all means, hire someone else. You're wasting your time, though.'

A client, she guessed, and a persistent one, judging from the raised voice coming down the phone. The words were muffled, so she couldn't make them out, but she could tell the caller wasn't happy.

Olivia picked up the cup of coffee he had poured for her, took a sip as she watched him, everything stirring inside. He had accepted her scars, no question or hesitation, and it had bolstered her confidence. Now she had overcome that hurdle, she was keen to make up for lost time. Had he been game, she would have played hooky from work and called in sick. Perhaps a good job then that he hadn't been. Roger was already annoyed that she had been out of the office. Best not to upset him further.

Besides, Noah seemed busy. He had mentioned he had an early start and seemed keen to get moving.

The doorbell made her jump and Noah spun around, looking taken aback that she was standing there in the kitchen. He was frowning at Olivia, didn't seem overly pleased that she was there. 'I have to go,' he snapped at whoever was on the phone.

'It's okay, I can get it.'

It would be his work partner, Dan. Noah had mentioned that Dan was picking him up. Olivia hadn't met him yet, and she was keen to get to know the people in Noah's life.

'No! Wait!' He took a step towards her, looked a little flustered.

The bell rang again. Dan was impatient.

'It's fine. I've got it.' She was gone before he could say anything else, the sound of him angrily trying to end the call fading as she headed down the hall towards the front door.

Noah had said little about Dan, blatantly ignoring Olivia's previous attempts to meet him, which was ridiculous really because why would he be anxious about his girlfriend meeting his work partner? Olivia was easy-going enough and Dan sounded like an okay bloke.

She pulled open the front door, expecting to find a thirty-something nerdy guy, maybe with glasses and a puppy-dog smile, because Noah had told her Dan was the computer brains of the business and that was what IT geeks looked like, right?

She got the thirty-something bit right, the 'hi' greeting freezing on her lips, as she came face to face with Dan. Yes, definitely thirty-something, but there was nothing nerdy at all. This Dan had long glossy hair and breasts, and what might have started off as a friendly smile was rearranging itself into an amused smirk.

Maybe Olivia was wrong. This wasn't Dan. It was someone else who just happened to be stopping by at ridiculous o'clock in the morning.

'You're Olivia. Or Liv as Noah calls you.'

'And you're Dan?' Olivia phrased it as a question, though she already knew the answer. She waited expectantly.

'Daniella. He shortens names. Bad habit of his. It's good to finally meet you.'

Noah would have disagreed with that, obviously did, as he came charging into the hallway. 'Dan, you're early. We said seven-thirty.'

'You know me, I like to get an early start.'

Dan... Daniella, sauntered into the house, ignoring the annoyance that was rolling off Noah. Olivia wasn't quite sure what it was he had to be annoyed about. She hadn't been the one deceiving people. No, that was all on Noah, which had Olivia wondering why exactly he had lied to her.

Okay, to be fair to him, he had never actually referred to Dan as 'he', but Olivia had on more than one occasion, so why the hell had he not corrected her? Had he seriously believed she would never find out?

She wasn't the jealous type, would not have had a problem with him working with a woman – an attractive woman – she noted, as Daniella stripped off her damp jacket to reveal a toned, svelte figure. The deceit of the situation had her wondering if perhaps she should be.

Damn it. She had just bloody slept with him, trusted him enough to show him her scars. He had some serious explaining to do.

But explaining would have to wait. Right now, she needed to go home and get changed, so she wasn't late for work. 'It's nice to finally meet you too, Daniella.' Olivia found a smile, though it felt a little bit forced. 'If you'll excuse me, I need to go get my things together.'

She glowered at Noah as she passed him to go upstairs, heard his brief snappy exchange with Daniella, then footsteps on the stairs as he hurried after her. Olivia was hunting through her bag for her car keys when he entered the room, kept her back to him as he closed the door.

'Are you pissed off at me for something?'

Seriously, he was going to play innocent here? She whirled around, fire heating her cheeks and her hissed tone. 'She has breasts, Noah! Dan has fucking breasts.'

Although he looked a little taken aback at her outburst, green eyes widening, he held his ground. 'Okay, and...?'

'And? Seriously? So, did you not think it would have been a good idea to tell me that Dan is a woman?'

'I never said she was a man.'

'No, but you let me carry on thinking that she was. You never attempted to correct me.'

'You're overreacting!'

That was it, the torch paper was lit. 'I am not bloody overreacting. Damn it, Noah. I trusted you to be honest with me. Why the hell didn't you tell me?'

'What difference does it make who I work with?'

'It doesn't make any difference, but don't lie to me about it.'

'I never lied to you.' His tone was calm, but his eyes were heated.

'Okay, you didn't lie, but you deceived me. Same thing.' Olivia grabbed her bag off the bed. She couldn't do this right now and just needed to get out of the house. The car keys were in her bag somewhere. She would find them when she got outside.

Noah caught hold of her arm as she brushed past him. 'Liv, damn it. Wait!'

She shook him off, hurried down the stairs and to the front door, grateful that Daniella had made herself scarce. Quickly pulling on her coat and boots, she yanked open the front door and dashed through the rain to her car. Hunkering down in the coat, she rummaged through her bag again for her car keys. *Where the hell are they?*

The rain was pounding hard, soaking her through, the sound masking Noah's approach. 'Looking for these?'

Olivia swung around. He had put on a T-shirt and slipped his feet into trainers and stood before her, hair plastered down to his forehead and neck, as he held out her keys.

As she went to snatch them, he took a step back, held them out of her reach.

'Don't be a dick, Noah. Give me my keys.'

'I'm gonna come over tonight and we can talk about this, okay?'

'There's nothing to talk about. Now give me my damn keys!'

'Look, I'm sorry, okay. I should have told you. We can talk tonight.'

When Olivia ignored him, made another swipe for the keys, he held them higher. 'Tonight, Liv. Say it?'

She scowled at him, soaked to the skin and thoroughly peed off.

'Say it.'

'Maybe,' she muttered grudgingly.

'No maybe. Definitely.'

When she tried again for the keys, he caught hold of her with his free hand, yanked her against him and kissed her hard on the mouth. Lust sparked through her, her body betraying her as she melted against him, but she managed to stubbornly hold on to her anger, pouting at him as he released her.

He studied her for a second, green eyes still heated, though the corner of his mouth twisted into a half-smile. 'I'll see you tonight.' He pressed the car keys into her hand, then leaving her in the rain, he turned and went back into the house.

* * *

Molly had just stepped out of the shower when she heard the front door close. She didn't bother to call down, instead peering out of the front window just to be certain it was Olivia's car. She was still a little annoyed that Olivia hadn't bothered to tell her she planned to stay out all night. Molly had received a message saying she had gone out, assumed it was with Noah, though Olivia hadn't elaborated, but it hadn't mentioned that she wasn't coming home.

Consequently, Molly had faced an unsettling evening alone, then a worrying night panicking in case Olivia had been in an accident or something had happened to her. Even her late-night message asking if Olivia was okay was ignored. She had finally received a reply an hour ago, full of apologies for scaring her. Too little too late. Learning that Olivia had stayed at Noah's was just the icing on the cake. There was something about that man that Molly didn't trust. She couldn't shake this nagging suspicion that he was up to something and it bothered her that Olivia was falling for him.

She had just finished dressing and was straightening her hair when there was a knock at her bedroom door.

'Yes?' Her tone was a little sharp, but she couldn't help it. She didn't bother to turn round, continuing to style her hair, watching Olivia in the reflection of her dresser mirror as she peered round the door, a contrite smile on her face. Her hair was damp and frizzing from where she had been out in the rain.

'Hey, I just wanted to say sorry about last night. I should have messaged you again to let you know I was staying out all night.'

'I was worried, Livvy. I thought something had happened to you.'

'I know. I'm sorry.'

'You had sex with him, didn't you?' Molly hadn't meant to blurt that out, knew it was none of her business. Despite her reservations, Olivia was thirty-one and perfectly capable of making up her own mind who she slept with. Noah Keen set all of Molly's alarm bells off though. She couldn't explain why. Just call it a hunch. She had learnt over the years that her hunches were rarely wrong.

Still, she had to be careful. She didn't want to sound like a lecturing mum. 'Sorry, I shouldn't have asked that,' she added by way of apology. 'I know it's none of my business.'

The last thing she wanted to do was drive Olivia away.

Olivia stepped into the room, sitting on the edge of Molly's bed. 'I really am sorry I worried you. I got caught up in the heat of the moment and forgot. But that's no excuse, I should have messaged you to say I wasn't coming home.'

Her wide grey eyes were full of apology and something else. Worry?

'It's okay.' Molly was aware her tone was still a little stiff and she made a conscious effort to soften it. 'I'm being an idiot. You can stay out all night if you want. It's none of my business. I think I am still a little bit jumpy after Friday, then when I got your message saying you had found the door open and thought someone was in the house, I kept hearing noises outside. I guess I was paranoid. That's why I was worrying where you were. I kept hoping you would come home. I think I spooked myself.' She forced a smile. 'I'm just an idiot.'

Olivia had paled. 'You heard noises outside?'

'It was probably just the cat. You know I've been a bit jumpy.'

'Mol, I was so certain someone was in the house before I went out, but there was no one on the camera.'

'What? Are you serious?'

Molly set down the straighteners, twisting round to face Olivia. She held her breath, barely daring to release it as Olivia explained how she had gone through the footage with Noah.

'So how did the back door get open?' she whispered, her eyes widening.

'I honestly don't know.'

'It wasn't me. I remember closing and locking it before I left for the gym.'

'Okay.'

Molly could tell from her expression that she was still doubtful, and it annoyed her that Olivia didn't trust her.

'You don't believe me. I remember locking it. I swear.'

Olivia shook her head. 'I'm sorry. I do believe you. I... I don't know what to think. I really freaked out and then looked like a complete idiot in front of Noah when there was no one on the camera. Someone was messing with the Echo too, changing the music.'

'What? Are you serious?'

'Noah said that could have just been a technical blip.'

'That doesn't sound like a technical blip. It's never done that before.'

'There was no one on the camera, Mol. But intruder or no intruder, I shouldn't have left you alone, knowing what had happened. I'm so sorry.'

Molly caught her hands, squeezed tightly. 'Stop apologising. It's okay. You're paranoid, I'm paranoid. It's probably nothing. I guess that's part of the peril of living in a big old house. Creaking floorboards and cats that like to make you jump probably aren't the best combination, eh?' She was silent for a moment. 'So you really like Noah then?'

Something passed over Olivia's face. Was that doubt? She took her time answering the question too, but then the slight frown softened into a smile. 'I do.' She was silent for a moment. 'Why don't you trust him?'

'I don't know. Gut instinct, I suppose. Something feels off.'

'So it really is just gut instinct? There's not anything else?' When Molly didn't reply, she pushed for an answer. 'There's no other reason?'

While part of her was curious to know why Olivia was asking, Molly knew she didn't actually have an answer to give her, which, she realised, made her look a little bit petty and stupid. This was Olivia and she mattered. Molly couldn't afford to lose her friendship. Somehow, she was going to have to find a way to get over the whole Noah thing.

Instead of answering the question, she hesitantly offered a truce. 'Look, I know he is important to you, so I will make more of an effort, okay?'

'Thank you.'

Olivia smiled. It looked a little tight. Was she upset about something? Molly was about to ask, but then Olivia got up from the bed.

'I need to finish getting ready or I'll be late for work. Have a safe trip.'

My work trip. Olivia had remembered.

'Thanks, I'll see you at the weekend.' Molly watched her reflection in the mirror as she left the room, musing about their conversation as she finished straightening her hair. Something seemed to be a little off with Olivia, but there was no time to find out what as she needed to make a move or she would be late. Perhaps she could figure out what was going on when she got back later in the week.

As for Noah, unfortunately there was no getting around it. It seemed he was here to stay, whether she liked it or not. She promised herself that she would make an effort to get along with him for Olivia's sake. She would give him a chance, try to get to know him a little better. But she wouldn't drop her guard completely.

Her gut instinct was rarely wrong and she intended to keep a close eye on him. If she discovered that he was up to anything devious, then she wouldn't have any hesitation in trying to get him out of Olivia's life.

19

The job they were out on wrapped up much quicker than expected and finding his afternoon free, Noah decided to check the footage on the cameras he had set up at Olivia's house.

He hadn't missed the 'told you so' look Daniella had given him when Olivia had stormed out that morning, and wasn't in the mood to be lectured.

'So that went well then,' she had announced, stepping into the hallway as he slammed the front door and pushed his dripping hair back off his face.

'It would have done if you had shown up when you were supposed to.'

'Hey, don't blame me. This mess is all of your own making. It was inevitable we were going to meet eventually.'

He hadn't liked that, partly because she had warned him this would happen and also because he knew she was right. She had followed him into the kitchen, where he picked up his now cold coffee, took a sip, grimaced, then threw the rest down the sink.

'Adam Somerville left another message on my phone. He's still trying to get hold of you. You need to call him back. You can't just keep ignoring him.'

'I spoke with him this morning and reminded him that the job is off.'

He glanced at Daniella as he sluiced his mug under the hot water tap, gave her a challenging look when she arched one eyebrow. 'I've been more than fair with him and he wasn't billed, so he needs to get over it. The job's a dead end.'

'Is it really though? I would say that, given recent events, Adam has every cause to be concerned.'

Noah set the mug on the drainer, turned to face her. 'Look, I made the call and I stand by it. Adam Somerville is no longer our client. If you have a problem with that, then you'd better give me a good reason why.'

Daniella's eyes flamed, anger flushing her cheeks, reminding him of why very few men dared cross her. 'You know exactly why. You've taken your eye off the ball, Noah. You and I, we make a pretty good team, and we always get the job done. But this last couple of months, since you got wrapped up with Olivia, you've been thinking with your dick, and it's affecting our business.'

'Leave Olivia out of this.'

'This isn't about Olivia. This is about you and this job. I need you thinking up here.' She tapped her forehead to make the point.

'My focus is fine.'

'Is it really?' She picked up an apple from the fruit bowl and bit into it as she fixed him with another one of those challenging glares.

Noah reined in his temper, knew if he said anything else it would lead to a bigger fight. 'I need to go get dressed or we'll be late,' he eventually said, ignoring her question. He had pushed past her, skulking upstairs for a shower, the bad mood he was in sticking like glue all morning.

They didn't speak again about the fight. He had worked with Daniella Curry for three years, going into partnership after they left the police force around the same time, and, while they were both hot-headed and quick to temper, they made a good team. They were also professional enough that any words spoken in the heat of the moment were quickly brushed aside when they were on a job.

Her accusation stuck though. Truth was, he hadn't wanted Olivia and Daniella to cross paths and, yes, it might have been inevitable, but he had pushed that problem to the back of his mind as something to deal with later. Now he had to figure out a way to handle this.

Olivia had given him her phone to view the cameras, but hadn't realised that he had only gone through the pretence of transferring the footage to his Mac. He already had full access to the cameras and had done ever since he had first installed them. He suspected she would have a hissy fit if she found out. If someone was harassing her though, he intended to find out who the hell it was.

He fixed a sandwich and poured a coffee, then he took them through to his office, sat down at his Mac and opened the program. While he waited for it to load, he glanced at his phone, noted Olivia still hadn't replied to the message he had sent her late morning, which suggested she was still mad at him, and he couldn't really blame her. He would leave her to simmer down for a bit.

She had trusted him last night, opened up to him, and then slept with him, only to find out he had lied to her. *Not lied*, he corrected. *Just hadn't told her.*

The scars had been a revelation and he had a lot of questions about those. Last night hadn't been the time to talk; he had been too distracted. Olivia finally had her clothes off and he wasn't going to risk her putting them back on. When he had told her the scars didn't bother him, he had been telling the truth. She was beautiful with or without them, and he wanted to punch the arsehole who had knocked her confidence.

He wondered if she had considered the connection between Gary's death and her own accident. She had been lured to the house in Honington Lane to watch a man burn and was now being taunted by the killer. It all seemed too coincidental and had to be linked to what had happened to her when she was a teenager, but why, if it had just been an accident, and where the hell did Gary Lamb fit into this?

For now, he turned his attention to the cameras on the screen, replayed the motion detected footage from the front camera first, wanting to be certain he hadn't missed anything, then forwarding through the actual camera footage from about 4 p.m. the previous day. As he ate his sandwich, he watched Molly leave again, Olivia arrive home. A guy walked past with a dog and a couple of cars, plus a delivery van drove down the road. There was nothing suspicious, no one approaching the property. Switching to the back camera, he repeated the process.

Olivia said the door had been open. While he didn't doubt her, her emotions were running high, the events of the past week having taken their toll, and he couldn't discount the possibility that Molly hadn't just left the door unlocked, that maybe it hadn't closed properly. There had been a breeze last night, along with the unrelenting rain, so it could have possibly blown open. As for the song, could it have just been a blip with her Echo?

Busy musing different explanations, he almost missed the flicker on the screen.

Rewinding, he watched again. Was that something, someone moving in the garden to the side of the house? He paused the footage, rewound again, zooming in and slowing down the video feed.

A dark shadow approaching the house, only part of the figure visible. Jean-clad legs, dark jacket, just one sleeve visible, head down and face obscured by a mask or hood. The figure didn't approach the back door though. It disappeared to the side of the house where the gate led to the driveway.

Noah checked the time stamp and flicked back to the front camera, forwarding the footage to the same point. If the figure went through the gate, the front camera would pick them up.

He watched the footage three times, slowing down and zooming in again, just to be sure.

Whoever had been in the garden had not left via the back gate.

They hadn't approached the back door either. So where in the hell had they disappeared to?

He returned to the back camera, took some screenshots and spent some time blowing them up further and adjusting the picture quality. There was no way of identifying the intruder. Even the clothing was dark and nondescript.

There was no sign of entry to the house, but the timing was too much of a coincidence, and he now fully believed Olivia's version of what had happened. Whoever had sent her the notes appeared to be upping the stakes, breaking into her house and taunting her with mind games. Given that her tormentor had chained a man to a chair and set him on fire, Noah didn't like that idea one bit.

20

Make sure you message me once you have news.

Howard scowled at his phone, wishing Fern St Clair would get swallowed up by a giant hole. The woman was getting on his nerves and had already sent three other messages since he had left her house last night, seeming unconvinced that he would do as instructed and make contact with Gary's girlfriend.

She was right to doubt him. Howard had left Fern's with no intention of seeing her or Janice again, and certainly had no plan to contact Rita Works. But then he had arrived home to find the door of his flat ajar, the lock clearly tampered with. From what he could see, nothing had been stolen, none of the furniture even disturbed, but then he had gone into the bathroom and found the word 'murderer' written on the mirror in red paint, and he had nearly shit himself.

His first instinct had been to call the police, but then he had stopped and thought about what Fern and Janice had said. Although he had disagreed with them at the time, had been certain the police would shrug off what they had done, the word 'murderer' worried him. What if Janice was right? What if they did go to jail? The thought filled Howard with dread and he decided he couldn't take the risk of involving the police.

He toyed with messaging Fern, but the woman was already crazy and controlling. This would only encourage her with her deluded plans to find out who was harassing them.

Instead, he had spent half an hour scrubbing at the offending word until the paint was finally gone. He couldn't risk Daisy showing up and seeing the graffiti. It would invite too many questions. Besides, it was too early on in their relationship. Finding out her new boyfriend was being accused of murder would only scare her off and he didn't want that, especially since they had their first romantic getaway booked for later this week.

Daisy wanted to spend some quality time together and it hadn't taken much to persuade Howard to book a log cabin with its own hot tub. He figured it could be her Christmas present. That would save him the worry of what the hell to buy her.

The timing of this whole situation was bloody inconvenient. *And more than a little stressful,* he concluded, glancing at his reflection in the mirror and frowning when he spotted a white hair in his eyebrow. He used tweezers to pluck the offending hair, brushed his teeth and moisturised, aware self-care was important, especially now he was in his thirties.

He had gone to sleep hoping to dream of Daisy in her bikini in the hot tub, but instead his dreams were filled with Fern and Janice and Gary, and he had woken in a foul mood to a message from Fern reminding him of what he was supposed to do.

Now as he sat at his work desk, reading her latest message, he resigned himself to the fact he was backed into a corner. He was going to have to go along with her plan.

He logged on to Facebook, clicked on to Gary's profile and found Rita in his friends list. Opening up a message, he debated what to write, toyed again with not bothering to send anything, figuring he could lie to Fern and pretend he had if she asked. But then what if she wanted to see it?

No, he would have to do this.

Hi Rita. Sorry to hear about Gary. We went back a long way. I don't suppose we could meet up for a chat? Howard.

There. Keep it casual. Hope she didn't read too much into it.

He hit send, part of him hoping she wouldn't see it or respond. I mean what the hell was he supposed to say to her if she did agree to meet him? Did Gary mention anything about this bad thing we did when we were fourteen years old?

This was stupid. Rita Works was not going to be able to give them any answers and Howard was wasting his time contacting her.

Still, he fired a message back to Fern, knowing she would just keep pestering him if not.

I messaged her and asked if we could meet. Will let you know if I hear anything.

He read through the message, amending 'if' to 'when', then hit send.

Hopefully the bloody woman would leave him alone now.

* * *

Janice wasn't getting anywhere with her attempts to track down Rachel Williams.

She had volunteered for the task, hoping to score brownie points with Fern, convinced finding their old friend would be easy, but instead she kept hitting brick walls.

Her first attempt had been to hunt through all of the profiles belonging to people called Rachel Williams on Facebook, but there were so many, it was a daunting task. It had taken ages to send messages to each one who looked like a plausible option. A handful of the Rachels pinged back straight away and she crossed them off the list, but most of the messages were still unread.

While she waited for more replies, she scoured her friends list for anyone who might have known Rachel, figuring she would find out if they were still in touch. The problem was Rachel had gone to a different school, lived in a different county. Janice, Fern and Howard had only met her during that one trip, and, although they had been bound by the secret they shared, none of them actually knew her well at all.

Still, Janice gamely continued with her quest, pinging off messages to the handful of friends she had gone to school with and who had been on the trip, asking them if they remembered Rachel.

Again, it was a dead end. Not a single person could help.

Google offered nothing and neither did any of the other social media sites. Janice even went back as far as her Myspace account in her attempts to find her. It was as if Rachel Williams hadn't existed.

She scrubbed her hands over her face, frustrated. Fern was going to kill her if she didn't come up with the goods, especially after she had bragged about being good at finding people. There had to be a way to track the woman down.

Then she had an idea. She had tried her own school friends, but what about Rachel's? There had been other kids from her school on the trip and they would have known Rachel better. Perhaps some of them were still in touch.

The next hour was spent wracking her brain, vainly trying to remember the names of the kids on the trip. Rachel and Kelly had been the only two who had hung out with Fern's group, the other kids sticking to their own friends. She remembered a couple of their first names, but that wasn't going to help her find them on Facebook.

On a whim she typed the name of the school into the search bar. Most schools had a page and maybe she would recognise the names of some of the followers.

That was how she found Julie Voorhees, remembering instantly as she saw the name that Fern had taken the piss out of the girl because she shared a surname with the killer from the *Friday the 13th* movies. She sent Julie a message, explaining that she was trying to get in touch with Rachel Williams and asking if they were still in contact.

Julie's reply came within ten minutes, abruptly ending Janice's search.

They hadn't really stayed in touch, but she did know through local gossip that Rachel Williams had become Rachel Colton, though the marriage had been short-lived. She also knew that Rachel had passed away after she was involved in a fatal accident.

A car accident, Julie told Janice, though she was unable to offer any further details.

It was with the name change that Janice was eventually able to find a handful of local news reports on Rachel's death.

A car accident was correct, though it wasn't as Janice was expecting. There hadn't been any other vehicles involved and the car had actually been stationary, sitting in the driveway at the time when it caught fire. In what reports claimed was a freak accident, Rachel Colton had been unable to free her seat belt, burning to death inside the vehicle.

Janice started hyperventilating. This was bad. Kelly, Gary and Rachel were all dead and they had all died in fires.

She needed to tell Fern.

* * *

Tracking down Olivia Blake was easier than Fern had anticipated. They had once been the best of friends, but things had abruptly changed after the accident and the two of them hadn't seen each other in years.

Olivia had a Facebook page and they shared a handful of mutual friends. Sending a message wouldn't work though. They had parted on bad terms and chances were, Olivia wouldn't read, certainly wouldn't respond, to any messages Fern sent. Her profile gave nothing away. There were just a few public posts, and there was nothing to suggest where she worked.

Fern knew that Olivia's mother, Elena, owned The Riverside Inn in Thorpe St Andrew, so figured that was as good a place to start as any.

She wasn't sure if Elena Blake would recognise her when she entered the restaurant on Tuesday lunchtime, but knew from the instant scowl on the woman's face that she did.

The place was reasonably busy with half a dozen tables occupied, the delicious aromas hitting Fern's nose and reminding her she had only had an apple and a muesli bar to eat that day. She toyed with getting a table and treating herself to lunch, but business was business, and she needed to find out where Olivia was. Besides, she didn't trust Elena to not spit in her food. Instead, she made her way to the bar, blinked in surprise when the bartender looked up and she recognised him as Olivia's brother, Jamie.

He had certainly improved with age, no longer spotty and gangly, instead filled out in all the right places, his Italian heritage clear in his dark eyes and olive skin.

'Fern St Clair, what a surprise.' He didn't sound or look any more pleased to see her than Elena, but they both recognised her, so that was a start.

'Hello, Jamie. You're looking well. Long time, no see.'

'What can I get you?'

No pleasantries, but no insults either. Jamie was sticking to being professional.

Fern made him wait while she perused the drinks menu. 'I'll have a glass of dry white wine please.' She could have just the one, and it was nearly Christmas.

'Small or large?'

'Tempting as large is, you'd better make it a small or I will have to leave my car here.'

She attempted a flirtatious wink, but he blanked her, turning to the fridge.

With Jamie working in the inn, she wondered if Olivia was there too, but unless she was out back in the kitchen, it appeared to be just Elena and Jamie manning the place.

'Well this is a nice little family affair,' she commented, as he poured the wine. 'Does your sister work here too?'

'She helps out occasionally.' He didn't make eye contact with her, his tone neutral, though she could tell from his body language that he didn't particularly like her. Shame, as Olivia's little brother had suddenly become a lot more appealing.

'That's £3.75.'

Fern waved her card over the reader. 'That's a shame, as I was hoping to catch up with her.'

'I doubt she'll want to see you.' That was from Elena, who had joined them at the bar. 'So, what brings you here, Fern? Not just a glass of wine, I'm guessing.'

That was Olivia's mother, straight to the point. She was viewing Fern with the same kind of indifferent dislike that Jamie had, though Elena also seemed curious.

'I thought maybe we should bury the hatchet.'

'After all this time?'

Fern decided to lay it on thick. 'We used to be so close and yes, I get that we haven't spoken in years, but I've done a lot of growing up in that time. Things happen and make you realise life is short. I don't want—'

'You know about Livvy's accident?'

Accident?

Fern managed to keep her expression neutral. Instead of blurting out, *'What accident?'* she twisted her mouth in what she hoped was a sympathetic smile and asked gently, 'How is she, Elena?'

'Cuts and bruises, but she's okay. I think the shock of finding Gary was the worst bit for her.'

'I can imagine.'

Thank God she was a good actress, because Fern's heart was thumping so hard she was surprised Elena and Jamie couldn't hear it.

Olivia had found Gary Lamb?

She remembered reading that a woman had discovered him, but there had been no name given. There was no way this was a coincidence. Olivia was up to her neck in this.

Was she the one who had been sending the notes?

'I would really like to see her. I've been thinking about her a lot these last few days.'

Elena's lips twisted as she considered. 'Why don't you leave your phone number and I can pass it on to Olivia when we next speak?'

Seriously?

'I was hoping to surprise her with flowers. Maybe if you could just let me have her address?'

'Send the flowers here. I can pass them on.'

Realising that she was getting nowhere, Fern left her number, gulped down her wine, and thanked Elena through gritted teeth. Swearing under her breath about the woman, she stepped out of the warm restaurant into the cool December air, pulling her coat a little tighter as she walked over to her car.

With the engine running, the heater on full, she googled Gary Lamb, looking for any news articles that mentioned the woman who had found him. Olivia's name wasn't anywhere, but one of the articles did refer to an estate agent on a viewing being the one to discover him. Further googling eventually revealed the name of the estate agent the property had been listed with.

Dandridge & Son. So that was where Olivia worked. Fern knew where their office was. Finally, she was getting somewhere.

She glanced at her watch, saw that she needed to head back to work, but that was okay: she would head down there after she had finished.

Despite Elena's reluctance to give up her daughter's location, the lunch break had been more productive than she could have hoped. Not only did she now know where Olivia worked, she had also learnt her former friend had found Gary's body.

It was time to figure out what the hell Olivia was up to.

21

To Olivia's relief, Esther was back at work on Tuesday, which meant she didn't have to endure another day with just Roger and Jeremy for company. She had been dreading facing Jeremy after their uncomfortable encounter, though recent events with Noah had taken her mind off that.

Her fears resurfaced as she walked through the door, wondering if Jeremy would say anything about how he had spooked her the previous night.

But he acted as if nothing had happened. She was pleased about that, but also found it a little unnerving. As the day wore on, she did start to wonder if she had overreacted. The two of them had never gelled and recent events had Olivia more on edge than normal. Perhaps it had just been Jeremy being a dick.

Not in the mood for joining in with any office banter, she kept her head down, willing the work day to pass quickly, her mind replaying the encounter with Dan, or Daniella as she now knew her, and Noah's reaction to it.

He had acted like it was no big deal. The apology she finally had received seemed more like a token effort to pacify her. Why had he felt the need to mislead her?

Other than a message that she hadn't bothered to respond to, she had not heard from him all day. He had said he was coming over to hers that night, that they would talk.

Part of her wanted to tell him not to bother, but also she was curious to know what he had to say. He had betrayed her trust, something she didn't give easily, and he was going to have to work hard to win that back. Plus, although she didn't want to be a coward, knowing Molly was away was making her dread returning home. Last night's incident was far too clear in her mind. Okay, so the cameras hadn't picked anyone up, but Olivia hadn't imagined what had happened.

Even if there was a rational explanation for the back door being open, and Molly had insisted she had locked it, Olivia didn't buy Noah's theory about the faulty Echo. And for it to start playing the same Christmas song that she had heard in the kitchen at Honington Lane? That was a stretch.

What if someone was hanging around the house trying to spook her? It would be dark when she returned home and the thought of being there alone frightened her more than she cared to admit. As the office clock ticked closer to five-thirty, her fear escalated.

She glanced at her phone, saw that there were no missed calls or messages from Noah. And okay, she had blanked his last message, but surely he should be grovelling or something? After all, he was the one in the wrong. She toyed with messaging him, asking if he was still coming over, but pride stopped her.

Maybe she should stop by the restaurant, see her mum. She could always stay the night there. But there was Luna to consider. She would have to return home first to feed her, plus get a change of clothes for the morning.

Pondering what to do, she said goodnight to her colleagues and stepped out on to the busy road, fishing in her bag for her car keys. As she began the walk back to her car, she was aware of someone falling in step beside her.

'Hello, Olivia.'

She glanced up and for a moment thought she was seeing a ghost. Although she hadn't seen Fern St Clair in over fifteen years, the woman was instantly recognisable, all sharp cheekbones, thin smirky lips and black hooded eyes. There were harsh lines around her mouth, which gave her more of an edge, and her blonde hair had been bleached almost white in colour, but Olivia would have known that hard face anywhere.

'Fern, what are you doing here?'

'I came to see you.'

'What? Why?' Olivia had stopped walking now and turned to face her former friend, was vaguely aware that the two of them were blocking the pavement, as people bustled around them.

'I thought we should have a catch-up. Fancy grabbing a glass of wine?'

'I don't think that's a good idea.'

'Oh, come on. Don't you think it's time we buried the past?'

Was she serious? Olivia wanted nothing to do with her. 'You are my past. And honestly, I'd rather you stay there.'

'Would it help if I said I was sorry?'

'Are you?'

That smirk deepened. 'It was a long time ago. We were just kids.'

'So the answer's no.' Why did that not surprise her? Fern had never been remorseful for anything in her life. 'Look, I don't have time for this, so you go your way and I'll go mine, and let's just pretend we never had this conversation.' Olivia started to walk away and was annoyed when Fern followed.

'Of course I'm sorry, Livvy. There you go, is that what you want to hear?'

The woman couldn't sound any more insincere if she tried.

Olivia kept walking, cutting off down a side street and picking up her pace, the clatter of Fern's heels following.

'What happened to forgive and forget? I thought you would be gracious enough to accept my apology.'

Ignore her. Don't bite.

'You're being pathetic, you know, keeping up a stupid grudge.'

'I'm not keeping anything up, Fern. I don't want you in my life, period.'

'That's cold. And people say I'm the bitch. Well I'm not. I'm trying to be the bigger person here. I'm the one offering an olive branch and doing the right thing.'

'The right thing?' Olivia stopped again, her temper rising. 'The right thing would be to go away and leave me alone. I have moved on and you should too.' The car park was just two minutes away and she started to walk away again, knowing that once she reached her car she could lock herself inside and get away from Fern.

'Have you really moved on, Livvy?'

Ignore her. Olivia turned into the side alley that led to where her car was parked, picked up pace again.

'Seems to me you are right in the thick of things.'

'What the hell is that supposed to mean?'

'You were there in the house that day with Gary when he died. Bit coincidental, don't you think?'

Olivia whirled on Fern, anger burning through her. 'What the fuck are you implying?'

'Don't tell me this isn't connected. You have this stupid grudge about what happened when we were kids. Are you really going to try convincing me that you didn't play a part in this? That what happened to Gary wasn't some stupid revenge prank that went wrong?'

What? Olivia couldn't believe what she was hearing. 'You think I did that?'

'I know you're behind it, Livvy. You might as well own up.'

'You're bloody crazy.' Olivia was reeling with both shock and disbelief. Was this one of Fern's sick games? 'Get away from me.'

As she went to walk away, Fern caught hold of her wrist, tightened her grip. 'A long, long time ago, you did a bad, bad thing.'

Olivia's heart was thumping, her mouth dry. 'What did you say?'

'You recognise those words, don't you?'

Had Fern sent her the notes? 'It was you?' Yanking her wrist free Olivia took a step back. 'You crazy bitch. Stay the hell away from me!' She bolted for the car park, trying not to stumble in her heels, freezing when she spotted the figure leaning on the bonnet of her car.

As she tried to plot her next move, aware Fern was still behind her and, not sure which direction contained the most danger, the figure rose, moving towards her and into the light of a lamp post.

Noah.

Relief skittered through her as she ran towards him. He met her halfway across the car park, the bunch of roses in one hand a reminder that she was still mad at him, and she took a step back when he went to pull her into his arms. He didn't get off that lightly.

'What are you doing here?'

'I heard yelling. Are you okay?' he asked, ignoring her question. 'Who's that?'

Olivia glanced behind her, dismayed to see that Fern was skulking her way across the car park. 'She's no one.'

'We need to talk, Olivia. Now!' Fern's voice was shrill.

Goddammit, the bloody woman just didn't give up! 'I told you I have nothing to say to you. Go away.'

'Who are you?' Noah demanded.

Fern glared at him before refocusing her attention on Olivia. 'I suggest you come somewhere quiet where we can talk before I start spilling all your dirty little secrets in front of your friend here.'

'Go ahead.' Olivia stuck her chin out defiantly. 'He already knows everything.'

That made Fern hesitate, though only briefly. 'So he knows you've been harassing your old friends, threatening us?' she asked, slyly.

'What? I haven't threatened you. You just threatened me.'

'Okay, seriously, who the fuck are you?'

Fern glanced at Noah again. 'Fern St Clair. I'm a friend of Livvy's.'

Olivia saw the penny drop. He didn't look impressed.

'Was a friend,' Olivia added. 'A long time ago. But not any more. Never again. Not after what you did. Noah, can we go, please? I'll explain in the car.'

'What threats?' he questioned.

There was another hesitation, this time longer. Fern seeming to debate whether she wanted to have this conversation with a stranger. 'My friends and I have been threatened.'

'And what has that got to do with Olivia?'

'She is behind it.'

'Really? How have you reached that conclusion?'

Fern shifted from foot to foot, for the first time looking uncomfortable. Was she really going to own up to what she had done? 'Revenge,' she muttered eventually, looking Noah square in the eye.

'For what?' He wasn't letting her off lightly and a little part of Olivia thawed. After all this time she wanted to hear Fern admit what she had done. Was Noah about to help her get that?

'It's not relevant what for. It was a stupid childhood prank and it certainly doesn't justify her sending us notes, letters, threatening us,' she answered eventually.

Fern had received notes? Olivia's blood ran cold. She exchanged a brief glance with Noah.

'What notes?' he asked.

'Maybe you should ask Livvy that! She sent them.'

'No, I didn't. I thought you'd been sending them to me.'

For the first time Fern looked a little unsure. 'No.'

'Yes, Fern.' Olivia turned to Noah. 'She knew what was written on them, so she must have sent them.'

'No, you silly cow. I know what is written on them because you... okay, some fucker has been sending them to me.' The fight left Fern, her shoulders sagging. 'You really didn't send them?'

'No! Seriously, I have better things to do than send you stupid notes.'

'So if you didn't send them, who the fuck did?'

22

'She was delightful.'

'She's a grade-A bitch.'

Olivia leaned back against the headrest. They were in Noah's car, having left hers in the car park to collect later, and on their way to get food. Noah was trying to win her over with flowers and dinner and, although she had softened her stance and appreciated how he had stuck up for her with Fern, she was biding her time as she awaited his explanation about Daniella, before deciding whether she would let him into her bed later.

'So are you going to tell me what she did to you?'

Olivia closed her eyes, not up for this conversation right now. She had made her peace with what had happened, no longer felt embarrassed by it, though when she thought back to that day, it was so easy to remember the burning humiliation and how at the time she had wanted to curl up and die. She would never forgive Fern for what she had done all those years ago.

'I don't want to talk about it right now. Can we just go have some dinner and forget about it for a while?' She found a smile for him.

'Sure.' Taking one hand off the wheel, he covered hers in her lap, gave it a squeeze.

Seeing Fern again had been a shock. The woman hadn't changed and

Olivia doubted she ever would. Part of her had always thought, hoped, that the spiteful girl she had gone to school with might have matured into a compassionate woman, but some people didn't change. Fern always put herself first.

It was understandable that Fern St Clair might be targeted by someone looking for revenge, but what the hell had Olivia done wrong? She certainly couldn't think of anything which would connect her to Fern.

Although she wanted nothing to do with the woman, Noah had taken Fern's number. While that had made Olivia bristle a little, deep down she knew he had only done it because he wanted to find out who was tormenting her. Sometimes Noah couldn't help going into cop mode, even though he denied it whenever she accused him of it.

She wondered where he was taking her, tired eyes watching the blurring fields pass by as they headed out of the city and into the country. After about fifteen minutes he pulled off the road into the large car park of a cosy pub.

'They have restaurants in the city, you know?' Olivia pointed out wryly as she stepped out of the car into the cold night. She marvelled at how silent it was in the countryside, the clear sky littered with stars.

'I know, but this place has good reviews, and it will be quieter. We can talk.'

About us or about what had happened with Fern? Olivia wondered.

Still, she took his hand and let him lead her inside, the homely interior with comforting smells, low lighting, soft music and giant Christmas tree instantly soothing her.

Noah ordered himself a pint and Olivia a large glass of wine while they waited at the bar for their table. 'I can't drink all that. We have to get my car remember.'

'Well, I was thinking you could leave your car for tonight. I'll give you a lift into work tomorrow.'

Her eyebrows lifted. 'That's a little presumptuous. I haven't invited you to stay over.'

'You will.' He gave her a wolfish grin when she opened her mouth to protest. 'Besides, Molly's away, isn't she? I'm sure you don't want to be there alone.'

He was right about that, she grudgingly conceded, though she didn't admit it out loud, instead remaining non-committed. 'We'll see.'

The atmosphere in the restaurant was informal and relaxed, and not wanting to ruin the moment, Olivia tried to keep conversation light until they had eaten. As the waitress cleared their plates, she studied Noah across the table.

With Toby cheating on her, then the incident with Dominic, she had lost her confidence. Too scared to date again she had resigned herself to a life of being single, convinced no other man would accept her for who she was. When Noah had blitzed into her life, he had knocked straight through all the barriers she had put up. She hadn't set out to find him. He had just appeared one day with Jamie and hadn't left her alone from that day on. And yes, okay, at first it had just been as friends, but then things had progressed, and the whole time, all Olivia could think was how damn lucky she was, because he was kind and confident and interested in her, and he made her laugh, plus of course, he was bloody gorgeous. It seemed crazy that he wanted her, but he did, and so she didn't question it, just went along with it, convincing herself that good things sometimes really did happen.

This morning had been a reality check, making her question everything.

Had she really been swept up in a web of lies or was there a more innocent explanation for why he had deceived her?

What did she know about him? She hadn't questioned the truth of what he had told her. American dad – he had the weird accent going on, mostly British, but pronouncing some words with a lazy American lilt; British mother and one brother and one sister, though Olivia hadn't met any of them – it was far too early in their relationship. And she hadn't questioned why she had yet to meet any of his friends. He was mates with her brother, so she had taken everything she knew about him at face value.

She knew that he had grown up as an army brat, his dad moving the family all over the place, and that they hadn't settled in the UK until he was in his teens. All of his family were based in Devon and that was where he had lived until he moved to London and joined the Met. A relationship had brought him to Norfolk five years ago, which had involved a transfer with the police, but then he had left to set up his own surveillance business. The relationship had also fallen apart, and he had been single for nearly two years, never married. Again, this was all what he had told her, so she had presumed it was true.

There were things she did know for certain. He liked rugby, Mexican food and live music, he drank his coffee black, and he was fairly anti when it came to social media, not even having a Facebook account. Oh, and of course her mother adored him. But seriously, that was it.

Had she been swept up too quickly, blinded by his charm? Had she overlooked any warning signs?

'You've gone quiet. Should I be worried?'

The corner of her mouth twitched nervously. Was she really that obvious? 'You said you picked here because we could talk.'

'Which we have been.'

'Yes, though not about the elephant in the room. You owe me an explanation, Noah. You deceived me.' When he frowned, she quickly added, 'I'm not mad about it any more, I don't want to fight, but I do need to understand why.'

The frown softened slightly, as he toyed with his glass, and for a moment Olivia wondered if he was going to ignore her, but then he looked up and met her eyes.

'Okay. I wasn't sure how you would react if you knew I had a female partner.'

Seriously? 'What? You thought I would be jealous?'

'You acted that way this morning.'

'Because you hadn't been honest with me, not because Dan is a woman.' Olivia threw her hands up, exasperated. 'Don't throw this back on me. In fact, dial back to before this morning. Have I ever acted jealous or possessive? Why would you assume that I am the jealous type?'

'Look, it's been an issue before with women. Dan and I, we have to work closely, and she's a pretty girl.'

'She is, but you should have trusted me.'

'I know, you're right, I should have done. I'm sorry. At first I didn't say anything because I didn't know if things were going to get serious between us, then as they did, I guess the timing never felt right. I'd mentioned her a couple of times and you had assumed she was a guy. After that it was difficult to correct you.'

Was it really as simple as that? Olivia studied his face for any trace of a lie. His clear green eyes held her gaze, not backing down, and she found it difficult to doubt him.

'So do you forgive me?'

'Are you keeping any other secrets from me?'

He didn't hesitate. 'No.'

'Okay, but I want to get to know Daniella. You're an enigma, Noah. I have never met any of the people in your life.'

He grinned crookedly. 'You've met your brother.'

'Well, yes, but apart from Jamie.'

'Okay, I will talk to Dan. Sort something out.' He glanced up at the waitress who had returned with dessert menus then looked at Olivia. 'Do you want anything?'

'I'm fine.' Olivia smiled at the waitress. 'Dinner was lovely, thank you, but I'm full.'

'Just the bill please,' Noah added. As the waitress left, he reached across the table, took hold of Olivia's hands. 'So we're good, yeah?'

A half-smile played on his lips, dimples threatening.

Damn it, those dimples got her every time.

'We're getting there.'

'Good, so while we are doing serious, are we going to talk about what happened tonight with the grade-A bitch? I could tell you really hate her, so I know she must have done something pretty bad.'

Olivia's face fell. She didn't want to talk about Fern. Had been trying her best to forget her. 'Do we have to ruin the evening?'

'She's been receiving notes too, Liv. I know you don't like her, but if whoever is tormenting you, is going after her too, we need to question why. You said she was friendly with Gary Lamb?'

'Well more so with Howard Peck. He was Gary's best mate at school. But yes, they were all friendly enough.'

'Gary was set on fire and you were involved in an accident where you were badly burned. I think there's a connection. Can you talk me through your accident and how it happened?'

Although his tone was gentle, tension bristled in her shoulders. This had been a nice evening and now they had talked through Daniella, she didn't want to dredge up the past. 'Do we have to do that tonight? Can't we just go back to mine and have hot sex?'

The green eyes heated briefly, his lips curving. 'Don't worry. We're going to do that too.' He turned her hands over, running his thumbs over the soft skin of her wrists, and little flickers of lust flamed in her belly. 'But first, tell me what happened. It could be important.'

Olivia pouted a little, relieved when the waitress returned with the card reader. As Noah settled the bill she reached for her coat and slipped it on. At his raised brow, she managed a smile. 'Look, let's get back to mine, okay? Luna's not been fed and she's going to be hungry. We can talk there.'

She was quiet on the ride home. The two glasses of wine had numbed the edges of her tension, but remembering the night of the accident brought back sharp and painful memories.

As Noah pulled off the road and into the dark driveway of her house, which seemed empty and unwelcoming, she was grateful to have him with her. In the summer it was the perfect home and she loved the south-facing secluded garden, how it was set apart from the other properties in the street, giving plenty of privacy. In the warmer months it was a haven to relax in, have barbecues and entertain friends, but at this time of year, and especially if she was alone, she was aware of every shadow and every creak the house made.

It was an old building and they had been lucky to get it for a good price. The place had needed a fair bit of work, and the ugly décor had put a lot of people off. Cosmetically, they had changed what they could as quickly as possible, fitting a new kitchen and bathroom, replacing carpets and decorating throughout, but there were still plenty of jobs that needed doing, ones that had gone on hold after the break-up. Olivia had managed to buy Toby out of the house, but it had left her on a tight budget. For now, the additional work would have to wait.

As she unlocked the door and stepped inside, reaching for the hallway light, Luna appeared, snaking around her legs and meowing in protest of her empty dish. While Olivia fed her and found a vase for her flowers, Noah opened a bottle of wine. When she went to join him in the living room, the curtains were drawn, the table lamp on, and the place was feeling a lot more homely.

Taking the glass he offered, she sat down on the sofa beside him, drawing her legs up under her and took a long sip. It didn't escape her attention that she had been drinking more in the last two weeks than she had done in months, and she blamed it on the stress of recent events, mindful she would have to cut back. For tonight though, if Noah wanted to talk about her accident, she needed the wine.

She took another sip, enjoying the pleasant buzz, and set the glass down, shifted her position slightly so she was facing him. Best get this over with, then she could make him fulfil the second part of his promise.

'We were on a school trip when it happened.'

'Okay.'

'It was almost Christmas, around about now actually. There was a place near the coast, a converted farm, and our school organised a trip. It was a pre-Christmas thing, five days away.'

Her mind went back as she remembered the place, how beautifully it had been decorated with glittering lights and festive cheer. And how, naively, she had believed it was going to be the perfect lead-up to Christmas.

How wrong she was.

23

It was late afternoon when the coach arrived at Black Dog Farm, dusk already settling, and fourteen-year-old Olivia Blake was looking on in awe as they rode up the long driveway towards the large building that was covered in twinkling lights.

She had been unsure about coming on the trip. Things had been a little fraught with her best friend, Fern, in recent weeks and they had been fighting a lot. Fern had always taken the upper hand in their friendship, with Olivia meekly following her along, but gradually she was finding her own voice, her confidence growing, and she was starting to question some of the things Fern did. Of course, Fern hadn't liked that and by way of punishment she had started to hang out more with Janice Hardesty, keen to show Olivia that she was expendable.

With both Fern and Janice on the trip, and Janice desperate to take Olivia's place, Olivia was worried the week would be a complete nightmare. So far though, the three of them had been getting along okay. Fern had sat next to Olivia on the coach, relegating Janice to the seat behind, and banter between the three of them had been easy-going and fun, reminding Olivia of the good old days. She had been considering cooling her friendship with Fern, maybe finding some new friends, but for now, while things were good, she wouldn't rock the boat.

On arrival they had been welcomed by Mrs Simon, who ran the place with her husband, enjoying home-made lemonade and biscuits, while the Simons shared with them the legend behind the farm, which had been named after Black Shuck, or Old Shuck, as Mr Simon called him, regaling them with tales of how travellers had seen the giant saucer-eyed dog standing in the roads that ran close to the farm.

He had a twinkle in his eye, but Olivia wasn't sure if he was teasing or not.

After the welcome, they had been shown to their dorm rooms in the converted barn at the back of the house. The place was huge, set over several acres, Olivia heard her teacher, Miss Patterson, say, and although it was no longer a working farm, there were plenty of activities lined up to keep the students amused over the coming days.

There were two schools occupying the farm, with forty students from each. The coach that arrived with the pupils from St Nicholas High School in Essex didn't arrive until just before dinner.

The first time Olivia spotted Margaret Grimes was in the dining room that first night. She had wandered into the room behind a male student, eyes darting about warily, then keeping her head down as she joined the dinner queue, looking like she didn't want to draw attention to herself, her shoulders slumped.

'Oh my God, look what that loser is wearing.' Fern was pointing and giggling, not particularly discreetly at the girl. 'I think my mum used to have a pair of jeans like that.'

The jeans were old-fashioned, Olivia had to admit that. High waisted and made of a stiff looking dark blue denim. They were worn with a shapeless T-shirt tucked into them, making them look even more dated.

'I bet your mum wore them much better than that too,' Janice simpered up to Fern.

She was such a creep.

'Hey, you.' Fern whistled loudly, half the room looking in her direction. The girl she was taunting wasn't one of them, which seemed to irritate her. Fern did not like to be ignored. 'Frumpy girl in the dinner queue. I'm talking to you.'

Hesitantly the girl glanced up, meeting Fern's eyes. She didn't speak.

Fern's lips twisted cruelly. 'What the hell are you wearing? Did Stevie Wonder help pick your outfit?'

A couple of girls in the queue behind the girl started to snigger, while the boy who was before her turned and scowled at Fern through bottle-rimmed glasses.

The girl didn't respond, simply turning away. Olivia didn't miss the look on her face though, resigned, already defeated.

'Hey, don't ignore me. I was talking to you.'

'Leave her alone, Fern.'

'Butt out, Olivia.'

Miss Patterson picked that moment to stop by the table. She gave Fern a warning look. 'Is everything all right here, ladies?'

'Everything is fine, Miss Patterson.' Fern smiled snidely at her.

'Good, good. This is a wonderful opportunity to form new friendships, not create enemies, Miss St Clair. Remember that. We are not too far from home. If you cause any trouble, I won't hesitate to get the coach to take you back early. Understood?'

'Yes, Miss Patterson.'

Fern saluted her back as she walked away. 'Great, now look what that frumpy bitch has done.'

'She hasn't done anything,' Olivia pointed out mildly. 'You started it.'

'It was just a stupid joke. Jesus, lighten up, Livvy. You're no fun these days.'

Olivia wanted to say more, but decided it was best to hold her tongue. She caught Janice's gloating smile, knew she would be pleased that there was some friction between her and Fern.

Annoyed and a little embarrassed by Fern's behaviour, she picked at her dinner, wondering if this was going to be a difficult week after all.

She watched the girl in the queue get her food and cutlery, before going to sit down at the end of one of the quieter tables. The two other students who were already there didn't speak to her and they didn't look overly impressed that she had picked their table. She sat far enough away though and made no attempt to join in on their conversation.

The boy with the glasses, the one who had been standing behind her, picked up his tray and started walking straight towards the three of them, a blank expression on his face.

'You can't sit here,' Fern told him, the second he set his tray down opposite her.

He didn't attempt to sit, didn't speak. He leant forward and picked up the bowl of spaghetti Fern had in front of her.

'Hey, what the hell are you—'

She didn't get to finish the sentence, instead gasped in shock as he tipped the hot food into her lap.

Calmly, he stood back up, picked up his tray and walked away, as if the incident hadn't happened, leaving Fern, Olivia and Janice staring after him, open-mouthed.

And that was their first encounter with Malcolm Grimes.

Margaret and Malcolm were twins, Olivia soon found out, though they looked nothing alike. Margaret soft and fair with a pretty heart-shaped face, while Malcolm was bulkier, darker and sharper around the edges. He wore a constant frown and although he had stuck up for Margaret in the dining room (at least that is what Olivia had assumed he was doing), the pair didn't seem that close.

To be honest, Malcolm Grimes scared Olivia a little bit. There was something cold and shifty about him and he had a cruel mouth. Luckily, he seemed to have just one goal for the week and that was to avoid everyone. Meanwhile, Margaret joined in the activities, though tried her best to keep a low profile.

Olivia felt sorry for the girl, knew she was an easy target for people like Fern because she offered little resistance, so when she saw her in the Tuesday afternoon craft group, she headed for the table where Margaret sat alone.

'Is it okay if I sit here?' She waited and when Margaret gave a shy nod, slung her bag down.

There were a choice of activities and Olivia had favoured crafting Christmas decorations and cards over ice skating with Fern and Janice. To be honest, after what had happened at dinner the previous night, she was grateful for the time away from them.

'You're Margaret, right?'

Another nod.

'I'm Olivia. It's nice to meet you.'

This time she got a hesitant smile, though still no words. Olivia guessed she couldn't blame Margaret for being wary of her. She had been sitting with Fern at dinner, after all.

'I'm really sorry about what my friend said last night at dinner. Sometimes she can be really mean. I don't like it when she's like that. It's embarrassing.'

'So why are you friends with her then?'

The fact that Margaret had a voice, plus the directness of her question, threw Olivia for a moment. 'I guess we– we've known each other for a long time.'

It wasn't really a proper answer to the question, but it did get Olivia thinking as the pair of them worked together, mostly in silence at first, but Margaret gradually lowered her defences as the afternoon progressed. Initially the conversation was a little awkward, Olivia asking all the questions, Margaret seeming reluctant to talk about herself, almost embarrassed that Olivia was interested and doubting at first if she was being genuine, but slowly she thawed, and by the end of the activity they were even having a laugh together.

Olivia liked her. Margaret was painfully shy and had been conditioned to believe she was irrelevant. She was kind and seemed smart, and she was quite funny, making Olivia laugh a couple of times. It had been a pleasant afternoon and Olivia was feeling much better after what had happened in the dining hall the previous evening.

As they headed along the hallway together discussing the Christmas cards they had made, Olivia heard a sharp taunt. 'Have you been doing some charity work, Livvy?'

She glanced up in dismay, recognising Fern's voice. She was heading towards them, hips swaying in her low-waisted jeans, flanked by Janice and two girls from Margaret's school. All of them laughed in delight at the poor attempt at a joke.

Olivia felt her temper rise a notch. Glancing disdainfully at Janice, who was still openly sniggering, she shot Fern a cool look. 'I could ask the same of you.'

Temper flashed in Fern's eyes, while Janice's mouth flapped open and shut like a goldfish at Olivia's insult. 'I'm hardly charity work!' she snapped indignantly.

Beside Olivia, Margaret seemed to shrink in stature. 'I should go,' she whispered.

'What?' As Margaret attempted to slope off, Olivia caught hold of her clammy hand. 'No, stay.'

'Yes, stay,' Fern agreed. 'We need to have a little chat about what your freak of a brother did to me. Kelly and Rachel here have been telling me all about you and your weirdo family.'

Another snigger from Janice. 'Weirdo is right. You tell her, Fern. I think she owes you a new top.'

When Fern took a menacing step towards Margaret, Olivia stepped in between them.

'Oh for God's sake, you two are pathetic,' she snapped, having had enough. 'Margaret's done nothing to either of you, so stop being so bloody nasty.'

'Really, Livvy? You are taking this loser's side over mine? What happened to best friends forever?'

'That was before my best friend turned into a bully and a bitch.'

There was a moment of silence as Fern and Olivia sized each other up, neither prepared to back down. Eventually Fern's lips twisted. 'You really want to do this?'

'Do what, Fern? Act like the bigger person?'

'You're making a mistake, Livvy.'

Margaret muttered something. It was barely audible.

Fern looked at her with disgust. 'What did you say, freak? Speak up.'

Margaret cleared her throat. 'I said you don't have to fight because of me. I can just go.' She tried to pull her hand free and Olivia gripped tighter.

'You're not going anywhere. If Fern can't be nice then we are done here.'

Fern's face reddened. Her shocked expression a clear indication that she didn't expect Olivia to call her bluff. 'You're right, Livvy,' she spat. 'We are done.'

She scowled at Janice and the other two girls, Kelly and Rachel, Olivia was sure she remembered her saying their names were. 'Come on, let's go. We don't want to spend any more time with these losers.'

Kelly and Rachel at least had the good grace to look mildly embarrassed as they passed Olivia, both averting their eyes, but Janice was loving it, a smug expression on her face as she sidled close to Olivia. 'You're pathetic,' she smirked, knocking her hefty shoulder into Olivia's before chasing after Fern.

'You didn't have to do that,' Margaret said, when the four of them had disappeared from earshot. 'I never wanted you to fall out with your friends.'

'They're not exactly good friends though, are they?' Olivia replied tightly.

At the moment she was being carried by temper, but she knew eventually it would simmer down and it bothered her that she would regret the fight with Fern. Had she just made herself a social pariah?

No, she had stuck up for someone who needed sticking up for, someone who she doubted had ever had a real friend. She had done the right thing. Her mother had always taught her to stick up for the underdog. Fern St Clair was a bully and Olivia couldn't continue to stand by and watch her hurt people.

Word spread quickly about their fight and, while several of her classmates were giving her the cold shoulder, Olivia was relieved to learn that Fern's influence was not as powerful as she liked to think, with a handful of students congratulating her on standing up against her former best friend.

Dinner was bearable and she ignored the snide comments from Fern's table, going to sit with Margaret and a few other classmates. Night-time was the worst though. She shared a bunk bed with Fern, was in a dorm with both her and Janice. Of the twelve girls in the room, only a couple of them were talking to her. Olivia kept her head down and ignored the bitchy comments.

As the week passed, she spent more time with Margaret, understanding her better and realising that her home life wasn't exactly a picnic either. Olivia's heart went out to her as she learnt about her domineering father, distant mother and her difficult relationships with her brother and sister.

Margaret was gradually coming out of her shell and the time spent with her was far more rewarding and interesting than hanging out with Fern.

She was kind-hearted, interesting to talk to, and wise beyond her years, and Olivia hated that she was tormented for something as shallow as wearing the wrong clothes.

The old farm was big, which was a godsend, as it meant it was easy to avoid Fern. The Simon family had invested a lot of money into converting the place for visitors, with plenty of activities, both indoor and outdoor, from go-karting and archery to trampolining and a bowling alley. In the woods surrounding the property there were tyre swings and tree houses, and although these were designed more for summer use, Olivia and Margaret explored every inch of the farm. That was how they first discovered the creepy old cottage.

24

The building was in the heart of the woods and had long been abandoned, the windows and doors boarded up. Olivia and Margaret had been walking one of the trails on Thursday morning and debating their plans for the rest of the day, aware they would be going home the following morning. There was a farewell Christmas disco planned for that night and Olivia had been persuading Margaret to borrow one of the two outfits she had brought with her.

As they headed towards the border of the property, deeper in the woods than they had been before, Margaret caught hold of her arm. 'Look.'

Olivia's eyes followed to where she was pointing, spotting the building in the clearing surrounded by a broken picket fence, a tall chimney jutting out of the roof, and her heartbeat quickened.

Did someone live there?

Curiosity took them closer and she spotted the wood panels covering the windows, the missing tiles on the roof and the weeds growing up around the board covering the front door.

'An abandoned cottage. I wonder if we can get inside.' Margaret seemed thrilled, not scared. She had told Olivia of her dream to become a horror writer and while she was meek around her peers, little seemed to phase her when it came to the macabre.

Olivia was more wary, but allowed Margaret to lead her forward. She had seen a couple of scary movies that had scenarios with creepy cottages in the woods and wasn't sure she wanted to go inside, but this was the most excited she had seen Margaret and she didn't want to dampen her enthusiasm.

As they approached the cottage, Margaret hoping for a way in, Olivia keeping her fingers crossed that the boards were all nailed down tightly, a bang came from within.

Olivia's heart jumped into her mouth and she let out a squeal, anchored only by Margaret's firm hand on her arm. If it hadn't been there, she would have started running back through the woods.

Still, Margaret exchanged a cautious look with her and hesitated.

Did someone live here? Olivia couldn't see how, with the place being all boarded up, unless it was a homeless person. Or maybe it was Margaret's brother, Malcolm.

Although he never spoke and wasn't at all close to Margaret, he was always lurking on the periphery, watching, and, she was certain at times, following them. Honestly, he gave Olivia the creeps.

A second louder noise was followed by footsteps crunching on broken wood, then the unmistakable peal of boyish laughter. The girls exchanged another look as they heard shuffling round the back, more footsteps, then voices.

Olivia unfortunately recognised them. She scowled as Gary Lamb and Howard Peck stepped into sight. Gary sneered when he saw them, while Howard didn't look impressed.

'What the fuck are you two doing here?'

'I could ask you the same thing,' Olivia retorted.

Howard Peck was Fern's on–off boyfriend. He and Olivia had never seen eye-to-eye, even before she had fallen out with Fern. Olivia found him shallow and two-faced, while Howard thought she was snooty.

'Staying away from losers like you, Blake.'

Gary sniggered at that.

'Come on, let's get out of here, pal. Have fun with your new friend.'

Howard pushed past them, Gary pausing to spit at Margaret as he passed.

She flinched, took a step back, though held his gaze as the glob of saliva fell at her feet.

'Later, losers.'

Olivia watched them go, relieved when they disappeared out of sight. She glanced at Margaret. 'Are you okay?'

The girl nodded. 'They're idiots.'

No kidding, Olivia thought. 'I guess we should head back too. It will be lunch soon.'

Margaret wasn't listening to her, stepping over weeds as she followed the path towards the back of the cottage, from where Howard and Gary had emerged.

'Where are you going? Margaret?'

'They were inside the house. They must have found a way in.'

Oh great. 'I don't think we should go in there.'

'It'll be fine. I just want to have a quick look.'

Olivia wanted to propose that she waited outside and kept a lookout, just in case Howard and Gary returned, but that would be wrong. She couldn't let Margaret go into the cottage alone. Not that Margaret seemed bothered. It was amazing how her confidence had grown out here alone in the woods. Reluctantly she followed, heart sinking when she spotted the open window, which Margaret had already scrambled through. A broken board of wood lay on the ground and Olivia guessed this was how the boys had gained access. They must have broken in. No wonder they made a quick exit.

'Olivia, are you coming inside? It's well creepy in here.'

Brilliant. I can't wait.

She clambered through the window, glad she was warmly dressed, though she wasn't sure if the shivers she had were from the cold. The inside of the cottage was dark thanks to the boarded-up windows, the only light coming from where she had just climbed in and cracks in the other boards, where thin lines of sunlight spilt through. The air was damp, musty and stank of dirt, and it was evident no one had lived here in a long time. Wallpaper was peeling off the walls. The furniture was sparse and mostly broken. On the far side of the room was a sofa with fabric ripped off the seat cushion so the springs poked through.

'Margaret, where are you?'

She heard the crunch of footsteps over broken glass and her friend appeared in a doorway. 'Come and look. This kitchen is ancient, but there are still cups and plates in the cupboards.'

Hesitantly, Olivia followed her into the room. The place was in such a state of decay, it was probably full of rats and spiders. 'You really like all this stuff, huh?'

Margaret turned to her and even though her face was immersed in shadows, Olivia could see her eyes shining. 'It's brilliant. There is so much history here. I wonder about the people who lived here and what they were like, what happened to them. Don't you?'

Not really. 'We should head back. It's nearly lunchtime.'

'There's an upstairs. I want to see it.'

Olivia didn't. 'I'm hungry and we don't want to miss out on food.'

'It will only take five minutes.'

'We could always come back tomorrow morning, I mean, if there's time before the coaches leave.'

The compromise seemed to work.

'You promise?'

'Sure, if there's time.' Olivia hoped there wouldn't be, but didn't say that to Margaret. 'Come on, let's head back.'

It was after lunch that Rachel Williams had approached them. Olivia had spotted the girl sitting alone, had heard Fern make a bitchy comment behind her back. Had Rachel fallen out with Fern, Janice and Kelly?

Fern really was making enemies fast.

Olivia was with Margaret in her dorm, as Margaret rifled through her case looking for something suitable to wear to the disco.

'I told you, why don't you try on one of the outfits I brought. I have two with me and we're about the same size. You can pick which one you want. I like them both, so I don't mind.'

'You don't have to lend me stuff, Livvy. I'm sure I have something I can wear.'

'Okay, well the offer's there.'

'I know, thank you. I don't really want to go to the stupid disco anyway. I hate things like that.'

If Olivia was honest, she wasn't looking forward to it either. The idea of spending their last evening in the company of Fern and her cronies didn't exactly appeal. But what other choice did they have? They could hardly hide out in the dorms. That would make them look like cowards and Fern would love that.

Both girls looked up as the door opened and Rachel entered the room.

She glanced hesitantly at them before making her way over to her own bunk, lying down on the bed and facing the wall.

Olivia and Margaret continued their conversation in hushed tones, though Margaret glanced over a couple of times. Eventually, closing her case, and admitting Olivia was right, she had nothing to wear for the disco, they got up to go back to Olivia's dorm to look at her outfits.

Margaret glanced at Rachel again and hesitated. 'Are you okay?'

When Rachel didn't reply, she tried again. 'We saw you sitting on your own at lunch.'

More silence, then Rachel rolled over to face them. She sat up, glaring at Olivia. 'Your friend, Fern, is a bitch.'

You've only just figured that out? 'Yes, she is, though she is no longer my friend. What has she done now?'

'She's turned Kelly against me.'

'I'm sorry.' That was from Margaret, who really was too nice for her own good. Rachel had picked on her, but now she had been ostracised, here was Margaret offering her sympathy.

Really? Olivia wasn't sure that she bought it.

Rachel must have been tuning in on Olivia's thoughts because her face suddenly crumpled and she looked like she might cry. 'I'm sorry too,' she whispered. 'I've been mean to you for no reason. You don't have to be nice to me. Fern is a nasty bully. I wish I hadn't listened to her about anything.'

Was this for real? Olivia couldn't decide. Yes, Rachel had been sitting alone at lunch, but the whole situation seemed awfully convenient. She couldn't help wondering if Fern was up to something.

'It's okay.'

Margaret was too quick to forgive. Rachel had been a bitch. Olivia would have held out, at least for a little while.

'You can hang out with us this afternoon if you want.'

As Rachel's eyes brightened, Margaret looked to Olivia for confirmation. 'That's okay, isn't it, Livvy?'

Great, now she had been put on the spot. 'I guess so, though we're not really doing anything exciting.'

'Are you sure?' Rachel sounded hopeful. 'I don't want to push in.'

Jesus. Did Rachel not have any other friends she could go pester?

Margaret smiled happily. 'We're sure.'

Olivia suspected that having two friends might be a first for her. She just hoped Rachel wasn't playing games. She didn't want Margaret to regret her decision.

The afternoon passed more pleasantly than Olivia had expected. There were no encounters with Fern, who had disappeared off somewhere with Janice and Kelly. Rachel joined in with Olivia and Margaret and appeared to genuinely have fun, as the three of them spent the afternoon in the bowling alley.

Olivia admitted she had misjudged the girl. She seemed sorry for how she had treated Margaret, eager to make it up to her and put things right.

After bowling, the pair of them had helped Margaret put an outfit together for the disco, using spare items from their own cases, and Rachel, who turned out to be something of a style queen, straightened the kinks out of Margaret's blonde hair and did her make-up. Dressed in Olivia's low rise flared jeans and one of Rachel's cropped tops, the transformation was staggering. Margaret was a knock-out.

All it had needed was a makeover and a little bit of friendship to give her confidence.

Heads had turned when they entered the dinner hall that night. Fern was already there, sat between Janice and Kelly, her face a picture when she spotted Margaret.

Olivia saw her whispering behind her hand to Kelly, but chose to ignore her as she joined the dinner queue behind Margaret and Rachel. The three of them took their trays to a table in the corner of the room, where some of the other girls from Olivia's school were sitting, and all were quick to compliment Margaret on her new look.

From the corner of her eye, Olivia was aware Fern was watching them and she didn't look happy. She allowed herself a smug smile. Was her former friend finally getting her comeuppance?

It was Margaret's idea to go back to the cottage. She had been talking with Rachel and telling her about the place they had discovered. Rachel saying how creepy it sounded and that she would love to see it before they went home.

Margaret had told her about Olivia's suggestion they went back in the morning and Rachel had joked about how creepy it would be to go there at night.

Well of course, Margaret had taken her seriously, loving the idea. 'Why don't we go now?' she suggested as they left the noise of the disco behind, heading down the hallway to the loos.

'Don't be silly. We can't.'

'Of course we can, Olivia. It's a clear night and it's dry. It's perfect. This disco is pretty boring anyway. It will be fun and super creepy.'

Rachel exchanged a look with Olivia that suggested she hadn't been expecting this response.

'You really want to go now?' she questioned hesitantly.

'Why not?'

'Well, we're not really dressed for a midnight stroll in the woods,' Olivia pointed out.

'So we can change.'

'And it's pitch-black outside. We won't find our way there in the dark.'

'I saw torches in the stockroom,' Rachel piped up. 'I'm sure they work.'

'Come on, please,' Margaret begged. 'It's our last night and it will be so much fun.'

Olivia was still dubious. 'I don't think the teachers will let us go.'

'We don't have to tell them. No one will know we've gone and it's still early. We can be back before the disco finishes. What do you say, Olivia?'

What could she say? Okay, she could let Margaret and Rachel go together, but that would leave her stuck at the disco by herself. And the idea of a night-time adventure was quite fun. She had been hesitant earlier when it was just her and Margaret, but with three of them it felt like safety in numbers. She nodded. 'Okay. Let's do it.'

It was bitterly cold outside and Olivia was glad she had changed into a jumper and thick socks. Her winter coat was zipped up, her scarf and gloves offering little resistance to the elements.

Margaret had borrowed three torches from the stockroom and she led the way into the woods, confidently striding ahead, while excitedly telling Rachel all about the earlier adventure.

Olivia stuck close to Rachel, not liking the sounds of snapping twigs she kept hearing in the distance. It crossed her mind that maybe Margaret's creepy brother had followed them. He seemed to keep tabs on Margaret and if she had disappeared from the disco, he would be wanting to know where she had gone. The idea of him being out in the woods with them was a little unnerving.

Of course it could just be an animal; maybe a badger or a rabbit. It was so quiet and dark, every noise was magnified.

'It's just ahead up here,' Margaret called back to them. She was in her element. No sign of the shy, nervous girl Olivia had met that first day.

Rachel seemed a little anxious, growing quieter as they went deeper into the woods. As her torch picked up the outline of the cottage, she grabbed Olivia's arm. 'We don't have to do this. Maybe we should turn back.'

That sounded like a pretty good idea to Olivia. 'I would like that, but I don't think Margaret will.'

'Hey, you two. Are you coming?' Margaret had stopped walking and was shining her torch back on them. 'We're almost there.'

'I just said to Olivia. Perhaps we should come back in the morning. It's really quite creepy out here.'

'Seriously?' The disappointment in Margaret's voice was clear. 'We're almost there. Come on. It will be fine.'

Rachel exchanged a resigned look with Olivia. 'I'm sorry.'

'It's okay. I knew you were joking when you said about coming out here. I didn't realise she would take you seriously.'

'Come on!' That was Margaret again and she sounded impatient. She had already disappeared round the back of the house when they arrived and Olivia led the way for Rachel, finding the window with the missing board. 'Here goes nothing.'

She climbed in the window, shone her torch around for Margaret, saw the faint flickering light from the room up ahead and started to walk towards it. 'Margaret?' she hissed. 'Where are you?'

'I'm right here.'

Margaret's voice came from the right, making her jump as she stepped out of the kitchen.

Olivia shone the beam on her face, trepidation knotting in her stomach. 'If you're here, what's that light coming from ahead?'

'Where?'

Margaret shone her torch ahead, spotting the flicker of light that Olivia had seen.

'We should go,' Olivia hissed. 'Someone's here.'

Ignoring her, Margaret edged forward.

'Margaret! Come on, let's go.'

She stepped through the doorway. 'Shit, Olivia. Look.'

Olivia didn't want to. She stood between the doorway and the window, not sure whether to grab Margaret or whether to bolt. Suddenly it crossed her mind that Rachel wasn't there.

Where the hell had she gone?

Turning back towards the window, she smashed into something hard, and everything went black.

25

'I don't remember anything after that, not until I woke up in the hospital.'

Olivia shrugged, was silent for a moment as she picked up her glass and took a sip of wine. She always tried to play it casual, as if talking about what had happened didn't bother her, but of course it did. She might not remember everything from that night, but reliving those last moments with Margaret, knowing what had then happened to her, was never easy.

'You okay?' Noah squeezed her free hand. She didn't even remember him taking hold of it because she had been so caught up in the past.

'Yeah, I just wish I could remember exactly what happened.' She saw kindness in his eyes, but also that he had questions, that cop brain of his working overtime.

'Who pulled you from the fire?'

'Rachel. I hit my head on something – a beam, the police thought – and knocked myself out.'

'She was in the cottage with you? You said you didn't know where she had gone.'

'She had been outside, hadn't plucked up the courage to follow us. She saw the flames. Managed to get me out, but the fire was too strong. She couldn't get to Margaret.'

He nodded slowly at that. 'And how did the fire start?'

'There was a paraffin lamp in the front room. The police said the place had been used by vagrants. They think they must have left it burning.'

'But there was no one else there at the time?'

'I don't... not that I remember.' She studied his face. 'Do you think this is connected?'

'Come on, Liv. Tell me it hasn't crossed your mind.'

Had it? Possibly she had considered it. What had happened that night had left deep scars, mental as well as physical. The possibility the past was coming back to haunt her was just too much to deal with. Besides, she had done nothing wrong, well, nothing other than surviving, so why would a killer now be targeting her? 'But why though? What would be the motive?'

'Gary Lamb was there.'

'And? What does that have to do with what happened to Margaret?'

'Talk me through again who was there on the trip with you.'

Olivia's shoulders tensed. 'I just went through everything.' She was aware her voice was getting high-pitched, made an effort to calm it. 'Don't make me do it again.'

'I just want you to remind me who was there on that trip, the ones who you and Margaret came up against. Gary Lamb, obviously, and Fern St Clair, Howard Peck and Janice Hardesty. Plus Rachel and Kelly?'

'Yeah, Rachel Williams and Kelly... I don't remember her last name, though they didn't go to our school.'

'And you didn't keep in touch with any of them?'

'Nope. Why would I?'

It was a fair question and he acknowledged it with a half-smile.

'What's the point of this, Noah?'

'Keeping you safe,' he answered simply.

Okay, he may be wide of the mark, but she couldn't argue with his motives.

'What did she do to you, Liv?'

When her eyes widened, even though she knew what and who he was referring to, he elaborated. 'You hate Fern so much. Tell me why.'

In her head the incident was as clear as day. While parts of the accident with Margaret were blurry, what had happened ten months later never faded.

Due to her injuries, she had missed the rest of the school year, had wondered at one point if she would ever be well enough to return. Therefore, she was grateful to be able to attend her final year of high school.

Scrub that. Grateful and nervous.

She hadn't seen any of her classmates since the accident, was understandably worried about her return.

It had gone as well as could be expected, some students shunning her, probably because they didn't know how to react, others with a welcoming smile, but too many questions. High school was suddenly overwhelming.

She didn't see Fern until the afternoon of her first day back. Although they had parted on bad terms, Olivia had been both surprised and hurt that Fern hadn't tried to make contact. Given the magnitude of everything that had happened, she had foolishly assumed she might put their fight to one side.

She was sat at her desk in the afternoon history lesson when Fern walked into the classroom. She made eye contact with Olivia for the briefest second.

'Hi.' Olivia gave her a small smile, conscious of the tension between them.

Fern didn't respond, her stony expression giving nothing away. Ignoring Olivia, she went to the back of the room and took her seat.

The snub stung, but perhaps was to be expected. Fern had never been one to kiss and make up if she fell out with someone. She was stubborn, self-righteous and if she felt she had been wronged, she wouldn't back down, certainly not without a grovelling apology.

There was no way Olivia planned on giving her one of those. And anyway, was it really that big a deal if her friendship with Fern was over? Fern was familiar, and yes, familiar was comforting, especially after everything that happened, but she wasn't a nice person. Maybe it was better for Olivia if she had a fresh start.

The first couple of weeks back passed without incident. Olivia ignored Fern and Fern ignored Olivia. Janice Hardesty was still on the scene, following after Fern like a lapdog. The first time she saw Olivia she had gushed about her accident, and then shut down abruptly after receiving a look from Fern. She hadn't spoken to Olivia since.

But there were other friendships to be made and life settled into a new sort of normal as Olivia studied for her exams.

It was into October when Fern started tormenting her. Initially it was playground stuff: flat bicycle tyres; walking into class to find 'Olivia Blake is a bitch' scrawled on the blackboard.

Olivia had no proof it was Fern, though the smirks and whispers gave her old friend away. Besides, who else would it possibly be? Olivia was reasonably popular and had received a fair amount of sympathy and support from her peers. She rationalised that maybe that was why Fern was now reacting so pathetically.

In her mind, Olivia had never been punished for her betrayal and it no doubt rankled Fern that she had found new friends.

The rumours put paid to a few of those friendships. Spiteful gossip did the rounds insinuating that Olivia had been saying nasty things behind people's backs.

Of course, when confronted with the gossip, Olivia denied it, but she could tell from the doubtful looks and wary smiles that the trust was broken.

Eventually she decided to have it out with Fern. This had turned out to be stupid and regrettable. Of course, Fern denied everything while wearing a smirk that confirmed to Olivia that her suspicions were right. Fern had then goaded her, playing the victim very well when Olivia lost her temper and slapped her.

The battle lines were drawn and the numbers on Olivia's side were dwindling. That would have been enough for most people, but not Fern St Clair, who still had her cruellest card to play.

Returning to the changing room one afternoon after hockey, Olivia waited until her classmates were finished showering before she dared strip out of her PE kit. This had been her practice since returning to school. She was too self-conscious of her burn injuries to shower with the other students.

She took her time soaping herself down, taking extra care around her scars, knowing that as it was the last lesson of the day, she had a while before the caretakers started locking up the building. Finishing up, she turned off the taps, pushed her dripping hair back off her face, stepping out of the communal shower and reaching for her towel.

It wasn't there.

At first she felt only frustration as she checked under the bench, in case it had slipped off, then padded her way back through to the locker room, leaving a dripping trail, as she went to the cupboard to see if there were any spare towels.

The door was locked.

Frustration turned to annoyance now. Where the hell was her towel? Was this one of Fern's stupid games, forcing her to get dressed without drying off first?

She stomped to her locker, not relishing the idea, but figuring it was only for the walk home. Apprehension and the first sliver of fear knotting her belly as she realised this door too was locked.

What?

The locker had been open, she was sure of it. Her bag and all of her clothes were in there.

She rattled the door, the frustration and anger that had morphed into fear, now sending skittering waves of panic through her. She was naked and had nothing to cover herself up with.

That would have been mortifying at the best of times, but her burn scars, the ones she desperately tried to hide from people, were exposed and on show.

What the hell was she going to do?

Fern had done this, of that there was little doubt, but she wouldn't be so cruel to keep it up. She was probably just trying to freak Olivia out.

Slowly she edged towards the main door of the changing room, tentatively eased the door open and sticking her head out into the corridor. There was no one around, the pupils having already left. There would be a few teachers and the caretakers on site, but she could hardly go looking for them while she was naked.

Assuming Fern was hiding close by, wanting to see her reaction, she called out, 'Very funny, Fern. I know you did this. Well, you've had your fun. Can you please give me my locker key and towel back?'

She was met with silence.

'Please, Fern. I'm officially freaking out here. I just want to get my stuff.'

Still nothing.

Maybe Fern wasn't there. Perhaps she had taken Olivia's towel and key, and left.

The idea filled her with dread.

'Hello! Can anyone hear me? I need some help.'

Still nothing.

She was going to have to wait in the changing room. When she heard the caretaker come to lock up, she would quickly run to the door to stop them walking in on her then ask them to find her a towel or some old clothes.

Reluctantly she closed the door and returned to the lockers, perching herself on the edge of the bench. The steam had cleared now from the shower and she shivered against the chill on her damp skin, her teeth chattering. As she hugged her body, rubbing her arms, her fingertips ran over her burnt flesh and she grimaced, knowing the accident had changed her for life.

Fern hated her, she got that, but this was going too far.

A loud bang on the door startled her and she leapt up, seeing the handle turn.

Oh God, NO!

She flew against the door before it could open, pressed herself against it.

'Don't come in. Please. I don't have any clothes on.'

Silence.

Her body was trembling now, partly from the cold, partly from the fear of being caught naked. Hesitantly she eased the door open, saw no one.

So who the hell had knocked on the door?

'Hello? Who's there?'

And then she spotted it, further up the corridor. Her towel. It was draped over the banister of the stairs that led up to the English department.

Olivia swallowed hard, glancing around. She was trapped in the changing room and needed the towel, but could she bring herself to go get it? She debated for a moment, called out again. 'Hello? Can anyone hear me? I really need some help.'

Perhaps she should just wait for the caretaker, as she had initially planned. Problem was, she could be there for another forty minutes or so. No one was around and she really needed to get the towel.

She judged the distance, figured it would take her just seconds to get to the staircase. Once the towel was around her, it wouldn't be so bad. Yes, the scars would still be visible on her arm, but at least the ones all down her side would be covered, as would her nakedness.

Ten seconds there, grab the towel, go find a teacher or the caretaker. She could use the phone in the secretary's office to call her mum. Get her to bring some clothes.

What if someone stepped into the corridor while she was going to get the towel? The humiliation would be unbearable.

So will the waiting around. You have to do this.

Drawing a couple of quick breaths, psyching herself up, she stepped into the corridor, nervously glanced around again then bolted for the towel.

A flash of movement up ahead, a figure crossing the corridor, grabbing the towel as they went, disappearing into a classroom.

Olivia froze, realised she had been tricked. As she turned to flee back towards the changing room, the door closed and she heard the unmistakable twist of a key in the lock. One hand covering her breasts, the other protecting between her legs she backed up against the wall as a figure wearing an old *Scream* mask slowly, deliberately walked towards her, phone raised and pointing at her.

She was being filmed.

The figure might be masked, but she recognised the walk and the bubble of muffled laughter, knew it was Fern.

'Stop it! Just give me my towel back, please!'

Humiliation burned and she tried to snatch the phone as Fern came closer, but the girl quickly stepped back and out of her reach.

Hearing more laughter behind her, knowing that Fern wasn't alone, she bolted along the corridor and into an empty classroom. She could hear footsteps following, quickly crossed the room to the store cupboard, stepping inside and locking the door behind her. Sinking to the floor, she curled into a ball and waited.

They quickly grew tired of tormenting her, leaving her alone in the store cupboard, and she waited there for what seemed like an hour, but was probably only minutes, until she heard the footsteps of the caretaker.

Her mum was called, bringing clothes to the school, pacing furiously as she waited for the head teacher to arrive so she could vent her fury.

Olivia couldn't prove it was Fern, but her mother was determined her former friend would pay, and the head teacher promised the matter would be dealt with. Embarrassed and miserable, Olivia didn't care. It was all too little, too late. She was never going to live this down.

She never watched the video footage, despite having it sent to her by a dozen different people, but she knew every student had seen her walk of shame. Returning to school two days later was one of the worst and most humiliating experiences of her life.

Olivia had managed to hold her head high, and ignored the stares from those who were curious, having seen the extent of her injuries, just as she ignored the spiteful taunts from some of Fern's gang, calling her Freddy Krueger.

Elena wanted her to change school, but it was her final year and there had already been too much disruption. Olivia knew she somehow needed to focus and get through her exams.

She dealt with the stares and the comments, ignoring most of them, and finding her own acidic putdowns to throw back at those who behaved the worst. Eventually the furore over the video died down and she was left in relative peace.

Fern was never punished for what had happened, as Olivia couldn't conclusively identify her, but she did back off on her campaign of harassment. Olivia heard that the head teacher had spoken with her and made a number of threats, one being expulsion, if it ever came to light she was responsible, and Fern had spent the rest of the school year giving Olivia a wide berth.

Olivia hadn't seen her since high school and the encounter tonight had shocked her.

So many years had passed, but she would never forget the humiliation of what Fern had done to her and certainly never forgive her. She wanted to forget the woman even existed.

But why were they both now being targeted? It made no sense.

The idea that she was being punished for something connected to Fern, made Olivia feel a little bit sick. She took another sip of her wine, set it down again, feeling defeated, her shoulders sagging. 'So there you go. You now know everything about me. Last chance to run away.' She said it jokingly, but recounting what had happened had sobered her up.

Noah had listened without interruption, his expression stony. Now it softened. 'Trust me, that isn't going to happen.'

'I don't get it. Why her and why me?'

'That's what we need to figure out.'

'You're still convinced it has something to do with that night, aren't you?'

'I think there are too many coincidences to discount it.'

'Okay.' If he was right, was there something she had done during the school trip that had upset someone? Other than Fern of course. She had been sitting with Fern that first night when she had taunted Margaret, had been right there when Malcolm had reacted. It was reasonable to assume he might have judged her on that first encounter, but he had seen her with Margaret, knew they had become friends. Why would he want revenge against someone who had stuck up for his sister?

Olivia scrubbed her hands over her face. She was tired and frustrated, fed up of all the recent fear and worry. 'I don't like any of this, Noah. I just want it to stop. I'm sick of being afraid, of knowing that someone is on some kind of twisted revenge mission against me. I just want to go back to my boring life where I'm not scared of being home alone or frightened someone might be watching me whenever I leave the house.'

'I know.' He slipped his arm around her, pulled her in close, and she leant into him, steadied by the rhythmic beat of his heart and his warm familiar scent. He stroked his fingers through her hair, pressed a kiss against her forehead. 'I'll stay with you until Molly is back. You don't have to be afraid. We're gonna figure this out, Liv, I promise. I'm not going to let anyone hurt you.'

She believed he meant it, knew he would try to keep her safe, but how could he fulfil that promise when they still didn't know what they were fighting against?

Everyone's past catches up with them eventually, including yours. Soon.

It was that last word that was freaking her out. What the hell did *Soon* mean?

She thought of Gary Lamb, tied to a chair and screaming as the flames ate his flesh, and she closed her eyes, hugged Noah a little tighter.

Soon.

26

It was the dream that woke Olivia. A dream featuring Toby of all people.

With everything going on, why the hell was she dreaming about her ex-boyfriend, especially when she hadn't seen him in over a year?

In the dream he had been pestering her to get back together. Of course she didn't want to because she was with Noah now. Except she couldn't find Noah. She looked frantically everywhere, with Toby in hot pursuit, gradually wearing her down until she agreed to give him another chance. Then she walked into her bedroom and found Toby in their bed with her. The slut with the red hair. She was riding him, just like she had done in the video Olivia had seen, long wild hair falling across her face, but then she shoved it back and looked directly at Olivia, smiling, and her face was Fern's. Beneath her on the bed, Toby had glanced up to see who Fern was smiling at and his face had morphed into Noah's.

That was when she had woken with a start, for a split second convinced it had been real, and that Noah really had cheated on her. Relief washed over her as she realised it had just been a dream.

She couldn't settle after that, lying in the dark for a while, listening to Noah's even breathing, needing to pee and desperate for a glass of water (*damn you, red wine*) but too lazy to move, Toby's betrayal all too clear in her mind.

She didn't regret breaking up with him, no longer felt that raw aching hurt, but the anger still burned at how he had cheated on her and the crass, humiliating way in which she had found out about it. How the video that had been uploaded on to his Facebook account had been seen by all their friends and family, many of them viewing it before Olivia had.

Toby had of course deleted it as soon as it came to his attention, but by then the damage was done. Besides, people had downloaded it, a few so-called friends helpfully forwarding it to Olivia, just in case she had missed it. She had watched it a dozen times or more. Toby on his back, the redhead riding him.

Of course he had tried to apologise, called it a mistake and a regret, but the damage was already done. She had kicked him out, called time on their relationship, clawed the money together to buy him out of the house.

She had no idea if he was still with the redhead, doubted it, as Toby had been livid about the video, but honestly, she didn't care what he was doing now or who he was with.

Why the hell then was she dreaming about him?

She checked her phone, saw it was just after 3.30, which meant she had only had a couple of hours sleep. Throwing back her side of the duvet, she eased herself out from under Noah's leg, which had somehow made its way over both of hers, and quietly crept across her bedroom, careful not to step on the discarded clothes that littered her path to the door.

She had been stressed and a little bit emotional about the notes, her encounter with Fern and talking about the past. Noah's solution had been to distract her with sex and, to give the man credit, he had certainly managed to do that.

Olivia unhooked her dressing gown from the back of the bedroom door, slipped it on, and glanced back at him. The light from the moon shone through a crack in the curtains and she could see he had his face mashed into one of her pillows and was looking very comfortable in her bed. She had to admit that she liked seeing him there. Letting herself out of the bedroom, she used the bathroom before tiptoeing downstairs, not turning any lights on until she reached the hall. Although Noah seemed dead to the world, she didn't want to wake him.

The heating having long gone off, the house was freezing, the tiled floor cold beneath her bare feet as she padded into the kitchen, and she wished she had put her slippers on.

She quickly got her drink of water, gulping down a glassful, then refilling it to take upstairs. As she made her way back along the hallway, a loud creak came from the lounge.

Olivia froze.

Was that a footstep?

Is someone in there?

She stayed where she was, not daring to move, barely daring to breath. *It's nothing,* she tried to convince herself. *It's an old house and old houses creak.* She was seriously getting paranoid.

But what if it wasn't nothing? What if someone was in there?

She could quickly run upstairs, though that would involve passing the doorway, and irrational as it was, she couldn't shake the thought of something, someone stepping out of the darkness of the living room and grabbing hold of her as she tried to flee up the stairs.

If she screamed for Noah she would likely wake him, but how quickly would he react? And how stupid would she feel if it turned out to be nothing?

She found out the answer to both questions just a few seconds later when she decided to brave it and go for the stairs, creeping a couple of steps forward, holding her breath and fearful of letting it out. As she was about level with the doorway to the lounge, there was another much louder creak and something banged, then footsteps.

She didn't hesitate this time. She screamed, dropping the glass and running for the stairs as it smashed. Her toe caught the bottom step and she tripped, landing face first on the stairs.

As she frantically tried to get to her feet, noises came from above.

'Liv?'

Noah charged downstairs, jeans half on, was with her before she had even pulled herself up from her spectacular faceplant.

'What's wrong?'

'The living room,' she whispered. 'I heard someone in there.'

He hauled her to her feet. 'Go wait upstairs.'

'Be careful of the broken glass.' Olivia whispered the warning as he approached the room and reached for the light. She didn't do as told, staying where she was, leaning against the wall to support her trembling legs, eyes on Noah's back.

As light flooded the room, he disappeared, and she held her breath, waiting.

No voices, no sinister sounds. Then he was heading back into the hallway with Luna in his arms, a neutral expression on his face, as he handed her over.

Seriously, it had been the fucking cat?

Olivia held Luna close for a moment, burying her face in the warm soft fur of her neck, putting her down when she wriggled. Embarrassment heated her cheeks. She had freaked out and woken him up over nothing. She really was starting to lose the plot.

'I'm sorry. I really thought...' She tailed off, glancing at the smashed glass of water. 'I need to clear this up. Go back to bed. I'm sorry I woke you.'

He touched her cheek, pressed a kiss to her forehead, but didn't say anything as he headed back upstairs. Jesus, she really needed to get her shit together. Noah had been more than patient with her, but he was going to start thinking he had a complete basket case for a girlfriend.

He was still awake when she returned to the bedroom and she felt a fresh wave of guilt for disturbing him as she crawled back under the duvet. 'I'm sorry,' she told him again, as he slipped his arm around her.

'It's been a difficult couple of weeks. Get some sleep, Liv.'

She closed her eyes, knew she had to try, though sleep seemed far away now. Instead images of Toby, the redhead, of Fern and Margaret, and of Gary Lamb burning in the kitchen of 8 Honington Lane, consumed her thoughts. She lay on her back for a few minutes then shuffled so she was on her side, her back to Noah.

After a moment he nuzzled in close, his warm breath on her ear. 'You're still awake.'

It wasn't a question.

'I have too much going on in my head. I can't switch off.'

He didn't comment on that, was quiet for a few moments, then she felt his hand on her thigh, fingertips lazily tracing circles on her skin, sending little sparks down through her belly. 'We should do something about that then,' he whispered, gently nipping her earlobe between his teeth.

'It's the middle of the night. I have to go to work in a few hours.' It was only a token protest, her body already responding to his, as she arched back against him giving his hand easier access to her front.

'Mmm, but you can't sleep, remember?'

His fingers dipped lower, though not close enough to where she wanted them, slowly tormenting, and she shivered in pleasure as his mouth trailed hot kisses down her neck. Craving more, she tried to roll towards him, but his arm held her in position against his chest as he teased, torturously slow and relentless, and her need intensified until she was squirming against him, could think of little else but him and what he was doing to her.

The shrill ring of the landline telephone cut through the silence and Olivia froze.

Noah's hand stilled. 'Seriously? It's the middle of the night.' He loosened his hold around her, easing back, and gave her a gentle prod with his knee when she didn't move. 'Should you not answer that? It could be your mum or Jamie.'

'But what if it's...'

She didn't have to finish the sentence. He knew who she meant. 'Well it doesn't sound as if they're giving up.' Rolling Olivia forward, he leant over and grabbed the receiver held it between them. For a moment there was silence.

Eventually Olivia spoke, her voice shaky. 'Hello?'

More silence, then that menacing whisper. There had only been the one phone call and several days ago, but she hadn't forgotten the voice nor the chill that ran through her when her tormentor spoke. This time, though, it was just one word.

'Soon.'

'Who is this?' Noah demanded.

More silence and then the line went dead.

Olivia shivered, struggling to keep the fear out of her voice. 'I don't like this, Noah. It's really starting to give me the creeps.'

He didn't comment, instead clambering over her and out of bed, yanking the phone cable from the wall. A scowl on his face, he skulked round to his side of the bed and climbed under the duvet, wrapping himself around her.

The mood killed, he pressed a kiss against her hair, gently rubbed his hand up and down her arm. 'I'm gonna find out who's doing this, Liv. I promise.'

27

'She has motive. I know you don't want to hear that.'

Daniella had been right, Noah didn't.

Her comment stayed with him throughout the afternoon, which would probably explain his bad mood.

They had been on their way to meet a potential client, Olivia dropped safely at work, coffee and a long shower having taken the edge off his tiredness, when Daniella had made the comment. He was already a little irritable and snappy, annoyed that he couldn't get to the bottom of who was harassing Olivia, and the unwelcome suggestion only served to darken his mood further.

'She's hardly stalking herself.'

'You're blinkered, Noah, and you're too emotionally involved. Take a step back and look at it logically.'

When he simply ignored her, she took it as encouragement to continue. 'She was badly burned then tormented by her classmates. They humiliated her. What a way to get back at them and throw suspicion off herself at the same time.' Daniella was warming up now. 'You said this Fern woman thought Olivia had sent the notes. I tell you, she has motive. You might not want to admit it, but she does. She had the key, could have easily lured Gary Lamb to the house.'

'He was double her size for Christ's sake. Somehow, I don't see her overpowering him and chaining him to a chair.'

'Maybe he was drugged.'

'Which would have made him a dead weight. You've met her. Can you honestly see her hauling a seventeen stone man around the house?'

'Maybe he thought it was a game.' When Noah raised his eyebrows questioningly at that, she smiled. 'She's a pretty girl. If he thought his luck was in... Trust me, there are ways. Then the notes and the photo, they would have been easy to sort.'

She was annoying him now, what with her stupid sex game theory, intimating that Olivia might have lured Gary Lamb to the house intentionally, suggesting that she was that emotionally damaged she would actually commit murder.

Part of him wished he hadn't told Daniella about Olivia's burn scars and everything that had happened to her. In a way it felt like he was betraying her trust. It helped to have someone to bounce theories off, though he hadn't expected that Daniella's would bounce in this direction.

'What about the phone call? She hardly called herself last night.'

'True. But you're not stupid. You know there are ways she could have orchestrated that. And what a brilliant way to convince her boyfriend she is the victim.'

Noah pulled up at traffic lights, turned to face her. 'You're actually serious. You honestly believe she killed a man and is stalking herself?'

A half-smile played on Daniella's lips, her eyes dancing, amused. Most people gave Noah a wide berth when he was in a bad mood. Not Daniella. She found it entertaining and got off on pushing his buttons. 'No, probably not. I'm just pointing out that you need to take those blinkers off and look at it from every angle.'

Noah scowled at that. Hated knowing that she was right.

They parted company after the meeting, having secured the job. Daniella went off to do some preliminary work, while Noah planned to follow up on the information he had learnt from Olivia over the past twenty-four hours.

Daniella hadn't been overly impressed that he was shirking off, but it was almost Christmas and their workload was light.

He hadn't told Olivia about the footage caught by the camera of a figure in her back garden on Monday night; had no intention of telling her, aware it would further freak her out.

While she had been busy feeding the cat, he had discreetly checked the utility room that led to the corner of the house. There was a window, one that slid up with just enough room for someone to crawl through. Was this how her tormentor had entered the house?

He added it to his notes, flipped back a page to the names he had written down. Fern, Gary, Howard and Janice were all there, as well as Rachel Williams and Kelly Dearborn. He added Margaret Grimes to the list and circled it. They had all been on the school trip together and too many of them had suffered because of fires.

It was all connected and had him wondering how many others on the list had received notes.

He needed to track them all down, speak with them individually. Fern St Clair would be first. She was the easiest because she had given him her number and she was also the one he had done most research on.

She didn't answer his call so he left a voicemail, guessed she was screening when she phoned back almost immediately. 'I was hoping you would call.'

She sounded a little too pleased to hear from him and Noah reminded himself this was business. Olivia wouldn't like that he had contacted her, but if it meant keeping her safe then it was necessary. Besides, he had no intention of telling her, certainly not for the time being.

'We need to talk. Can we meet?'

'I haven't taken my lunch break yet if you can do now.' Her tone was hopeful.

Best to get it over and done with. 'Sure, where do you want me to meet you?'

Fern was based in an office block on the outskirts of the city, far enough away from Olivia's workplace that he didn't have to worry about being caught.

He waited outside for her, hunkered down in his jacket, glad he had his scarf, gloves and hat on. The wind chill factor was freezing. Luckily, she didn't keep him waiting long, appearing at the top of the entrance steps in a blood-red coat, her smile widening to a grin when she spotted that he was alone. Noah guessed she hadn't been sure if she was meeting just him or if Olivia would be with him, wondered if the lipstick she wore that matched the coat had been an effort on his behalf. He faked a smile for her that he hoped disguised his contempt and reminded himself that this was purely to get information, so to play nice.

'There's a little café on the corner,' she pointed out.

'Sure, okay.'

If it had been a milder day he would have preferred to walk, but it really was cold. He would buy her a coffee and hopefully get her to talk.

* * *

'So, Olivia sent you to talk to me on her behalf, did she?' Fern said the words with a half smirk as Noah set down the coffees and removed his jacket, before pulling up a seat opposite her. As he did, she caught the pleasant scent of light spicy aftershave, her lips curving in approval. 'Talk about holding on to a grudge. It's been years and she still won't speak to me.'

Noah angled her a cool look. 'I can't imagine why.'

Was that a trace of sarcasm?

Olivia had done well for herself Fern had to admit as he pulled off his hat, ran his fingers through messed-up tawny brown hair. He really was quite attractive, all that scruffy stubble and angular features, with a generous mouth and those fascinating wide-set sharp green eyes. *He is wasted on someone as dull and damaged as Olivia.*

'What's the deal with you two anyway?' She blatantly stared at his empty ring finger. 'You're not married. Are you engaged, living together, or is it more casual than that?'

'We're not here to talk about my relationship with Olivia.'

'No, I guess we're not. Livvy said she had been receiving notes too. Is that true?'

'It's true. You seem surprised by that. How come?'

Fern opened her mouth then shut it again, took a sip of her milky coffee as she considered how to answer, realising that she hadn't really thought this bit through and understanding that however she did reply, it wasn't going to paint her in a particularly good light, especially as she didn't know what Olivia had told him about the past.

'It's a simple question, Fern.' He stirred his coffee, set down the spoon and sat back, studying her. 'Why would you think Olivia is the one targeting you?'

'How much has she told you?' she countered.

'About?'

Ooh, he is good. He's not going to give anything away. Yes, he is definitely wasted on Olivia. 'We were friends, she betrayed me, and then we weren't friends,' she answered eventually. 'We played a few silly pranks on her and she didn't react well. It was high school.' She shrugged. 'What do you want me to say? It happens.'

His expression darkened at that, but if he knew about the video he didn't say. 'It's a little extreme though, don't you think, assuming she would be targeting you over a *silly* prank all these years later.'

She didn't appreciate the way he emphasised the word *silly*, and glowered at him. 'Maybe, but I was exploring all possibilities. As you've pointed out, it wasn't Olivia, so it's all irrelevant anyway.'

'You said last night that you and your friends had received notes. Who else are you talking about?'

She had said that, and although it had been in the heat of the moment, she guessed there was no harm in him knowing. 'Janice and Howard, they're both friends of mine.'

'What did they say?'

Fern glanced around, worried someone might overhear them. 'Same as Livvy. Something about how we'd done a bad thing a long time ago,' she told him, her voice dropping to a whisper. 'And how the past is about to catch up.'

There was no way she was telling him about the other note. The one that had called her a killer.

'And what about Gary? Did he receive any notes?'

'I wouldn't know. I hadn't seen Gary in a long while.' Fern hesitated. 'Howard was still matey with him. He's trying to make contact with Gary's girlfriend.'

'Rita Works.'

He already knew. Seemed Olivia's boyfriend had been doing his own investigating.

'Have you spoken to her?'

'Not yet. You were on the school trip with Liv, the one where she was injured.'

'I was.'

'Can you tell me about that?'

Jesus, that's a loaded question. She toyed with her coffee cup, again considered how best to answer, unsure how much he knew. 'Livvy and her friends went into the woods. I don't know the exact details, but there was an accident, a fire, and one of the girls died.' She narrowed her eyes. 'You know all this though, so why ask?'

'Who was there? You, Liv, Gary Lamb, Janice, Howard, Rachel Williams, and Kelly Dearborn. Have I missed anyone else from your little gang? Her eyes widened slightly as he ticked the names off using his fingers. He knew about all of them.

'It was hardly a gang. We were fourteen, just kids.'

'Margaret Grimes was the girl who died.'

'And?'

'And she burned to death; Gary burned to death.'

'Your point being?'

'Something happened that night, something that is connected to what is happening now, and I want to know what it is.'

Fern didn't appreciate the abrupt barrage of questions. It reminded her of... Her eyes narrowed suspiciously. 'Are you a cop?'

'Ex.'

Her blood heated and she tried not to look flustered by that, knew she would play her cards close. 'Figures.'

His lips twisted. 'Look, I'm here as Olivia's boyfriend. Nothing else. I want to know what happened so I can figure out who is harassing her. You are going to help me with that.'

'Really?' That was rather presumptuous. Truth was, Fern wanted exactly the same thing. She had no intention of spilling any of her dirty secrets to Noah though.

'If you're getting notes too then it's in your interest to tell me what you know.'

He had a point, but she would wait to see what else he asked.

'Tell me about Margaret Grimes.'

Fern thought back to the wimp of a girl she had met at Black Dog Farm all those years ago with her questionable dress sense and zero personality. It still galled her that Olivia had picked this complete loser over their years of friendship, had turned on Fern just because she had made a few harmless jokes at Margaret's expense.

She was sorry that the girl had died, Fern wasn't that heartless, but it had been an accident. No point in pretending she had liked Margaret just because she was dead.

'She was a nobody,' she said simply, hoping he wouldn't judge her for telling the truth. But her temper was stirred by his barely disguised look of contempt. She crossed her arms defensively. 'Think what you want of me, at least I am being honest. Margaret Grimes was pathetic and cowardly and Livvy turned her back on me to hang out with her. Do I feel bad about what happened to her? Of course I do. I don't wish anyone dead. But did I like her? No.'

'So what did happen that night when she died?'

'I already told you, Livvy, Margaret and Rachel snuck off. I don't know any more than that.'

'Really?'

'Really!' He was starting to annoy her now with his judgemental attitude and all these questions. 'I'm really not quite sure what the point of all this is, so if you'll excuse me, I'm going to head back to work.' She reached for her coat, started to get up.

'Sit down!' Although his voice wasn't loud, his steely tone caught her off guard, had her pausing, open-mouthed. 'We're not done yet.'

'You can't boss me around. Who the hell do you think you are?'

'I know more about you than you realise.' His tone was even as she slipped on her coat. 'You've been sleeping with your boss, Peter Collins.'

That had her freezing, eyes widening.

'You're hoping that he'll leave his wife, but he won't. How safe do you think your job will be if she finds out?'

How did he know that? She studied his face for any sign of a lie. 'You're bluffing. You wouldn't tell.'

'Want to take that bet?'

'What do you want?'

'Information, the truth, so sit.'

She wavered, knew she didn't have a choice, reluctantly dropping back down into her chair, her heart hammering.

'What really happened the night of Liv's accident, Fern? I know you're hiding something.'

She studied him for a moment. *He doesn't know. No one could.*

Except the person sending the notes.

Fern pushed that little detail to the back of her mind. Noah didn't know. He might have suspicions, but they amounted to nothing, and he certainly had no proof. No, he was calling her bluff. If he really knew, they wouldn't be sitting here having this conversation.

'I told you the truth. I don't know.'

'I don't believe you.'

'Well that's your problem. What do you want me to do? Make something up?' When he scowled at that she added, 'Look, you've got me. You know about Peter. Go to his wife if you don't believe me. There's nothing I can do to stop you. I've told you the truth and there's nothing more I can add.'

'You're really something.' He sat back and regarded her, his expression both faintly amused and scornful. 'Does it not bother you that your friends are dying? That they are being murdered?'

'Only Gary was murdered. Kelly and Rachel's deaths were accidents.'

She blurted the words out quickly without thinking, expecting him to be shocked by her revelation that Kelly and Rachel were both dead, surprised when he didn't react, just studied her with those cool green eyes. 'You already knew that.'

It wasn't a question and he didn't respond to it.

Fern sized him up cautiously, suddenly wary. She suspected there was more to Olivia's boyfriend than he was letting on.

28

Howard's romantic getaway with Daisy wasn't quite going to plan.

Firstly, Daisy's boss had called her into work on Thursday. She worked as a personal assistant for some hotshot solicitor who thought she should be at his beck and call, and although Howard had protested, grumbling about it ruining their time away together, Daisy had stuck up for the man, justifying his request. All it had done was cause their first fight.

Eventually they had agreed that Howard would go on ahead to the cabin and she would join him later that evening.

Then just as he was loading up his car, Fern had messaged, demanding to know what was happening with tracking down Rita Works.

Truth was, nothing. Howard had messaged her and the woman hadn't replied. Hadn't even read his message from what he could see.

He hadn't attempted to track her down, wasn't really that interested, so decided the best course of action would be to ignore Fern.

Big mistake. By the time he had driven to the forest park on the Norfolk/Suffolk border, he had two further messages and three missed calls from her. He checked in, drove his car down to the cabin and parked outside, pleased he had chosen a lot on the outskirts of the park. Although the place was fairly empty – unsurprising given that it was so close to Christmas – the forest location gave that extra layer of privacy. Howard planned to have lots of sex in the hot tub and didn't want anyone disturbing them.

He hauled his stuff into the cabin, felt his phone vibrate in his pocket and plucked it out, frowning at the new message from Fern.

STOP FUCKING IGNORING ME!

Annoyed, he fired a brief message back.

I'm not ignoring you. Rita hasn't replied. There's nothing to tell.

He saw the three dots, indicating that she was typing, his heart sinking. This was not how he had planned for this day to go. He'd had visions of arriving at the cabin with Daisy, stripping her out of her clothes then drinking prosecco in the hot tub. A sparring session with Fern hadn't featured.

The dots disappeared and he let go of the breath he hadn't realised he had been holding.

Then the phone rang instead.

Damn it, Fern.

Knowing she wouldn't stop pestering him, he reluctantly answered the call.

'Where the hell have you been? I've been trying to get hold of you.'

'I know.'

'So why have you been ignoring me?'

'I haven't, Fern, honestly. I've been driving.'

'You need to get hold of this Rita Works woman. That was part of the deal. Maybe you should speak to Gary's mum. She might know who she is.'

'I can't right now.'

'Why not?'

'I'm away.'

'You're what?' She sounded livid, and while that annoyed Howard – because it was none of her damn business how he used his time – his bowels were also knotting. Fern had always scared him a little and confrontational situations like this made him want to go to the toilet.

'Why the fuck have you gone away when we have this problem to deal with?'

'It's a work thing,' he lied, not yet ready to tell her about Daisy. In a way it was lucky Daisy wasn't there yet.

'Really?'

'Honest, Fern. Really.' Fuck, she'd better not call his office to check. As he'd had no holiday left, he had called in sick. He needed to talk his way out of this fast before she got him into trouble. 'Look, I know this is important and I will be back in a couple of days. Why don't you get Janice on the case? She likes tracking people down.'

That was good. Get Janice to find this Rita woman. She had jumped at the chance to track down Rachel Williams. Which reminded him, he should ask how she was getting on. If he started showing an interest in Fern's little investigation, she might cut him some slack.

'How did Janice get on, by the way. Did she manage to find Rach?'

There was a pause. 'Yes. And she's dead.'

'She's what?' Howard thought he had misheard her for a moment.

'She's dead, Howard. And guess how she died.'

He wasn't sure he wanted to know. 'Go on.'

'She burned to death in her car.'

No, he really didn't want to know. For the first time since all this had started, a ripple of unease stirred in his gut. 'You're kidding, right?'

'No, I'm not kidding. So that's Kelly, Gary and Rachel who have all died in fires.'

'What are the chances of that?' He muttered the comment more to himself, but Fern must have heard because she huffed down the phone.

'Are you actually going to take any of this seriously, you idiot? There were six of us there that night and three of us are dead. Someone is doing this intentionally. Those notes we've received are no joke.'

She was right. Kelly and Gary he could put down to coincidence, but three of them? That was too much of a stretch. Was someone seriously punishing them for a stupid prank? He didn't understand how. No one else had been there that night. Well, apart from...

'Did you talk to Olivia Blake?'

'I did. And guess what? She's been receiving notes too.'

'Really? Why would she get notes? She didn't do anything.'

'Beats me.' Fern was silent for a moment. 'She has a boyfriend and he seems a little too interested in what is going on. I'm not sure I trust him.'

'What, why?' This conversation had Howard's full attention now. He flopped down on to the sofa, kicked his shoes off and put his feet up on the cushion.

'He wanted to meet with me and he started asking loads of questions. I can't be certain, but I think he might know what we did.'

'How is that possible? No one knows. Just us.'

'You haven't blabbed to anyone?'

'No, of course not.'

'Howard? Are you sure?'

'I'm sure. I've never told anyone what happened, swear on my life.' It was the truth. It was hardly the kind of thing he wanted people to find out about. They could be so judgemental. 'What about Janice? Could she have told? She always did have a blabbermouth.'

'Janice would never do that.'

Oh nice. So Fern trusts Janice, but she doubts me. 'Well, I never told either. So what does this bloke, Olivia's boyfriend, know? What has he said?'

'It was just some of the questions he was asking. He says he knows something happened that night, but I don't know if he is bluffing. He's an ex-police officer. I don't like that.'

'Oh.' Howard wasn't sure he liked that either. Although he had been all about going to the police initially, he had thought better about it over the past couple of days.

'He may try to talk to you too. His name is Noah Keen. If he does approach you, I need you to promise you won't say a word.'

'I won't say anything.'

'You promise, Howard?'

'I promise.'

The conversation had him unsettled for the rest of the afternoon, the revelation that Rachel was also dead knocking it home that maybe this was more serious than he had been taking it. Fern had told him that Rachel had been briefly married and her surname had been Colton. He spent a little time googling her, reading about what had happened, trying to convince himself that maybe it really had been a tragic accident. But deep down he knew that wasn't true.

In isolation it was an accident; but put together with Kelly's death and Gary's murder, plus the notes they had all received, it suggested they were all in danger.

Howard didn't like that one little bit.

He toyed with driving back to Norwich, calling off the getaway with Daisy, but he loathed losing the money he had shelled out for the cabin, even if he had got a cheap deal on it because of the time of year. Deciding to make the most of it, he unpacked. It was only just gone 4.30 p.m., and knowing that Daisy wouldn't be with him for at least another couple of hours, he opened one of the bottles of prosecco he had brought with him, and took it out to the hot tub.

It was already dark, the surrounding woodland looking more spooky than romantic, and he put on the outside lights, before quickly shedding his towel robe, nipples hardening in the cool air before he sunk into the hot bubbles of the tub. He pulled up a favourite playlist on his mobile, slipped in earphones and, taking a healthy swig of prosecco, ordered himself to relax.

It was all going to be okay.

He must have drifted off, because he awoke with a start, bubbles from the hot tub up his nose, as he spluttered the mouthful of foamy water he had swallowed.

What an idiot! He could have drowned.

He felt for the plastic seat, eyes blinking furiously as he struggled to pull himself up.

Firm hands were suddenly on his shoulders, shoving hard, and he fell forward again.

What the fuck?

Before he could even register what was happening, that someone was with him, there was a pressure on his head, pushing down as he tried to break to the surface.

Howard's arms and legs flailed as he started to choke, his lungs desperate for air, panic taking over as his brain registered that someone was doing this to him on purpose.

Someone was trying to kill him.

As he took in more gulps of water, fought frantically against his attacker, desperate to free himself, his body started to convulse. And then there was just blackness.

* * *

Howard's first realisation was that he wasn't dead. Somehow he had survived being drowned. The second realisation was that he was really bloody cold. Scrub that. He was freezing. Every part of him was like ice and he was shivering uncontrollably, teeth chattering. Or at least they would be if there wasn't something preventing them from touching.

His head was pounding and for a moment he thought he was going to be sick. He needed to lie down, wanted to curl up and try to get warm. His limbs weren't working though: something was forcing him into this standing position. As awareness gradually came back, he understood why. He was tied to a tree. Wrists yanked back, metal digging into them, legs spread wide, cuffs cutting into his ankles, and rough bark cutting into his back. Something was pressing against his head, pushing it back against the tree, forcing him to look straight ahead, but casting his eyes downwards he could see enough to understand he was naked.

Panic taking over, he screamed, the sound coming out as little more than a mumble, and he realised the reason why his teeth weren't chattering was because there was something roughly pressed between them. Some kind of rough cloth that tasted chemically, like petrol, had been forced into his mouth.

He struggled like a madman to free himself, felt the pain of metal cutting into flesh, blood dripping down into his eyes from whatever was holding his head in place.

And then, holy fuck, if he wasn't frightened enough, something moved in the shadows up ahead. Was that a figure heading towards him through the trees?

He almost passed out from the fear as it came closer, the plain white mask illuminated in the darkness, a can of something in one gloved hand.

'Please, please don't do this.' The words that were clearer in his head, were caught up in the gag, seeming less coherent, but the figure tipped its head to one side as it regarded him, seeming for a moment to consider, before shaking its head.

And then the lid was off the can, the unmistakable smell of petrol trickling on the ground around him, over his feet and his legs, over his cock and up his belly, the last of the can splashing on to his hair and his face.

He attempted to scream again, salty tears mingling with the petrol, rolling down his cheeks and dampening the gag.

This could not be happening. He could not die like this.

The figure reached into a pocket, pulled a box of matches out, flicked one alight, and he lost control of his bladder as he saw the flame, the screaming in his head intensifying.

But then the flame went out and the figure laughed.

He recognised the sound. Blinked in horror as the figure removed its mask and smiled at him.

It couldn't be. It wasn't possible.

'Surprise, Howard. Now, are you comfortable? We have a lot to discuss before we get to the main event.'

29

It had been Elena who had called, suggesting that they meet up for dinner on Thursday night. They needed some family time, she had said, and she would arrange extra staff to cover the restaurant. She booked a table at one of the neighbouring pubs, arranging to meet Olivia and Noah there at seven. It wasn't until they were sitting down at the table and Jamie made a passing comment, that Olivia realised this had all been Noah's idea.

Initially she wasn't sure how to feel about that, a little bit miffed that he had taken it upon himself to decide what was best for her, but also touched that he had tried to cheer her up.

As they ate, the wine flowing liberally and Elena entertaining them with anecdotes about the restaurant (most were stories that Olivia and Jamie had heard before, but still found amusing) she realised Noah had been right. She had needed this. For the first time in days her mood was lifting and she was less on edge, her laughter genuine. As the plates were being cleared, she caught his hand under the table and gave it a squeeze, mouthing a 'thank you' when his eyes met hers.

As they perused the dessert menu, Elena excused herself to the ladies, leaving instructions to order her the tiramisu. She ruffled Noah's hair affectionately on her way, leaning down to whisper (not too discreetly) in his ear, 'You did good.'

Jamie stretched his arms behind his head, sat back in his chair and gave a wide grin as she disappeared. 'You scored yourself double brownie points tonight, mate.'

'Added bonus.' Noah winked. 'Though I wasn't actually doing it for your mum.'

Jamie immediately sobered, looking at his sister. 'How are you holding up, Livvy?'

The reminder of what she was escaping from had the smile dropping from Olivia's face. She forced it back. 'I'm okay. Tonight's been nice.' She refrained from saying more as the waitress arrived to take their dessert order.

'I meant to say, Fern stopped by the restaurant looking for you earlier in the week,' Jamie said as the waitress left. 'She was looking super skanky. We didn't tell her where you were. Figured you wouldn't want to see her. She left her number with Mum to pass on, but I think Mum binned it.'

Olivia smiled tightly. 'Unfortunately, she found me.'

'Oops. Sorry about that.'

'It's okay. I made it clear I didn't want anything to do with her.'

'How are you doing apart from that?'

That was a loaded question. Olivia exchanged a brief glance with Noah, recalling her mini meltdown on Tuesday night. Should she admit to her brother that right now she was scared of being in her own home alone? She was assuming Noah hadn't told Jamie or Elena about that, knew her mum would be freaking out big time if she knew about the notes and the phone calls.

'I'm okay. It's been a tough few days.'

Her phone pinged in her bag and she plucked it out, avoiding further scrutiny. It was a Facebook notification. A friend request from Howard Peck.

Why the hell was Howard trying to friend her? She hadn't seen him since she was sixteen. She stared at the screen, unsure whether to delete it or accept it. While she had no interest in being friends with Howard Peck. He had been mates with Gary, so could possibly be connected to everything that was going on. Fern had mentioned that some of her friends had also received notes. Did that include Howard? He had been on the school trip.

'You okay, Liv?'

'Yeah, um...' She glanced at Noah. 'I have a friend request on Facebook from Howard Peck.'

'Fern's friend?'

'And Gary Lamb's,' Jamie pointed out. 'Didn't those two used to hang out together all the time? Maybe he's trying to contact you about what happened with Gary.'

'Maybe.'

'Are you going to accept it?'

Honestly, Olivia wasn't sure. She was saved from answering the question when her mother returned to the table, immediately wanting to know if the waitress had taken dessert orders and had Jamie remembered to order her a tiramisu.

As was her way, Elena took over the conversation again, steering it in a completely different direction and, relieved, Olivia, glanced at her phone again, made the decision that she didn't want Howard Peck in her life, even if it was just on Facebook, and she hit decline, slipping the phone back in her bag.

The desserts arrived, followed by coffee then Elena asked for the bill, paying for all four of them, despite their protests. 'It's my Christmas treat,' she had insisted. As Olivia and Noah had yet to call a taxi, she suggested they head back over to the Riverside Inn for drinks.

'Did you accept Howard's friend request?' They were walking hand in hand a little behind Jamie and Elena, Noah's voice not much more than a whisper as he asked the question.

'No, I declined it. Why?'

'He was on the school trip with you and a friend of Fern's. I think it's worth finding out if he knows anything. You're not the only one being targeted.'

'I don't really want to have anything to do with him.'

'Okay, so let me talk to him then.'

Like you wanted to talk to Fern, Olivia thought, though didn't say it out loud. It had been a nice night and she didn't want to ruin it.

She hadn't been happy about Noah taking Fern's number. He was still hellbent on the idea that the notes and Gary's death were all connected to that night in the woods, and, although she knew he was just trying to help, she didn't like the idea of him being in contact with her tormentors from the past.

'I'd rather you didn't,' she told him a little stiffly.

'You can't keep ignoring what's happening, Liv.'

'I'm not ignoring it, but I do think you're clutching at straws.'

'At least think about it, okay?'

'Can you just drop it, please?' Olivia pulled her hand free. 'You're ruining a nice night.'

'You two okay back there?' Her mum had stopped walking, must have heard Olivia's heated tone, as she was looking at them curiously, waiting for them to catch up.

'I will. For now,' Noah agreed in a hissed whisper. He caught hold of her hand again, held on tight when she tried to pull away again, smiling broadly at Elena. 'We're fine. Aren't we, Liv?'

Olivia might not want anything to do with Howard Peck, but he was persistent. The restaurant was almost empty by the time they returned, the last table settling their bill. Elena spoke with the two staff members working, then left them to lock up, herding her brood upstairs and into the family living room. While she poured brandies, Olivia nipped to the loo. As she was drying her hands, her phone beeped in her bag again.

She had six new notifications, all from Howard.

He had resent the friend request, plus five message requests.

She sat down on the toilet seat, her mouth dry as she opened up Messenger and read through them.

Long time, no speak, stranger. Don't you want to be friends? 🙁

I have something really important to show you.

Hey, earth to Olivia. Don't you want to see? I promise it's really good.

The fourth message was a video that she was hesitant to click on, in case it contained a virus, her eyes skipping instead to the fifth message.

You did this. This is YOUR fault. Boo hoo. 🙁

Her heart was racing, the dinner she had not long eaten heavy in her stomach. She didn't want to watch the video, but knew she had no choice. Her fingers were shaking as she pressed play.

At first it was just darkness, then the sound of music playing. Olivia recognised the Christmas song, was immediately transported back to the house on Honington Lane. Her mouth was dry, fear gripping her throat.

The screen lit up and she could see trees. A wood or something. And what was that? Something standing in front of one of the trees. A man... was that Howard Peck with his back pressed against the trunk of a thick tree, and stark naked? Something was wrapped around his head... it looked like barbed wire, cutting into his skin, blood running down his wide forehead from where he had been struggling against it, and the way his arms and legs were pulled back suggested that they too were bound behind the tree.

He was sobbing and screaming into the cloth that covered his mouth, the words that she assumed were pleas to his captor, nothing more than a muffled moan.

Olivia wanted to stop the video, had an awful feeling that things were about to get a whole lot worse. She tried to call for Noah, but found she couldn't speak, as she sat there on the toilet seat, compelled to keep watching.

Whoever was filming was now walking round the tree, the camera footage shaky.

As they came full circle, Howard was frantically struggling, his eyes now open and wide with terror as his tormentor stepped back and a gloved hand held a lit match tauntingly in front of the camera.

As it dropped to the ground, igniting the trail of petrol at lightning speed, Olivia found herself screaming along with Howard.

The last thing she saw was the tree and the man tied to it as it went up in flames.

30

There were four in the bed and the little one said, roll over, roll over.
So they all rolled over and one fell out.
There were three in the bed...

I am enjoying this, you know. I didn't think I would. It is a job that needs to be done, making the guilty pay for their sins. It's been a necessity, but I didn't realise it would be so much fun.

Remember when we were kids? You were always the good one, I was forever in trouble. Dad said I was a bad seed. He just didn't understand me. He kept trying to fix me. The path I am on was never a choice, it was a compulsion. Twenty strikes of a belt was never going to take away that need to pull the wings off butterflies or the urge to light the match.

For years after you died I tried so hard to be the normal child, to replace the one they had lost. When I understood I was being offered an opportunity to put things right it scared me a little. I had buried my true self so deep. But the guilty had been judged and they have to atone. It was how we were taught; an eye for an eye and a tooth for a tooth.

I was put on this path for a reason and, as I walk among them, the wolf in sheep's clothing, the thirst for the next kill is growing. I play my part well and they have no idea, but the craving is growing. I need to experience it again, the moment of revelation, the moment of understanding, the moment of true fear. I feel their terror, I feed on it, and I need it. Dear God, I need it.

There are three left to pay, three wicked girls who need to repent.

And their time is soon.

31

It had been gone two in the morning when the police and the paramedics had left and Noah and Olivia were in a taxi on their way back to his place on the west side of the city.

Elena had tried to persuade them to stay the night, but Olivia had been reluctant, shaken and upset, wanting space and quiet, needing time to process everything. Noah got that.

Her mother and brother now knew about the notes and the phone calls, had both viewed the video after Olivia had been found passed out on the bathroom floor. She had bashed her head on the sink, and they were understandably rattled.

Noah soon learnt that Elena became hyper when stressed. She asked too many questions, her tone high-pitched, as she scurried around, forcing sweet tea on Olivia who had been in shock as she struggled to talk to the police officers.

Noah got her out of there as soon as he was able, taking her back to his place, then holding her and soothing her until she fell asleep.

He had stayed awake for some time after, his mind working overtime trying to slot the pieces of the puzzle into place, before he finally drifted off. When he eventually awoke, he was surprised to see it was almost nine in the morning.

Olivia was still fast asleep and he got up, careful not to disturb her. He put on a T-shirt and a pair of sweatpants, and took his phone downstairs. He spoke to her boss first to say she wouldn't be in, then he called Daniella.

'What's up?' she asked, foregoing any kind of greeting.

He briefly explained what had happened, as he filled the kettle, his tired mind in desperate need of coffee. As much as she had annoyed him yesterday with her observations about Olivia being a potential suspect, he knew he needed her. He was too close to the situation and his feelings for Olivia were now clouding his rationality and judgement. Daniella would offer a fresh pair of eyes and focus.

'So what do you want to do?' she asked when he had finished explaining about the video.

'I want to go out to Black Dog Farm. Something doesn't sit right with this.'

'Okay, well we can do that this morning if you want.'

Noah thought of Olivia upstairs asleep in his bed. He didn't want to leave her alone, but he had to. She would be safer in his house though. Safer than she would be at home. 'Pick you up in an hour?'

'Sounds like a plan.'

Ending the call, he finished his coffee, got out a clean mug and poured another cup, then took it upstairs, setting it down on the bedside table beside Olivia. She stirred as the mattress dipped when he sat down beside her and he stroked the hair back from her face as her eyes opened. She looked exhausted, her grey eyes haunted.

'What time is it?'

'Just after nine.' When she started to sit up, panic on her face, he eased her back down. 'I already called your boss. He knows you won't be in.'

'He's going to sack me. He's already unhappy about last week.'

'It's one day. He'll be fine. You've had hardly any sleep, so why don't you get some rest.' He nodded to the mug beside her. 'I brought you coffee.'

She seemed to waver over the work thing, looking troubled for a moment, then heaved out a sigh. 'Okay. I guess that's maybe a good idea. And thank you.'

As she sat up, bringing the duvet with her, Noah passed her the mug. Her light brown hair was mussed up, there were dark smudges under her eyes, and her normally olive skin was too pale, but she was still beautiful to him, his heart squeezing as she bit down on her lip, a contemplative look on her face.

That look suddenly turned to one of alarm.

'What's wrong?'

'Luna. I forgot about her. She hasn't been fed. Can you drive me home?'

For a moment there she had actually worried him. Noah stifled his smile, certain that Luna would cope for an hour or two. It was actually sweet how much Olivia adored her cat.

'I need to go out for a couple of hours this morning. Give me your key and I will nip in and feed her, okay?'

'You're going out?' She was frowning slightly at that. 'Then I should go home. You can drop me off on the way.'

'It's a work thing.' His smile widened to cover the lie. 'But I won't be too long. I'd rather you stay here. It's safer.'

Olivia's face paled further. 'You really think I'm in danger.'

It wasn't a question. They both knew after what had happened to Gary and Howard that she couldn't take any chances. 'I'll be happier if you stay here.'

'I don't have anything with me.'

'There's a spare toothbrush in the bathroom cabinet; you can borrow a pair of my old sweats. If you can't sleep, I have Netflix, and there's food in the fridge. I'll be back this afternoon.'

'You promise?'

'I promise.'

* * *

'You're better off to stick to the bypass, you know.'

'I need to make a detour.'

'Where to?' Daniella was looking at him expectantly.

'Liv's place. I promised I would feed the cat.'

She nodded, smirking at that. 'Okay.'

'It's her pet cat. I can't let it starve.'

'No, absolutely, I agree.'

They rode in silence for a few minutes longer.

'So you really are falling for her?'

Noah clenched the steering wheel, his own smile tight. 'I like her, yes, but you already know that, right?'

'Right.' The smirk remained and this knowing little look that irritated him, but he refrained from commenting further, deciding that his relationship with Olivia was none of Daniella's business. Instead, he turned up the radio.

Five minutes later and he was pulling into Olivia's driveway. The cameras were up, but the seclusion of the property still bothered him. It was a quiet lane with the high hedge separating it from the other houses in the street. He decided there and then that he didn't want her returning home alone, at least not until whoever was harassing her had been caught. He wasn't sure how she was going to react to that.

Luna greeted them, impatient for her breakfast and, while Noah tended to her, Daniella snooped around. He found her in the living room picking up photographs from the mantel. 'You okay in here, Miss Marple?'

'Just looking around. Cat sorted, Dr Doolittle?' She waggled an eyebrow, lips twitching into a smile, as she set down the photo frame and moved on to the bookcase, eyes scanning the titles.

'Fed and watered. You ready to go?'

'Yup.' Daniella pulled out a book, smile widening to a grin. 'I didn't know Olivia was a Bible-basher.'

'What? She's not... I don't think.'

'Well she has her Bible sitting right here. Wedged between *The Shining* and *Fifty Shades of Grey,* if you can believe that. I'm surprised the whole bookshelf hasn't gone up in flames.' She chuckled at her own joke, slipping the book back and turning to go. 'You know we should probably snoop while we're here.'

'We're not snooping. Besides, I've been staying here. There's nothing to see.'

'Yes, but when you're here, Olivia's here. She's not now.'

Daniella sauntered past him, heading for the stairs and Noah charged after her, catching hold of her arm and pulling her back. 'No you don't.'

'Spoilsport.'

He narrowed his eyes when she pouted. 'I already told you, she has nothing to do with this.'

'What about the lodger though?'

'Molly?' Noah thought of Olivia's uptight friend and stifled a laugh. 'Now you're clutching at straws.'

'How long has she been living here?'

'About a year, I think. They were friends before that. I'll give it to you that she's a bit *Single White Female*, in that she's a bit odd, but seriously she's way too up her own arse to pull anything like this off.'

'She hates you though. I remember you telling me.'

'And? This isn't about me. I think she might have non-friend, friendly feelings for Liv though.'

'Really? Which head are you thinking with there? Are you sure that's not just wishful thinking?'

'Remind me why I work with you again?'

'Because I keep you entertained and I sometimes make you brownies. Come on, Noah. We should at least go peek.'

She pulled on his arm and he made a show of reluctance as he let her drag him up the stairs. Truth was, he was now curious to see what the ice queen might be hiding.

It turned out to be a disappointing waste of five minutes. Molly's room was boringly plain with only a couple of personal knick-knacks, a simple jewellery box that was practically empty, containing two pairs of simple stud earrings, and a framed picture of Olivia and Molly stood together, Molly with her arm around Olivia. The rest of her stuff was toiletries.

'Wow, she likes the colour black,' Daniella commented, rooting through her clothes. 'I get now why you call her the grim reaper.'

'She has the personality to match.'

Noah pulled open the drawer of the bedside table, found it contained a box of Kleenex tissues, a packet of Polos, a reporter's notebook and a couple of pens. Curious, he pulled out the notebook, quickly flicked through it. The pages were empty. As he went to put it back, something fell out and landed on the floor. A photograph. He picked it up and flipped it over, saw Olivia's face looking back at him, and his chest tightened. He recognised the picture, knew it was one Olivia had used on her Facebook profile. Not that she knew Noah had a Facebook account. He was careful to use an alias. She had found it amusing when he told her not long after they first met that he didn't do social media. It was true he wasn't a fan, but the account was still necessary. It helped him keep tabs on things.

'Oh, look. She keeps a picture of your girlfriend in her bedside drawer? How sweet,' Daniella commented dryly, peering over his shoulder. 'Maybe it's not just your wishful thinking after all, eh?'

It would certainly go some way to explaining Molly's dislike towards him. She had always been a little off, but since Noah had become involved with Olivia, her coolness had intensified into open hostility.

Placing the photograph back where he had found it, he slipped the notebook back into the drawer and closed it.

Part of him wished he hadn't snooped, not liking that he had been right, and he wondered if Olivia had any idea how Molly felt. Not that he planned on telling her. She would be mortified if she knew they had been in Molly's room, going through her stuff. Besides, he had to get Molly onside. It was a stupid unrequited crush and he needed her help regardless. Olivia shouldn't be alone and with Molly's job taking her away a lot, he needed to familiarise himself with her schedule, so he could make sure he was around whenever she wasn't.

'Come on, there's nothing here. Let's go.'

* * *

Black Dog Farm was located just outside the village of Roughton, in the heart of the North Norfolk countryside, not far from the coast, its long driveway set back off the main road and the old welcome sign hidden behind an overgrown verge. Noah almost missed the turning, braking sharply once he had checked the road was clear. As he eased the car down the bumpy drive, it was clear no one had been out this way for quite some time.

He had done his research, knew the place was named after a local legend, a ghostly dog called Black Shuck, that roamed the coastal roads of Norfolk. He also knew that the farm had closed its doors a couple of years after the fire.

The Simon family had tried to shake off the bad press and keep their business going, but schools were put off visiting, the farm quickly gaining a bad reputation, and they had finally given up and moved away. The farm had gone up for sale, but there had been a lack of interest until a property developer had bought it a few years back. He had been battling to get planning permission to build luxury homes, but had so far been unsuccessful, and the place was standing abandoned and neglected.

Noah pulled to a halt near the main house, killed the engine, and he and Daniella climbed from the car. The place was bleak, and with its boarded-up windows, missing roof tiles and weed-riddled borders. It was hard to imagine it in its heyday, lit up and welcoming as Olivia had described it.

'This would make a great place for a Halloween party. I bet it's spooky as hell at night.'

Knowing Daniella as well as he did, he knew she was only half joking. She loved all things ghostly, had even done a couple of organised overnight tours with mediums, where she had sat in dungeons and crypts summoning the dead. Noah had taken great delight in ribbing her about that.

'Maybe you should nip back home and get your Ouija board, Dan. See if you can get us some answers about what really happened here.'

'Don't knock it till you've tried it.' She picked her way over broken glass, heading towards the main house. 'So this was where they all stayed then?' She let out a low whistle. 'I looked up photos online. It didn't look anything like this.'

Although he had come to see the cottage where the fire had taken place, Noah was curious too, following Daniella along the perimeter of the main house. A couple of the boards round the back had been torn away from the windows, suggesting vandals or vagrants and, had there been more time, he would have been tempted to explore inside.

He wasn't keen on leaving Olivia alone for too long and this wasn't where the fire had happened. 'We should go find the cottage,' he told Daniella.

'Lead the way.'

They headed towards the woods, Noah following the path he had seen on the aerial view of Google Maps.

The cottage, he had read, dated back to the seventeenth century and had come with the farm when the Simon family had bought it, though it was set so far away from the rest of the buildings, they had never bothered to do anything with it.

Despite the intensity of the fire, much of the cottage was still standing, though it had been devastated, and it looked a sorry sight as they approached the clearing. The chimney was broken and part of the roof missing. The shell of the building remained though the intervening years had not been kind and it was a sorry sight, surrounded by wire fencing and 'Danger. Keep Out' signs.

There were a couple of large gaps in the fence. Noah guessed the signs had been up for a while and they weren't the first ones to come exploring. The place had a grisly history and was probably on the bucket list for a number of local urban explorers.

Climbing through the fence, Daniella hot on his heels, he followed the path down the side of the cottage, the one he knew Olivia and Margaret had gone down all those years earlier, looking for where they had gained access.

The window was still accessible and what did strike him immediately was how high up in the wall it was. He clambered through, and finding himself in a room with blackened walls and a bare floor covered in rubble, glanced back at the open space of the window and offered a hand to Daniella.

'Jesus, this place was incinerated. I can't believe it's still standing,' she commented, brushing her hands down on her jeans.

'Just be careful, okay. The building probably isn't that safe.'

'Yes, Dad.'

Olivia said Rachel Williams had dragged her out of the cottage. She was unconscious at the time so wouldn't have remembered. Rachel had been a short and slight fourteen-year-old girl, and Olivia would have been a dead weight. Noah had heard of people managing incredible acts of strength in times of desperation, but was that really what had happened here? The window was high up. Too high to drag her and push her through. Rachel would have had to lift Olivia, and somehow he couldn't see her being capable of that.

'Come here and lie down on the ground for a moment.'

'What?' Daniella looked at the filthy floor, her expression horrified. 'You want me to lie down there?'

'Just for a second.'

'No way, it's filthy. Do you know how much I paid for this jacket?'

'Your jacket's black. It'll be fine.'

'It'll stink. Besides, there are probably rats in here.'

'You're not scared of rats.' Noah grinned. 'All that ghost hunting stuff and you're frightened of a rodent?'

'Hey, we all have our phobias. You're not too keen on snakes from what I remember.'

'Touché. I'm sure that in the five seconds you'll be on the floor, you won't see any rats.'

'Why do I have to lie on the floor?' she sniffed.

'Because I'm going to pick you up.'

'You're gonna do what?'

'I need to check something out and see if it's possible.'

'What? Why?'

'Rachel Williams supposedly got Liv out of the fire through this window. Personally, I don't see how. Liv would have been unconscious, a dead weight, and Rachel was not a big girl.'

Daniella nodded and he could see her thinking it over. 'What were they, fourteen at the time? You're a thirty-four-year-old man, Noah, and you weigh a hell of a lot more than a teenage girl, so it's not really a like-for-like. For starters, you'll be able to lift me no problem, and you're what, six one? You'll easily be able to get me through the window.'

'Yeah, but I can at least gauge how easy it would be for me and how difficult it would have been for Rachel.'

'Not really. However…' She smiled slyly. 'If you're Olivia and I'm Rachel…'

'You want to pick me up?' Noah fought to hide his grin, knew he had failed when he saw the indignant look on Daniella's face.

'I work out with weights, you know. I'm stronger than you think.

Besides, you said Olivia would have been a dead weight, so Rachel would have had to carry a heavier weight than her. At least it's a better comparison.'

'Okay, be my guest. This I can't wait to see.' Noah dropped to the floor, shaking his head. 'Go for it.'

She struggled, as he expected, but to give her credit, she didn't give up easily, finally managing to lift him up off the floor after her third attempt, staggering towards the window, grunting in determination.

It was the grunting that amused him most, had him bursting out laughing before they reached their destination, which of course started Daniella off too.

Carrying she could just about do, but laughing and carrying was impossible, and she lost both her grip and her balance at the same time, the pair of them crashing to the floor.

'You okay?'

'I'm fine,' she told him, getting to her feet and brushing herself down. 'I'm used to a bit of rough and tumble.'

Noah pulled himself up. 'So that didn't quite go according to plan.'

'At least I proved I could pick you up, though.' Daniella flexed her arm. 'See, stronger than I look. We can do it again if you want.'

'No, really, it's okay. Having you sweep me off my feet once was more than enough.'

'Ha ha, charmer.'

'I think we can safely say you would have struggled to lift me out of the window. And bear in mind the place would have been full of smoke. The odds would have been stacked against Rachel.'

'Yeah, I guess you're right,' Daniella admitted.

He was. There was no way Rachel could have got Olivia through the window. So, if that was the case, how the hell did Olivia get out of the fire?

32

Olivia dozed for a bit and on waking took a few seconds before realising she was in Noah's bed. She remembered that he had gone out, then recalled the video she had been sent from Howard Peck's phone. Nerves and sickness immediately returned, along with the image of him tied to the tree as it caught fire.

Whoever had killed Gary and Howard was blaming her for their deaths and the guilt was weighing her down. She hadn't liked either man, but that didn't mean she wanted either of them dead. What the hell was she supposed to have done to result in them being so cruelly murdered?

Although she was still tired, her mind was restless and working overtime, and she knew she wouldn't be able to get back to sleep. Throwing back the duvet she climbed from the bed, shivering, though Noah had left the heating on. After showering, she rummaged through his chest of drawers, found a long-sleeved T-shirt and a pair of sweatpants. They were both far too big for her, but they were warm and comfortable, and they smelt of him, or at least whatever washing detergent he regularly used.

Her phone pinged and she picked it up, saw he had messaged her to let her know Luna had been fed and was okay, and she smiled, grateful he had done that for her. Truth was she was a little bit nervy about returning home alone. It was different when Molly was there or when she was with

Noah, but alone, the house felt too big, and every creak and shadow had her jumping. She hated that the place that was once her sanctuary now felt unsafe.

Downstairs she made coffee, peered inside his fridge, unsure if she was hungry or not. Her belly kept growling, but then a vision of Howard would come to mind and she would lose her hunger pangs. But she headed for the fruit bowl and managed to eat a banana while she waited for the kettle to boil. Her coffee made, she went through to the living room with her phone, her plan to do a bit of investigating. Settling herself down in the corner of the oversized sofa, legs tucked beneath her, she logged into Facebook.

Her feed was full of decorated trees and posts about drunken antics at work parties, and it occurred to her that she still had most of her Christmas shopping left to do. She had started late November and would usually be finished by now, but with everything that had happened, it had slipped her mind. She really needed to get on with it, but couldn't drum up the enthusiasm. Instead, she pulled up Gary's Facebook page, looked again at the friends who had commented most on his profile updates.

She needed a pen and paper, realised it would be easier to write everything down as she went.

Noah would have both in his office.

Although she had never been in there, she knew it was the room opposite the lounge. She went to open the door, but was surprised to find it locked. She tried the handle again, frowning. He lived here alone. Why would he need to lock the door to his office?

Unless he wants to keep me out. Olivia considered that possibility, not liking it one bit. If that was true, did that mean he didn't trust her?

Unsettled, she went through to the kitchen, rooted through the drawers, finally finding a pen and some Post-it notes. They would have to do.

Still, as she gathered the names of Gary and Howard's close friends, it niggled away at her that she had let Noah into every aspect of her life, yet he didn't trust her alone in his house.

On a whim, as much to distract herself as anything, she looked up Malcolm Grimes to see if he had a Facebook account. There were a handful of men under that name, but none had a profile picture that resembled the boy she remembered. It could have been any of them or none of them.

She recalled Margaret telling her they had an older sister, though couldn't remember the girl's name. Annie or Abigail or something like that.

Next, she typed 'Malcolm Grimes' into Google, curious to see if anything came up.

The results that did were mostly old. It appeared Margaret's twin brother had been in trouble with the police quite a bit during his late teens. The articles she clicked on mostly in local newspapers. There were no photos and, aside from a reference to the twins' father, nothing about the family.

She was about to give up when a search result at the bottom of the page caught her attention. Malcolm Grimes had been arrested in connection with a fire when he was eighteen.

Olivia read the article, her heart in her mouth, as it reported how Malcolm had set a fire in the conservatory of the family home. Although the flames had taken hold, destroying part of the house, the fire brigade were able to get the blaze under control.

Malcolm Grimes had been at Black Dog Farm when his sister had died. Was he taking revenge against the students who had been on that trip?

The idea left her cold. She had been Margaret's friend. Did Malcolm blame her for what had happened to his sister. Had he been responsible for what had happened to Gary and Howard?

She was still sitting on the sofa and pondering when Noah arrived back around lunchtime.

'You okay?' he asked as he sat down beside her, leaning in to kiss her on the mouth and she turned slightly so his lips instead brushed her cheek.

'Fine.'

'What are you up to?'

She tilted the Post-it note she had been writing on so he couldn't read it. 'Stuff.'

He gave her a measured look, didn't push it. 'I'm gonna put the kettle on. Do you want another coffee?'

'Okay.'

She ignored him as he picked up her mug, though she was aware he paused in the doorway, looked ready to say something, then thought better of it.

Hearing him moving around the kitchen, turning taps on, opening cupboards, carrying on as if everything was fine, her temper snapped and she stomped through, trying her best not to trip over the bottoms of his sweatpants which were far too long for her.

'Why is your office door locked?'

He glanced up. 'What?'

'Your office door. It's locked. Do you not trust me?'

His eyes narrowed. 'Of course I trust you, though why would you even need to go in my office?'

Ha. He was twisting it back on her. Well, it wasn't going to work, because she had a valid reason. 'I needed a pen and paper.'

'Okay. Well you got those from in here.'

'That's not the point...'

He didn't seem to be taking her particularly seriously, finishing making the coffee and peering into the fridge, as if she wasn't even there.

'Noah?'

'What?' He closed the door, looked at her, the corners of his mouth twitching into a smile, which only served to irritate her further.

'What's so funny?'

'You are. Those sweatpants are drowning you.'

'It's not my fault your legs are so long! Can you please take me seriously for a minute?'

'Of course.'

'Why is your office door locked?'

'Why are you so bothered about it being locked?' he countered.

'Because you live here alone. You have no reason to lock any doors unless you don't trust me.'

'You're being ridiculous.'

'Really? Because I have shared everything with you; my past, my scars... hell, I even trusted you to go into my house this morning and feed Luna.'

A flicker of something – was that guilt? – passed over his face before his expression hardened. 'I did that to help you, to keep you safe. I didn't realise we were keeping a scorecard.'

'We're not, but you don't trust me.'

'I do bloody trust you, Liv.'

'So why lock the door?'

He threw his hands up in exasperation. 'Habit, I guess. I haven't always lived here alone and there are confidential files in there. You're really being irrational over this.'

Was she being irrational? Olivia wavered for a moment. She was tired, stressed and paranoid, her emotions all over the place. Maybe she was overreacting. It was Noah's house, so it was totally up to him if he kept doors locked. She was coming across like a bit of a diva.

The fight went out of her. 'You're right, you're right. I am being irrational. It's this situation, I'm sorry. It's your house. I have no right to make demands.'

Noah studied her for a moment before grabbing his keys up off the counter. 'Come on.' He caught hold of her hand.

'Come on where?' He was already pulling her into the hallway, Olivia struggling in the sweatpants as she followed.

He paused outside the office door, twisted a key in the lock and pushed it open, nudging her inside. 'There you go, just a regular office. Nothing really to see.'

It was a small room with a desk in front of the window and a couple of filing cabinets. A Mac was set up on the desk and shelves were filled with books. Like the rest of his house it was uncluttered, the furniture masculine. He was right: there was nothing really to see.

He placed his hands on her shoulders, eased her around and back out into the hallway, closing the door again. 'Now you've seen inside. No secrets, okay?'

'Okay.' She returned the kiss he pressed against her lips, trying to ignore the nagging little voice in the back of her mind when she heard him twist the key in the lock again.

He's still hiding something.

33

'Maybe we should get away for a bit,' Janice suggested, nursing her vodka and Coke as she watched Fern pace up and down her kitchen. 'We could go to Tenerife. That has a good temperature all year round.'

Although Janice Plum was worried by everything going on, the one silver lining of this situation was that her friendship had been rekindled with Fern. She was back in the zone. It wasn't that she didn't have friends. No, she had all of her Zumba pals and the local mums, but Fern had always been one of the cool ones. Fern St Clair didn't hang around with just anyone.

Of course Fern's friend options were being killed off. Howard had always come higher on the pecking order than Janice, but he was gone now. The police had been in touch with Fern not long after Howard's phone was found in the woods out near Fritton. As she had been the last person Howard had spoken to before his gruesome death, they had needed to ask her some questions.

Fern had been careful not to reveal any details of why the killer might be targeting them. If the police found out the truth about that night at Black Dog Farm, the pair of them could be in a whole heap of trouble. Janice wasn't sure what was worse: being targeted by a stalker or spending her days in a prison cell.

Getting out of the country seemed to be the only way they could stay safe. Plus of course, it would be nice to have a girls' holiday, a pre-Christmas break. Martin wouldn't begrudge her that: she worked hard looking after the house, and he could take care of the kids for a couple of weeks.

'Get away?' Fern stopped pacing, stared at her incredulously. 'Are you seriously that stupid that you think a holiday is going to fix this?'

'Well, it can't hurt. And at least we would be safe while we tried to work out a longer-term plan.'

Fern dragged her fingers back through her hair, resumed her pacing. 'How did I get left with the idiot of the bunch?' She muttered this to herself, but it was loud enough for Janice to hear.

She bristled. 'Hey, I don't have to be here, you know! I do have other friends.'

'Whatever.' The outburst brought Fern to a halt though. She paused by the counter, picking up her own drink. Janice had watched her pour at least three shots of vodka in the glass and was starting to wonder if her old friend had an alcohol problem.

'What we need to do is find out whoever the hell is doing this and put an end to it.' Fern paused, considering. 'Have you managed to track down that Rita Works woman yet?'

'Not yet. I'm still trying, but honestly, Fern, the woman is like a ghost. I've sent her three messages and she hasn't even opened them.'

'What about Gary's mum and his friends? I told you to talk to them.'

'I have.' Speaking with Gary's mum had been a difficult conversation. As she wasn't on any social media and Janice didn't have a phone number for her, she'd been left with no choice but to track down her address and pay her a visit. Doreen had been a mess, not coping at all well with her son's death, and hadn't been much help with Janice's questions. When the woman had collapsed sobbing, her husband had come to the door and angrily insisted that Janice leave.

The only thing she had managed to ascertain was that neither of Gary's parents had ever met Rita Works.

Gary's best friend, Keith, had been a little more helpful. He had been in the year above them at school and remembered Janice. They'd met for a drink at Gary's local, where she also got to speak with a few of Gary's other friends. Again though, none of them had met Rita. Keith knew that they had hooked up via the dating site Plenty of Fish, but wasn't sure if the relationship had ever made it offline.

Janice told Fern, 'He reckoned Gary was planning to meet up with Rita in the real world the night before he died, but apart from that—'

'I thought you said you were good at finding people?' Fern pouted, knocking back more vodka.

'I usually am. I'm trying my best.' A thought occurred to Janice and her eyes widened. 'Oh my God, Fern. What if she was the one who killed him? Keith said they were meeting up. Maybe they had a fight and Rita killed him by accident.'

'By chaining him to a chair and setting him on fire?'

'Maybe it was a kinky game that went wrong.'

Fern shook her head. 'A kinky game? Would you listen to yourself? What do you think, she only meant to burn his cock off, but the match slipped?'

'I'm just coming up with suggestions, there's no need to be sarcastic. All I'm saying is, if Rita was supposed to meet him just before he died and she's suddenly disappeared, maybe she killed him. She could be a female serial killer. They exist. Maybe Gary's death had nothing to do with the notes.'

'So explain why Howard died? Did Rita kill him too?'

There it was, the giant-sized hole in Janice's theory. She had momentarily forgotten about Howard. She was quite liking her Rita idea. Deflated, she sipped at her drink. 'Maybe we should start a list.'

'A list?'

'A list of potential suspects.'

Although Fern turned her nose up, she didn't rubbish the idea, reaching into one of her kitchen drawers for a notebook and pen. 'Here you go.'

Janice opened the book, picked up the pen. 'Who should I put on it?'

'Olivia.'

'I thought you said Olivia had received notes too?'

'That's what she said. I don't trust her though, so put her name down.'

'We should add Rita too.'

Fern rolled her eyes. 'Whatever. And add Noah Keen, Olivia's boyfriend. There was something about him I don't trust.'

Janice started to write the name, pausing as another thought occurred to her. 'Do you think him and Olivia could be in on it together?'

It definitely held up better than her last theory. Olivia had motive and her boyfriend seemed too interested in what was going on. Maybe he was helping her to get revenge.

Although Fern didn't actually say the words, Janice could tell that she thought it was a plausible idea too. Olivia had been there when Gary had died; she could have been lying about the notes. After all, it made no sense that she would be targeted too, especially as she hadn't done anything wrong.

Janice thought back to the cruel prank they had played on Olivia in high school. Although they had never been formally identified, Olivia knew who was behind it. Even if she couldn't remember what happened the night of the fire, she probably hated them all for the video.

Janice did feel bad about that. Fern had been hellbent on revenge, still wanting to punish Olivia even after everything she had already been through. None of them had expected to see Olivia back at school and Fern had been so bitter when she returned, unable to see that she had suffered enough.

Janice had willingly gone along with her revenge plans at the time, only now considering how awful they had been to her.

Does Olivia hate us that much that she wants to see us dead?

'We should check out Margaret's brother too,' Fern said, interrupting her thoughts. 'I had forgotten about him. Malcolm Grimes, I bloody hated that kid. He was fucked up in the head enough to do something like this.'

Another plausible suspect, though Malcolm Grimes had been a hot-headed kid. If he knew what had happened the night his sister had died, he wouldn't have left it seventeen years before getting revenge, Janice was sure of it. She added him to the list anyway.

They spent another half an hour considering suspects, but the list remained at four names. Fern was insistent that Janice be the one to check out Malcolm Grimes, wanting to keep tabs on Olivia and Noah herself.

Janice intended to do her own investigating anyway, figuring it wouldn't hurt.

Fern didn't bother to see Janice out. She stayed at her kitchen counter drinking a fresh vodka and Janice told her she would message her once she had news, before saying goodnight.

She buttoned up her coat and put on her scarf, knowing it was cold outside and a sharp frost was forecast. Letting herself out of the front door, she made sure the latch caught as she pulled it shut, and clicked her keys at her car. As she walked towards it, the outside light came on, illuminating the words scratched into the bonnet of her Toyota.

YOU'RE NEXT

34

It was coming up to the one day of the year that Malcolm always dreaded.

As he stared at the one photograph he had of Margaret, his mind drifted back to the fire that had claimed his sister's life. It was the catalyst for many things to come and it had changed everything, setting him on a new path that would determine his future and ultimately result in vengeance and murder.

Christmas was never much fun in the Grimes household. Gerald and Marie Grimes took their faith seriously and much of Christmas Day revolved around the church. Although the children received a few gifts, all were practical in nature – a new Bible, clothes, maybe a book bag for school – and the majority of the day was spent in prayer or Bible study, firstly at the church then later at home. The only highlight of the day was Christmas lunch (though as always Gerald was watching closely, ready to deliver punishment for the slightest wrongdoing) after which they were allowed to listen to a few Christmas songs. Nothing too modern, mind. There would be no Slade, Wham! or Mariah Carey in the Grimes house. Marie had an old-fashioned record player and the family would listen to a selection of songs by artistes such as Bing Crosby, The Andrews Sisters and Perry Como.

Christmas Day 2003 was a more sombre affair than usual. Malcolm had heard his mother sob that first night he was home, but other than that his parents had remained dry-eyed and stony faced in the days following Margaret's death, completely emotionless and of little comfort to their two remaining children.

This did nothing to help the burning grief eating up Malcolm. Margaret hadn't just been his sister, she had been his twin. They had come into the world together and, although she was the good to his bad, the lightness to his dark, and they'd never had much in common, she had always been his constant. Without her, he was lost. Knowing how she had died filled him with a rage he had no outlet for.

Margaret was mentioned in the prayers of the Christmas morning church service then the Grimes family returned home.

It was during lunch that Malcolm really noticed the change in Alice.

His older sister had always been defiant and uncontrollable, getting worse in the last year, but since his return from the school trip, she had seemed like an empty shell. At first Malcolm had put it down to grief, but now he sensed it was more than that. There was an atmosphere between Alice and his parents, something unspoken between them, and it was as though her spirit had been crushed.

She was even on her best behaviour – no snide looks or rolled eyes, and no answering their father back – and for the first time in Malcolm's life, Alice was actually doing exactly as she was told.

It was as if she had been replaced by a robot.

Malcolm didn't like it. Margaret had always been the good child, the one who tried her best to please their parents. Alice was the rebel and Malcolm, well he was beyond saving, according to their father. Alice's complete change of personality... no, not change, more like *lack* of personality was unsettling.

He couldn't help but wonder if something had happened during the week he had been away.

Over the coming months Alice remained in the same zombified state. There was no more sneaking out at night and she became a loner at school, losing interest in friends, boyfriends and all social activities, instead studying hard. Malcolm tried to talk to her about it on several occasions, but each time she shut him down.

And so he did the rebelling for both of them, acting up and causing as much trouble for his parents as possible, as he desperately tried to evoke some kind of emotion or reaction in them, so bloody angry that Alice had submitted to their will, almost moulding herself to replace Margaret, while sweet, dead Margaret seemed to be wiped from their lives. The beatings from his father became more frequent, but Malcolm didn't care. At least when Gerald hit him, he could feel.

Unlike Alice, who passed all of her exams and went to university, Malcolm failed every one of his. It wasn't that he couldn't do them. Despite what his father thought, he was a relatively intelligent boy and knew he could have passed had he wanted to. He just didn't bother to show up.

Of course Gerald had been furious about that, but Malcolm was growing fast, almost six foot and muscular with it, making it difficult for his father to physically punish him.

He managed to secure work in a local supermarket and as soon as he was able to afford it, he left home, moving into a bedsit on the rougher side of town.

It was while he lived there that Alice made contact from university.

At first her messages had been tentative, but the more they talked, initially by text, eventually by phone, he understood about her change in personality.

They had both lost Margaret and they both grieved for her, and they both hated their parents with a passion, but Alice was also terrified of them. And now Malcolm knew why. He was furious with his parents, disgusted with what they had done to Alice.

That was why the match had been lit. Malcolm had wanted to see Alice when she returned from university for her summer break, but things had ended so badly with his parents, he knew they wouldn't let him in the house, and each attempt to see her outside and away from their control, kept being thwarted. Malcolm suspected that his father was monitoring Alice's phone, which is why she wasn't replying to his messages or answering his calls.

He was so angry, so blinkered with hatred, he had sat outside the house waiting for his parents to leave then had broken in once he knew it was empty.

As he watched the flames rise, taking hold of the conservatory blinds, he had stood mesmerised, drawn back to the night of Margaret's death. He was so caught up in the past, he hadn't initially heard Alice's voice, hadn't realised she was in the house.

'Malcolm, what the fuck are you doing here?' Her tone had been sharp, she had been so angry with him. They had fought, the police and fire brigade had arrived, and Malcolm had been arrested.

He didn't see his parents or Alice again.

Now, as he sat at his laptop and studied the news reports, he knew it was time.

Kelly Dearborn, Rachel Colton née Williams, Gary Lamb and Howard Peck. Four had paid for what had happened to Margaret. Four sinners had been burned alive.

An eye for an eye. A tooth for a tooth.

Time was running out as it grew closer to the eve of Margaret's death. The instigators were going to be next. He closed the laptop and grabbed his duffle bag.

It was time to finish this.

35

The Grimes family had been next on Noah's list to look into. As it turned out, Olivia had already started doing the legwork on that for him.

Of course she had to be persuaded to share what she had been up to, mostly because she was pissed off about his office being locked. That was a problem in itself, but one he would have to deal with later. He had been ignoring it for long enough. Another week wouldn't hurt. Eventually she had yielded, telling him about the article she had found on Malcolm Grimes and his arrest for arson.

It certainly made Malcolm a viable suspect, but was it really that straightforward?

Olivia had been friends with Margaret, so it made absolutely no sense that Malcolm would be targeting her. But Fern and her friends were a different story and almost certainly involved in what had happened to Margaret. Fern might have denied it, but it had been written all over her face.

Following Howard's murder, Noah intended to talk to her again, hoping she might now start taking things more seriously and agree to tell him what really happened the night of Margaret Grimes' death. That would have to wait though. He didn't want to leave Olivia alone and he couldn't take her with him.

Instead, he waited until they were back at her place and Olivia decided to have a bath. Once she was out of earshot, he placed a call to an old police pal, who he knew had a loose mouth, to find out what information he could on the Howard Peck murder.

There wasn't much to go on. Howard's burned remains had been found in woods near Fritton, where he had hired a log cabin. His killer had recorded his murder on Howard's phone, sent it to Olivia, then dumped the phone before fleeing the crime scene.

At the moment, the police were trying to track down Howard's girlfriend, Daisy Angel, who was supposed to accompany him on the break. According to messages on Howard's phone they had decided to travel to the cabin separately, as Daisy had been called in to work. Although she had arranged to meet him at the cabin, it seemed she had never showed up.

Noah added Daisy's name to his list of people to speak to.

He then found out what he could about the Grimes family, firstly using trusty Google, skimming over the article Olivia had told him about. There was no point putting in a request for the police report on the arson attack. There just wasn't time. Noah knew how the system worked and that it would take weeks, if not months, to get it. His best bet would be to speak with the officers and the solicitor who had worked the case.

Hearing the bath water draining, he fired off a quick message to Fern, telling her that they needed to talk again, before slipping the phone back in his pocket and heading upstairs.

'You want to get takeout tonight?'

***

Olivia was in her bedroom, naked and one leg up on the bed as she used her towel to dry herself. She hadn't heard Noah come up the stairs and jumped at his voice, immediately conscious that her burn scars were clearly visible, snaking a jagged path down the side of her body. Quickly she pulled up the towel to cover herself. 'Sure. Okay.'

They had been sleeping together all week and the scars didn't seem to bother him, but she was still self-conscious of being naked around him out of bed. Catching her from behind, he trailed kisses down her neck, tugging the towel away when she relaxed back into him.

'Don't do that,' he said.

'Don't do what?'

'Hide from me. I like seeing you naked.'

She tensed slightly at that, catching her breath when he ran his hands down her sides, his fingertips tracing a pattern over the roughness of the scars, before he slid his arms around her, pulling her tight against him, and nibbling at her earlobe, warm breath on her neck.

Her insides pooled as her body instantly reacted to his, betraying her as she attempted to hold on to her rational thoughts. This wasn't good. She was falling hard for a man with secrets; a man she was beginning to wonder just how well she could trust.

'So what do you fancy?'

'I don't mind. Surprise me.' She managed to ease herself out of his arms, grabbed the towel, prudishly wrapping it around herself, her legs still a little wobbly, and angled him a look. 'What have you been up to? I heard you on the phone.'

She could tell from his expression that he hadn't realised she had heard him. 'I was talking to an old friend.'

'In the police?'

'Yes.'

'About Howard?'

He hesitated at that, seeming unsure what to tell her. 'I didn't find out much.'

'Okay, so what did you find out?'

She listened as he told her about the log cabin and the phone, wondering if there was anything he was holding back. Although he had been talking quietly, the bathroom door had been ajar and she had been able to make out parts of his conversation, understood that he hadn't wanted her to hear him. She asked a few more questions, trying to sound casual, hoping to trip him up, and was annoyed when he gave nothing else away.

Her unease stayed with her into the evening, as she thought back to how Noah had kept Daniella a secret from her. At the time, she had believed it was simply because he didn't want her to know Daniella was a woman, but was it really as simple as that? Then there was the locked office door and the secretive phone calls, plus the fact she didn't actually know that much about him – well, only what he had told her about himself.

She trusted him in so much that she didn't think he would ever hurt her, certainly didn't think he was behind the notes and knew he hadn't made the phone calls, but the secrets were starting to bother her. What was he trying to hide from her?

* * *

To Olivia's relief, Molly returned home on Saturday. She needed a little time out from Noah. Things were getting too intense and she couldn't think straight around him. He had slept in her bed all week and, while she appreciated that he was staying with her to keep her safe, having him there was too much of a distraction. Now Molly was home there was no need for him to stay.

She used her lodger as an excuse to have a night apart, telling him she wanted some catch-up time with her friend. It wasn't actually a lie. Molly worked for a tour operator, inspecting and contracting hotels. While her job involved a lot of travel, she was usually only away for a night or two at a time. This trip had been one of her longer ones and Olivia had missed her.

They spent the evening catching up over Mexican food and beer, Molly telling Olivia about the awful hotel she had stayed in, then Olivia updating her friend about everything that had happened in her absence, from the run-in with Fern to Howard's murder.

As she expected, Molly was wide-eyed with shock and had plenty of questions.

'So somehow this is all connected to your past and to these people. Jesus, what did you do, Livvy?'

'Nothing.' Olivia bristled a little, not appreciating the hint of accusation in Molly's tone. 'I have no idea why I'm being targeted.'

Molly scooped a dollop of salsa on to her nacho and popped it in her mouth. 'You were all friends though, right?'

'No, well, with Fern for a while, but we haven't spoken in years. Not since Margaret…' Olivia trailed off. She didn't want to get into the past and the night of Margaret's death again. She had never shown Molly her scars and her lodger didn't know about the fire she had survived.

'Who is Margaret?'

'She was a friend.'

'Was? Have you fallen out with her too?'

'No, no. Margaret passed away.'

'Sorry, I didn't realise. What happened?'

'It was just an accident. It happened years ago.' Olivia waved her hand dismissively as if it wasn't a big deal, kicking herself for mentioning Margaret's name. She should have known it would lead to questions.

Luna was skulking around the coffee table, where they had set out the dishes of cheese, sauces and chicken for the fajitas, nose raised as she debated whether to chance her luck in jumping up. Searching for a subject change, Olivia grabbed hold of her, pulled her close for a cuddle. 'This little shit scared the living crap out of me a couple of nights ago.'

'She did?'

Relieved to move on from Margaret, Olivia recounted how she thought someone had been in the living room. At the time she had been scared then embarrassed, but now she could laugh at it, and it was a safer topic of conversation. At least she thought so until she mentioned Noah's name, immediately kicking herself.

'Noah's been staying here?'

'He just…' Damn it. Why was she pussyfooting around Molly? This was her house. 'I didn't want to be alone,' she said simply.

'Probably a wise idea, especially with everything that's been happening,' Molly agreed, picking up her beer and taking a healthy swig.

Olivia stared at her friend. Had she had a personality transplant? Molly hadn't even flinched or sneered at Noah's name.

'What?'

'You hate Noah.'

Molly's smile was easy, and she let out a laugh, seeming amused. 'You asked me to give him a chance and I promised you I would. Besides, regardless of my reservations about him, I don't think you should be alone. Two of your friends have been murdered.'

'They weren't my friends.'

'Whatever. You know what I mean. You shouldn't be alone and so yes, I do think it was good that Noah stayed. How are things with you two anyway?'

'They're good.'

'You don't sound so sure about that. Anything you want to talk about?'

With Molly? Is that really a good idea? She was finally being okay about Noah and Olivia didn't want to ruin that, but damn it, she needed someone to talk to about him. She was probably being paranoid and overreacting, but her mind was so muddled right now with everything else going on, she needed a second clearer opinion. 'I met Dan.'

'Who's Dan?'

'Noah's partner in his company, who he works with, remember?'

'Oh yeah, I do, and what's wrong with Dan? Is he an arsehole?'

'No, not an arsehole. Not a "he" either.'

'What?' Molly's eyes widened.

'Yes, Dan is Daniella. She's a woman.'

'Okay. And why hadn't Noah told you that?'

'He was worried I might be jealous. Apparently, his last girlfriend didn't like him having a female partner.'

'But he introduced you, right?'

'Not exactly. It was Tuesday morning, just before you left.' When Molly narrowed her eyes, Olivia quickly added, 'I didn't say anything before you left, as I was still trying to process it. She showed up early. He wasn't happy.'

'That you met her? So what is she like?'

'She seemed nice enough.'

'Is she pretty?'

'Yes.'

'Do you think they're sleeping together?'

'Molly!'

Molly threw her hands up. 'Hey, I'm just asking the question. He kept her a secret.'

'No, they're not sleeping together. I think she might be married.'

'So why all the cloak-and-dagger shit then?'

'I don't know.' Olivia hesitated, decided to take a leap of faith in Molly. She might as well know it all. 'Noah seems to have a lot of secrets.'

'He does? Such as?'

Another pause. Was she really going to tell Molly everything? After working so hard to get her to accept Noah, it felt like she was throwing him under a bus. She was now offering her friend all the ammunition she needed to hate him. Was she crazy?

But Noah's secrets were getting to her. He was hiding something and she no longer felt she could trust him. She needed to talk to someone before she went completely crazy.

To Molly's credit, she listened without passing judgement as Olivia told her about the locked office door and the phone calls she wasn't supposed to overhear. Saying it out loud, she couldn't help wondering if she was overreacting, and when she was finished, Molly surprised her by saying pretty much the same.

'Keeping his office door locked is a bit over the top, but he does work in security.'

'It's more than that. I know it is. It sounds stupid, I know, but there's something in that office he doesn't want me to see. I just know there is.'

'You have no proof of that. Just a hunch.'

'Hunches are sometimes reliable.'

'Okay, well, instead of getting worked up about this, have you considered just sitting down and talking to him about how you feel?'

'He gets defensive. Besides, what about the phone calls. I know he waited until I was out of earshot before he made them. And he seems far too interested in Gary and Howard's murders.'

'Have you ever thought that it's maybe because he's worried about you. You've said yourself. He's an ex-cop. He probably can't help but investigate.'

That was true. Olivia wasn't sure from Molly's expression that she really believed that though. Still, she continued to fight Noah's corner.

'And you are his girlfriend. You witnessed one murder, received a video of another. For whatever reason, whoever murdered your friends is targeting you. Are you sure there is nothing you have done? There has to be a reason why whoever is doing this is focusing on you specifically.'

That was the second time Molly had referred to Gary and Howard as

Olivia's friends, which was starting to annoy her. 'For God's sake, I told you, they weren't my bloody friends!'

She snapped out the words a little harsher than she'd intended, immediately regretted them when she saw Molly's hurt expression.

That was the thing with Molly, she often spoke without thinking. Olivia should be used to her by now, but yet again she was overreacting.

Just as you did with Noah.

Had she overreacted? This whole situation was taking its toll on her. 'I'm sorry, I didn't mean to snap,' she apologised. 'I'm so on edge with everything and now the Noah stuff as well... It's not your fault. I shouldn't take it out on you. I know you're only trying to help.'

'It's okay.' Molly's tone was sympathetic. 'Look, you're tired. I can see that. Why don't you go have an early night and I'll clear everything away?'

'That's not fair. You're the one who's been travelling. No, I'll clear away.'

'Livvy, you're my friend. Please let me help you. You've been through a lot these last few days. Seriously, go get some rest.'

Olivia briefly closed her eyes, could feel the tiredness. And she had the start of a headache. Molly was right. She did need to rest. 'Okay. Thank you, and I owe you.'

'You don't owe me anything. We're friends, right?' Molly got to her feet as Olivia did, pulled her into a hug. 'This is what friends do for each other.'

'Thank you.' Olivia returned the hug, tried to ease back, was stopped from doing so when Molly tightened her grip.

'It's going to be okay, Livvy. We'll figure this out, the two of us together.' She turned her head slightly, so her face was pressed against Olivia's hair, her breath warm against her ear, one hand starting to rub her back, while the other trailed down lower over her arse, cupping her bum cheek, her fingers kneading.

Olivia jerked back, forcibly removing herself from Molly's hold. *What the hell was that?*

'Are you okay?' Molly was wide-eyed at her reaction, seeming shocked and not acting at all like what she had just done was wholly inappropriate. Should Olivia call her on it?

'I... I'm fine. Tired. I'm gonna go to bed. I'll see you tomorrow.' Olivia left the room before anything else could be said, knowing she was a coward and that she should have said something. Though seriously, what the hell was she supposed to have said to what had just happened?

Her bedroom was cold and she quickly undressed, slipping under the duvet. On the bedside table her phone showed an unread message, and she glanced at it quickly, seeing it was from Noah, checking in with her. She quickly fired a reply, telling him she was okay, before settling back against the pillow.

Her body was so tired, but her mind wide awake as she replayed the scene with Molly.

Had she overreacted?

No, it hadn't been just a friendly hug, it had definitely been more. Had Olivia given her the wrong signals? She thought back over the time she had known Molly. There had been no boyfriends (though no girlfriends either) and she had never really shown interest in anyone. And she knew Olivia was straight. When they had met, Olivia had been dating Toby, and now she was with Noah.

That was the other thing. Molly had always hated Noah. Olivia remembered Molly's reaction when she first found out Olivia was involved with him. She had gone from cool indifference to downright hostility. Had it been because she had feelings for Olivia herself?

No, this was stupid. It was the situation that was making her overthink everything. Tiredness and worry was leading to paranoia and she was doubting everyone around her. Noah was just trying to keep her safe and Molly was being no more than a good friend.

She repeated that mantra as she closed her eyes, willing sleep to take her, but her last coherent thought before she finally drifted off was...

Trust no one.

36

A good session of Zumba was going to help Janice's mindset no end.

Although there were no classes on a Sunday, one of her exercise pals, Gretchen, had messaged, proposing a pre-Christmas get-together at the community centre for Sunday night. The plan involved alcohol and maybe a few unhealthy snacks, as well as the dancing.

A night with some of her friends, lots of dancing and fun... It was exactly what Janice needed after the shock of Howard's death.

Gretchen had apparently spoken with one of the Zumba instructors about using the hall. She hadn't mentioned alcohol, of course. The community hall was quite strict on that, but Janice figured what they didn't know wouldn't hurt them. There was only one camera at the hall, overlooking the car park at the front. Janice and her friends would just need to sneak the drinks inside hidden in bags.

Kissing Martin goodbye and leaving him with Sky Sports and a takeaway, she set off for the community centre, a plastic bag containing mince pies and some cans of gin and tonic swinging by her side. Beneath her coat she wore her favourite exercise outfit, a black T-shirt emblazoned with 'Zumba Babe' in big silver letters, and a pair of leopard print leggings. For a laugh she had stuck Rudolph earrings with flashing red noses in her ears and silver star deely boppers on her head. It was almost Christmas after all, and she knew it would make the girls smile.

The community centre was only a five-minute walk from her house, the roads well-lit, and as she walked, she messaged Gretchen to say she was on her way. She wondered who else had been invited, had asked Gretchen the question in an earlier message, but her friend had simply replied with a smiley face, saying it was a surprise.

Janice assumed it would be the usual crew, maybe Charmaine, Kirsty, Helen and Sue.

Whoever was there, she was determined it was going to be a fun night. The last two weeks had been so stressful and, although she was aware the problems weren't going to disappear, she just needed to switch off from the worry for one evening.

Fern didn't seem to be coming up with any decent plan to catch their tormentor. Instead she was getting snippier, drinking heavily and nit-picking at Janice, trying to make everything her fault. Which was rich, given that Fern had been the instigator, the one who had hatched the plan to get back at Margaret. And yes, Janice had gone along with it which, she could admit now, had been a foolish thing to do, but Fern was the one who was mostly to blame. If anyone had a right to be mad, it was Janice.

Instead, she felt like she was taking the brunt of everyone's frustrations.

Even Martin had been furious when he had seen the words scratched into the car bonnet. Of course, he had wanted to know what it meant and Janice had been forced to lie to him, saying that Fern was having trouble with an ex-boyfriend and that the message had probably been intended for her.

That had almost backfired because he had wanted to call the police, but luckily she had managed to talk him out of that.

She desperately wanted to tell Martin the truth, but Fern had warned her not to, and while the threat of Fern's wrath wasn't a complete deterrent, knowing that Martin might not forgive her if he learnt the truth, was. They had been together for so many years. How would he feel if he found out what she had done and also that she had never told him?

No, she had to keep this a secret. Martin could never find out.

In less than two weeks it would be Christmas and they were planning to go to North Yorkshire to stay with Martin's sister over the festive period. For Janice, the break couldn't come soon enough and she wished she could bring it forward; anything to get away from this situation with the creepy notes and Gary and Howard's murders. At least in Yorkshire she would be safe from whoever was stalking them.

As she wondered if they could get away earlier, and as she worked out Martin's last day of work and how many spare holiday days he had left, the welcoming security lights of the community centre car park came into sight.

There were no cars outside, which suggested Gretchen had kept the invitation local. Unless of course any of the girls were getting a taxi. It was going to be a boozy night, after all. Janice realised she was the first one there. She glanced at her watch. Gretchen had said to meet at eight and Janice was right on time (she didn't do tardy). Helen was a bit of a stickler for timekeeping, but Charmaine and Sue were often running into the Zumba class at the last moment.

She tried the door, guessed Gretchen was already there when it opened. The hallway light was on and the kitchenette at the end of the hall was also lit up. 'Helloooo? It's only me, mate. Am I the first here?'

She closed the door behind her, made her way down to the kitchenette, surprised when she peered in and found it empty. Frowning, she crossed to the double doors that led down to the main hall where they did Zumba, a smile on her face as she recognised Christmas music.

Gretchen must be setting things up.

Janice unzipped her coat, dumping it on one of the chairs in the corridor before pushing her way through the door, doing a silly dance as she wiggled her arse and her boobs, and shook her deely boppers. 'Guess who's here?'

It occurred to her as she jigged around in the middle of the room, doing a little twirl, that she was all alone. Gretchen wasn't in the hall. It was just Janice and a portable record player set up on a table. 'It's beginning to look a lot like Christmas' echoing around the large room.

'Gretchen? I'm here. Where are you?'

The lights were all on and the music playing. She had to be somewhere.

Wandering back through to the main hallway, Janice paused to put her mince pies and gin in the kitchenette, before poking her head into the different rooms of the community hall, calling for her friend.

All of the rooms were empty.

Wherever Gretchen was, she couldn't have gone far, as she had left the building unlocked and the music playing. Back in the kitchenette, Janice helped herself to a mince pie and opened a can of gin.

No point in waiting to get the party started.

Cramming the mince pie into her mouth, she fished in her bag for her mobile phone. She decided she would send Gretchen a selfie of herself, kitted out with her reindeer earrings and deely boppers, with the caption;

Starting the party without you.

Back in the hall, she wiped crumbs from her mouth, took a couple of large sips of her gin, and raised the phone, clicking on to the camera and smiling in approval at her image. Not bad for thirty-one. The Cherry Crush dye covered her premature grey hairs and with the right filter none of the lines were visible around her eyes.

She angled the camera, trying to hold the phone far enough away from her so that she could get the deely boppers fully in.

In the background Perry Como sang, 'It's beginning to look a lot like Christmas.'

She glanced back into the camera, scrunched up her lips, and froze, eyes widening as she took in the masked face behind her.

37

Olivia had spent much of Sunday running away from her problems, playing things cool with Noah and giving Molly a wide berth.

The first had been easy enough, as aside from a few messages checking she was okay, Noah had pretty much left her alone. Olivia lived with Molly, though, which made things more awkward. So being the coward she was, she had made a point of getting out of the house early, heading into the city to do some Christmas shopping.

The streets had been filled with fellow shoppers and buskers, including Norwich's well-known street performer, the Puppet Man, who had been performing one of his favourite songs by the Beatles as Olivia walked by, with what looked like a blue-capped duck on his hand, and for a short while she had managed to lose herself in the festive atmosphere, though her problems had never been far away.

Rather than return home – she was still worried about facing Molly – she had stopped by to see her mum and Jamie. Elena had already been fretting about the video Olivia had been sent and had a dozen questions, wanting to know what the police were doing. Truth was, Olivia didn't know. She had given them a statement, and they knew where to find her if they needed anything else. For now, they were investigating Howard's death and would be focused on finding out who had murdered him.

The questions were annoying, but they were better than what she worried about facing at home, and she didn't want to cave and go to Noah's, so she let her mum talk her into staying for dinner.

It also gave her a chance to talk to her brother, who was the one link she had to knowing who Noah really was. Unfortunately, his answers had done nothing to reassure her. 'How did you say you met Noah again?' she had asked, trying to sound casual, as she chatted to him between him serving customers at the bar.

Luckily Jamie was preoccupied enough not to question her curiosity. 'We met in the gym,' he told her, as he pulled a pint.

That agreed with what Noah had told her and she was going to leave it at that, but another question niggled. 'Have you known him long?'

'Since earlier this year. I had seen him around, but we'd never really spoken before, then he came over and started chatting one night.' Jamie had looked up at her then, dark eyes narrowing. 'Why are you asking? Is everything okay with you two?'

'Of course. Everything's fine. I was just curious, that's all. He never talks about his family or friends much.'

'You know his family all live in Devon.'

'Yeah, I know.'

'I think he's close with his brother and sister, but from what I gather he has a bit of a love–hate relationship with his dad.'

'The authority thing. He's mentioned it. His dad was in the US Air Force, wasn't he?'

'Yeah, the colonel. I think he was pretty strict. Very religious. You know Noah. He rebelled against that every step of the way.'

'He never mentions his friends around here. He must have some.'

'I think he still sees some of his old police mates. And he's friendly with some of the other guys at the gym. We've all been out a few times. Then of course there's Dan.'

'Yes, Dan. Of course.'

Jamie didn't elaborate on whether he knew Dan's sex, so Olivia didn't comment. He must have noted her tight expression though. 'He's a good guy, Livvy. He won't dick you around like Toby did.'

'I know.' She had smiled to keep her brother happy, but still the questions niggled. She had thought Jamie and Noah had known each other longer than a few months. The fact that Noah had walked himself into Jamie's life, the same as he had hers, bothered her more than she cared to admit.

Molly had messaged while she waited for her mum to serve dinner, worried and wanting to know where she was, and Olivia had felt a surge of panic and guilt, quickly firing back an apologetic message saying she wouldn't be home until late and asking her to feed Luna.

She had hoped Molly would be in bed when she returned that night, as it was almost midnight, but her lodger was on the sofa, drinking wine and watching TV, and she had looked up suspiciously when Olivia walked in the house. 'Everything okay?'

'Everything's fine. Thanks for feeding Luna. I'm beat, so I'm gonna go straight up to bed.'

She started to walk away, tensing when Molly spoke. 'Are you sure everything's okay? You're acting really strange.'

'Honestly, I'm fine. Just tired and worried about everything. I have work tomorrow, but we'll catch up in the evening, okay?'

'Okay, sure.' Molly shrugged, turning back to the TV. 'Night.'

Olivia slept restlessly, guilt and worry fuelling her dreams.

Molly wasn't acting like she had done anything wrong. Had Olivia overreacted to what had happened? And the whole Noah thing was starting to bug her. He had tried to call her when she was driving home and she had sent him a message before going to sleep, but he hadn't replied.

She needed to clear the air with Molly and she needed to talk to Noah. She was back at work in the morning though and would no doubt have to face Roger's wrath for skipping work on Friday. Yet another stress to add to her list. Molly and Noah were both going to have to wait if she wanted to keep her job.

* * *

She was exhausted when her alarm went off on Monday morning and, after a night of tossing and turning, wondered how the hell she was going to make it through a full day of work. Glancing at her phone, she was a little unsettled that Noah still hadn't replied to her message.

He had got into the habit of messaging or calling her most mornings and the fact he hadn't replied to her had her worrying a little. She was tempted to call him, but told herself off, resisting the urge to pick up her phone.

This was good. He was giving her some much-needed space, so why was it bothering her so much that she hadn't heard from him?

She managed to get ready and out of the house with little interaction with Molly, who was in the kitchen when she came down the stairs. Olivia shouted her goodbyes from the hallway and let herself out of the house, stopping off at Costa for a coffee and croissant, before heading to the office.

To her dismay, Jeremy was the only one already there, greeting her with a slimy smirk as she took off her coat. She still had twenty minutes before the office opened and had hoped to eat her breakfast in peace.

'Nice of you to grace us with your presence today, Blake.'

'Oh, did you miss me, Jez?' She settled down at her desk, pleased that her use of his abbreviated name brought a scowl to his face.

'Well, I can't say you not being here made any difference to the sales,' he told her nastily.

Olivia ignored him, unwrapping her croissant and taking a bite, as she waited for her computer to fire up.

'You're in Roger's bad books you know,' he told her when she didn't react, sidling over and planting his bum on the edge of her desk. He picked up one of her pens, started clicking the end. 'He was pissed off that you didn't show up for work on Friday.'

'He knows why I wasn't in.'

'Yes, your boyfriend called and explained. Have to say that was a surprise, you having a boyfriend, Blake. He must have the patience of a saint.'

Olivia's temper rose a notch. Normally she would fire back a smart remark, but her head was pounding from lack of sleep and she wasn't in the mood for Jeremy, the suffocating smell of whatever aftershave he had showered in, or that bloody clicking pen.

'Look, do you actually want something or did you just come over here to insult me?' she snapped. 'Because I had hoped to eat my breakfast in peace.'

'Ooh, tetchy.'

'No, just tired and not in the mood for your shit today.' She was biting, but couldn't help it, and she could tell he was loving it from the grin on his face.

'Bad attitude for a Monday morning, Blake. I can see you're gonna work your way right into Roger's good books.'

Olivia made a grab for the pen, clutching at thin air when he held it out of her reach, that shit-eating grin widening.

'Look, just piss off, okay.'

'What, or you'll set me on fire like your other friends?'

There was a moment of stunned silence as she stared at him, his pale eyes were challenging, a snide smile on his thin lips. Olivia was incredulous, barely able to believe his nerve. 'You low-life son of a bitch. You have no idea.'

'It's true though, isn't it? Those men are dead because of you.'

'Just fuck off, Jeremy. Seriously, just fuck off.' Although she snarled the words, her tone was louder than intended.

'Everything okay here?' Roger stood in the doorway, a scowl on his face.

'Fine,' Olivia and Jeremy both muttered at the same time. Thankfully Jeremy got up from her desk, sauntering back to his own side of the office, giving her a taunting smile as he sat down at his monitor.

'Olivia, nice of you to join us today.' There was nothing nice about Roger's tone, which was downright sarcastic. The look he levelled her was a warning that she was testing his patience.

Olivia didn't try to justify her reasons for being off on Friday. Roger already knew and she didn't want to talk about what had happened in front of Jeremy. Keeping her head down she logged into the server and entered her password, trying to be discreet as she finished eating her breakfast.

Roger had managed to find another old database he wanted sorting through and, although the work was mind-numbingly boring, she threw herself into the task with as much enthusiasm as possible, aware she was on thin ice.

She had her head down and was focused on her work, so didn't hear

Noah enter the office, wasn't aware he was there until he dropped down into the chair facing her desk.

'Can I help you?' That was from Jeremy, who had assumed he was a customer.

Olivia glanced up in surprise, panic quickly taking over when she saw Roger looking in her direction, a frown on his face. 'What are you doing here?' she hissed. 'I'm working.'

'We need to talk.'

'I can't now. Can't it wait until lunch?'

'No, we need to talk now.'

'Well I...'

She trailed off as Roger approached her desk. 'Is everything okay here, Olivia?' He didn't look happy.

Noah rose to his feet, eyes not leaving Roger's face as he offered his hand. 'Noah Keen. We spoke Friday morning.'

'Oh yes, Mr Keen.' Roger shook Noah's hand. 'Is there a problem?'

'I need to borrow Olivia.' When Roger frowned, he added, 'Ten minutes. It's important.'

Roger wasn't happy, but he didn't argue. 'Go,' he snapped at Olivia. 'Ten minutes, though.'

Olivia wanted to protest, but Noah's expression was grim and it occurred to her that something might really be wrong. Her heart started to thud as she grabbed her coat and followed him out of the office, ignoring the stares of Jeremy and Esther.

'What the hell's going on?' she demanded as soon as they were outside.

He took her arm, walked with her a few feet, leading her off the narrow pavement and away from the pedestrians. There was an empty bench set back from the street and he guided her to it, sitting down beside her and taking her hands.

'Noah, you're scaring me. What the hell's going on?'

'Janice Plum was attacked last night. Someone set her on fire. She's in intensive care.'

'What? How do you know that?'

'One of my old police mates. Did anything happen last night? Any phone calls? Any videos or notes?'

'No, nothing. I would have told you.'

First Gary, then Howard and now Janice. This was real, someone was really targeting them all. Despite the notes, the video and the phone calls, part of her had been in denial, believing that what had happened to Howard and Gary was perhaps a coincidence. But not any more. Twice was stretching it. Three times was too much.

Her legs were trembling and she was glad she was sitting down. 'Is Janice– is she going to be okay?'

'It's too soon to say. She's in the best place, and she is the best chance the police have of identifying who is doing this.'

Olivia thought back to Gary, chained to the kitchen chair, and Howard burning alive on the video she had been sent. There was no way either of them would have survived what had happened to them.

'Why did he leave Janice alive?'

'The community centre caretaker happened to be driving past and saw lights on. He went to investigate, found Janice on fire, and reacted quick enough to douse the flames. Her attacker must have heard him coming and fled the scene.'

God, the poor woman. Olivia had never liked Janice, but she would never wish harm on her.

Noah rubbed his hand up and down her arm. 'Are you okay?'

Shocked, scared. Olivia didn't say either of those words, though. She just nodded numbly. 'It's a lot to take in.'

'I know. The police will want to talk to you again. They will probably call you, but I didn't want to risk them showing up and catching you by surprise or you seeing it on the news later, and I didn't want to tell you over the phone.'

'I appreciate that.' She honestly did. Wasn't sure how she might have reacted if she had heard the news from Jeremy or if the police had arrived unexpectedly.

'I need to go back to work.'

'You sure you're up to that?'

'I don't really have a choice. I'm already in the doghouse with Roger for taking Friday off.'

'I'll talk to him.'

'No don't, please. You'll just make this worse.'

Noah huffed out a sigh. 'You know, your boss is a bit of dick, Liv. Do you really like working there?'

'No,' she admitted. 'But now's not the time for a change.' She managed a small smile. 'Maybe when this is over I can look for something else. Right now though, I need this job to pay the bills. Which means I do have to go back.'

'Come and stay with me tonight.'

She had promised herself she would be strong, take a step back from Noah until she had sorted her head out, but there he was sitting in front of her being all kind and thoughtful, and looking so damned good while being kind and thoughtful, that, had her head not been reeling with the shocking revelation about Janice, she would have wanted to jump all over him. He messed with her head and she couldn't think straight when he was around. He made niggling little alarm bells seem like they were not such a big deal.

'I can't. I promised Molly we would spend some time together tonight.'

'You spent Saturday night with Molly.'

'I know, but...' She debated telling Noah what had happened. 'Molly and I need to have a chat.'

His eyes narrowed at that. 'Why, did something happen?'

Would he think she had overreacted? Olivia realised she did need a second opinion on this. 'Okay, I don't want you to laugh because this is really embarrassing.' Her cheeks were already flaming. 'I think she hit on me.'

Noah's green eyes widened, but he remained straight-faced. 'You think?'

'Saturday night. We'd both had a few drinks and as I went to go up to bed she gave me a hug.' God, it was mortifying saying this out loud. 'Well... It started out as a hug, but then was a little bit more than that.'

When Noah stared at her, not speaking, she elaborated. 'She caressed my bum.'

His lips twitched at that and, when Olivia slapped him on the arm, annoyed at his reaction, he burst out laughing.

'Damn it, it's not funny. I've been avoiding her ever since.'

'All the more reason then why you should come and spend the night with me.'

'I need to talk to her, Noah. We live together and it's really uncomfortable.'

Plus of course she needed more time to sort out what to do about Noah and his secrets. Now wasn't the time for that conversation and she had to get back to work, but she knew if she stayed the night in his bed, she wouldn't be able to think objectively about him.

'Okay,' he agreed. 'But I'm going to meet you here after work and walk you down to your car then follow you home.'

When Olivia opened her mouth to argue that it was unnecessary, he pressed his finger against her lips. 'No arguments. I won't stay and I won't pressure you to stay with me, but I need to know you're safe. Okay?'

It was a compromise she could live with, and she would feel safer having him with her when she walked down to get her car. 'Okay.'

38

Killing Janice was supposed to be easy.

It had started out that way. I didn't even have to subdue her. The silly bitch passed out in shock when she realised I was behind her. Hauling her considerable weight into a chair had been more of a problem and I was doing that when I saw the flash of headlights and heard the car outside.

The plan had to be adjusted, petrol doused, the match lit. I couldn't leave her alive. To keep things on track, she needed to die.

She was still out cold. Didn't flinch as the liquid trickled over her. She only reacted when the flames caught hold, anguished screams crying out as the fire melted her flesh.

I had wanted to wait, make sure the job was finished, but there had been no time. The handle already turning on the door I had broken earlier. Instead, I fled for the window and I was outside before anyone entered the room.

I am safe now, no one saw me, and that is the priority. I need to be safe because I have to finish this. But I am frustrated. Last night didn't go to plan.

Janice never repented for her sins. She never knew why she was being punished. And Olivia was supposed to see. But I have no video, no photo, not even a recording of Janice's screams.

I only had one chance to kill Janice and last night I failed.

Of course, I only realised quite how badly I had failed when I heard the news today, learned that Janice Plum hadn't actually died. She is in a critical condition in hospital.

It is okay in that, if she ever wakes, she won't be able to identify me. The mask has taken care of that, but how am I supposed to kill her now?

She has to die or the sequence will be messed up, but she will be in hospital under secure protection. I have missed my opportunity with her and can only hope that her injuries are so severe she won't survive.

Frustration burns. I haven't had closure with Janice. I have let you down.

That is the bit that stings the most. After everything that happened to you, the awful way your life ended, this was my chance to put things right and settle the score.

It was fate that I learnt the truth about what really happened that night and it was fate that put me on this path... but it will be karma that ends this.

The guilty have to pay and I cannot afford to lose sight of the final goal. There are two left to be punished. The instigators, the ringleaders. The final two are the reason you died.

Their time is almost here.

Soon.

39

The first Fern knew of the attack on Janice was when she was contacted by the police on Monday afternoon.

She had been trying to get hold of Janice, calling when she didn't receive replies to the message she had sent late last night or the two angry ones she had sent earlier that morning. When she learnt what had happened, and that her old friend was in the hospital and might not survive her injuries, Fern's first thought was, *'Have I said anything incriminating in my messages to Janice?'*

If she had, the officer didn't make comment, though she did want to know when Fern had last seen Janice. Then she confirmed that Fern had known both Gary Lamb and Howard Peck, and said another officer would be in touch with some follow-up questions.

Now Fern was really panicking. Not only was some psycho bumping off her friends, the police thought she might be involved.

She toyed with confessing all, admitting what had happened all those years ago and hoping that the police would take a sympathetic view, and offer her protection.

It was so risky, though. What if they decided to press charges against her? With Gary, Howard, Rachel, and Kelly all dead, and Janice on her way to joining them, Fern would have to stand trial alone.

She couldn't bear the thought of that.

What had happened had been an accident, and yes, okay, her actions may have led to that accident, but it was not her fault.

It didn't help that Olivia Blake's boyfriend was still snooping around, either. He had sent Fern a couple of messages over the past few days, both of which she had ignored, but she knew she couldn't avoid him forever. Noah Keen had struck her as the persistent type and she was surprised he hadn't yet turned up unannounced and demanding answers. He had said in the messages that they needed to talk again, which had her fearful. Had he found something out or was he still digging?

There was simply one solution.

She needed to get away.

When Janice had suggested the idea of fleeing, Fern had scorned her, but now, she was the last one left. Well, apart from Olivia, and Fern wasn't too sure she believed Olivia's bullshit story that she too was being targeted. No, Fern was now the sole survivor. She was the only one now who really knew what had happened that night, and she was the only one left to target.

She had to disappear somewhere where the killer wouldn't find her, away from her tormentor, away from the police, away from overly inquisitive Noah Keen and bloody Olivia Blake, who had kick-started all of this, by stubbornly befriending Margaret Grimes, just to piss Fern off. It was Olivia's fault all of this was happening. Not Fern's.

She would have to start over, but was she really leaving that much behind? A mum and a sister, neither of whom she was close to, and who probably wouldn't even miss her, a boss who had broken her heart and been avoiding her, his regret at sleeping with Fern written all over his face. She didn't really have many friends. Okay, there was Meg, and maybe Fern could confide in her, perhaps even let Meg have her location once she knew she was safe.

She spent the rest of Monday afternoon using her work PC to Google potential destinations. The office was already winding down for Christmas and the rest of her team were busy stuffing their faces with festive buffet snacks and getting excited about swapping their stupid Secret Santa gifts.

Fern switched off from them, not interested in their inane banter, as she tried to figure out where she could go. Abroad was too tricky and would be far too easy to trace, but she could get a room in a guesthouse somewhere until she figured out a longer-term plan.

Coming up with a shortlist of potential destinations, she scribbled them down, careful to wipe the search history from her PC before logging off.

Tomorrow she would call in sick, use the time to close her bank account and draw the balance out in cash. It would be easier that way. No one would be able to trace her. She would need to ditch her phone too, trade it in for a cheaper pay-as-you-go model.

There was so much to think about, and she knew she would have to leave a lot of stuff behind.

It was the only way she could be sure of being safe, though.

She would visit the bank and get a new mobile phone tomorrow, pack what she needed, then hopefully she could be out of Norwich no later than Tuesday afternoon.

* * *

Noah had spoken with Martin Plum at the hospital, while the man was waiting on news of his wife. His methods had been a little unethical, pretending to be a worried fiancé, whose wife-to-be had been involved in a car accident, but needs must.

Striking up conversation with the man who seemed relieved to have someone else who could relate to what he was going through had been easy, and Noah had left him half an hour later with plenty of additional information about Janice and the lead-up to her attack.

Perhaps he should have felt guilt about taking advantage of Martin Plum at such a vulnerable point, but there was no time for that. If he was going to keep Olivia safe, he needed to find out who was killing her old classmates.

Janice had gone to the community centre to meet up with friends. Martin had told Noah that his wife was obsessed with Zumba and a group of them regularly worked out together. This wasn't an organised event, though. Janice's friend, Gretchen Self, had arranged the meet-up, and the women had been planning to have a bit of a pre-Christmas party with food and plenty of alcohol.

The police had spoken to Janice's friends, but none of them had known anything about the get-together. According to what Martin had been told, no one had been able to trace Gretchen either.

Back home, Noah opened up the document where he had listed the dead friends. Kelly Dearborn, Rachel Colton, Gary Lamb and Howard Peck. He added the seriously injured Janice Plum to the list, writing Gretchen Self in brackets next to Janice's name.

It bothered him that the police hadn't yet been able to track down Howard's girlfriend, Daisy Angel, or Janice's friend, Gretchen. Had the women been involved in what had happened to Howard and Janice, or were they unwitting pawns? In which case, should the police be looking for more bodies?

The Grimes family was still his main focal point.

Gerald and Marie Grimes were retired and had moved from Essex to live in the countryside of the Chiltern Hills. Gerald now spent much of his time in a wheelchair, having fallen off a ladder when he was fixing a broken roof tile, which ruled him out as a viable suspect. Marie was short and slight in build, and Noah couldn't see her being capable of overpowering two grown men. That left Margaret's sister and brother. Alice had gone on to train as a therapist, moving to the States when she was in her early twenties. There was little trace of her after that.

Malcolm, meanwhile, had stayed in Essex, working his way through a number of positions, mostly involving physical labour. He was a bit of a loner, no longer in contact with his family and had few friends, and he appeared to have completely dropped off the radar about six months ago after leaving his job working in a warehouse.

Malcolm Grimes seemed almost too convenient a suspect. He had the physical strength and he had been at Black Dog Farm when Margaret died, which suggested he had the motivation too, but was he really behind this?

Noah glanced at his watch, mindful of the time, wanted to make sure he was at Olivia's work before she left off. It was Monday 14 December, three days to the anniversary of Margaret Grimes' death. If the killer was working to an endgame, Thursday would be the crucial day.

Olivia was insisting on staying home tonight and he hadn't pushed her on that, knew she was still a little mad at him. He had given her the weekend to stew, had hoped she might have thawed by now. She was coming around, but slowly.

He knew it was because of the secrets; Dan and now the locked office door, plus of course it hadn't helped that she had overheard him on the phone. He couldn't have her find out the truth yet, not before Thursday, so he would need to find a way to win her over, persuade her to stay with him from tomorrow night so he could keep a close eye on her.

* * *

Olivia was dreading returning home Monday evening, but knew she couldn't put off having a conversation with Molly any longer.

She had gone over what she planned to say a dozen or more times in her head, figured she would have to be clear that Molly had got the wrong impression and there was nothing between them but friendship. She had agonised, worrying if she had ever encouraged Molly or done anything that could be misconstrued as leading her on, but there was nothing she could think of.

The whole scenario was just so odd. Olivia was in a relationship and, given that the pair of them had been living together for the past year, Molly had never done anything to suggest she had feelings towards her before. They had both been drinking on Saturday night. Had it really just been a spur-of-the-moment thing?

Chances were, Molly was embarrassed as hell about it as well. That's why it was important that they cleared the air and started over.

Still, she nearly chickened out, tempted to ask Noah to stay after he followed her home. He got out of his car to see her to the front door, drawing her in for a long lingering kiss that completely scrambled her brain.

'Come over tomorrow night after work. I've missed you.'

Olivia hesitated, aware that she was out of excuses to say no. At least not without voicing her concerns about his secrets again, and she wasn't ready for that conversation, not on top of the one she was already dreading having with Molly. 'Maybe.' She shrugged, non-committedly.

'No maybe. I'll cook for you.' He grazed his fingers down her cheek then back into her hair.

'You're going to cook?'

'Hey, I'm not that bad in the kitchen.'

'Really? What was the last thing you cooked?'

'I can throw a meal together,' he protested, ignoring the question. 'And now I am going to prove it to you, tomorrow night. Okay?' He tugged gently on her hair.

'Okay, though let me see how tonight goes first.'

'I would love to be a fly on the wall for this conversation.'

When his grin widened, Olivia pushed him away. 'Yes, I bet you would. Now go. I need to get this over and done with.'

'Call me if you need support. I can come over.'

'I think the last thing Molly is going to want is you in the house.'

'Well, at least now I know why she hates me. I'm competition.'

'Go.' Olivia gave him another shove, though couldn't help smiling herself.

'Message me later. I'm going to want to know details.' Noah stole another quick kiss, before backing away.

Olivia watched him get in his car, turn on the engine before unlocking the door and stepping into the lion's den.

Molly wasn't downstairs and she chided herself for feeling relief, as all she was doing was delaying the inevitable. After kicking off her shoes and hanging up her coat she went through to the kitchen and put on the kettle, was greeted by a purring Luna who had come wandering through, looking for dinner.

Olivia picked her up and gave her a cuddle, burying her nose in the cat's soft fur. As she turned around, she jumped, hadn't heard Molly come downstairs over the noise of the boiling kettle.

She stood in the doorway, dressed in her gym gear, giving Olivia a tentative smile. 'Was that Noah I heard outside?'

'Yeah, he insisted on following me home.' At Molly's raised brow, she elaborated. 'There was another fire last night.'

'Someone else was killed? Oh my God, Livvy.' Molly's eyes were wide.

'She's not dead. She's in the hospital, but I think it's pretty bad.'

Although not comfortable to talk about, the subject was easier ground to cover, given what was to come, and Olivia was relieved that for a few minutes the tensions eased as she updated Molly on what little she knew about Janice.

'Noah could have come in, you know. I'm not an ogre,' Molly eventually commented. 'I told you I would give him a chance.'

'I know that and I appreciate it, thank you.'

'So... I take it things are okay between you two now?'

'We're getting there,' Olivia lied. She was regretting blabbing to Molly on Saturday night, wishing she had kept her worries and suspicions about Noah to herself.

This was the perfect opportunity to bring up Saturday night and clear the air. She thought back over her well-rehearsed speech, as she put a pouch of food in Luna's dish, trying to pluck up courage to actually say the words.

'Is that why you've been quiet the last couple of days?' Molly asked before she had a chance to speak. 'I was beginning to worry that I had done something to upset you.'

What? Olivia took a deep breath. 'Well... I'll be honest, I have been feeling a bit weird about what happened on Saturday night.'

'About Saturday night? Why, what about it?'

'About what you... about that hug.' Olivia's cheeks flamed at Molly's confused expression.

'Livvy, what are you on about?'

'The hug.'

'Yes, you said. But why would you feel weird because I gave you a hug? That's what friends do.'

Was Molly messing with her? Did she seriously not remember? 'You grabbed my arse.'

'No I didn't.'

'Yes, you did.'

'Livvy, I'm pretty certain I would remember if I grabbed your arse.

Jesus, I know you had a couple of beers, but I didn't realise you were that pissed.'

'I wasn't pissed.' Anger was taking the edge off Olivia's embarrassment and she couldn't quite believe that Molly was denying what had happened. 'And that was not a platonic hug!'

'So what you're saying is that I hit on you?' Molly was smirking now, not seeming in the least bit uncomfortable. 'You're pretty, but I hate to disappoint you, you're also not my type. I like men.' She shook her head, laughing to herself. 'Maybe the hug you are remembering was one in your dreams.'

'I was not dreaming.'

'Well, I honestly don't know what else to say.' The smile dropped from Molly's face, replaced with a look of pity. 'Look, I don't quite know if I'm mad at you, amused, or if I just feel sorry for you.' Her voice took on a sympathetic tone. 'You've been through a lot the last couple of weeks, I get that, I really do. Have you been sleeping well? You've looked like a zombie the last few days.'

Olivia stared at her friend, lost for words. It was bad enough that Molly was denying what had happened, but what was worse, she was now actually starting to question if she had overreacted. If maybe it had just been an innocent hug after all.

'Have you thought about talking to someone?' Molly suggested gently. 'Perhaps a counsellor? It might help to talk things through. You've been under a lot of strain and sometimes the mind does play tricks. You thought there was someone in the house last week, remember? And you're convinced Noah is keeping secrets from you.'

'I don't need to talk to a counsellor.'

'Okay. Well, I'm here if you want to talk to me about anything, okay?' When Olivia simply stared at her, she added. 'And how about we put this conversation behind us, forget we ever had it.'

How was she supposed to react to that? Should she continue to dig her heels in or try and accept that maybe she was wrong? 'Okay,' Olivia agreed grudgingly. She finished making her tea and picked up her cup. 'I'm going upstairs for a shower.'

'Fine, well I'm heading out to the gym. There's chilli in the saucepan if you want some. I made plenty.'

Molly already had her back turned, heading to the front door, as Olivia murmured, 'thank you.' She remained in the kitchen for several minutes after the door shut, sipping at her tea and replaying Saturday night and then the conversation she had just had with Molly. That had not gone at all how she was expecting.

Was she really starting to go crazy? She had been convinced someone was in the house that night before she went to Noah's, but there had been no one on the security camera. And it was true, she was becoming paranoid about Noah and his secrets. Had she really imagined the incident that had happened with Molly?

Suddenly she was no longer certain of anything.

40

Fern's heart sank when she returned from the bank on Tuesday morning to find Noah Keen parked on her driveway.

Her case was packed, her handbag contained enough cash to see her through to the end of January, and she had a new mobile phone ready to go. She had messaged Meg that morning and updated her on her plan to leave town for a while. Now all that was left to do was load her car and leave. But she couldn't do that while Olivia's boyfriend was sniffing around.

For a moment she was tempted to drive past her house, give it half an hour and hope he had moved on, but he was leaning against the bonnet, arms crossed as he waited for her, and she was fairly certain he had already seen her.

As he had rudely taken over her drive with his Audi and she didn't want to block him in (God forbid she give him any reason to stay longer than necessary), she left her car parked on the street, clicking her key to lock it as she marched purposefully towards him, chin raised and heels clipping against the pavement.

'Is there a reason why you're blocking my driveway?' She scowled at him, annoyed when the insolent smirk on his face widened. He really was far too attractive for his own good. Wisps of tawny brown hair poked out from under the woolly charcoal hat he wore; the olive-green scarf wrapped around his neck highlighted the colour of his eyes; even his smirk gave him appealing dimples. And that annoyed her also.

If circumstances were different and he wasn't harassing her, she would have liked the opportunity to get to know him better.

But as it was, he was proving to be an obstacle in her mission to get away.

'If you had bothered to answer my calls and messages, I wouldn't be here.'

'I didn't answer as I have nothing to say to you, so run along. I have things to do.'

When she strode past him to the front door, key ready in her hand, he stood up from the bonnet and followed. 'That's where you're wrong. You and I have a lot to talk about.'

Fern unlocked the door, stepping into the house and wheeling on him. 'No, you're wrong. So just piss off, will you?'

'Or what? You'll call the police?'

Her heart thumped uncomfortably. He knew that wasn't an option for her. Annoyed, she attempted to slam the door in his face, irritation and fear flitting through her when he wedged his boot in the doorway and pushed his way into the hall. 'Get out of my house! I will make that call.'

Unperturbed, he shut the door behind him, following Fern into the kitchen as she made a show of pulling her phone from her bag, intending to call his bluff.

Leaning back against the counter he studied her calmly. 'We both know you're not going to call them.'

'Don't test me.'

'Okay, go ahead. Make the call.' He shrugged. 'It's no odds to me. I'm not going anywhere.' To make his point, he unzipped his jacket, loosened his scarf, and pulled the beany hat off his head, running his fingers through his dishevelled hair, before staring at her pointedly.

Fern swore under her breath, furious with him for catching her out. He was right. They both knew she wasn't going to call the police. She slipped the phone back in her bag, which she put down on the counter, not daring to look at the edge of her suitcase poking out from under the breakfast bar. 'So come on, then. What the fuck is it you want from me?'

He stared at her for a moment, the smirk turning to a look of contempt. 'The truth,' he told her, his tone dangerously soft.

'The truth about what?'

Because he was unnerving her a little, she busied her hands, reaching into the cupboard for a bottle of vodka. Her go-to in any stressful situation.

Noah watched her set it on the counter, one eyebrow raised. 'Bit early for a drink, isn't it?'

She threw him a scowl, though his comment reminded her that she had a long drive ahead. She couldn't afford to get stopped for drink-driving. Leaving the bottle where it was, she moved to the breakfast bar and leant against it, trying to discreetly move her suitcase further out of sight with her knee.

'What do you want?' she repeated. Of course she knew what he wanted. She wasn't stupid. He had said 'the truth' and she knew exactly what truth he wanted. She didn't plan on giving it to him though.

'What really happened the night of Olivia's accident, Fern? What did you do to Margaret Grimes?'

'We've already had this conversation and I told you.'

'We did, but now I want you to tell me the truth. Janice is in the hospital; Howard, Gary, Rachel, and Kelly are dead. That leaves you and it leaves Olivia. It's time to confess what really happened.'

'I said I already told you.'

'Yes, but you're lying. I want the truth.'

'I'm not lying!'

'You're testing my patience, Fern.'

'Do you think I give a shit?'

'You should. You really should.'

Fern didn't like his tone. For a moment it crossed her mind that he actually knew what had happened that night in the woods. That he just wanted her to say the words. 'What the hell is that supposed to mean?'

Those green eyes studied her intently and she couldn't help squirming a little. Saying nothing, he slowly, deliberately walked towards her, pressed his palms on the counter and leant forward until his gaze was level with hers. 'How about I call the police? Tell them you're planning on disappearing.'

'What?' Her voice came out high-pitched and more shocked than she had intended. 'What do you mean?'

'You know exactly what I mean.' He nodded down to where her case was hidden under the breakfast bar. 'Your stuff is packed. You've cleared your bank account.'

'How do you know about that?'

'I followed you.'

'You did what?' Anger bit through the panic. 'You had no fucking right to follow me anywhere! Does Olivia know what you've been doing? I know her. She would never agree to that.'

'I'm doing it for Olivia,' Noah told her coldly. 'I wonder what she would think if she knew you were skipping town. I wonder what the police would think.'

'They never said I had to stay.'

'Trust me, they are not going to be happy if you leave.' He pulled his phone out of his jacket pocket, tapped at the screen, and fear coiled in Fern's belly.

'What are you doing? You can't call them.'

'Tell me the truth then.'

'I told you—'

'No more bullshit, Fern. I can make this call and have them here before you've even left the city.'

He had neatly backed her into a corner and she realised she had nowhere left to go. 'If I tell you, you have to promise to let me leave. You can't tell the police.'

Noah seemed to consider that. Nodded. 'Okay, but no more games, no more messing around. What really happened?'

Fern drew a breath, resigned. She had planned on taking this secret to the grave. 'You have to understand, it was an accident.'

She waited for Noah to say something, but he was silent as he stepped back, resumed his position leaning against the counter, eyes still on her, watching, she suspected, for any sign of a lie.

'And Livvy, if she hadn't betrayed our friendship, if she hadn't treated me like a piece of dirt, then I would have left Margaret alone. She's as much to blame.'

A flicker of annoyance creased his brow at that, but he remained quiet, waiting for her to continue.

'They had found this house, Livvy and Margaret. Well, Howard found it first. He told me how he and Gary had been exploring it and when they came out they ran into Livvy and Margaret. We got talking and thought it would be funny to scare Margaret. There was a storage room on the farm and it was full of loads of props. Masks, cloaks, fake weapons. We just needed a way to lure her out to the cottage.'

Fern tapped her fingers nervously against the counter, wishing she had poured the vodka, the memory clear of that final night, how Rachel had fooled Olivia and Margaret into thinking she had fallen out with Fern. How a group of them had gone out to the cottage late that afternoon and hidden costumes, matches and a couple of paraffin lamps, how they had plotted how best to scare Margaret and make her pay, how funny the whole situation would be.

Rachel had talked Olivia and Margaret into going out to the cottage during the final night disco and Fern had snuck out ahead of them with Howard, Gary, Janice, and Kelly.

'Are you sure they're going to come?'

Janice was whining yet again, her words slightly muffled behind the clown mask she wore. Although she was supposed to appear scary, and probably would do to Margaret who wouldn't realise it was Janice behind the mask, she actually looked rather comical. The whining was getting irritating though and Fern rolled her eyes, almost wishing she hadn't brought her.

They had only been in the cottage fifteen minutes and so far Janice had been worried someone might find them trespassing. She had needed the loo, had been too scared to go outside and pee, had been tired, had aching legs, oh, and she had been too cold.

Fern had cursed Olivia again for her betrayal. Janice hadn't exactly been her first choice for best friend.

Howard and Kelly were fooling around upstairs, giggling and sharing jokes as they tried to spook each other, and Fern yelled up to them to shut up.

From his position in the corner by the window, Gary called through. 'I just saw a light. I think they are coming.'

Fern hissed again for silence, excitement building and overtaking her annoyance with Janice. If they managed to pull this off, it would be epic.

After a couple of minutes of silence, she heard footsteps and excited chatter. That was definitely Margaret's voice she could hear and yes, that was Rachel and Olivia too.

Across the room, Janice sniffed and shuffled her feet.

'Stay bloody still,' Fern whispered, her tone harsh. 'If you mess this up, I will never speak to you again.'

'Sorry.'

There was no more sniffing or shuffling, but Fern could still hear Janice breathing.

She bit down on her irritation.

The voices grew louder and there were crunching footsteps over stones and glass. She took a step forward, peering through the doorway, and saw a shape clambering through the window. Realising it was Margaret, she quickly stepped back again, seeing a torch flashing in her direction. Olivia was behind her and she was the one who immediately spotted the faint glow from the paraffin lamp.

And then it happened quickly. Margaret was stepping forward into the room where Fern and Janice were hiding and Gary had hold of Olivia, who let out a scream before falling silent.

As Margaret glanced back in panic, Fern and Janice ambushed her, Kelly and Gary stepping forward to join them, Rachel close behind, having put her own mask on.

For a moment Fern had wondered why Gary was there. His job had been to incapacitate Olivia and hold her back while they tormented Margaret. Why wasn't he with Livvy? What had happened to her after she screamed?

But then they had Margaret surrounded and she was turning in circles, wide-eyed, her face pale, and Fern was feeding on her fear, forgetting all about Olivia. Margaret didn't scream, seeming more stunned than anything, at least until the hood went over her head, and then her cries were muffled and panicked as between them they managed to bundle her up the stairs to where Howard and Kelly were waiting.

As they tried to restrain her she fought like a wild thing, breaking free and charging blindly around the room, the hood still on her head, tugging in panic as she tried to find the drawstring to free herself.

The accident happened so fast. One moment they were trying to grab Margaret, the next the second paraffin lamp was on the floor, flames igniting the wooden boards.

'Fuck! We need to get out.'

That was from Howard who was already hurtling down the stairs with no consideration for the others.

Fern glanced at the rapidly spreading fire, heart in mouth, as she quickly followed.

It wasn't until they were outside and the cottage was ablaze that she realised Margaret and Olivia were both unaccounted for.

It would have been foolish to go back inside. They had probably both already succumbed to the flames.

The implications of that were clear in her mind.

'We have to go. We have to get out of here.'

'What?' Kelly had ripped off her mask, looked horrified. 'They're still inside.'

'What are we supposed to do? The place is on fire. They're dead!' That was from Howard, who was trying hard to sound authoritative, but his shaky voice betrayed him.

'What happened to Olivia?' Fern turned on Gary, pointing a finger at his chest. 'You were supposed to stay with her. Make sure she didn't intervene.'

'I shoved her against the wall. I think she hit her head.'

'You what?'

'I don't like this.' Rachel was crying now, setting Janice off too, who until now had been silent. 'We have to get them out.'

'Are you thick? It's too late!'

Fern glanced at Howard. He was right. There was nothing they could do for Margaret or Olivia. It had been an accident, a terrible accident. The police might not see it that way, though. 'We need to go. We need to get out of here fast.'

'What?' That was Kelly and Rachel in unison now. They sounded appalled. 'We need to get help!' Kelly added.

'They wouldn't get here in time. There's nothing we can do and if we stay we will be in so much trouble. Seriously, we need to go.'

Howard and Gary didn't need any encouragement, already heading back down the woodland path, Janice hot on their heels, fearing she might be left behind.

Kelly and Rachel were still looking at Fern, seeming uncertain. 'So you're just going to leave them to burn?' Rachel accused.

'They're already dead!' Guilt and fear were fuelling Fern's anger now. 'You want to save them? Be my guest.' She took a step back, shook her head, before turning and racing after the others.

'You left them there to die.'

Fern wasn't sure what was worse, Noah's disgusted tone or the way he was looking at her like she was something he had just scraped off his shoe.

She had never told anyone what had happened that night, shared the secret only with those who had been there, and they had vowed to never tell a soul.

They had managed to sneak back into the farmhouse without being seen, had kept a low profile as the place became bedlam as word of the fire spread. The fire brigade tackled the blaze for most of the night and the police were there speaking with the owners.

Rachel was the only one who had stayed behind, trying vainly to get back in the cottage to help Olivia and Margaret, and she had been found wandering disorientated in the woods, covered in soot and suffering the effects of smoke inhalation, in shock from what had happened.

She was the one weak link, the one who could expose the rest of them. But Rachel never told, despite throwing daggers at Fern when she saw her briefly before being taken away in an ambulance.

Word of Margaret and Olivia had spread by breakfast. The staff were doing their best to keep a lid on the situation as they worked closely with the police and the fire brigade, but rumours were spreading quickly. Some of the students had noticed that Margaret and Olivia were absent, while others had overheard that two bodies had been pulled from the fire and quickly put two and two together, given that both girls had been seen with Rachel Williams the previous night.

It wasn't until later when she was home that Fern learnt Olivia had survived the fire, though she was in hospital and in a critical condition.

'It was a prank. A stupid, childish prank,' she spat at Noah. How dare he stand there and judge her? They had been fourteen, just kids. It could have happened to anyone.

'Margaret Grimes died. Stop calling it a prank or using your childhood as an excuse.'

'Well what do you want me to call it? Murder? Do you honestly think I wanted them to die? If I could go back in time, we would never have gone to that stupid cottage. It would never have happened. But it did. It was an accident and I feel bad that Margaret died, that Olivia was hurt. There, is that what you want me to say?'

'You felt bad for Olivia?'

'Of course I did. I'm not a monster.'

'So bad that you made her life hell when she returned to school? After everything she had been through, after what had happened to Margaret, you still continued with your spiteful pranks.'

Fern narrowed her eyes. 'What has she told you?'

'I know about the video, Fern. I know what you did to her. And yes, dress it up any way you want, you are a monster.'

'Get out of my house. We're done here.'

'Oh, we are definitely done here. But first I have one more question.' Noah pushed away from the counter, took a step towards her and she straightened, jutting out her chin. She was done with his judgemental bullshit and there was no way she was going to let him intimidate her.

'What?'

'You know what is happening now is connected to that night. You've stood by and watched someone burn your friends in revenge for what happened to Margaret. Who else might know what happened that night? Who would want to punish you?'

'I don't know. Your girlfriend has pretty good motivation, I would say.'

'Olivia didn't do this.'

'So you keep saying.'

'Where was Malcolm Grimes when you were baiting his sister? Olivia says he used to follow them everywhere. How certain are you that he wasn't there that night in the woods, that he didn't see what you did to his sister?'

Honestly? Fern had toyed with the idea of it being Margaret's creepy-arse brother, but she hadn't given it that much thought. She had worked on the basis that one of the group had blabbed and that whoever they had told had decided to punish them. Had Margaret's brother followed them that night? If so, why take so long to come after them?

'It's possible,' she conceded. 'But why would he wait until now?'

'Maybe he wanted to make sure he got everything right before he took his revenge.'

Noah smiled coldly. An odd expression passed over his face and a chill passed down Fern's spine, her spider sense tingling, warning that something wasn't quite right. He had threatened, intimidated, and tried to blackmail her, but this was the first time she had actually been scared of him.

'How did you say you and Olivia met again?'

'I didn't.'

For a moment they sized each other up. Was there something familiar in that green stare?

'I think we're done here now. I answered your questions.' Fern moved quickly, giving him a wide berth as she went into the hallway, keen to have him out of her house. Opening the door, she faked a smile at him as he followed, relieved when he simply scowled at her before leaving.

She closed the door after him, locked it, watching through the peephole as he climbed into his car and started the engine, not letting out a sigh of relief until he had pulled out of her driveway.

Was it possible he was behind all of this?

Even if he wasn't, she couldn't trust him not to call the police. She had told him what he wanted to know, but there was still too great a risk. Noah Keen was a danger to her however she looked at it. She needed to get her stuff together and leave as soon as possible. She had already picked a location, figuring she would head for Wales and the Pembrokeshire Coast.

Quickly she hauled her case out from under the breakfast bar, dragging it into the hallway, then fetched her car from off the road, moving it on to the driveway and loading the boot.

Back in the kitchen she filled a canvas shopping bag with a few non-perishable items and the bottle of vodka, then poked her head in the fridge, debating on what might survive the journey.

Hearing a noise behind her, she started to turn and caught a glimpse of a familiar figure just a second before something smacked her hard across the face and her world turned black.

41

Dinner was steak, tomatoes, and mushrooms, served with chips that Olivia suspected might have come from a bag in the freezer.

Un-fuck-up-able, and not quite what she would call cooking, but to give Noah credit the food was good, and he had tried to make an effort, low lighting, slow and sexy old-school mood music playing, and he had bought her favourite red wine... which had scuppered her plans to drive home. She had planned to use the excuse of needing a good night's sleep, telling him she had been awake much of the night. What she didn't tell him was that she hadn't slept great because she was starting to doubt herself, worrying if she was slowly losing her mind.

She wondered if Noah suspected she might try to get out of staying, which was why he had pulled his sneaky wine trick. Truth was, she was reluctant to sleep with him again until she knew whether she could trust him, knew that once she was in his bed, she wouldn't be able to think straight. He had weakened her defences with the long lingering kiss he had given her in the kitchen before pouring her the wine, pushing her up against the counter with his body, hands in her hair, then roaming down her back and over her bum, while he used that talented mouth of his to distract her.

She had needed the wine after that kiss, and drank the first glass too quickly, while convincing herself that maybe his secrets weren't that bad after all. Which is how she found herself flat on her back on his sofa a couple of hours later with most of her clothes on the floor.

'I wasn't going to stay tonight,' she protested, her lips swollen from rough stubbly kisses. She arched her back, sucked in a breath as he trailed more kisses down her neck, her resolve weakening further.

'Hmm, but you've had too much wine to drive and you're already mostly undressed,' he reminded her, breath warm against her ear as he unhooked her bra, easing her out of it. 'You're better off here.'

'I didn't sleep well last night.'

'Well, you've been through a lot this last couple of weeks.'

'It wasn't that.'

'So what was it then? Molly?'

When she tensed beneath him, Noah raised his head, his sharp green gaze studying her. 'I thought you said you resolved things?'

That was what Olivia had told him, terrified to reveal what had really happened, in case he told her he agreed with Molly, that maybe she was losing her mind, because the truth was she no longer trusted herself to know what was real and what wasn't. So she had glossed over it, telling Noah that Molly hadn't even realised what she was doing, and that she had been mortified when confronted, confirming, 'We did resolve things, kind of.'

'Kind of?'

'We're good. Honestly.' She hooked her arms around his neck, pulling him closer and distracting him with a kiss.

Tonight she decided she would forget her problems, stop worrying about her sanity and the secrets he was keeping from her, and just feel. Tonight she would take what he was offering and pretend for just a few short hours that everything was okay.

* * *

It was just gone four in the morning when she awoke, taking a moment to realise she was in Noah's bed and not her own. Noah was sound asleep, rolled away from her, all messy hair and broad shoulders, with one arm wrapped around the pillow his face was buried in.

Olivia listened to his steady breathing for a few minutes, reminding herself it wasn't a good idea to fall for a man with secrets, yet knowing it was too late. She was already halfway in love with Noah Keen.

Thirsty and needing to pee, she eased back the duvet and crept from the bed into the bathroom, careful not to disturb him. The house was silent except for her and after using the loo, she snuck back into the bedroom, grabbed Noah's discarded T-shirt from the floor and slipped it on. She watched him sleeping for a moment. Her movements hadn't disturbed him and he was dead to the world.

What she would give for such a restful night's sleep. The middle of the night pee and drink thing was becoming the norm for her.

Tiptoeing from the room, she pulled the door closed and went downstairs.

Her mouth was parched – her own fault for drinking too much wine – and she found a tumbler in the kitchen cupboard, filled it with tap water, drinking greedily. As she rinsed it out and set it down on the drainer, her attention was drawn to the countertop, where Noah's keys sat, next to the microwave, the small silver key to his office slightly set apart from the others on the ring, almost glinting at her as if it was taunting her.

Olivia chided herself that her first thought was of snooping in the locked room. She knew she couldn't do that. It would be an awful betrayal of trust.

She hated that Noah had secrets and that he insisted on keeping the room locked, but it was up to him to share them with her. That was just the way it had to be. With one last look at the keys, she turned off the light, started to head back down the hallway to the stairs.

She hesitated as she reached the locked office and glanced up the dark stairs. Noah was sound asleep; his office and whatever he was hiding in there from her was driving a wedge between them. She could have a quick look inside and he would never know. No harm would be done.

Curiosity wrestled with guilt. It was wrong, but she wouldn't sleep for the rest of the night knowing she had missed this opportunity. Tomorrow, she would kick herself for not taking the chance.

* * *

The catch of the lock clicking as the key turned cut through the silence, and Olivia caught her breath, waiting for any noise or movement from upstairs. If Noah heard her, if he found her snooping through his things, she would have no defence.

She questioned again if she was really going to do this, knew, though, that she had to find out why he kept the office door locked. Yes, she was betraying his trust, but if their relationship was to survive, she had to know why he was keeping secrets.

Carefully she eased the door open, her heart thumping as she stepped inside and softly closed it behind her. In the darkness her fingers felt for the light switch, casting light on the small room.

She recognised the desk, the Mac, the bookcase and the filing cabinets from when he had briefly shown her the room, before hurrying her out again, but this time she was able to take it all in, from the titles on the bookshelf to the wide corkboard that took up part of the door wall and was covered in Post-it notes.

Her attention was drawn to two photographs tacked to the board. One was of a group of people. Olivia recognised Noah in the picture. There were four other people, two male, two female, and she suspected it was probably his family. Curious she studied the older couple, could see where Noah had his father's height and build, though he looked more like his mother. The younger couple she assumed were his brother and sister. They all had the same tawny brown hair. His brother was portlier, but his sister shared the same wide, crooked grin.

The other photo was of Olivia. She recognised this one, knew he had taken it of her a few weeks before they got together, when they were still in the friend zone. They had been walking down by the river and he had caught her off guard, snapping a couple of pictures of her feeding the swans. The shot he had pinned on the board was when she had just realised he was taking her picture, surprised, a little embarrassed, but grinning at him, caught in the split second before she tried to look away.

She remembered at the time wondering why he would want her

picture, part of her secretly romanticising and hoping that he had done it because he liked her.

Seeing the photo pinned to his board, her heart swelled and a fresh wave of guilt burned through her. She shouldn't be in here. It was wrong.

She was about to take heed of her guilty conscience, when one of the Post-it notes caught her attention.

Two names. Hers in capital letters and underlined, then underneath, Adam Somerville, a mobile number, and a date, 28/03.

Why was her name written on the note and who was Adam Somerville? More worrying though, why did Noah have her name written on a Post-it note that was dated several weeks before she had actually met him?

She tried to give him the benefit of the doubt. Maybe it wasn't a date or if it was, perhaps it was relevant to something else, but a quick glance at the other Post-it notes showed dates on all of them.

How did Noah Keen know who she was before he had actually met her?

She thought back to that day in the restaurant when she had met him. He had never given any indication that he knew of her. No, she remembered quite clearly, she had spotted him walking through the door behind Jamie, laughing at something her brother had said, and he had glanced in her direction with that sharp green gaze, his crooked smile widening to a grin as he winked at her, and stupid as it sounds, she had been flustered and shy, her legs like jelly and butterflies nervously fluttering in her belly. When Jamie had introduced them, Noah had feigned surprise that they were brother and sister and she had been excited then secretly flattered when he kept showing up unexpectedly after that first encounter, always interested in what she had to say, seeming to want to get to know her better.

Had it all been fake?

She had showed him her scars, shared with him her past, told him things she trusted very few people to know, and she had slept with him, falling so hard for his bullshit.

For a moment she struggled to breathe, sickness swirling in her gut as she tried to process the betrayal, tried desperately to think of a way to prove she was wrong, that he hadn't used her.

Turning her back on the board, she tried the desk drawers. They weren't locked. She guessed if no one could get in the office in the first place, there was no need to worry about locking the furniture inside.

Not that there was anything worth hiding in there.

She turned her attention to the filing cabinet, pulling open the top drawer. The hanging files were alphabetised, each with a name, and she flicked through them, knowing before she came to it that her name was going to be in there.

There it was. Blake, Olivia. Was this what their relationship came down to, a formal file?

She plucked it out with shaking fingers, sat down on his office chair and closed her eyes for a moment as she readied herself, aware that this was going to be the death knell on their relationship.

Tentatively she opened the file.

* * *

She got dressed before waking him. Her clothes were all still strewn on the lounge floor, which made it easy. It had only been a few hours since he had slowly stripped her naked, fucking her on his sofa, then later carrying her up to his bed where they had fucked again before falling asleep, but it felt longer.

It made it easier to think of it as simple fucking, even though at the time it had felt more than that. Feelings hadn't been involved. At least they hadn't been on Noah's side. He had been using her. She understood that now.

Part of her, the cowardly part, wanted to leave without saying anything. He had hurt her, betrayed her, and broken her stupid pathetic heart. She should never have been foolish enough to believe that someone like him would fall for someone like her.

Kudos to him though, he had taken his work seriously, and she couldn't help wondering if he slept with all of the women he investigated. He had been so cool, so laid-back about her scars. Had he known about them already?

Olivia hadn't found anything in the file to indicate he knew about the fire and she recalled that brief moment of surprise when she had shown her scars to him, so perhaps not. She had been so relieved when he didn't reject her, having no idea that she was just a job to him and that he had probably had to suck up his revulsion.

It was easier to think that way, let the anger stamp over the hurt and the humiliation, and it was the anger that carried her up the stairs and into his bedroom.

She wasn't quiet this time, flipping on the light then marching round the bed to yank up the blind, pushing open the window, and letting a blast of cool air into the room, as he grunted and swore, not looking happy at being abruptly woken up.

'What the fuck, Liv?' He blinked at her as his eyes adjusted, a frown on his face. 'Why are you dressed? It's the middle of the night.'

'Who's Adam Somerville?'

'What?'

'Who the hell is Adam Somerville, Noah, and why did he want you to investigate me?'

He actually had the good grace to look sheepish for a moment. 'I can explain.'

'Really? You can explain? How are you going to explain all of this?'

She hurled the file at him, saw his expression darken as he realised what it was.

'You broke into my office?' He looked so annoyed that for a moment Olivia felt guilty. She quickly stamped that down though, reminded herself that her wrong was nothing in comparison to what he had done.

'You used me. You lied to me. You betrayed me. Thank God I did break into your office. At least now I know it was never real, that I was only ever a job to you.'

'That's not true.'

She took a step away from him as he got out of bed and found his jeans, hopping into them.

'Look, you need to calm down. Just sit down and I will explain everything.'

'What? Tell me more lies you mean? You were investigating me? Everything that's happened between us, it was all bullshit. I trusted you. I believed it was real. You tricked me into thinking I really mattered.' Her voice cracked on the last word and she sucked in a deep shaky breath. She would not get upset in front of him, she would not show him how much she cared. Anger was better and she would hold on to that.

'I never tricked you. It was real. It *is* real. You do matter to me.'

'Stop lying to me!' She held up her hand towards the window and Noah's eyes widened as he realised she had his keys.

'Liv, give those here.'

'Or what?' She arched her eyebrows, gave him a challenging stare as rage simmered through her veins, desperately wanting to hurt him and get him back for what he had done. 'What are you going to do, Noah?'

'Give me my keys!'

He moved suddenly and she sidestepped him, hurled the keys as far out of the window as she could before making her escape over the bed, just out of his reach.

'For fuck's sake, Liv!'

The keys only distracted him for a brief second then he was after her, charging down the stairs. She had pre-empted him. The front door was already ajar and her car unlocked with the keys in the ignition.

As she ran down the front step towards her car, she was aware of him gaining, heard him swear as the front door slammed shut behind him. She felt a flicker of satisfaction as she realised he had locked himself out.

His fingers brushed the car door as she slammed it shut, locking herself inside.

As she started the engine, he dropped down against the driver side window, and she stared straight ahead, chin jutted out, refusing to look at him.

'I know you don't believe me, but I never faked anything with you. Yes, it started as a job, but then I got to know you. I quit the job, Liv. I quit it because I was falling in love with you. I know you don't believe that, but it's the truth.'

He sounded convincing, but she now knew that it was just an act. All the lies he had told her, she had gullibly fallen for every single one, but not any more. She was done with his bullshit.

Blinking back the tears that kept threatening to fall, she floored the accelerator and pulled off the drive, aware he had chased into the street after her, but refusing to look back.

42

It had taken over forty minutes to locate his keys. Barefoot and dressed only in his jeans – hardly ideal clothing for a cold December early morning – and without his mobile phone, Noah had been forced to ask for help from his neighbour.

He had lived next door to Suzie Arnold for the last couple of years, knew she had a soft spot for him that he played on now and again. As she ushered him inside, she hadn't seemed at all put out that it was not yet five in the morning, insisting on making him tea that was too weak and too milky, and fussing around him while he called Daniella, relieved she had a number he had been able to memorise.

While he waited for his partner to arrive with his spare key, he learnt that Suzie had been curtain twitching, that she thought he could do better than a 'haughty madam' like Olivia, and that she had recently 'dipped her toe' back into the dating world, registering with a number of online sites.

Noah had declined the offer to see her profile pictures, not liking the way she kept blatantly staring at his chest.

Thankfully Daniella hadn't kept him waiting and, having endured death stares from Suzie for relieving her from her caretaking duties, she had let Noah back into his house, chuckling to herself about how Suzie must have thought all of her birthdays had come at once when he had knocked on her door.

As Noah went into his office and slammed the filing cabinet drawer shut, she lingered in the doorway.

'You might as well say it, Dan. I know you are desperate to.'

'Well.' She stepped into the room, dropped into his office chair, and swung around to face him. 'I did warn you this would happen.'

'I was going to tell her.'

'So why didn't you?'

'Because of this... exactly this. Tomorrow is the anniversary. I need to keep her safe. I swear I was going to tell her after.'

'Well, that's gone tits up, so what's your plan now?'

'I don't know.' Noah scrubbed his hands over his face. He had feared this would happen, couldn't believe he had been stupid enough to leave his keys out. Now Olivia hated him, no longer trusted him, and that gave him zero chance of keeping an eye on her, of making sure she was safe.

Skulking upstairs he finished dressing, then torch in hand he went outside, Daniella hot on his heels, to find his keys.

While he appreciated her bailing him out, he was tired and irritable, and not in the mood for her perkiness and smug 'told you so' attitude this early in the morning.

'You would be best to wait until daylight rather than hunting around in the dark,' she pointed out from the sidelines as he rooted through an overgrown border.

'Actually, what would be best is if you could perhaps give me a hand looking for my keys, instead of just standing there dishing out advice.'

'Ooh, you're all about using up the favours this morning, aren't you?' Although she grumbled, it was good-natured, and she pulled out her phone, using the torch, to help him look. 'You owe me breakfast after this.'

Noah grunted a non-committal response. Breakfast would have to wait. His only focus was on finding the keys and getting over to Olivia's to fix the mess he had created.

'You're planning on going after her, aren't you?'

Add 'mind reader' to Daniella's list of annoying talents.

When he didn't respond, moving on from the border he had been searching in and casting his torch beam further down the garden, she took that as a yes. 'You need to let her cool down, Noah. There's no way you're going to resolve anything while she is still worked up.'

'There isn't time to let her cool down.'

'She won't talk to you. It's too soon.'

'Just keep your nose out, Dan. I can handle it myself.'

'Of course. Because you're doing a great job of handling things so far.'

Noah ignored her sarcastic comment and they worked in silence for a while as he brooded over what had happened and tried to figure out how the hell he was going to resolve everything.

His brooding was eventually interrupted as Daniella triumphantly snatched up the keys. 'Now you definitely owe me breakfast.'

When he went to grab them from her, she held them out of his reach. 'Promise me, Noah, you're not going to drive over there. You need to leave things, let her simmer.'

'Give me the keys, Dan.'

'Look, at least give her a few hours. I know you're worried about her, but she'll be going to work in a couple of hours. While she's there she's safe and she will also have time to process what happened. Go meet her after she has finished. Hopefully she might have calmed down a bit and be ready to listen to what you have to say.'

It annoyed him that she was right. Olivia hadn't been interested in listening to him as she was running out of the house. He needed to wait until she had blown off some steam.

Grudgingly he agreed to Daniella's suggestion. 'Okay. I'm not cooking you breakfast though.'

'Hell no. You need to thank me, not punish me. I'll put the kettle on while you go clean up, then you're taking me out to eat.'

She had done it to make sure he kept his word, sticking with him (and annoying the hell out of him in the process) until he had calmed down, aware that if she turned her back on him, he would probably go straight to Olivia. She had been right to do so.

He bought her breakfast, knew he owed her, and over two plates of full English she rationalised with him, helped him come up with a practical approach to win Olivia back, then went over the details he had learnt from Fern, their former colleagues in the police, and trusty Google.

'Fern St Clair is key to this. She was the ringleader and whoever is doing this knows that. That's why she is being left till last.'

'Along with Liv,' Noah pointed out, sipping at his second cup of coffee, the caffeine finally kicking in and helping him feel more alert. 'That's the bit that still doesn't make sense. She was Margaret's friend, so why is she being targeted?'

'That's what we need to figure out. It would help if we could talk to Janice's friend, the one who messaged her about the Zumba night, find out what happened.'

'Good luck with that. No one can find her.'

'What did you say her name was?'

'Gretchen Self.'

Daniella was silent for a moment and Noah could see her mind buzzing.

'You said that Fern had a case packed, that she was planning on leaving.'

'What about it?'

'Did she say when?'

'Imminently, I guess. Why?'

Daniella nodded. 'I think we need to speak with her again. Let's see if we can catch her before she leaves.'

* * *

Olivia had tried her best to be quiet when she arrived home, creeping into the house and softly closing the door, but she had still managed to wake Molly. Her lodger had appeared at the top of the stairs in her pyjamas, her sleep-heavy eyes quickly widening when she realised things were wrong.

'Livvy, it's the middle of the night. What's going on?'

Olivia had promised herself that she wouldn't cry, knew Noah didn't deserve her tears, but the anger and the harsh realisation of what he had done to her, made it impossible to hold them back.

She wished she had punched him before she had left wanting him to hurt as much as she was hurting now and cursing herself for being foolish enough to fall for all of his lies.

'Livvy, what the hell is wrong?' Molly had rushed down the stairs, quick to console, their earlier fight forgotten as the truth had come spilling out.

'He was investigating you?' She sounded horrified. 'I thought he ran a security business?'

'So did I. Apparently that is just part of what he does.' Olivia's tone was sarcastic, anger rising again as she recalled seeing the stack of business cards in his office, the words 'Private Investigator' clearly typed under his name.

'But why you? Have you done something that I don't know about? Who would be hiring him?'

'Someone called Adam Somerville. His name was on the Post-it note and in the file.'

'Adam Somerville?' Molly repeated slowly. 'Do you know who he is and why he would be wanting you investigated?'

'No.'

Olivia was kicking herself. She should have brought that file home with her. She had only read the first few pages, enough to see all the notes Noah was keeping on her, the photographs he had taken as he followed her. Then the red mist had taken over, fuelling her rage. When she had taken the file upstairs to confront him, she hadn't planned on throwing it at him. If she still had it, it may have offered more clues as to why Adam Somerville had hired him. Certainly, it would have given her the man's contact details. At the very least she should have jotted down his mobile number.

She was such an idiot, acting without clearly thinking things through. She could see Molly's mind working overtime. 'What are you thinking?'

'Those cameras he fitted. He couldn't wait for an excuse to install them. Do you think he has been watching you, us?'

Olivia hadn't thought about that, but Molly was right. If Noah had been following her, taking photos, he had almost certainly put the cameras up to keep tabs on her. She had believed he had done it to protect her, to keep her safe, but no, the truth of his betrayal was becoming worse by the second.

Backhanding away tears she got up from the sofa and went through to the kitchen, Molly close behind. 'Livvy, what are you doing?'

Holding the hammer from her toolbox, she unlocked the back door and stepped outside so she was facing the camera positioned over the door. 'Are you watching me now, you bastard?' She raised the hammer and smashed it into the lens repeatedly.

'I think it's dead,' Molly commented dryly after Olivia had hit it half a dozen times.

Olivia stepped back, let out a breath that was shaky with anger, and went to the front of the house, Molly following and watching as she repeated the process on the camera above the front door.

'Do you feel better for that?'

'I do.'

There was no way she could sleep, so instead Molly sat with her until daylight finally broke, agreeing with her during the moments of rage and offering words of comfort when the fresh tears came.

* * *

Noah didn't expect to find Fern home, assumed after their talk yesterday she would be long gone, so he was surprised to see her car in the drive.

When she didn't answer Daniella's persistent knocking at the front door, they made their way round the back. Alarm bells went off when they spotted the open patio door and the food spilling from a plastic bag across the kitchen floor.

Noah glanced at Daniella, before using the arm of his jacket to ease the door open, stepping inside. 'Fern?'

He waited a beat, walking further into the house when he was met with silence. He urged Daniella to follow. They found Fern's suitcase in the hallway, her bag beside it and her mobile phone on the side table. Her keys were in the front door.

'We need to alert the police.'

Noah nodded in agreement. 'I'll make a call from the car. Tell them I spoke to her and think she's a flight risk.'

He picked up Fern's mobile, saw a message on the screen. It was from someone called Meg.

Have a safe trip.

He swiped the screen, but a lock code came up. Knowing he didn't have time to break it, he wiped the phone clean of prints and set it back down on the table.

A quick check round the rest of the house established that Fern definitely wasn't there, and they made their way back to the car.

'You think he has her?'

Noah glanced at Daniella as she started the engine. 'Yeah, I do.'

And he didn't like that one bit. If the killer now had Fern, Olivia would be the next target.

* * *

It had taken a huge effort for Olivia to drag herself into work.

She was exhausted, her eyes were stinging and the thought of spending the day with Roger, Jeremy and Esther filled her with dread, but she had already had too much time off recently. Besides, work would help take her mind off Noah. He hadn't called, messaged or shown up banging on the door. Of course he had been locked out of the house and Olivia had no idea how long it had taken him to get back inside, but she had expected to hear something by the time she left for work. But there was nothing. No apology, no attempt to argue his case.

In the harsh light of the morning she understood that there would be no contact because the feelings hadn't been real. She had just been a job to him.

Touching up her make-up in the car, trying her best to disguise her red-rimmed eyes, she gave herself a pep talk. She was stronger than she realised. Toby's betrayal hadn't floored her and neither would Noah's. She would put on her big girl pants, go into work, and be professional, not let on to her colleagues that anything was wrong.

Aside from Jeremy, who gave her a few sly glances, no one seemed to suspect anything was wrong. Olivia kept her head down, initially throwing herself into her work, though as the morning wore on, lack of sleep caught up with her and she found it tough to keep her focus.

Her phone was on silent, hidden out of sight beneath her monitor stand. She couldn't help herself checking it every so often. She was not sure if she was relieved or disappointed that Noah hadn't tried to make contact.

She really hadn't mattered to him at all.

Even though it had all been a lie, the finality of it hit her hard.

Knowing she couldn't concentrate on work, she decided to Google Adam Somerville. Who was he, and why the hell had he hired Noah to look into her?

There were a handful of people with that name, none of them local to Norfolk, and only three she could find who were based in the UK. She read up as much as she could on each of them, looking at websites and social media. One Adam was based in Wales, another in Yorkshire, while the third was down in Oxfordshire. It was while looking on Facebook at the third Adam and scrolling through his mutual friends that she made the connection.

Adam Somerville was friends with Kelly Dearborn. She recognised the name, realised it was the same Kelly she had met at Black Dog Farm all those years ago.

She clicked on Kelly's profile, recognised her immediately. Adult Kelly didn't look much different to child Kelly, with her dark hair and long, narrow nose.

It was after studying her picture that she spotted 'Remembering' above Kelly's name. Shock reverberated through her as she realised it was a memorial page.

Scrolling through comments under photos that people had shared, she soon learnt that Kelly had died eighteen months ago. She had been killed in a house fire.

For a moment Olivia couldn't breathe.

'Are you okay?' Esther had her glasses lowered, was looking across the room at her with a mix of suspicion and concern. Her question had Jeremy and Roger raising their heads too.

Olivia quickly minimised the Facebook page, managing a smile. 'Just a dizzy spell. I'll be fine.'

She gulped at the glass of water on her desk, grateful when they all turned back to their work. Then she discreetly slipped her phone in her jacket pocket and got up to go to the loo.

Once locked in the cubicle, she pulled out her phone, clicked back on to Adam Somerville's Facebook page and flicked through his photographs. Had he been involved with Kelly?

There were pictures of him with a woman, but it wasn't Kelly. She looked familiar though and the tag was of a Rachel Colton.

The tag was inactive though, didn't link through to a profile.

Olivia scrolled through the photo comments.

'Thinking of you.'

'Call us if you need anything.'

Was Rachel Colton Rachel Williams? Why would Rachel's boyfriend have hired Noah to look into her?

She googled 'Rachel Colton', already having a bad feeling about this.

The top stories that appeared, confirmed her suspicions.

Rachel Colton had been killed in a freak accident after her car caught fire.

This was bad. Kelly, Rachel, Gary, and Howard were all dead, and Janice was in the hospital.

Noah had to have known about Rachel and about Kelly, yet he had played along, pretending he was helping Olivia figure it all out.

Did he know who was threatening her? Or why she was being targeted?

A sharp knock on the toilet door made her jump. The phone almost slipped from her grasp.

'Olivia?' It was Esther. 'Roger wants to know if you're okay. You've been in here awhile.'

'I'm fine.'

She slipped her phone back into her pocket, made a show of flushing the chain. Somehow she was going to have to get through this afternoon, then once she was home she would see what else she could find out about Rachel Colton and Adam Somerville.

* * *

Tempting as it was to go straight to Olivia's workplace and insist on taking her somewhere safe, Noah knew it would only cause a scene, would likely get her in trouble with her boss, and probably earn him a punch in the face.

Daniella was right. It was too soon after their fight and Olivia would still be reeling from the revelation that he had lied to her.

Instead, he drove home, following up on a couple of leads for the job they were currently working on. Then his intention was to be waiting outside Olivia's office when she left work.

She wouldn't like it, but he would come clean about everything and make her hear him out. It was the only way he knew he could keep her safe.

With a couple of hours still to kill before he needed to leave, he returned to her case and the list of the victims, and went over everything he knew about them.

Kelly Dearborn had been the first to die, in a house fire eighteen months ago. She had lived alone, had a drink problem, and from the few family and friends Noah had spoken to, she was very much a loner, spending a lot of time in therapy for anxiety and depression.

The fire was supposedly an accident.

Noah had tried to track down the two doctors who had treated Kelly. Doctor Phillips had been the first and she had been his patient for a number of years before he was taken ill, eventually passing away. She was then referred to Doctor Miller, who was currently on gardening leave. Not that it really mattered. Patient confidentiality meant he would never learn why Kelly had been seeing a therapist.

The last person to see her alive had been her brother, James. He had visited her at home and expressed concern about her drinking. They had fought and Kelly had kicked him out.

The next to die had been Rachel Colton, six weeks after Kelly. Again, the fire that killed her had been ruled an accident. The last person to see Rachel had been her fiancé, Adam Somerville. She had left his to go home where she was planning on meeting a woman, Peggy Wick, who was purchasing some items Rachel had been selling through a Facebook group. A freak accident with her car had caused it to explode on her driveway. It was unclear if the buyer had ever shown up.

Then there was a sixteen-month break before Gary Lamb had died. It was unclear who had been the last person to see him. There were rumours he had a date the night before his death with his girlfriend, Rita Works.

Howard Peck was supposed to be on a break with his girlfriend, Daisy Angel. The last person to see him alive had been the receptionist, Grant Savage, who had checked him in and given him the keys to the cabin.

Then Janice had been lured to her local community centre, supposedly by her friend, Gretchen Self, while Fern had vanished, her last known contact with anyone had been a WhatsApp exchange with someone called Meg.

Noah went on to Fern's Facebook page and looked through her friends. A Meg Gentile was the only Meg or Megan showing. He jotted the name down. Studied the list, rearranged it.

Realisation dawned.

Never did he think a childhood growing up in a strict religious home would pay off.

He ran a Google search to confirm his suspicions and the first clue finally fell into place.

Turning his attention to the Grimes family, he again ran searches on Malcolm and Alice, coming up empty, before turning to Gerald and Marie Grimes.

Gerald had been an only child, but Marie had two sisters. He ran searches on them both.

There was little information on the older sister, but Christine Hargreaves, the youngest, was active on Facebook. Her friends list was set to private, but several of her photographs could be viewed.

He scrolled through them, quickly tiring of the endless selfies. Christine in the garden, Christine out with friends, Christine eating dinner.

He almost didn't persevere, would have clicked off her profile if he didn't have time to waste, still needing a distraction from Olivia.

It was a photo posted in 2009 that stopped him in his tracks, one of several that Christine had posted when she had first joined Facebook, so

Noah estimated it had been taken a couple of years earlier. It was Christine's wedding to her third husband and there was a shot of her posing with a man he recognised to be Gerald Grimes. There were three other people in the photo; a woman and two teenagers. Marie, Alice, and Malcolm Grimes. It had to be.

He studied the photo, almost did a double take, saved it to his desktop and zoomed in close.

It couldn't be.

Heart in mouth, he closed his MacBook and grabbed his car keys.

43

Needing to confide in someone now Noah was out of the picture, Olivia turned to Molly, letting her friend cook her dinner, which she mostly pushed around her plate, too anxious and upset to eat.

While she pushed the food she came clean about everything that had been going on, telling Molly about the notes, the photo, the video and the phone calls. Molly had at first been shocked, but that shock had quickly turned to annoyance.

'I can't believe you kept all this from me.'

'I'm sorry. I just wasn't comfortable with people knowing.'

'But you told Noah,' Molly pouted.

'Well... yes.'

Olivia hadn't counted on this reaction.

'I share a house with you, Livvy. If someone has been threatening you then I think from a safety point of view, I had the right to know.'

'I'm sorry, I—'

'That night in the garden. Do you think whoever was outside, whoever knocked into me, is the same person doing this?' she whispered.

'I don't know. I guess, maybe. Look, I'm sorry I didn't tell you. You're right. I should have. You deserved to know.'

'You said you don't know why you're being targeted. Is that really true?'

That was a loaded question.

Olivia sighed deeply, aware that now Molly knew some of it, she may as well find out the rest. The thought of going through everything again was exhausting, but Molly was right, she did deserve to know.

She shifted her chair back and got up from the table, lifting her jumper to reveal her scars. Molly's eyes widened as she waited for Olivia to speak.

Olivia drew in a deep breath. 'When I was fourteen there was an accident.'

Molly didn't say anything while Olivia went over everything that had happened, but her expression did change from shocked to angry to horrified.

'So that's it. That's everything that happened.' Olivia gave a shrug as she finished. She was still uncomfortable talking about the past. 'Noah is convinced what is happening now has something to do with what happened to Margaret. I had my doubts, but knowing that Rachel's boyfriend hired Noah to look into me suggests it is all connected.'

'Have you thought about contacting him?'

'Adam Somerville?'

'Maybe you should confront him and find out why he was having you investigated.'

Olivia had thought about it, had kicked herself for not making a note of Adam's telephone number, but that had been in the heat of the moment. Now she had calmed down a little, knew he was connected to Rachel, so was another unwelcome connection with the past, she was more hesitant. Molly was right, though, she should confront him and demand answers.

She had already established that he was a freelance web designer and had got his mobile number from his website, so making contact should be easy enough.

'I will try and get hold of him tomorrow.'

Molly nodded, glancing at where Olivia had pulled her jumper over the scars. 'Does it still hurt?'

'Not really. I have some numbness, but I didn't lose all feeling.'

'It looks painful. I can understand why you hide it. Do you think Noah was really okay with it or just pretending?'

'I don't know.' Olivia's tone was tight. She had shown Molly her scars in confidence and didn't appreciate having it pointed out how unsightly they were. 'I was just a job to him, so probably not.'

'I'm sorry. I was thinking aloud and it was insensitive.' Molly pulled a face and tapped the side of her head. 'I really need to think before I open my big mouth.'

She did, but Olivia knew her well enough by now to know she was blunt, brutally so at times.

Dominic had made her paranoid about her scars and knowing how Noah had just used her made things far worse. They were her demons though and she would fight them. 'Look, I'm really tired. It's been a long day and I need to get some sleep.' Olivia pushed back her chair, started clearing the table. 'Thank you for cooking me dinner tonight. I really appreciate it.'

She saw Molly glance at her barely touched meal and thought she was going to comment; but instead she nodded. 'No problem.'

As soon as Olivia closed the bedroom door she glanced at her phone. She was annoyed, frustrated, and hurt that she hadn't heard a word from Noah. Which was what she kept telling herself she wanted, of course. The relationship was over. Still, she had expected something; an explanation, an attempt to put things right, or an apology, at the very least.

But there had been no messages, no phone calls, and he hadn't shown up at her home or work, which was what she had been readying herself for all day.

A tiny part of her was tempted to message him, tell him exactly what she thought of him, just to get a reaction. It was a stupid idea, though, and she knew it was an act she would regret in the morning.

She lay awake for an hour, unable to find a comfortable position, too hot under the duvet though it was freezing outside and aware of every creak in the house. Her mind worked overtime as she mulled over Noah's betrayal and why Rachel's fiancé had hired him. And all the time she was acutely aware that if she didn't get to sleep she was going to face another exhausted day in the office.

Eventually sleep pulled her under, but it was restless and dream-fuelled. Fern was filming a naked Olivia as she tried to escape down a corridor of locked doors that never seemed to end. Eventually she came to a door that opened and she found herself in a room with Gary, Howard, Janice, Kelly, and Rachel gathered around a huge fire. Margaret and Noah were both dead on the floor, their bodies still burning, and the gang had Molly surrounded. She was screaming for Olivia to help her as they pushed her into the flames.

Olivia turned to run, found herself face to face with Fern, the door slamming shut behind her. Her smile was macabre. 'You're next.'

Olivia spun around, as the group gathered around her, hands grabbing, pulling her towards the flames. The smell of thick smoke and cooked flesh filled her nostrils, making her gag, and the heat of the fire and the thick smoke stinging her eyes.

'NO!'

She woke up, sat up in bed, heart racing, covered in sweat and the sheets tangled around her. Through the blackness of the room, she heard Luna meow in protest at being disturbed.

'Fuck.'

She reached through the darkness for her bedside light, clicking it on, the warm comforting glow lighting up her bedroom, and she blew out a breath.

'It was just a dream.' She muttered the words aloud, needing to convince herself. It had felt so real.

She grabbed her phone. Still nothing from Noah. The time was 3.15 a.m. Somehow, she had to get back to sleep.

Not sure what she feared most, staying awake or slipping back into the nightmare, she sank back down into the pillow and closed her eyes.

* * *

Twenty miles north, in a dark and chilly room, Fern St Clair attempted to shift position, wincing when the metal cuffs cut into her wrists and ankles.

She had no idea how long she had been here. The way everything was aching from her uncomfortable position, she suspected a couple of days. She had drifted in and out of consciousness and her only way of telling time was the small grate in the bottom of the wall. At times sunlight filtered through it, bathing the empty room in shadows, while at other times she was in complete darkness.

She knew she had lost control of her bladder twice because the bastard had just left her. She had seen him moving around outside but he had left her alone in the cold, no food, no water, and no toilet. She wasn't sure what scared her more: meeting the same fate as Gary and Howard, or being trapped here to slowly die.

Her last recollection was of being in her kitchen, getting ready to leave. That was how he must have got her, sneaking into her house. She had then woken here, her face pressed against a hard, damp, and dirty floor, and her head throbbing in pain. There was complete silence, other than the slow drip from a faraway tap, that taunted her, a constant reminder of how thirsty she was. Even if she could find a way to manoeuvre herself towards the source of the water, the thick musty cloth that filled her mouth would prevent her from drinking.

Her initial reaction had been panic and she had fought like a wild animal to free herself. Escape had been impossible though. Her wrists and ankles were both cuffed and linked by a further chain that forced her shoulders back and prevented her from doing little more than rolling from side to side on her stomach.

So she had no choice but to lie there and wait, her muscles cramping, desperate for water, her belly raw and aching with hunger, and shivering, both from cold and fear.

She had learned his identity before it turned dark, waking from an uncomfortable sleep, for the briefest second in ignorant bliss, before a fresh wave of despair had hit, and she remembered she was trapped and at the mercy of a monster.

Footsteps had cut through the silence, growing closer, and she had whimpered into the gag, wanting to be freed, but terrified that if her captor came in the room, worse would happen.

Her shoulder blades had screamed as she snaked an inch closer to the grate, pushing her face against the bars and she had blinked against the light as her eyes adjusted.

Dark laced boots, long jean-clad legs. The low position of the grate didn't allow her a full view, but she could tell that the person who had taken her was male.

What was he going to do to her? Fern remembered Gary and Howard, Janice too. She squeezed her eyes shut as she trembled uncontrollably. Waited.

It couldn't end this way for her. It just couldn't.

But then the footsteps were fading. He was leaving her again.

Her eyes sprang open, catching a glimpse of the man from behind. The jeans, the dark jacket, and hair poking out from underneath a beany hat. He turned in the doorway and she caught his profile, eyes widening in horror.

Noah Keen.

She had suspected Olivia, been suspicious of Noah's motives, but she hadn't actually believed he was behind everything.

She watched as he disappeared, wondering why he was doing this. What was Noah's connection to Margaret Grimes?

Unless he was helping Olivia and she was in on it too.

Her mind worked overtime as she tried to ignore the fact she needed to pee again, her bladder straining against her tight jeans. Eventually she drifted off to sleep, awoke sometime later, aware of shuffling close by.

Was that a fucking rat?

The room was completely black, every muscle in her body weeping as she tried to roll into a more comfortable position, crying against the pain in her arms and legs.

As she rested on the floor, tried to calm herself as a fresh bout of tears threatened to take hold, the shuffling noise sounded again, this time growing closer.

Something furry brushed against her face and she scooted back and then jolted as it scurried over her belly.

Oh God, it was a rat.

Fear trembled through her as she held her breath, praying it had gone away.

She wondered where Noah was, whether he was close by, and how much longer he was going to leave her like this.

All she wanted was for the nightmare to be over, but deep down she knew the worst was yet to come.

44

It was Thursday afternoon when Daniella Curry made contact with Olivia.

Suffering the effects of another restless night, Olivia had had to force herself into work and was struggling to keep her eyes open as she tried to focus.

Roger was on a day off and Jeremy was out on a viewing, so it was just her and Esther in the office and they hadn't seen a customer all day.

She had called Adam Somerville's mobile while on her lunch break, but there had been no answer, so she had left a rambling message. She wasn't sure if he would call her back, so when her phone vibrated, she had snatched it up, expecting it to be either him or Noah finally calling to apologise.

It was an unknown number, and given that she had already stored Adam's in her phone so would know if it was him calling, she let it go to voicemail, annoyed when the caller didn't leave a message.

A few seconds later though, a text flashed up from the same number.

Olivia, this is Daniella, Noah's partner. I need to speak with you. Can you call me? Thanks.

She stared at the message, her heart racing. Had something happened to Noah? Although she had resolved not to talk to him if he made contact, she hadn't counted on Daniella getting in touch.

Daniella would have been involved in the investigation commissioned by Adam Somerville. While Olivia resented her for that, she also wanted to know why she was calling, knew she wouldn't be able to settle if she didn't speak with her.

Esther was peering over her glasses in her direction.

Olivia held up her phone. 'Missed call from the police. I need to ring them back.'

There wasn't much Esther could say to that and it wasn't like she was Olivia's boss. She also wasn't a snitch like Jeremy. Wanting privacy, Olivia got up from her desk, took her phone through to the back corridor and stepped into the tiny kitchen. She hit 'call' on Daniella's text message, her insides twisting, anxious to know what the woman wanted.

Daniella answered almost immediately. 'Olivia, hi. Thanks for calling me back.'

'What's wrong?'

'Is Noah with you?'

Olivia hadn't expected that question. 'No, um... we had a fight. We're actually no longer together.'

There was silence on the line for a moment. 'So he didn't come to meet you after work last night?'

'No.' *Had he been planning to meet me after work?* 'I haven't seen him or heard anything from him since yesterday morning.'

Another pause. 'Okay, well I was supposed to pick him up this morning to meet a client and he wasn't home. I assumed he was with you.'

'Nope, he's not with me.' Although Olivia tried to keep her tone casual, a sliver of fear licked her belly. She had left him locked out of his house in the bitter cold, wearing just a pair of jeans. Was he okay? 'When did you last see him?' she asked, not liking the guilt that was now creeping its way in.

'Yesterday. He called me after your fight. I have his spare key. We had a job then I left him around lunchtime. He's not answering his phone; his car isn't here. That's why I figured you had made up. He said he was going to talk to you last night.'

Okay, well that is at least something. Olivia's guilt eased slightly knowing she wasn't responsible for him dying of hypothermia. And he had planned on coming to see her. She wasn't sure how she felt about that. Would she have been calm enough to listen to what he had to say? Daniella obviously knew about the investigation, seemed to think Olivia might have forgiven him. Would she be able to give her some answers? And where the hell was Noah? She shouldn't care. He was no longer any of her concern, but still, the news from Daniella was making her more than a little anxious. 'I haven't heard anything from him.' Olivia paused. 'Are you at his house right now?'

'I am. It looks like he might have been looking into the fires and Fern's disappearance before he vanished.'

'Fern is missing?'

Another longer pause. 'Where are you now? At work?'

'Yes. What's going on, Daniella? Why was Noah investigating me?'

'Can you come over to his house? I think it's time we had a talk.'

* * *

Olivia told Esther that the police needed to speak with her in person and fled work early. As she drove into Noah's street, memories surfaced of the last time she was here, and the hurt she had felt at his betrayal.

For a second it crossed her mind that this might be a trap. What if Noah was home and had persuaded Daniella to help lure her over so he could talk to her.

It was an elaborate ruse though and Olivia didn't think Daniella had faked her concern on the phone.

She didn't need to ring the bell. Daniella had seen her arrival and already had the door open. As Olivia stepped into the house after her, it felt weird that it wasn't Noah letting her in.

'I'll put the kettle on.'

Olivia nodded, followed her through to the kitchen, hovering by the door frame. She wasn't patient enough to wait for the kettle to boil. 'Why was he investigating me?'

Opening the cupboard, Daniella pulled out two mugs. 'We were hired by a man called Adam Somerville.'

'I know that, but why?'

Daniella seemed to be purposely taking her time to answer. Olivia wasn't sure if it was because she was searching for the right words or delaying telling her the truth.

She watched as the woman spooned coffee into the mugs, and shook her head when asked about milk and sugar. Daniella had been another of Noah's secrets and she really was very pretty. She had a key to his house, knew her way around and looked perfectly at home here. Were they more than just work partners?

A pang of jealousy gnawed in her gut and annoyed, she tried to push it down. It was no longer any of her concern if Noah and Daniella were involved.

'Adam was the fiancé of Rachel Colton. I believe you knew her as Rachel Williams.'

Olivia already knew about Adam and Rachel, but she kept quiet. She just wanted to get to the truth. 'Go on.'

'Rachel died in an accident last year. Or rather what was considered an accident. Adam wasn't so sure. He wasn't happy when the police closed the case. Rachel had still been in touch with Kelly Dearborn and he found it too big a coincidence that they were both killed in fires just six weeks apart.'

'What has that got to do with wanting me investigated, though?'

'Rachel had a conversation with Kelly about a week before she died. I say conversation, Adam described it as a blazing row. They were in the garden at Rachel's house and he said he was keeping his distance, staying indoors, but that it was impossible not to hear what they were talking about with all the windows open. Rachel was agitated because she didn't want Kelly to tell her therapist about something. Adam overheard her saying that the truth could never get out, that Olivia Blake must never find out what really happened with the fire.'

'What did happen?' Olivia asked quietly, her mind working overtime. 'What didn't they want me to find out about?'

'Kelly stormed out,' Daniella continued, ignoring the question. 'And Adam tried to talk to Rachel about the fight, but she was really cagey. Then Kelly died and when he pushed the subject again, Rachel was tight-lipped, refused to say a word. A while after she was killed, he was sorting through her stuff and came across a letter she had started to write. It was addressed to you at your mother's restaurant.'

'What did it say?'

'Not much. She had only written the first few lines, saying that you probably didn't remember her. She mentioned Kelly had died and said she had something she had to talk to you about. She never finished the letter. Adam was convinced you were key to finding out what had happened.'

'So why didn't he approach me himself? He had my mum's address. I could have saved him the effort of hiring bloody private investigators. I have nothing to hide!' Olivia was aware she was getting a little high-pitched, but honestly she couldn't help it. The man had hired people to look into her based on an overheard conversation and a part-written letter. It was ridiculous.

Daniella seemed unbothered by Olivia's outburst. She took a leisurely sip of her coffee before she continued. 'Adam Somerville is very particular. He has a lot of money and he prefers to get other people to do things for him. He wanted us to discreetly find out what your connection to Kelly and Rachel was, work out if you had any involvement in what had happened to them.'

'He thought I might have killed them?'

'Well, he never actually came out and said those words.' A brief smile crossed Daniella's face. 'But yes, I think he convinced himself you had.'

'I wouldn't even know what they looked like now. We were just kids.' Olivia shook her head, finding it all hard to take in. 'So that was why Noah showed up in my mum's restaurant, because he was investigating me?'

'It was. We had looked into you. Couldn't find a connection to Kelly and Rachel. I have to say your mother did a good job at keeping your name out of the press after your accident. We were going to call it quits, tell Adam Somerville he had it wrong, then Noah realised he had seen your brother – Jamie, isn't it? – in the gym. He didn't know him well, but figured he could change that, somehow get introduced to you, try to get to know you a bit.'

He had certainly bloody well done that. Daniella's words opened a fresh wound. 'He used me.'

'He did.' Daniella's bluntness stung. 'But only at first. Getting involved with you was never part of the plan. When he realised he had feelings for you, he wanted to call it quits on the job. We argued about it and I told him he was being unprofessional. He didn't listen to me though. He never bloody does. He called off the job. Adam, I tell you, that man was not happy. I got an earful over that. Noah didn't charge him. Told him you were clean and to go away. I was bloody livid about working for free.'

She eyed Olivia with a half-smile again, a challenging flash in her dark eyes. While Olivia was quite sure Daniella hadn't liked working for free, she got the impression that she hadn't really been that mad about it.

Was the woman being honest with her though? She found herself wavering, part of her thawing towards Noah, but she was still mad that he had befriended her under false circumstances. 'Why didn't he come clean and tell me the truth?'

'Exactly because of this. He feared you would react this way.'

'And he kept you a secret.'

'Because he was scared if you met me you might find out the truth.'

'So our relationship was built on a lie.' Olivia set her mug down. She had barely touched the coffee which was now cold. She had heard enough.

'I know you hate him, but he has genuinely fallen for you. None of that was a lie and he put a halt on the investigation before he let himself become involved with you.'

'But you said he was looking into the fires, into Fern's disappearance.'

'Because of you. Adam Somerville is no longer our client. Noah's interest in the fires is now purely personal. He just wants to keep you safe.'

It was a lot to take in. Had she been too hard on Noah? Daniella had answered all her questions, had no reason to deceive her. But even if she had been truthful, it didn't change the fact that her relationship had been built on a lie.

'Has he been in contact with Fern?'

Olivia saw the flicker of wariness on Daniella's face. She had just done a pretty good job of defending him, so obviously didn't want to throw him under a bus. She took her time answering, clearly wanting to get her words right. 'We were both at her house yesterday,' she admitted. 'My idea. I felt we needed to talk to her, but she wasn't there. Her bag, phone and suitcase were, though, as well as her car, and the French doors were open. Today is the anniversary, right, of Margaret's death? Noah has been worried that today it ends, that you are in danger. With Fern gone, that just leaves you.'

'But I didn't do anything. I still don't understand why I am being targeted.'

'I think at this stage we need to accept we're dealing with someone who is clearly deranged. For whatever reason, you are in their crosshairs. Noah was conscious of that, which is part of the reason why he planned to meet you after work last night. He didn't want you being alone. That's why I'm worried as hell about him right now. He wouldn't just disappear like this. It's not his style.'

No, it wasn't. Olivia was in complete agreement over that. And while she wasn't ready to forgive him, wasn't sure if a relationship that started so deviously could be saved, she still cared enough about him to want him to be safe. She was involved whether she wanted to be or not. 'Okay, so what do we do now?'

45

There were three in the bed and the little one said, roll over, roll over.
So they all rolled over and one fell out.
There were two in the bed...

46

Malcolm Grimes listened to the news, learning that Janice Plum, the woman who just four days ago had been badly burned in a vicious attack, had passed away from her injuries.

He turned off the radio, sat in silence in his car for a few minutes, taking that news in. He was parked in a lay-by overlooking the entrance to Black Dog Farm. The place where his twin sister had died at the hands of cruel bullies. Bullies that had included Janice.

The farm was now run down, hadn't been lived in for years. Margaret's death had taken care of that.

Everything came full circle. It had started here and tonight it would end here.

And Malcolm was ready.

47

Olivia drove home from Noah's with her mind working overtime as she processed everything she had learnt from Daniella.

She was unsure how to feel about Noah's deception, knowing their initial friendship had been based on a lie and that, while she had been falling for him, he had been investigating her.

Knowing that he had called off that investigation before they had become involved, that he hadn't charged Adam Somerville, and that his feelings for her had been real did soften the blow. She wasn't ready to forgive him yet, still didn't know if she could, but she was cooling down to a point where she prepared to meet with him and listen to what he had to say for himself.

Well, that is if we can bloody find him.

Daniella was worried, and Olivia suspected she was usually unflappable. Daniella was also right. It wasn't Noah's style to just vanish. So where the hell was he?

Her own unease was growing. Regardless of what had happened between them, she couldn't just shut her feelings off. The idea that something might have happened to Noah, that he could be in trouble or worse, actually made her feel sick.

Molly wasn't at home, hadn't left the porch light on, and Olivia cursed her as she readied her keys, making the quick run from her car to the dark porch. She fumbled with the lock, pushing open the door and reaching for the switch, flooding the hallway with light before quickly locking herself inside.

The heating was on a timer and had kicked in an hour ago, so at least the house was warm. She instructed her Echo to tune in to her favourite radio station then walked through the house drawing the curtains and turning on all of the lights to scare away the shadows. *'I should invest in some timer lightbulbs'.*

After kicking off her shoes and hanging up her coat, she pulled out her phone, noting there was still nothing from Noah. It had now been well over a day since anyone had seen or heard from him and panic was gnawing at her gut. *Where is he?*

Needing to know he was safe, she dialled his number. He hadn't answered to Daniella, but maybe he would to her.

Or not. Her call went straight to voicemail.

She didn't leave a message, figured she would give it half an hour and try again.

Slipping her phone in her pocket, she called Luna, heard the familiar thump of paws hitting the wooden floor of her bedroom as the cat jumped off the bed. As she went through to the kitchen, there was a tap, tap, tap of paws on the stairs, and Luna appeared, slinking around Olivia's legs as she filled her bowl.

Molly often cooked before she hit the gym (which is where Olivia assumed she was), but the work surfaces were clean. *I'll make dinner,* Olivia decided. She owed Molly for being a good friend last night. Besides, cooking might take her mind off the worry about Noah.

After showering and changing into a fleecy top and her favourite pyjama bottoms, she tried Noah again, this time leaving a message that she was worried about him and could he please call her. Then she foraged through the fridge and cupboards, looking for potential ingredients.

Settling for a simple Italian dish, she began dicing vegetables, as her mind again ran over her conversation with Daniella. Together they had gone through Noah's notes, trying to figure out exactly what lead he might have been working on before he disappeared.

He must have left the house of his own will. His car was gone and there was no sign of forced entry. Daniella had taken his MacBook home and planned on hacking her way in. That way she could check his emails and also the footage from the cameras set up around his house.

When she had learnt there were cameras in his house as well as outside, Olivia had immediately panicked, questioning as casually as possible if Daniella knew where they were situated, as she recalled the various places where they'd had sex. She tried to keep her relief discreet learning there were just two: one in the hallway and the other on the landing.

They had left it that they would stay in touch with each and get in contact immediately if they heard any news, and Olivia had her phone on the worktop as she started making the tomato and garlic sauce, not wanting to miss any calls from either Noah or Daniella.

It occurred to her that Adam Somerville hadn't returned her call either, but as Daniella had said he was a man who preferred others to do his work for him, not wanting to get his own hands dirty. *Shame. I'd like to give him a piece of my mind.*

As she stirred, the radio cut into the local news. Distracted by her thoughts she was only half listening, but the name Janice Plum immediately caught her attention. The newscaster reported that she had passed away in hospital from her injuries and her attack was now being treated as a murder investigation.

Olivia's blood ran cold. Janice had been the fifth victim, which left just her and Fern. And Fern was already missing.

Maybe she should stay with her mum for a couple of days. It would be safer for her with more people around, plus Jamie there at nights, and probably safer for Molly too. Her lodger had already been surprised by an intruder in the garden. If Olivia stayed here, surely she was putting Molly in danger.

Her phone pinged and she snatched it up, overcome with relief when she saw Noah's name on the screen. She quickly swiped open the message.

Sorry I've not been in touch. I know you're still mad at me, but I have found something and I need to show you. Can you come meet me?

She read and reread the message, her heartbeat quickening. What the hell had he found that had caused him to go missing for over a day?

Hearing the sauce bubbling, she quickly removed the saucepan from the hob ring, pulled up Noah's number and hit 'call', going through to the front of the house and into the living room, pacing up and down.

It rang twice then went to voicemail.

Frustrated, she hung up.

What the hell was going on with him? Why wasn't he answering? He had just called.

Irritated, she fired a message back.

Where are you? Call me.

Nearly ten minutes passed before she heard from him again. No call. Instead another message.

Sorry, really bad signal. I'm at Black Dog Farm. Liv, you need to come meet me. This is really important.

Seriously? He was all the way up at Roughton? What the hell was he doing there?

She didn't like the idea of going to meet him, not alone. Okay, so it was Noah and she wasn't afraid of him, but she hadn't been up to the farm since the accident and it was already dark, plus it was in the middle of nowhere. She would feel better if she could just speak to him.

Again she tried to call him, hanging up when the voicemail message kicked in. Then she tried Daniella. Maybe Noah had tried to call her too.

Daniella's phone rang for longer, but also cut to voicemail. Frustrated that she couldn't get hold of anyone, Olivia left her a message. 'Hi, Daniella, it's Olivia. I heard from Noah. He's at Black Dog Farm. Don't ask me why. He wants me to go and meet him there, says it's important. Have you heard from him at all? Can you let me know? Thanks.'

She had just ended the call when she saw car headlights through the curtains, heard an engine. Even though it was probably just Molly, she automatically tensed. Peering through a crack in the curtains, she was relieved to see her lodger climb out of the car and told herself to get a grip.

Quickly she fired off another message to Noah, offering a compromise.

I'm not comfortable with driving up there by myself. How about I meet you halfway?

Remembering she had left the pasta sauce off the boil, she went back through to the kitchen, was at the stove when Molly walked in. She dumped her gym bag at the bottom of the stairs.

'Something smells good.'

'I thought I would cook. I owe you for the last couple of days.'

Molly wandered through to the kitchen, her eyes narrowing. 'Livvy, you look really stressed. Are you okay?'

Now that was a loaded question.

'I spoke with Daniella earlier. You know, Noah's business partner? Noah has been missing for the last day.'

Molly frowned. 'Okay, and that is your problem how? You broke up with him, remember?'

'Yeah, but I can't just shut my feelings off. I'm not a tap.' Olivia paused, her face contrite. 'Sorry. I didn't mean to snap. Anyway, that's irrelevant. He messaged me a few minutes ago.'

'Right, so he's okay. That's good for Noah, but...' Molly's expression was suspicious. 'Livvy, you haven't forgiven him for what he did?'

'No, well I... He's out at Black Dog Farm. You know where the fire happened. He says he's found something. Wants me to go meet him.'

'You can't go. You know that, right? What he's asking is ridiculous.'

'He says it's important.'

'Really? And what if it's just some stupid ploy to get you back?'

It wasn't. Olivia was sure of that. Noah might be a lot of things, but he wouldn't ask her to travel out to the farm unless it was serious.

When she was silent, Molly shook her head. 'You're gonna go, aren't you?'

'I don't want to go out there alone. I haven't been back there since the accident. But this sounds urgent. I just wish I could get hold of him to speak to. I don't want to just drive out there not knowing where exactly he is.'

Olivia glanced at her phone again. Noah still hadn't replied.

'Look, I'm not going to do anything rash. Let's eat and I will wait to hear from him again.'

'Have I got time for a quick shower? I still stink of gym.'

'Fifteen minutes? I just have to cook the pasta.'

'Can do.'

Noah's next message arrived as she was dishing up dinner.

If I could come to you I would, but you need to meet me at the farm. I'll explain when you get here.

Fuck! She didn't like this one little bit.

She told Molly as they ate, who immediately tried to talk her out of going.

'I'll try Daniella again. I'm really not keen on driving up there by myself.'

'Then don't go. If Noah wants to see you he will come to you.'

'He said it's really important.'

'And you believe him?' Molly shook her head in resignation when Olivia fell silent. 'Okay, look. Do you want me to go with you?'

Olivia's eyes widened in surprise. This was Noah they were talking about and although Molly had made more of an effort in the last week, she still didn't like him. 'No, you don't have to do that. I can go by myself.'

'I really don't think that's a good idea. I'm not letting you drive up there alone.'

Olivia hesitated. She really didn't fancy going alone. 'Okay, thank you.' Finished poking her food around on the plate, she cleared the table, sent another message to Noah.

Okay, I will come to you, but it had better be worth my time. Where will you be?

'When do you want to leave?' Molly asked.

Olivia glanced at her watch. It was almost seven. 'Give me ten minutes to get dressed and we'll leave straightaway. Hopefully that way we won't be back too late.'

As she went upstairs she figured she should update Daniella, sending her a quick message, letting her know she would head out to the farm with Molly.

Up in her bedroom she glanced out of the window. It was a dry night, but cold, the crescent moon offered little light. They would have to take torches and she would need something warm to wear. Quickly she changed into jeans and her thickest jumper, put on two pairs of woolly socks.

Noah replied to her message as she slipped on her boots.

I'll wait for you by the main farmhouse. See you in about forty minutes. This will all be over soon, Liv. I promise. Xx

Although the words were probably meant to be comforting, she couldn't help the sense of foreboding. Quashing it down she slipped her phone in her pocket and went downstairs to find Molly.

48

The final scene is perfectly set up. One bitch is already in place, aware of the terror that awaits her; the other is on her way.

I have worked so hard to fix things, to make the guilty pay for what they did to you all those years ago. Kelly and Rachel, Gary, Howard, and Janice, they have all been punished, and tonight the instigators will atone for their sins.

It seemed only right to return to where it all started, to bring it full circle, and I will make sure both of the bitches suffer, that they understand exactly why they are here. The wicked will repent before they die and they will beg for your forgiveness.

Tonight is for you, sweet Margaret.

Tonight is where it ends.

49

As the car headlights thrashed down the bumpy track, it was clear, even in the dark, that the farm had not been maintained in a long time. There were no welcoming Christmas lights or decorations, and no warm glow from the house itself. Instead, the windows were boarded up and the lawns overgrown with weeds.

Molly had driven, reasoning that her car was probably better for the terrain. Olivia had protested: she felt bad that not only was Molly accompanying her on what might be a waste-of-time trip, she was also now having to drive. But she had to admit it relieved her stress.

Returning to Black Dog Farm brought up many demons and although she was back in contact with Noah, they still hadn't seen each other since she had stormed out, which only added to her anxiety. She expected to find him waiting outside the main door for her as he had promised. His car was there, but he was nowhere to be seen, and that cranked up her irritation. She fired off a quick message letting him know they had arrived and demanding to know where he was.

He didn't realise Molly was with her. As far as he was aware, she had driven out here in the dark all alone. Part of her was tempted to tell Molly to turn the car around and head back to Norwich. Screw Noah Keen and whatever game he was playing.

Molly had already turned off the engine, though left her headlights on. She exited the car, staring up at the abandoned farmhouse. 'This place is bloody huge. I can't believe it's just been left like this.'

'I think they had trouble selling it.' Reluctantly Olivia got out and went to join her.

'Where did the fire happen? Was it in here?'

'No, the cottage was over there somewhere.' Olivia pointed towards the dark woods that bordered the property. It was hard to believe that years ago, she had gone wandering into them with Margaret and Rachel. How much braver they had been back then. But then again, remembering the outcome, they had been foolish too.

Aside from the two of them, the place was completely silent.

'Where the bloody hell is Noah? He said he would be here.'

Molly's face was immersed in shadows. 'Let's wander round the building and see if we can find him. Maybe he's inside.'

Olivia wasn't sure she liked the idea of that, but they had just driven all the way out here and, other than sitting in the car and hoping he appeared, they didn't have a better plan. 'Okay,' she agreed reluctantly.

'I need to turn off the headlights. I don't want a flat battery. Have you got the torches?'

'They're in the glovebox.'

Olivia quickly fetched them, waited for Molly as she killed the lights and grabbed her jacket from the back seat before locking the car. As Molly zipped up the jacket and slipped on warm gloves, Olivia cursed, realising she had forgotten hers.

Hopefully they wouldn't be here long. Turning on her torch, she stuck her free hand into her coat pocket, hurrying after Molly as she headed towards the side of the building.

Without the full beam from the car, the place was even more creepy and her unease grew. Olivia realised it was probably because of the memories it evoked and that her shivering was more from the cold than being back here. She was thirty-one. Time to overcome her demons.

Molly was a few yards ahead of her and Olivia stepped over the uneven ground, trying to keep up, as her friend disappeared round the back.

'There are some missing boards here, Livvy. We can get inside.'

'Maybe we should just wait out here.'

She caught Molly up, peered through the dark window, following the beam of Molly's flashlight as it lit up a few empty chairs and tables. She cast her mind back, trying to remember what room this would have been. Was it the craft room where she had first got to know Margaret?

Molly was already clambering through the window, as Olivia pulled out her phone again. Noah hadn't replied to her message. In fact, she hadn't heard a word from him since agreeing to meet him.

What the bloody hell is he playing at? Not liking this at all, she slipped her phone back into her pocket and followed Molly into the building.

* * *

Fern's head shot up at the footsteps crunching against glass. Was the psycho coming back?

She held her breath, tried to still her racing heart, as she listened. Voices. Two of them. Female, she thought.

God, please let them find me.

Time was running out. She understood that when she had been moved to the swimming pool. Realised that unless she could escape, it was almost over for her.

When her legs were uncuffed had been her one opportunity to get away, but they had numbed from the pain of being forced back into such an uncomfortable position, and she had wept at the sharp burst of agonising pain, barely able to walk as she had been half dragged out of the room and down the corridor. That was when she had realised where she was, that she had been taken back to Black Dog Farm. Any hope she had been clinging to had dissipated as she had been kicked down into the old swimming pool, now empty of water. She had been unable to cushion her fall with her wrists still cuffed behind her back and her face and her shoulder had taken the brunt. From the way her nose throbbed, she was pretty certain she had broken it. Possibly dislocated her shoulder too.

She had cried as she spotted the crudely made crucifixion cross lying flat on the bed of the pool, but she had been in too much pain to fight as her wrists were uncuffed and her arms stretched out, tied to each side.

Then her ankles were bound together again and chained to the bottom of the cross. And she had become hysterical as she watched the canisters being dragged to the side of the pool, smelling the strong fumes of petrol.

It was going to happen. She was going to burn alive.

She tried to plead through the gag, begging for it to stop.

And then it had. The psycho had left her. That had been hours ago and the pool had long been plunged into darkness. As she struggled to free herself, knew better than to believe it was over, she heard the footsteps, could make out faint voices. If she was somehow able to make enough noise to alert them that she was here, maybe, just maybe, her nightmare might be over.

* * *

'This is the dining hall where we ate.'

The chairs and tables were still there, though covered in a film of dust, and the serving counter was still intact. The beam of her torch picked up the trays that were stacked up at the beginning of the line. It was weird seeing everything as she remembered, but in such a state of decay. Olivia recalled the room as being huge. It was a still a decent size, but not quite as big as she remembered it. The door behind the counter that led to the kitchen hung off its hinges and she wondered what kind of state the kitchen was in now.

The longer she spent inside the old farmhouse, the less scary it felt, but she was still a little on edge, not liking being in so much darkness. It wasn't the farmhouse that bothered her. More what she couldn't see.

Anyone could be in here.

Molly seemed to be loving it though, already wandering out of the dining hall towards the main staircase. 'Does this lead to the dormitories?'

'Yes. Our rooms were up there.'

'I'm going up to look.'

'Wait for me.'

As Olivia crossed the dining hall, she felt her phone vibrate in her pocket.

Noah!

Where are you?

Is he serious? 'Hold on, Molly. Noah just messaged.' Olivia hit call, frustrated when her phone lost its connection. She typed a reply:

I'm right here. Where the hell are you?

She waved the phone around until she had enough bars, hitting send, before rushing out of the room, annoyed to find Molly had already gone upstairs without her.

'Molly? I said to wait for me.'

There was no answer, just silence and Olivia picked her way carefully up the stairs, aware some of the floorboards were loose and worried about stumbling in the darkness.

She found herself on the landing, thrusting the torch in both directions, familiarising herself with the layout, remembering that both corridors were long and twisting, not liking that she was suddenly alone.

'Molly?' she hissed, her voice too loud in the silence. 'Where the hell are you?'

More silence followed and Olivia was aware of her heart beating too fast. She didn't like this one bit. Where was Noah and where the hell was Molly?

A scream pierced through the darkness, making her jump. She fumbled with the torch, almost dropped it. It was Molly, she was sure of it. 'Molly? What's wrong, where are you?'

She charged in the direction of the scream, torch beam flashing ahead, trying not to think about what had just happened. Maybe Molly had stumbled or seen a rat, or maybe been startled by Noah. Yes, that would be the best-case scenario. Then they could all get the fuck out of there.

'Molly?'

She shone her torch in the dorms as she passed, the beam picking up the old bunk beds they had slept in. When she reached the end of the corridor, Molly still nowhere to be found, Olivia pulled her phone out. She had a signal, but it was weak. Noah still hadn't replied she noted.

She called Molly's number, praying that she would answer.

In the distance she recognised Molly's ringtone. Holding her breath as she slowly walked towards the room where it was coming from.

She paused outside, the sound louder now. 'Molly?'

Again, no answer.

Olivia stepped into the room, moving closer to the sound.

Molly's mobile phone was on the floor, Olivia's name on the screen as it rang.

Fuck!

What the hell was going on? She didn't like this one bit.

'Molly?' She snatched up the phone, ended the call. Tried Noah again.

Straight to voicemail.

If it wasn't for everything going on, she would think this was some sick prank. Molly and Noah wouldn't do this to her, though. And certainly not together. They hated each other.

Okay, think, Liv. She rationalised with herself, deciding to get the hell out of the farmhouse and call for help. As she headed back down the corridor towards the stairs, her phone beeped.

This time it was a text from an unknown number.

Look behind you.

Olivia's heart was in her mouth as she slowly turned, shone the torch towards the darkness. There was nothing there.

She heard the creak of a floorboard, footsteps, and turned back just as something heavy whacked into the side of her head, screaming as she dropped the torch, losing her footing and tumbling down the staircase.

She tried to cushion herself against the fall, landing on her side as she reached the bottom. As she attempted to sit up, wincing in pain, footsteps descended the stairs. In the pitch black she couldn't see who it was, squinting her eyes at the harsh beam that was suddenly flashed in her face.

'Please don't—'

She caught the glint of something silver in the split second before it smacked into the side of her head, then there was only blackness.

50

Malcolm Grimes carried a lot of anger.

Towards his parents, towards the church, towards the world in general, and, for a long time, towards the people who had hurt his twin sister.

He knew the names of everyone involved in the prank that night at Black Dog Farm, the one that had resulted in Margaret's death. Understood exactly what had happened.

After Margaret left the disco with Olivia and Rachel, he had followed, curious to know where they were going, hiding in the trees to the side of the cottage as they went around the back and disappeared inside.

He had seen the fire, watched as Fern St Clair and her friends had fled the building. Recognised them all as they argued outside before bolting back into the woods towards the farmhouse. Margaret and Olivia had still been inside.

Rachel Williams was the only one who had stayed. She had been by the window when Malcolm had approached. Trying, he assumed, to pluck up courage to go back inside.

He had pushed her out of the way, desperate to get to his sister.

Clambering through the window he had found a motionless body, assumed it was Margaret, and managed to pass her back out to Rachel.

Distraught when he realised it was Olivia and not Margaret, he had attempted to go back for his sister, but the flames were rising, the smoke too thick, and it was impossible.

He had fled the building, ran crying in rage and grief into the woods, leaving Rachel and Olivia behind. The next morning, he learnt that Rachel Williams had taken credit for saving Olivia from the fire.

Malcolm hadn't called her out on it. Didn't want the attention on him. He could speak out and tell the truth about how Fern and her friends had pulled a cruel prank and then ran from the cottage. How they were responsible for Margaret's death. But if he did, questions would be asked. They would want to know why he had followed them, why he hadn't stayed with Olivia and Rachel. And worst of all, if Fern and her cronies stuck together, he could end up being blamed for the fire.

It was better to stay quiet. The guilty would get their comeuppance in the end. Malcolm was a big believer in karma.

And so he had adjusted to life simply as a brother, no longer a twin, shifting his sole focus to Alice.

That was the thing about Malcolm. People thought he didn't care, and yes, he tried to give that impression, but the truth was, when it came to the important stuff, he cared almost too much. Especially about his sisters.

He watched his parents mould the newly compliant Alice into the Margaret-sized hole, horrified at the change in his free-spirited sister.

When he eventually learnt what had happened to her during that week he was away, what their so-called parents had done, he was fuelled by disgust, knew whatever happened he would forever be there for his one remaining sister.

That was why she had broken his heart when she had shut him out, moving away.

Alice tried so hard to be normal, marrying well, getting a good education. On the outside she was an achiever, was respected and had a good life. But that was all a shell. She was broken, dead on the inside.

It was Malcolm's job to be there for her, to protect her, to fix her.

Margaret was gone, so he would do whatever it took to look after Alice.

51

Noah's emails threw up no clues and the cameras at his house showed him rushing out of his office and heading out in his car, but Daniella had no idea where it was he was going, knew only that it would have been too early to go and meet Olivia.

His search history had her narrowing her eyes. Why had he been looking at religious sites? She knew his parents were devout Christians, but Noah was atheist. It had been a huge bone of contention with his family.

Pondering, she turned her attention to the names he had jotted down. Five victims, all now dead, given that Janice Plum had succumbed to her burn injuries, plus Fern St Clair, missing since Tuesday.

Next to their names were those of the people who had presumably been the last to see them alive.

Daniella scrolled through the names. Peggy Wick, Rita Works, the receptionist, Grant Savage, who had checked Howard in, Gretchen Self, and the name Noah had added most recently against Fern. Meg Gentile.

Something jarred. What was it?

After dinner, she poured a glass of wine, locking herself away in the study and firing up her laptop as she pondered the names again.

Peggy Wick, Rita Works, Grant Savage, Gretchen Self, Meg Gentile.

Grant was the one that was out of place.

Howard had a girlfriend who was supposed to go with him to the cabin. Daisy Angel.

And Gentile. Wasn't that something to do with religion? Daniella was sure she remembered hearing that word in her religious education lessons at school.

She thought back to Noah's search history. Had he stumbled upon something? Pulling up the last site he had visited, her eyes widened.

The Seven Judgements of God.

Sins at the Cross.

Self-judgement.

Believers' Works.

Judgement of Gentiles.

Judgement of Israel.

Judgement of Angels.

Judgement of the Wicked Dead.

Self... Works... Angel... Gentile... Wick(ed)

It wasn't a coincidence. It couldn't possibly be. All five women had been in the victims lives then had conveniently disappeared after they had died. Of course no one had taken much notice about Peggy, a buyer off the internet, who may not have even turned up. They had looked for Rita, but she again had been an internet girlfriend. There was no proof Gary Lamb had met her, or even that she was real.

The police were tracing Daisy Angel and Gretchen Self. They had witnesses that had seen both women, so could verify they did exist, though both had disappeared straightaway after the deaths.

Meg Gentile was a new one to Daniella. She vaguely remembered a message from a Meg on Fern's phone. Noah must have looked into her, discovered her full name. Was this what he was working on? Had he figured it out before he disappeared?

Israel and Cross were missing. They had to be someone connected to Olivia.

She looked at the names again.

Peggy, Rita, Daisy, Gretchen, Meg.

And the second connection hit her.

All were variations of Margaret. Margaret Grimes.

How had they missed this?

She grabbed her mobile to send a text to Olivia, let her know what she had found, realised with horror that her phone had been on silent, and she had already missed a call and a text message from her.

She listened to the voicemail, then read the text message, learning that Olivia had headed out to Black Dog Farm to meet with Noah.

Realisation hit as she finally understood, knew who Olivia was in danger from. Slamming her laptop shut, she grabbed her car keys and ran from the house.

52

It was all so easy, luring her here.

I could have drugged her, or knocked her unconscious like I did with the other bitch, but that had been a lot of work. There had been risks involved getting her into the car without being seen, and have you any idea how heavy an unconscious person is?

I actually looked it up. It's not that they weigh more, it's all to do with the weight distribution, but I understand now why it's referred to as dead weight. I keep myself fit and healthy, and I have worked hard to build muscle, knowing I had to be in peak physical shape to pull this off, but the dead weight thing still shocked me.

No, it was easier to lure. More fun too, giving me a chance to feed off her reactions; the growing unease when she realised Noah wasn't there, then the blind panic when Molly disappeared and she understood she was all alone. Taking away her best friend had been unplanned, but it turned out to be an inspired move. I would have liked to toy with her for longer, but we are all here for a purpose. It was best to stick to the plan. Deviating could have resulted in me losing her and I couldn't risk that. Not after everything I have been through.

I have her now, though. She is all mine. Along with the other bitch. And soon they will understand real fear, realise that they need to pay for what they did to you. An eye for an eye, a tooth for a tooth. They are sinners, and sinners need to be punished.

It makes me so mad when I realise how they almost got away with it. If Kelly Dearborn hadn't crossed my path, I would have never learnt the truth. If I hadn't recognised her name, remembered that sympathy card she had sent after you had died.

She was seeing Doctor Phillips and after he went long-term sick, his patients were divided among the rest of us at the practice. Kelly hadn't been mine, but when I saw the list I did a little bit of digging, understood she had been the same Kelly Dearborn who had gone to school with you, so I swapped her name to my list on the computer. No one was any the wiser and her case file ended up on my desk.

I only took her on because of who she was. I remembered the lovely words she wrote following your death and I guess it was a connection to you. It almost felt like fate that I had come across her. Little did I know that I was about to uncover her terrible secret.

'Miss Dearborn, please come in.'

I remember welcoming the plainly dressed, dark-haired woman into my office. I knew from her case file that she was not much younger than me, but had I not known that, I would have thought she was at least ten years older. Time had not served her well.

'I'm Doctor Miller.'

Her handshake had been pathetically limp, her eyes never making contact with mine. My first impression of her, I admit, had been disappointment. Call me shallow, but I had built up an image of Kelly Dearborn from her kind words and it was nothing like the woman standing before me.

Her file told me she suffered from anxiety and depression, and notes from Doctor Phillips indicated that she had issues buried in her past. He had been working to get her to talk about those, and now he was gone, I was going to have to start from the beginning, learn how to gain her trust.

It took several weeks to persuade her to open up and when she finally did, telling me about the school trip to Black Dog Farm, even mentioning you by name, I had caught my breath, tried to even out my expression, aware she could never know who I was.

Your death had been ruled an accident and none of us ever questioned that, but as Kelly spoke about the secret she had sworn to take to the grave, I began to realise there was so much more to what had gone on that night, and I understood that somehow I was going to have to work on her to get her to reveal exactly what had happened.

The hardest thing had been to keep my face a blank canvas as the truth came out. How she told me about the two best friends from the school in Norfolk, Fern St Clair and Olivia Blake. How they had tormented you that first night in the dining hall. And how Fern and Olivia had fallen out, with you being dragged into it when Olivia befriended you.

It was so difficult to listen to, but little did I know that worse was to come. A plot had been hatched to lure you to the cottage in the woods so a prank could be played. Olivia and Rachel Williams were to bring you there, where Kelly, Fern and their other friends were waiting.

After you panicked, after the paraffin lamp had broken, setting light to the cottage, they had left you to burn.

I knew Olivia Blake and Rachel Williams had been with you, that Olivia had barely escaped the fire herself. But I didn't know about her betrayal.

She had led us to believe she was your friend, sending emails when she was well enough, distraught at your death. She tried to fool us. Tried to play the victim and the loving friend, when all along she had been part of the prank that got you killed.

After the session where Kelly had confessed the truth about your death, she had left my office looking lighter than she had in months. Her burden shared, but now weighing heavily on my shoulders. She honestly had no idea who I was. But then why would she? She didn't know that Miller was my married name, that I had eagerly taken it to get away from my own. Albeit, it was a name that came from a brief marriage. I had married a doctor who wanted to fix me, who didn't understand that I was beyond repair.

That awful night with my parents and their friends, so many years ago, taught me that. They had tried to fix me, to expel the evil. Of course, I let them believe they had, but my darkness runs too deep, so instead I have learnt to hide it well.

I understood that Kelly had to pay, that they all had to pay, but I acted rashly.

Over the days following our therapy session, I became consumed with rage. Eventually I had gone to Kelly Dearborn's house and, knowing she was inside, I had set fire to it. An eye for an eye, a tooth for a tooth. I wanted her to suffer the way she had made you suffer.

What I hadn't expected was the hollow feeling I was left with after she died.

Kelly had never learnt the truth; she hadn't realised she was being punished. I wanted her to understand. I wanted to see her suffer.

I knew what I had to do, that I had to get it right the next time.

I spent the next few weeks plotting, knew it made sense for Rachel Williams to be the next target. It was easy to create a fake Facebook profile and make contact with her on Marketplace. I didn't even put too much thought into the name, only finding it amusing that I used the pet name, Peggy, that Grandmother used to call you.

I made sure Rachel understood before she died that she had sinned, listened to her cry and apologise and tell me it wasn't her fault before I burned her alive in her car.

That's what they always do, protest their innocence while begging for my mercy. It sickens me and only makes me want to hurt them more.

I had planned to go to Norfolk next, wanting to end this before your last anniversary. Our bloody father ruined that plan though. When I heard he had fallen from the ladder, I hoped he was dead. But no chance of that. He survived the fall and my assistance was required.

You would probably tell me I shouldn't have gone, that I should have been strong enough to say no and continued on my mission to avenge you, but you have to understand, I really didn't have a choice. Since that night, knowing what they are capable of, I have never been able to deny them. Don't get me wrong, I desperately wish our parents didn't have this hold over me, but it is like a compulsion. I have to do as I am told. They are the only people in this world who genuinely scare me.

That month, spent at their new home, helping to nurse him, gave me a new perspective, allowed me time to plot and make sure I got this right. I understood that I didn't want to just watch them die, I wanted to get to know them so when the time came to kill them, they would feel that same betrayal. I decided not to rush things, taking gardening leave from my job and moving to Norfolk.

It was easy to befriend them all; Fern and Janice eager for friends, while Gary had been desperate for a girlfriend, frequenting every dating site. I hooked him on Plenty of Fish (get it?) and he was desperate for the connection, happy to talk, worried he might scare me away if he pushed me into meeting him too quickly. It was simple to set up his death. Olivia had been moaning about being stitched up with the property on Honington Lane and when I googled it, I knew it was perfect, while Gary was only too happy to participate in my kinky little game. The fat pig had become apprehensive when he realised how much chain I was using to bind him to the chair, but by then it was too late.

Howard had also been an easy pick-up, though far pushier. I knew I would have to sleep with him to keep his interest, but a girl's got to do what a girl's got to do, right?

Olivia Blake is the one I have always held mostly responsible though. I know it was Fern's prank, but Olivia is the one who tricked you with her fake friendship. If she had never done that, you would still be alive. We 'met' in a yoga class and it was easy to work my way into her life, starting with the occasional coffee date or drink after work. I had followed her for a few weeks before I introduced myself, found out what I could from social media about her likes and dislikes. I made sure I was fun to hang out with, interested in her boring life, and always there for her.

It was easy to put on a wig and lure her boyfriend, Toby, into bed, my phone hidden and recording everything. Even easier to transfer it to his phone while he was in the shower and upload it on to his Facebook profile. He was history once Olivia saw that, turning to her new best friend for comfort and support.

I look at her now, head down, chin against her chest. She is still unconscious, held in position by the cuffs that bind her to the chair. She is starting to stir, though, and I know I will soon witness that delicious moment of confusion, betrayal and fear as she comprehends what is happening.

'You crazy fucking psycho. Let me go!'

My shoulders tense as the other bitch speaks and I again regret removing her gag. Out here, with so much silence around us, I want to be able to talk to them, listen to them beg, and feed off their screams as they die. Fern hasn't shut up, though, going from sobbing to screaming in rage, and, honestly, it is starting to give me a headache. I glance over my shoulder at her, where she lies in the empty swimming pool, writhing on my crudely constructed cross. After two days with no food or water, I had hoped she would have a little less energy.

'We're just waiting for your friend to join us,' I tell her, trying to keep my voice calm. 'It shouldn't be much longer now.'

Olivia is murmuring now, trying to lift her head.

I open my water bottle, splash some in her face, and it shocks her into consciousness. She gasps, her eyes flying open and gradually coming into focus.

She looks at me, blinking, then at her surroundings and I see her taking it all in, the large dark room with a domed ceiling, lit by orange lanterns that cast flickering shadows across the wall ahead of her.

Fern is yelling abuse again and Olivia's attention drops to where her old friend is chained to the bottom of the pool. She looks back at me, her eyes widening in horror.

'Molly?'

She tries to move, realises she can't. Her struggles becoming more frantic.

'You're awake. Good.'

'Molly? What the hell's going on? Untie me.'

Instead of answering, I disappear behind her, liking this level of control as Olivia tries to twist round to see where I am.

'Molly? Seriously, what the fuck?'

'She's not Molly,' Fern tries to raise her head. 'Why do you keep calling her that? Her name's Meg. And she's a fucking psycho. I've been here for days. She left me tied up in a cupboard. No food, no water.'

'What?' Olivia is still in shock, trying to comprehend what the hell is going on, still attempting to understand that her best friend, the woman she has shared a house with for the last year, is about to betray her trust in the worst possible way.

That's okay. Shock is fine. Shock is good. She still has time to get used to her predicament, to understand why she is here. All I need from her at the moment are her eyes.

Fern's whining, though, is getting on my nerves. It is time for her to repent.

53

'I had to buy a new one of these,' Molly explained conversationally as she came back into the room carrying a suitcase. 'When I was interrupted with Janice, I was forced to leave my old one behind.'

Olivia watched her sit it down by the pool, opening the case to reveal a record player, her mind immediately going back to the kitchen of the house in Honington Lane, where she had watched Gary Lamb burn to death. In the deep end of the pool, Fern had started bawling her eyes out.

What the hell was Molly playing at? Was she really responsible for all of this? For the threatening notes and the murders?

And was her name even Molly? Olivia had known her for over a year, had shared a house with her, considered her a close friend, but Fern knew her too, had called her Meg, so who the fuck was she?

While she was distracted, Olivia tested her restraints more calmly. Not that she felt in the slightest bit calm, but panicking wasn't going to help her get out of this chair. Her wrists were cuffed behind her back and she could feel the chain twisting between the slats of the chair back, while her ankles were bound with rope to the front legs. She tried wriggling her hands free, but the cuffs were too tight. The only way she could get free is if she managed to break the chair. She tested the slats, but they held firm.

Noah was her best hope. She had come here to meet him and his car had been outside, so he had to be around here somewhere.

He had wanted to meet her here. Had insisted she come to him. It was important he had said.

She stilled, a terrifying thought occurring to her. *Is he part of this? Are Noah and Molly working together?*

No. She tried to convince herself it was a ridiculous notion. They hated each other.

Or had that been an act?

She thought back to Noah's messages, urgently trying to get her out to the farm, then Molly insisting on being the good friend and driving her out here.

Shit.

'Is Noah in on this with you?'

Molly removed a record from its sleeve, placing it on the player. 'Noah is no longer your concern.'

'Where is he? I want to see him. Is he here?' Olivia looked frantically around. 'Noah? NOAH?'

'Shut up!' Molly got to her feet. 'You're giving me a headache.'

'He's here.' Fern paused her sobbing, anger behind her words. 'I've seen him. Your arsehole of a boyfriend, he's in on it with her.'

Was that really true?

Where was he? If he was really in on it, she wanted to see him. Wanted to know why he was doing this to her.

'NOAH?'

Olivia's jaw cracked as Molly slapped her hard across the face, leaning in so her face was inches away. 'I told you to shut up.'

Anger bristled against the fear and Olivia rattled her cuffs, tried to lurch forward, pleased when Molly flinched. Unable to use her fists, she spat in Molly's face. 'Fuck you!'

The cold look Molly gave her chilled right through her, and she realised she no longer recognised her lodger at all. But she held her stare, tried not to react when she received another stinging slap.

Molly stepped back, eyes still on her as she slowly wiped the spittle from her cheek. She turned and walked back to the record player, lined up the needle. 'Right, bitches. Let's have some music while we have a little chat.'

Olivia knew what track was going to play, yet couldn't help the shiver down her spine as the familiar Christmas tune echoed around the room.

Molly sat herself down on the edge of the empty pool where she had a full view of both Olivia and Fern, and began to swing her legs back and forth. 'It's beginning to look a lot like Christmas. This was my sister's favourite Christmas song, you know. She always used to choose this one.'

Olivia watched her carefully, waiting for her to continue. Down in the pool, Fern had stopped sobbing, but was still moving restlessly on the cross. Olivia suspected that, like her, she had a feeling this story was going to end badly.

'Of course, she doesn't get to celebrate Christmas any more. But I think you both know that.'

Olivia exchanged a glance with Fern. Molly had to be talking about Margaret. She wracked her brain trying to remember the name of Margaret's older sister.'

Abigail? Anna? It began with A. Alison? No, not Alison. Alice.

'You're Alice,' she said quietly.

'Well done, Olivia.' Molly... Alice gave her a little clap. 'Finally, you're catching up.'

'What happened to your sister was an accident.'

Alice scowled at Fern. 'An accident?'

'We didn't kill her. We never caused the fire. Margaret knocked the lamp over and the place went up in flames. We tried to get her out, I swear.'

'LIAR!'

'It's the truth.'

Olivia watched the exchange, her mind reeling. Fern had been in the cottage that night? 'You were there?'

Fern's eyes widened as she looked at Olivia. 'We were just going to play a stupid prank. No one was supposed to get hurt.'

'You never said anything. All these years and you never said.'

'It was an accident!'

'Yes, but you left us.'

'Okay, stop.' When Olivia and Fern continued to eyeball each other, Alice clapped her hands together. 'Hey, bitches! Eyes to the front of the class.'

When they both looked at her, she smiled thinly. 'Better. I think we all know who is in charge here, so show me a little respect, please.'

'Fucking psycho.' Fern muttered the words under her breath, though it was loud enough for Olivia to hear, so Alice would have heard also.

Olivia watched as she jumped down into the pool, slowly wandering over to Fern, her gaze flicking between the pair of them. 'Might I remind you that you're not in a position to call me names. You might have got away with bullying my sister, but I won't tolerate it.'

She sat down, straddling Fern's legs, pulled something from her pocket.

Olivia thought she was going to be sick when she saw the blade, realising it was a flick knife. She watched as Alice ripped it downwards, tearing open the front of Fern's top. Wrestling against her cuffs, Fern started screaming, the blade carving a line across her exposed belly. Droplets of blood, that looked almost black in the candlelight, dripped on to the white tiles of the pool floor.

'That is for lying and pretending that you tried to save my sister.'

'I'm sorry, I'm sorry!' Fern was gasping and sobbing, trying to roll away as Alice drew another line of blood forming a cross on her stomach.

'Stop! Leave her alone!' Olivia hated Fern, even more now, learning about the prank, but she couldn't watch her being tortured like this.

Alice paused, glancing over at Olivia. 'So you do care what happens to her? I thought so. You try to pretend you weren't part of what happened to Margaret, but I know the truth. You lured my sister to that cottage that night. You pretended to be her friend and you betrayed her.'

'She *was* my friend.'

'Liar! Stop it with the lies or I will come and carve you up too.'

She was delusional. How was Olivia supposed to convince her that it simply wasn't true. Alice only wanted to believe her own twisted version of events.

The record had finished playing, and the only sound was coming from

Fern, who was still wailing, almost hysterically now, as she pleaded with Alice.

Olivia watched Margaret's sister, still trying to come to terms with the fact she had shared a house with her for a year. She had been living with a psychopath all this time and hadn't realised. All the times Molly had cooked for her, they had stayed in watching movies, sharing everything with one another. Had anything been true?

Molly... Alice, she had to keep reminding herself, could have poisoned her or stabbed her in her sleep. It was scary realising how vulnerable she had been all this time. Of course, Alice wouldn't have taken that easy route. She wanted her big finale, to watch Olivia suffer.

The thought of that terrified her to the core. She had seen what had happened to Gary, watched the video of Howard. It was better not to think about what Alice had planned. Better instead to focus on escaping.

It wasn't over until she stopped breathing.

'Will you shut the fuck up?' Alice smashed her fist into Fern's face, and Olivia flinched. 'I can't concentrate.'

She got up from the pool floor, shaking her head, went over the far side, picking up one of the three plastic canisters that Olivia had noticed, uncapping it and splashing the liquid over Fern.

The strong petrol fumes filled the room and Fern's sobbing and struggling intensified. 'No, Alice, please don't do this, please, I'm begging you. I'll do anything.'

Olivia yanked harder at her cuffs, trying to break the slats of the chair, as Fern was doused with the other two canisters. She squeezed her eyes shut, knew she couldn't watch this. She had been frightened when she first gained consciousness, understood she was dealing with a crazy person, but now knowing what was about to happen, she was terrified.

'Open your eyes, Olivia.'

There was no way she could watch someone else burn to death.

'I said, open your fucking eyes, bitch!'

'Don't do this to her, please.'

'Open your eyes, Olivia, or I will come over there and force you to watch.'

Hearing Alice moving towards her, Olivia complied.

'That's better. I don't want you to miss this.' Alice pulled herself out of the pool, walked towards her. She had the knife and Olivia stilled as she moved behind the chair, felt her scoop up her hair, twisting it around and pulling tightly, as she leant down to rub her mouth up against her ear. 'I enjoyed fucking with you,' she whispered. 'Stupid bitch, it was so easy. You thought you were going mad.'

Olivia held her breath, forcing herself to remain calm, not show any reaction, knowing that was what Alice wanted.

'You know I fucked your boyfriend. Screwed his brains out in fact.'

Alice had slept with Noah?

'All those years with you, he needed it.'

Toby?

'Didn't take much to make him stray.'

Olivia recalled that awful post on Facebook that had ended their relationship. 'It was you in the video.'

'I needed to get him out of your life,' Alice said simply, letting the knife slide round to caress Olivia's cheek. 'That way I could be the sympathetic friend offering a shoulder to cry on and the perfect lodger to help you afford the mortgage.'

Plus, it cleared the way for Noah. Olivia thought that, but didn't say it aloud.

Fern had said she had seen him at the farmhouse, but Alice hadn't confirmed he was helping her. And he hadn't yet made an appearance. Although it was looking increasingly likely he was involved in this, Olivia was still clinging to the faint hope he hadn't completely used her.

Alice dropped her hair, stepping away from the chair back over to the record player. She stared down at Fern who had quietened to a whimper, reset the needle on the record.

'Let's have some more music, shall we?'

Olivia knew that if she survived tonight, she would never be able to listen to this wretched song again.

She watched as Alice walked round to the far side of the pool. Fern was watching her too, frantically twisting her head to see where Alice was. Seeing the woman pick up one of the paraffin lamps, holding it over the pool, she went bug-eyed and started pleading again.

'Begging isn't going to help you at this stage,' Alice told her. 'However, unlike you I'm not a completely heartless bitch, so, any last words, for me, or for our captive audience, or for Margaret?'

When Fern let out a bloodcurdling scream in response, she shrugged, glanced over at Olivia and smiled cruelly. 'Okay. Don't say I didn't ask.'

And with that, she let go of the lamp.

54

There were two in the bed and the little one said, roll over,
roll over.
So they all rolled over and one fell out.
There was one in the bed...

It was a beautiful moment watching Fern burn on the cross and it was worth all of the time and hard work it took dragging her out here to the farm.

Their screams had echoed around the domed room; Fern in agony, Olivia in horror, and I had screamed with them, though mine was cathartic, knowing the wicked were finally being punished for their sins.

Do you know that the screams barely last a minute when you set someone on fire? Of course, each second feels much longer, but after around a minute, the brain shuts down and unconsciousness often takes over. It's a shame, as Fern St Clair deserved to suffer for longer for what she did to you. I take my comfort from knowing that it's not truly over for her, that an eternity in hell awaits her.

Olivia had tried to look away, so I had forced her head back, my knife to her throat, as I made her watch. I wanted her to witness every glorious moment of Fern's death. She had become hysterical, struggling against me and begging for it to stop, showing her true colours and proving her allegiance to her bitch friend. If she had really been true to you, Margaret, she would have wanted Fern to atone for what she did to you.

She is subdued now, in shock, I think, as we walk into the dark woods along the track that leads to the cottage. That is perhaps better as it makes her easier to control, especially as I am having to lug the record player with us. Her hands are still cuffed behind her, but I had to free her ankles as I needed her to walk. She is limping from where she fell down the stairs earlier and I don't think she can get away, but for added security I put a noose around her neck. Each time she slows down, I give it a tug to remind her it is there.

I wonder if she is remembering the last time she walked this path, when she was with you, playing the charlatan friend as she lead you to your death.

How fitting that I should now be doing the same to her.

This was always my destiny, I realise. My purpose for being here. To make the guilty pay for hurting you.

The darkness was always in me, even at a young age. Our parents showed me that. They tried to drive it out of me and I sometimes wonder if that was why you were taken from them, as their punishment for intervening, because the darkness is too strong.

I had just turned sixteen the winter that you died and life was all about discovery. I had a boyfriend, you know. Our parents were appalled, tried to stop us seeing each other, but we would sneak out and meet when you had all gone to bed. I thought I was being so clever, but I didn't realise that they knew. That they were watching and plotting against me.

That's why they sent you and Malcolm off to Black Dog Farm. It was all because of me. They needed you both out of the house so you didn't witness what they had planned.

I didn't understand at that point. I honestly thought I was just having fun. I didn't realise I had evil running through my veins.

* * *

Alice finished applying her make-up and ran a brush through her hair. It was Wednesday night and she had plans to meet up with Scott. Her parents had their church friends over and after making small talk with them to appease her dad, she had excused herself to bed. It was only half-eight, but it was a school night, so none of them really raised an eyebrow.

She would give it half an hour then sneak across the landing to Malcolm's bedroom. His room overlooked a sloping part of the roof, which she could shimmy down to reach the ground.

When Malcolm was home, he turned a blind eye when Alice used her escape route. As siblings they bickered, but they were drawn together by a mutual dislike for their parents. By way of thank-you for keeping quiet, Alice would stick her spare change in the glass bottle that sat on his desk.

She was excited to meet Scott tonight. He had told her he had a Christmas present for her and she couldn't wait to find out what it was. She hadn't had the opportunity to buy anything for him, but she still had something special to offer. Tonight she planned to give him her virginity. She had talked with her best friend, Jenny, about it, decided after four months of seeing Scott that she was ready.

He didn't know about it yet. It was going to be a surprise.

She listened downstairs to the chatter, could hear the clinking of cups and saucers as her parents' guests used her mother's best china, drinking tea and tucking into slices of her home-made Victoria sponge. Marie Grimes only ever baked for her church friends. Alice, Malcolm and Margaret were not allowed sweet treats.

Holding her breath, Alice twisted the door handle, readying herself to creep across the landing, hoping that the noise downstairs would mask the sound of the creaking floorboard outside her room.

The door didn't open.

Frowning, she tried it again, anger and frustration burning as she realised it was locked.

Seriously? Her dad had locked her in her bedroom? He hadn't done this in years and then only as a punishment. Which had her wondering, what had she done to deserve this?

A lick of fear heated her belly as it crossed her mind he might know she was planning on sneaking out to meet Scott.

He couldn't know. Surely it was impossible. She had been so careful not to get caught.

There was nothing else she could think of that deserved punishment, and worry turned to dread, in fear of one of her father's beatings.

Wiping the make-up from her face, she quickly undressed and crawled under the bedcovers.

If he thought she was asleep, realised he had got it wrong, maybe nothing would happen.

Alice lay there for over half an hour, unable to settle, knowing Scott would be waiting for her and wondering where she was. Her parents wouldn't allow her to have a mobile phone, so she had no way of contacting him and letting him know what had happened.

She also feared hearing the foreboding sound of footsteps on the stairs, prayed they wouldn't come.

As the minutes ticked by, she heard the familiar creak, knew her praying hadn't worked and it would be her father coming to check on her. She rolled on to her side, closing her eyes, trying to stop the trembling, as the key twisted in the door.

'Alice?'

She ignored him, pretended to be asleep.

'Alice, wake up.'

And it was then she realised her father wasn't alone, heard the other footsteps, the other voices.

She wanted to carry on pretending she was asleep, but shock had her rolling over as her parents' friends filed into the room, gathering around the bed.

There were eight of them in total, including Gerald and Marie, and they all had Bibles with them, their faces solemn. Mrs Rigby, her mother's closest friend, who was the most pious of them all, held a large crucifix in her bony hand, and...

Was that a whip her husband had?

Her father stood ominously at the back of the room by the door, preventing any escape.

'What's going on?' Her voice came out as a whimper, terrified they were planning on hurting her.

'Alice Catherine Grimes, you have been sinning against God,' Mrs Rigby told her, her lips thin. 'We need to drive the Devil from you.'

'No, please. I haven't done anything wrong.'

'Liar!' Marie Grimes stepped forward, her face like stone. 'I overheard you on the phone, talking about giving your virginity to that boy. Sinners need to be punished.'

'Please, no, I won't see him again. I promise. Please don't hurt me.'

Alice screamed as the duvet was pulled from the bed, hands grabbing hold of her and flipping her on to her stomach. Her nightdress was torn away and she struggled against them as they pinned her down.

She heard the key turn again in the door, understood her father had just locked her in the room with these monsters.

'Daddy, no, please!'

In a voice that was completely devoid of emotion, he responded with just one single word.

'Begin.'

* * *

The memory of that night still haunts me, even all these years later I can still recall the chanting prayers, feel the stinging burn of the whip. I tried so hard to become the daughter they wanted after you died. The thought of failing them again scared me half to death.

I hear choking, and a strangled sob brings me back to the present.

I have been so caught up in the terror of my absolution, I hadn't noticed Olivia stumble, but she is face down on the forest floor, the noose around her neck tightening as my hand yanks on the rope. Panic surges through me as I realise I have been so caught up in the past that I had forgotten about her. She can't die yet.

Easing some tension in the rope, I kick her hard in the ribs. 'Get up!'

I have frightened myself. Spending too long dwelling in the past is dangerous. All of this planning and I could have ruined it in one split-second. Tonight is about the present. Tonight is about making sure Olivia pays. And it can't go wrong.

She struggles pathetically to get to her feet, but she is still coughing from where I accidentally choked her, and with her hands bound behind her back it is difficult.

This time when I tighten the noose, I am careful not to crush her windpipe. 'Get the fuck up, bitch.'

She tries again, stumbles again.

Losing patience, I put down the record player case and grab hold of her arm, yanking her back to her feet. She staggers for a moment, but this time manages to keep her balance.

We are losing time so I grab the case again and push her forward, keen to get her to the cottage.

She knows where we are going. She becomes more agitated as our destination comes into sight and I guess it's because she understands that she will soon meet the same fate as her friends.

It has been a pain walking her out here, but this was where you died, Margaret. This is where she brought you and left you to burn to death. There really was no other choice. This has to be the place where it all ends.

Olivia doesn't want to go inside the cottage, but I push her round to the back of the property, to the window you climbed through all those years ago.

Knowing it will be impossible for her to climb inside herself, I part lift her, pushing her inside. She cries in pain as she lands on the floor.

I quickly clamber through the window, pull her to her feet, half dragging her through to the back room of the cottage, the place where they found your body.

When the light of my torch falls on the cross I have erected against the centre beam, her eyes widen in panic and she starts struggling again.

'No, Alice, please, no!'

I almost want to laugh when they beg. After everything I have done, all the work I have put into making this happen, do they really think they can reason with me and change my mind?

Sinners have to be punished. I was forced to realise that a long time ago. Made to understand that there could be no mercy.

I suffered, Margaret suffered. And now it is Olivia's turn.

55

The sound of footsteps outside had him pausing and he relaxed his wrists, let them rest for a second.

Was the bitch coming back?

He listened, pretty sure he could make out voices. Two voices in fact, both female.

That had his heart beating faster.

He had watched the sun going down, darkness filling the room, knowing that time was running out.

Pressing the sole of his boot against the radiator pipe, holding on to his handcuffed wrist with his free hand, he renewed his efforts to free himself, yanking on the cuff as hard as he could.

It had been the photo that had led him to her.

A young Alice Grimes.

Although she had longer, darker hair, was a little plumper in the face, there was no mistaking who she was. Those taunting eyes and that familiar sneer she thought passed for a smile.

Molly Cross. Olivia's lodger.

At that point Noah probably should have called the police, at the very least told Daniella or tried to warn Olivia, but in his usual rash way he had seen red and gone straight after the target.

Which in this instance was really bloody stupid.

The fact Alice had used aliases that related to the Seven Judgements told him she was batshit crazy, but knowing she had gone to the elaborate length of integrating herself into Olivia's life over such a long period of time warned him she was also determined.

Determined, crazy and dangerous.

Not a good combination.

She had passed him in her car as he was approaching Olivia's house, planning to confront her, and curiosity had him swinging his Audi around, tailing her out to Black Dog Farm.

It was then he understood this was where she would have brought Fern St Clair, would likely be the place she intended to end her twisted murder spree.

He had held back then, knowing he had to find Fern and get her to safety.

Alice had gone into the main farmhouse and he had followed at a distance, watching her erecting what appeared to be a giant crucifixion cross in the bottom of the empty swimming pool.

He should have gone after her then, taken her by surprise, but he didn't know where Fern was, feared Alice wouldn't tell him. He needed her to lead him to where she was keeping her.

While she was busy with her little DIY project, he had used the time to scope out the building, then he had followed her out to the cottage in the woods, where she had constructed another cross, hammering wooden planks to one of the vertical beams that had withstood the fire.

Two crosses, two more victims. He understood now how this was supposed to end.

While she was outside and distracted, he had snuck into the cottage, assuming that this was where she was holding Fern.

He had a plan. Rescue Fern, overpower Alice, call the cops.

What he hadn't counted on was Alice realising he was there. She must have seen him following her. He didn't hear her as she crept up behind him, realised she was there at the last second, just before the hammer had smacked against his skull.

That was how he had found himself cuffed to the radiator, with a throbbing headache and his keys and phone missing, wondering why she hadn't killed him outright.

Instead, she was waiting for him when he awoke, sitting on an old crate, the hammer swinging in her hands, and that irritating smirk on her face.

Noah wanted to throttle her, realised in frustration that he couldn't when his hand rattled uselessly against the pipe.

'Well, well, well. This is an unexpected delight.'

She had shifted the crate closer, keen to goad him, and tell him all about how she had duped both him and Olivia.

'It's over, Alice. I'm not the only one who is on to you.'

She regarded him for a moment, not seeming the slightest bit perturbed. 'I think if that was true we would have heard sirens by now. You followed me out here alone. My money says you didn't tell anyone where you were going. I know you too well, Noah.'

When he didn't respond to that, anger building, she added, 'Recklessness leads to stupidity. You were careless and look where that's landed you.'

Fucking bitch.

He rattled the cuff again in fury, tried to lurch towards her.

Although her eyes widened slightly, she didn't flinch, sitting just an inch out of his grasp and seeming amused by his efforts.

'Now let me tell you what's going to happen.' She absently tapped the hammer against her palm. 'You're going to stay right here and I'm going to go home to Olivia – who hates you, by the way – and I'm going to play the dutiful best friend. Oh, I forgot to say, I really do need to thank you for that. Your dirty little secret has really cemented our friendship. She was so mad at you, she even smashed up your stupid cameras, so I no longer have to sneak in and out of the utility room window.'

'I already have you on camera.'

That had her pausing, looking wary. 'No you don't.'

It was a semi-bluff. He did have her on camera, but unfortunately the image wasn't clear enough to make a formal identification. She didn't know that though.

'I went back over the footage. That night Olivia freaked and found the back door open, the camera picked you up in the back garden. You didn't get quite out of the shot. It's sitting right there on my computer. That's how you're going to get caught.'

Alice's eyes narrowed. 'I don't believe you.' But he could tell she wasn't sure, that he had given her something to think about. She held up his mobile phone, taunting, the smirk back, widening to a grin. 'I'm going to have fun being you.'

Noah mentally kicked himself. *Fucking stupid idiot.* He could only hope that Olivia was still too mad at him to answer any messages.

'You've made it so much easier for me to lure her out here tomorrow night. Lure her out here and hurt her the same way that she hurt my sister.'

'She didn't do anything to your sister. Olivia and Margaret were friends.'

'That is bullshit. Olivia Blake killed my sister.'

'You're fucking twisted. She almost died in the fire too.'

'Is that supposed to make me feel better? She survived and Margaret died. And it was all Olivia's fault. Tomorrow night I am going to fix that. And you get to be here for the whole thing. To listen to your girlfriend's screams and know you can do nothing to save her. Of course, you won't have to worry about living with the guilt that you helped me do this. I am going to burn this place to the ground.'

She was crazy, Noah could see that now. Wondered how he had never noticed it before. He had never liked Olivia's lodger, knew there was something off about her, but he hadn't expected this.

'I'm going to kill you,' he promised. 'I'm going to get free from this cuff and I'm going to kill you.'

She simply stared back at him, with eyes that were already dead.

Alice had left him after that and he had spent a frustrated night cursing himself for not telling anyone what he had discovered and worrying like hell about Olivia and what mind games Alice was playing with her, while trying to free himself.

There was a pile of wire on the opposite side of the room and he tried his damnedest to get to it, knowing he could use it to unlock the cuff. It was too far away though and there was nothing within reach that he could use to hook it. For a while, he focused on snapping the radiator pipe, but the damn thing was fixed solidly in place.

Eventually, tiredness had taken over and he had crashed and burned, falling asleep on the hard, dirty floor, renewing his efforts when the sun came up.

Now it was dark again, the evening of the anniversary of Margaret's death, and time was running out for Olivia.

Noah knew Alice was planning one murder at the farmhouse, the other in the cottage, and assumed she planned to kill Olivia here, as she had mentioned wanting him to hear her die.

His worst fears were realised when he recognised the voices of the two women, heard Olivia pleading with Alice to let her go.

'Olivia?'

His voice echoed through the cottage as he paused again with his efforts to free himself.

Unless he could find a way to break through the pipe, he couldn't help her, but he needed her to know he was here with her and she wasn't alone.

* * *

Alice had looped the end of the noose around the top of the cross she had Olivia pushed up against and was uncuffing her left wrist when the familiar voice had yelled out Olivia's name.

She paused struggling, her eyes widening. 'Noah?'

Alice smiled cruelly at her, the light from the candles she had lit making her look sinister. 'He can't help you now,' she whispered and Olivia felt something hard press up against her thigh as Alice leant against her. The pocket knife.

Her left arm temporarily free, as Alice tried to cuff her right wrist to the cross, Olivia reached down, feeling for the knife, her fingers touching the metal casing. She plucked it out, fumbling to flick it open. As Alice went to lock the cuff, she stabbed the knife down, aiming for the woman's neck, but catching her in the top of the arm.

It was enough to shock Alice into dropping the cuff, and as she started screaming, Olivia kneed her hard in the stomach, sending her flying back.

'Liv?'

It was Noah again. His voice was coming from somewhere above her.

Olivia struggled to remove the noose from around her neck, standing up on tiptoe and managing to loosen it, one eye on Alice who was still on the floor, already trying to sit up.

The loop now wide enough, she yanked it over her head, fleeing for the stairs as Alice's fingertips brushed against her ankle, knowing she only had precious seconds.

'Noah?' It was pitch-black upstairs, but his voice led her to one of the bedrooms. 'Where are you?'

'I'm right here.' The sound of a rattling chain. 'I'm cuffed to the radiator.'

Had he been here all this time?

'There's wire, Liv, to your left, down in the corner. I need you to pass it to me.'

As she felt her way to where he was telling her, she heard Alice's footsteps racing up the stairs, immediately tensing at the shriek of outrage that pealed from her lips.

The light from her torch cast a faint beam on the room.

Spotting the wire, Olivia threw it in Noah's direction, then she snatched up a loose piece of wood, slamming it into Alice's chest as she charged into the room. As Alice fell to her knees, Olivia hit her again, this time catching her hard across the face.

'Take that, you fucking crazy bitch.'

She turned to Noah, saw the wire had fallen just out of his reach. As she went to retrieve it, his eyes widened.

'Liv, behind you!'

56

Even with his arm extended as far as it would stretch and lying on the floor, the end of the wire was just out of the reach of his foot. Realising that he wasn't going to reach it, Noah sat back up, tried to figure out another plan.

It had been several minutes since Alice had knocked Olivia out cold and he had watched in frustration and despair as she had dragged her limp body back down the stairs. Apart from his initial yelling, the cottage was ominously quiet.

He suspected Alice was waiting for Olivia to wake up, understood that there was no satisfaction for her in burning the cottage down while her victim was unconscious. Once that happened it would be game over.

The one positive that he did have was the dropped torch on the floor that at least gave him a little light to work with.

He needed to get the wire – it was his only hope – and to get it he needed to find something that would reach. There was nothing close to him in the room that he could use. The piece of wood that Olivia had hit Alice with was in the doorway, again out of his reach.

He looked down at what he was wearing, debating whether he could use his boot laces or belt. Deciding the belt had most chance of success, he unhooked it from his jeans. He still couldn't get close enough using his free hand, so would have to use his foot.

Making a lasso with the belt, he used his boot lace to secure the end then stretched back out on the floor, lifting his leg and trying to hook the belt loop over the wire.

It was long enough, but it was exasperatingly difficult to catch hold of the wire.

From downstairs came music. He recognised the song, 'It's beginning to look a lot like Christmas'; knew this wasn't a good sign. Olivia must be awake.

He tried again with the lasso, catching the wire once and managing to yank it a couple of inches before losing it.

This just wasn't going to work.

He yanked on the cuff, swearing in frustration. Made another attempt.

This time the wire caught. He yanked the belt to him, grabbing the end of the wire and bending the end, so he could pick the lock.

An agonising scream from below told him he needed to hurry.

* * *

Malcolm Grimes entered the cottage just in time to see his sister using the knife.

Although he hadn't seen Olivia Blake in years, he recognised her, knew she was the girl who was tied to the cross, her arms stretched wide apart and held by cuffs, her feet bound together by rope. She was crying out in pain and writhing against her bonds as she desperately tried to escape the knife, her jumper ripped open and blood seeping from where Alice was carving into her stomach. All around them, candles and lanterns cast a spooky glow, while music played on a portable record player.

He recognised the track, realised it was Margaret's favourite Christmas song.

'Alice?'

His sister stopped her knife work, her shoulders tensing. 'Malcolm?'

She spoke his name as if she didn't believe it was really him, but then she turned, saw it was, and her face crumpled. Dropping the knife, she rushed towards him. 'Malcolm, I didn't know you were here.'

And then she was in his arms and his beautiful, damaged sister was sobbing like a baby.

'What are you doing here, Alice?' He glanced over her shoulder to where Olivia was watching him warily, unsure if he was friend or foe.

Alice eased away from him, her eyes shining bright. 'This is for Margaret. I am doing this for her. I know how she died, Malcolm. The sinners are being punished.'

'This is Olivia, though. She was Margaret's friend.'

Alice shook her head. 'No, you're wrong. Kelly told me. Olivia was part of it. She was the one who lured Margaret here. She is the one who is responsible for her dying.'

'Is that so?' Malcolm looked at Olivia again.

Her eyes filled with tears as she shook her head. 'It's not true. I cared about your sister. Please.'

'Liar!' Alice broke free of Malcolm's arms, stormed back over to Olivia, who tried to flinch away, pointing her finger at her. 'You did this. It's all your fault. And now you have to pay.'

Glancing wildly around, Alice reached for one of the canisters of petrol lined up just inside the door.

'Alice, what are you doing?'

'What I came here to do. I'm going to burn the cottage down. I told you. This is for Margaret.'

'Is this what Margaret would have wanted?'

Alice nodded. 'Of course it is. She knows this is all for her. I talk to her all the time, you know.'

Malcolm watched her pouring petrol around the edge of the room, his mind going back to that day he had caught her with the matches in their family home. He had taken the fall for her that day, remembering what Gerald and Marie Grimes had done to her and knowing how broken she was.

She was his sister. His responsibility. It was his job to help her, to fix her.

They only had each other.

'Alice?'

'Yes, Malcolm?'

'It's okay. I'm here now. I will help you finish this.'

* * *

For a brief moment Olivia had thought Malcolm Grimes was going to help her, that he understood his sister was completely deranged. He had appeared in the doorway, seemed truly shocked by what was happening. At first, he had seemed to rationalise with Alice, but now Olivia understood that he was here to help his sister kill her and panic took over.

Escape had seemed so close. She had found Noah, put up a good fight against Alice, but then the evil bitch had knocked her out cold. When she awoke with a banging headache and found herself tied to the cross, she understood it was too late.

There had been no more noise from upstairs and Olivia didn't dare call out to Noah or ask Alice about him, fearing he could already be dead.

Malcolm had been the cavalry. He was the last possible chance Olivia had of escaping, but Alice was his blood, and it was apparent he was now taking her side. Fighting against two of them, she had no chance of getting away.

She pulled uselessly on the cuffs that held her wrists to each side of the cross, watching as Alice doused the room with petrol, and trying not to remember the agonising deaths that Gary, Howard, Janice, and Fern had suffered.

After telling Alice he would help her, Malcolm had disappeared back outside, leaving Olivia alone again with his psycho sister. She wondered where he had gone, her terror building by the second. Knowing they now had her completely trapped, she just wanted the nightmare to be over with.

The last canister empty, Alice halted in front of her. She held one of the candles and Olivia tried not to react, not wanting to let the crazy woman feed on her fear.

'Any last words, Livvy?'

Protesting her innocence, telling Alice that her friendship with Margaret had been real was just going to fall on deaf ears. Olivia had already tried to reason with her and nothing would change Alice's stance.

She was crazy, plain and simple, and anger was the only defence left. 'Fuck you!' she spat, knowing that the words would rile Alice.

She was right, could tell from the sneer on Alice's face that the woman hadn't been expecting that and it hadn't been the reaction she had hoped for.

Malcolm picked that moment to walk back into the room and to Olivia's horror she realised he was holding an axe. She struggled frantically against her bindings as he strode towards her and Alice, fresh fear taking over.

'What are you doing with that candle?' he demanded. 'I told you I would help you finish this.'

'I'm sorry, Malcolm.'

Olivia's eyes widened as he disappeared behind the cross, her heart thumping in her chest. *Oh God, oh God, oh God.*

'Please don't,' she begged.

As the axe rose, Alice looked on in horror. 'No!'

* * *

Noah reached the bottom of the stairs just as Alice dropped the candle, the trail of petrol instantly igniting. His eyes went to where Olivia was bound to the cross and the man who was swinging the axe down behind her.

'Stop!'

Olivia was screaming, Alice was hysterical, dropping to her knees as she howled in anguish, and the flames were rising higher. The blade of the axe sliced into the wooden cross, tearing it apart and freeing the piece of wood that held Olivia's left arm.

Before any of them could react, a second swing freed her right arm, then Malcolm had dropped the axe, had fallen to the floor, his arms wrapped tightly around his sobbing sister.

'She was supposed to die, Malcolm. She has to die.'

The room was fully ablaze now and Noah rushed across to where Olivia was desperately trying to free her cuffs from the mangled wood. Her feet were still bound he realised, and he dropped to his knees, working to untie the knots, before grabbing her hand and pulling her towards the window at the back of the cottage.

'Come on, we need to get out of here.'

They soon discovered that escape was going to be impossible. The flames were already too high, thick smoke rising. Olivia was glancing frantically around her, the panic clear on her face, as she realised they were trapped.

Noah turned back, spotted the axe Malcolm had used to break up the cross. Quickly, he grabbed it. 'Come on!'

He dragged Olivia up the stairs, the only route left, and went back into the room he had become far too familiar with over the last twenty-four hours, kicking the door closed behind them. 'Stand back.'

Using the axe, he sliced it into the wooden board that was blocking the window.

'Hurry!' Olivia's tone was urgent and when he glanced back, he could see smoke seeping up through the floorboards.

Another swing of the axe splintered the wood, a third broke it open. Handing the tool to Olivia, he kicked at the remainder of the board, clearing a big enough gap to climb through. He peered out of the window. There was nothing to break their fall under the drop.

He caught hold of both her hands, cuffs still dangling from her wrists, and pulled her to the window.

'We need to jump. It's not too high.'

She nodded, glanced out of the window, and while he knew she didn't like the idea, she understood it was better than the alternative.

He caught the dangling cuffs, pressed them into her palms. 'Hold on to these, okay, so you don't bash yourself in the face with them. And keep your legs together,' he instructed. 'You want to try to land on the balls of your feet, then when you hit the ground, roll to the side.'

He helped her out of the window and lowered her as far as he could. 'Ready?'

When she nodded, he let go, held his breath, waited until he saw she had landed safely before climbing through himself.

Behind him he could hear the flames fiercely pounding against the door and knew he only had seconds.

Lowering himself down from the ledge, he jumped.

***

Olivia had landed with a thump and her body cried out in pain, but she knew it was from the bruises and injuries she had already sustained over the course of the night. Nothing had been broken. She rolled on to her knees, brushing herself down, and watched fearfully as Noah prepared to drop, terrified the building might suddenly collapse.

But then he was on the ground beside her and they were both safe. At least from the fire.

'You okay?'

She nodded, glancing fearfully around. She had been so preoccupied with escaping the flames, she had briefly forgotten about Alice. 'Where are they?'

Noah was silent for a moment. 'They were still inside. The fire's too fierce. There's nothing we can do for them.'

Olivia stared at the cottage, the enormity of everything that had happened all catching up at once. She didn't care about Alice. Yes, the woman had issues, was mentally unstable, but she had still been clear-minded enough to cruelly murder six people in cold blood. Malcolm was different though. While Olivia had initially thought he was going to hurt her, that hadn't been his intention.

'He saved me.' Her voice trembled when she spoke and was a no more than a whisper. 'I thought he was going to kill me, but he didn't. He saved my life. I would be in there right now if he hadn't cut me free.'

Noah crawled over to where she sat. 'I'm sorry, he's gone, Liv. They both are. There's nothing you can do. But you're here. You're safe, and you're going to be okay.'

She didn't protest when he folded his arms around her, held him right back, and together they sat and watched as the cottage burned.

57

Daniella had been the one who had called the emergency services when she saw smoke billowing from the cottage.

'Looks like I'm too late to save the day,' she had quipped, walking into the clearing and startling them both.

Noah had been relieved to see her, though he pointed out she could have arrived twenty minutes earlier.

He had forced Olivia into an ambulance, ignoring her protests because he knew that she needed to be checked over. Even if her injuries were mostly superficial, she had taken a couple of heavy bashes to the head, and he didn't doubt she was still in shock.

They had sat mostly in silence as they watched the fire burn, and she had let him hold her, but he wasn't fool enough to think things had been fixed between them, knew she may go back to hating him after everything had calmed down.

He had deceived her, he got that, and knew he had broken her trust. She was safe though and that was the most important thing. He told himself he would respect whatever decision she reached about their future.

Daniella had watched him with a smirk as the ambulance took Olivia away and he narrowed his eyes. 'What?'

'Didn't you get bashed over the head too? Seems to me you should have been in that ambulance with her.'

'I'll get checked out later.'

Noah had insisted on hanging around, despite the protests of the paramedics, though he had gratefully taken the bottle of water that Daniella had offered.

The bodies of Malcolm and Alice Grimes were never recovered, and the police had sent out a search and rescue team, in case they had made it out of the cottage and into the surrounding woodland. This was eventually called off without success.

Noah had kept tabs on both of them, was certain he would know if they made a reappearance. He wasn't too worried about it though, was certain there was a reasonable explanation. He remembered seeing the siblings huddled on the floor surrounded by flames, and found it unlikely that either of them would have survived.

He only saw Olivia once again after the fire. She had told him she needed some space and time alone to process everything that had happened and he had accepted her decision without argument, going to Devon to stay with his family over Christmas, then throwing himself into work when he returned in early January.

He had bumped into her brother, Jamie, at the gym a few times. The first encounter had been a little uncomfortable because Jamie now knew that he had been used to get to his sister. But he also knew that Noah had helped her escape from the fire. After some initial frostiness, they had settled back into a tentative friendship.

The ball had been left in Olivia's court so she could call when she was ready; but she never did. Although Noah was disappointed, he had promised to leave her alone, and resolved to do so.

His decision had upset Daniella, who kept grumbling about how miserable and bad-tempered he had become. She had attempted to fix him up with a handful of her friends, but there were no second dates. Noah always managed to find fault with every one of them.

'Why don't you just go and see her?' she suggested, one afternoon in early spring when they were out on surveillance.

Noah shot her a look, but didn't answer. They both knew who Daniella meant.

'Has it ever crossed your mind that maybe she is reluctant to contact you?'

'How have you reached that conclusion?'

'You met her under false pretences, and you've never really done anything to prove to her that she wasn't just a job.'

'I apologised for that.'

'But did you properly apologise and convince her that you cared about her? Look at it from where Olivia is standing. You only got close to her because someone had hired you to investigate her and when you became involved with her, you kept the truth a secret. Then, when she found out what that truth was, you never got in contact to convince her that she had it wrong and that you do really care about her.'

'I never got in touch with her because I was stuck in the middle of the woods cuffed to a bloody radiator.'

'Details.' Daniella waved her hand dismissively. 'You had time after the fire to have that conversation, but instead she told you she needed a bit of time and you just said "Okay, bye". She probably thought she was doing you a favour cutting you loose.'

Noah had scowled at that, dismissed her theory as stupid. Olivia knew he was sorry about everything that had happened. Still, Daniella's comments stuck with him, playing on his mind. The next time he saw Jamie, he swallowed his pride and asked after Olivia.

Initially, Jamie seemed reluctant to talk about it, but then he admitted, 'She's found it tough.' The truth had come out then about how much Olivia had struggled over the months following the fire, both with her confidence and with trusting people. Jamie suggested that what Daniella had said was true, that Olivia still believed she had just been a job to Noah. 'That's why she never got in touch. She figured if she really meant something to you, then you would have tried to fight for her.'

Jamie had looked contrite then, perhaps realising he had said too much. 'She's been doing a lot better in the last few weeks. She quit her job and has been working in the restaurant, and she's been going out and socialising with friends more. She's slowly building her confidence back up.'

'That's good. I'm pleased for her. Do me a favour and tell her I said hi, will you?'

'Sure.' Jamie hesitated. 'You know, you could always stop by and tell her that in person. I think she would like that.'

* * *

A lot of things had changed for Olivia following the fire, some bad and some good.

She had initially gone to stay with her mother, unable to face returning to the home in Salhouse which she had shared with Molly.

It wasn't just the memories, the house was just too big and empty, and she was far too jumpy. If the last few weeks had taught her anything, it was to practise caution and to be very afraid of the things that go bump in the night.

What had started as a couple of weeks over Christmas and New Year had turned into a much longer stay, and eventually she had realised that she couldn't move back home. Instead she had put the house on the market and stayed with her mum and Jamie while she considered her options.

She had also quit her job at the estate agents. She lasted two hours when she returned in the New Year for the first time since the fire. Roger's guilt-tripping that she had taken too much time off and Jeremy's snide looks and comments seemed so childish and insignificant given everything she had gone through and the idea of having to spend day after day with either of them was excruciating. It wasn't as if she was any good at selling houses anyway.

Elena had been delighted when Olivia had taken a waitressing job in the restaurant. It wasn't permanent, but it was okay for now while Olivia decided on her next career move.

She had always kept her circle tight, but since Christmas she had made it even smaller, scared to let anyone new in.

Molly... Alice's betrayal had left her reeling. The woman had managed to work her way into Olivia's life and had shared her house. Knowing that she had been so easily duped had really scared her. It would be a long time before she could trust anyone new again.

Noah's deception had been a little different, but no less hurtful. Olivia understood now that he had just been doing his job and that everything he had done was with the best of intentions. She had just been unlucky enough to be caught in the crossfire and to have fallen for him in the process.

He had redeemed himself in her eyes when he had helped her to escape from the cottage and she had clung to a hope that maybe his feelings for her were real and not just an act. But she had realised it wasn't to be when she had asked for a little space and he couldn't wait to give it to her. She hadn't seen or heard from him again.

It was late afternoon on a warm day in April, and she was setting the tables in preparation for the evening reservations. Olivia was alone in the restaurant, with Jamie on a supplies run and Elena was out back in the kitchen.

'I heard you quit your job.'

The door was propped open, so the bell hadn't sounded. She jumped at the familiar voice, swinging round to see Noah standing by the bar.

'I did.' She blinked at him, caught off guard and a little unsure how to react. He looked good, really good, his tawny brown hair its usual scruffy mess and those green eyes as sharp as ever. 'Selling houses wasn't for me.'

'So you're working here full time now?'

'For now, while I consider my options.'

Olivia put down the cutlery she was holding, moved closer, her heart thumping. She had thought after not seeing him for four months she might have started getting over him, but no, it seemed he still had the power to floor her, especially when his mouth curved up into that familiar crooked grin, his cheeks dimpling.

'Why are you here, Noah?'

He took a step towards her, caught hold of her fingers, his grip loose, allowing her to pull away if she chose to. She didn't. This close she could breathe in his warm, familiar scent, hadn't realised how much she had missed it.

'I wanted to see how you're doing.'

'I'm good, I'm fine.' She spoke the words lightly. It was easier that way.

'I've missed you.'

For a moment she couldn't speak. Four months she had waited for him to come and see her, to tell her that. Four months without a word. 'Well I've been right here,' she managed eventually.

'I didn't come because I thought you didn't want to see me.'

'Perhaps you should have at least tried.' Her voice cracked on the last word and she cursed herself.

Noah was silent for a moment and then he dropped her hand. She hated that she instantly missed his touch.

'You're right, I should have.' His hand went to her face, cupping her chin so that she was looking up at him, into that clear steady gaze. 'I should have come to see you and I should have told you how much you really mean to me. I nearly lost you in the fire and then I let you walk away.' The dimple cracked again. 'In case you haven't figured it out yet, I'm an idiot.'

'Yes, you are.'

'Can we try this again? No more secrets, no more lies, no more psychotic bitches.' His eyes twinkled at that. 'Just you and me?'

When she gave the faintest of nods, he closed the distance between them, kissed her nose and then her mouth. Soft, sweet and chaste, though she felt the fire beneath it.

'I've missed you, Liv.'

Olivia slipped her arms around his neck, pulled him towards her for another kiss.

'I've missed you too.'

EPILOGUE

It is late at night and the house is quiet, the occupants both asleep, and the only sound comes from the trickling of the contents of the canister as I walk the perimeter of the property, trailing liquid up the walls.

Round and round I go, like a teddy bear, the trickling sound soothing as the fluid falls. The heady smell of petrol fills my nostrils, making me giddy with anticipation. As I place the second empty canister down and study the house for a final time, I remind myself that I am just putting things right and that tonight I will sleep easier.

The match burns bright, an orange flicker against the darkness that grows quickly in intensity as the flames lick the house.

The flames rise higher and their passionate roar is like music to my ears as the heat warms my skin. Thick smoke billows into the air and I imagine what is happening inside the house. Can only hope the last moments are of terror and remorse.

Glancing at my watch I note the fire has only been burning for four minutes. The fire engines will still be at least five minutes away and by the time they arrive, it will be too late.

I smile to myself.

Living in the countryside isn't all that it's cracked up to be.

As I stand and watch the fire rage, I am aware of someone coming to stand beside me, taking hold of my hand.

I think of the people inside, the two religious school teachers, so pious and judgemental. They are to blame for what happened to their daughter, Margaret, and they are to blame for what happened to me too.

I turn to my brother and nod, understand now that he was right.

He smiles down at me, squeezes my hand. 'I told you, Alice. I'm here now. I promised I would help you finish this.'

ACKNOWLEDGMENTS

Friendship is important and I have had some great people in my corner offering me encouragement when I needed it most. To Trish Dixon, my writing buddy, who was always on the end of the phone when I needed a chat or to work things through, thank you. Your support has meant so much and I honestly don't know if I could have finished this book without you. Also to Jo, Paula, Ness, Andrea, Christine and Sally. Thank you for reading advance copies of the book and for giving me such in-depth feedback when you had finished. This was a huge help.

To my competition winner, Daniella Moorer Curry. I was thrilled when I drew your name as the winner, as you have been so wonderfully supportive of my books. I loved writing your character and I hope you enjoy reading about her.

Also to Kay Woods, who came up with the inspired name of Black Dog Farm. It is perfect for the story. And to Aileen Davis, I hope you are still enjoying your special mug.

To Mum, Holly, Paul, and Nicki, plus not forgetting the cat and dog crew of Ellie, Lola, Lily, Frankie, Bruce, Bodhi and Steve. You guys are the best.

Finally, thank you to my editor, Caroline Ridding, and all of the fantastic team at Boldwood Books for republishing this title for me.

ABOUT THE AUTHOR

Keri Beevis is the internationally bestselling author of several psychological thrillers and romantic suspense mysteries, including the very successful *Dying to Tell*. She sets many of her books in the county of Norfolk, where she was born and still lives and which provides much of her inspiration.

Sign up to Keri Beevis' mailing list here for news, competitions and updates on future books.

Visit Keri's website: www.keribeevis.com

Follow Keri on social media:

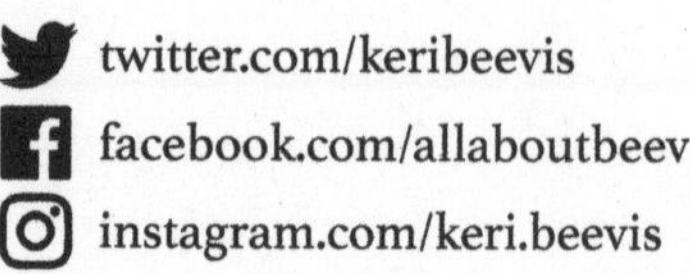

ALSO BY KERI BEEVIS

The Sleepover

The Summer House

The Boat House

Trust No One

Every Little Breath

THE *Murder* LIST

THE MURDER LIST IS A NEWSLETTER DEDICATED TO SPINE-CHILLING FICTION AND GRIPPING PAGE-TURNERS!

SIGN UP TO MAKE SURE YOU'RE ON OUR HIT LIST FOR EXCLUSIVE DEALS, AUTHOR CONTENT, AND COMPETITIONS.

SIGN UP TO OUR NEWSLETTER

BIT.LY/THEMURDERLISTNEWS

Boldwood

Boldwood Books is an award-winning fiction publishing company seeking out the best stories from around the world.

Find out more at www.boldwoodbooks.com

Join our reader community for brilliant books, competitions and offers!

Follow us

@BoldwoodBooks

@TheBoldBookClub

Sign up to our weekly deals newsletter

https://bit.ly/BoldwoodBNewsletter